# The
# Fifth Conspiracy

# Also by Ted Jones

## Grant's War
## Hard Road to Gettysburg

# The
# Fifth Conspiracy

a novel by
## Ted Jones

LYFORD
Books

The characters in this novel are fictitious. Any characters (except historical figures) resembling actual persons, living or dead, are purely coincidental. The dialogue and specific incidents described in the novel are products of the author's imagination and creativity. They should not be construed as real.

Copyright © 1995 by Theador E. Jones

LYFORD Books
Published by Presidio Press
505 B San Marin Dr., Suite 300
Novato, CA 94945-1340

Library of Congress Cataloging-in-Publication Data

Jones, Ted, 1937–
    The fifth conspiracy : a novel / by Ted Jones.
        p. cm.
    ISBN 0-89141-515-7
    1. United States—History—Civil War, 1861–1865—Fiction.
I. Title.
PS3560.05418F54  1995
813'.54—dc20                                        95-5726
                                                         CIP

Typography by ProImage
Printed in the United States of America

*For Tarin, who, at the age of eleven,
had the patience to read Grandpa's second novel.*

# ACKNOWLEDGMENTS

The written word is the tool of the writer; encouragement and assistance sustain the effort. To Jacquelin Kinzer, curator of the Rome-Floyd County Library who, knowing only a voice on the telephone, willingly provided valued source material on the Civil War period in and around Rome, Georgia. To Larry and Wanda Gould for their sustaining friendship and encouragement. And a special acknowledgment to all the people who read and enjoyed *Grant's War* and *Hard Road to Gettysburg* and took the time to write letters. In addition, I wish to express my gratitude to Dr. Dale Wilson, former Executive Editor at Presidio Press, for his friendship and dedicated assistance in editing not only *The Fifth Conspiracy,* but *Grant's War* and *Hard Road to Gettysburg.*

# PART 1
# THE RECEDING TIDE

# CHAPTER

# 1

An arrogantly rash secessionist thoughtlessly cranked open the floodgate—barely a crack, it seemed, just to send the message that the time for debate had ended. The unrelenting tide of war swept through the cleft and across the land, engulfing everything and everyone along its turbulent course. At this place, a spit of land at the entrance to placid Charleston Harbor, the federal government had maintained a small, unimportant fort called Sumter. It might have been anyplace that a Southern state coveted for its own, because it was the time and the rhetoric, not the territory, that controlled events. The time had come for the Southern people to look to the heavens. There they saw the light of the angel of redemption, spreading her wings across the whole of the Southland, proclaiming that the time of rebirth through a second rebellion had arrived. They may have lacked the means to sustain what they had unleashed, but, propelled by an inflexible belief that Providence was on their side, they believed they had the volition to endure. Now, a little more than two years later, fewer than the original number thought so. When the news of what had just concluded spread throughout the South, fewer still would cling to the dream.

So it goes in war: all are bravely spirited at its beginning, before the dying begins; then everything changes. Events erode men's resolve when good men are maimed or die. Glorious declarations of righteous indignation become hushed when the mind becomes numbed by never-ending distress. As passion fades, so too do all the truth and beauty of the noble cause that first brought it on. But strangely, inexplicably, the will to sustain the struggle lingers on, even as resources become exhausted. To end it, the tenacity of purpose must be violently torn away—swiftly if possible, slowly and methodically if necessary—until force of arms grinds everything of value into the dust, and the winds of war lift the shattered residue and scatter it to oblivion.

Much had transpired since that cool April morning in 1861, when a red-hot steel ball arced across the predawn sky. The projectile did no material harm, but the intent behind it ripped apart a nation. The long-repressed sentiment for rebellion took life in that eruption of fire and steel, leaving nothing the same forever. Yet the warring parties had accomplished nothing worth the pain and toil thus far exacted. Now, it seemed, the struggle continued more from gruesome habit than from any remaining doubt about the eventual outcome. Expectations of a victorious conclusion for the South had given way to a less ambitious striving for survival. Never more than now did even so modest an endeavor seem less attainable.

A few hours earlier, the hope of a fledgling nation, carried forth in the hearts and minds of more than twelve thousand brave Confederate soldiers, had stridently advanced across the field. Those devout warriors, wearing threadbare uniforms and shoes with soles of cardboard, resembled scarecrows more than the invincible machine of war that they collectively had become. On they had advanced, marching fearlessly down the distant, sun-drenched hill and across the mile-wide plain toward the anxious Union defenders. Surely such a force was invincible, many in both armies had thought. But the Union defenders were ready, many even eager, as they recalled a similar scene on a cold December morning more than six months earlier at Fredericksburg—except it had been them advancing against the unyielding rebels at the base of Marye's Heights.

When the smoke of battle cleared, the truth had unambiguously revealed itself to anyone who cared to look. The tide that had rumbled forth so confidently at Fort Sumter had reached its high-water mark less than a hundred yards from where young Union Lt. Col. Samuel Wade now stood, his gaze fixed on the right angle of the jagged rock wall, halfway down the center of the ridge they had just defended on the outskirts of Gettysburg, Pennsylvania.

The young officer had traveled a circuitous route to arrive at this place and time. He had been born far away, but he had no earlier memory than of his mother's farm less than a dozen miles north. He had whiled away his formative years here, nourishing the dreams born of a fertile mind and honing his character and conviction as he freely roamed the nearby fields.

About a mile down the valley he had honed his idealistic vision of battle and self-reliance, thinking of duty and honor as he climbed the massive rocks that littered the craggy slopes of the Round Tops—two hills that protruded like large, misshapen breasts from the surrounding fields. Sam Wade had no way of knowing of the alluvial origin of these protrusions, formed more than a hundred millennia before by a mile-high river of ice that had flowed this far and no farther, then deposited its residue as it began its long retreat north.

Six years earlier, the youthful farm boy had left his home and traveled to West Point. There, his idealism serving as a beacon, he had sought to master the art of war. He learned his trade well. He had performed his duty and tempered his honor. As with so many others, his country expressed pride in his accomplishments. In the two years since his graduation from the military academy, he had commanded an artillery unit, served as a spy behind enemy lines, occasioned the death of a beloved Confederate general, been captured twice and sentenced to death, and had been exchanged for others who were as prized by the South as the North prized him. In the process, he had advanced from lieutenant to lieutenant colonel. Finally, as a reward for his unswerving devotion to duty, his superiors had sent him to Maj. Gen. George G. Meade, the new commander of the Army of the Potomac, who gave him command of an infantry regiment. Forty-eight hours and the supreme battle of the war had passed since his arrival.

Try as he might to avoid it, his eyes were drawn to the wall. He had seen it often before without really thinking about it. That had changed. He still had not adjusted to the horrors of war. In his mind the wall had become his personal symbol of that horror.

Farther down the shallow grade from that rock wall, layered close to the ground and too ponderous to rise higher, the noxious, bittersweet smell of death clung to the trampled plain—an odor so thick that it seemed to have acquired a malevolent mass of its own. What was visible, of course, were the wavering remnants of radiant heat lingering in the aftermath of the oppressively hot day. The heat's weakening waves vibrated slowly in the elongated beams of evening sunlight. The ghostly tints—green, purple, and something akin to the color of a rotten lemon—were less seen than sensed as cautious litter bearers moved solemnly about, provoking the odor, forcing brief wisps upward, reminding them of the deeds carried out earlier by their hands. In humid air that cooled quickly as the sun slid below the western horizon, drops of dew began forming on the twisted grass—tempting poets to lament decades later at the dewdrops' likeness to God's plaintive tears upon his witnessing what man had done in the name of self-proclaimed righteousness.

Now and again, a doleful moan drifted across the plain, a sound certain to propel the sweaty, blue-clad figures to scurry toward it. Hope drew them to the unlikely utterance of life mingled with the carnage. The color of the uniform worn by a man still breathing meant nothing. Lingering life among so much death, they reasoned, must surely be a small miracle.

It was late evening on July 3, 1863. The last of the three longest, bloodiest days of this terrible war was giving way to a pink cloak of dusk settling over the now tranquil field. Despite the day's slaughter, many remained fearful that what had concluded that afternoon on this field represented nothing more than an interlude in a grievous struggle to the end. If the soldiers had been less weary, they might have worried about that. Few did. For the next several hours they would savor what they could of peace—and life. Even so, as they looked at a thousand flickering campfires hardly a mile to the west, many were thinking that nothing about General Lee's character remotely suggested he was a man who easily quit. So they kept their muskets at hand. They almost welcomed a conclusion, a supreme test of arms, with the survivors taking all. Then, at last, the war would end, and they could go home.

Nearly a fourth of the Union forces—about twenty-five thousand men—had been wounded or killed or were missing. After the Confederate charge that petered out with only a score or so of the ragged, gray-clad soldiers reaching the crest of Cemetery Ridge, the rebel ranks had dwindled by more than a third. This brought the total casualties, North and South, to more than fifty thousand.

Although many uncertainties remained, one truth was obvious: this battle had to end shortly. If not, both armies would soon be unable to function. Perhaps that would be best, thought young Lt. Col. Samuel Wade. His eyes closed as he let his head drop, but the angle of the rock wall remained etched in his mind. Hungry, unwashed, and bloody, weary to the core of his soul, he turned his back on the setting sun and walked diagonally up the shallow, battle-scarred slope to attend to his men.

# CHAPTER

# 2

"Hank," said a soldier after pausing to listen in the dark. "I think I hear a groan over by that pile of rocks."

"Let's have a look," said the other man, a corporal, raising a lantern to dimly light the area.

The two men threaded their way through the eerily misshapen forms that nearly covered the ground. "My God!" said the soldier. "Would you look at that dead Reb colonel. He has two swords stickin' in him, one from the front and t'other from the back." He shook his head slowly. "Lordy me. The way the bodies're piled up here, there must'a been some kind of fightin' goin' on."

"Where'd y'hear that groan?" asked the corporal.

"Must'a been near here," replied the soldier. The corporal moved the lantern from right to left. He flinched, then shuddered as from an icy chill when the yellow light reflected from the eyes of a dead Union sergeant. They seemed to be looking directly at him. He moved, but the piercing stare appeared to follow.

The men stood quietly, eyes closed, breath held, listening for the slightest sound.

The soldier's head turned when he heard a faint, muffled groan. He knelt. "Here, it's this'un, this Reb lieutenant colonel." The corporal moved closer, holding the lantern next to the wounded man's face, and the soldier placed a small mirror under the man's nose. The soldier looked up and smiled. "See. I told ya, Hank. He's breathin'."

"Get a stretcher over here," the corporal shouted. "And be quick about it. We got us a Reb officer." He squatted and peered down at the officer's face. "Don't look any too good, does he? Look at that pool of blood."

The stretcher bearers ran toward the light. "You found a live'un, huh?" asked an accompanying sergeant. "Which one is he?"

"Here," said the soldier, pointing. "It's this'un with the hole in his side." He shook his head. "I don't think he's gonna make it. The wound's drained him pretty good. He's white as a ghost."

"Well, roll him on the stretcher so's we can carry him back to the aid station," said the sergeant. "Go on, be quick about it."

"Major," asked a young lieutenant as he saluted, "do you have a moment?"

"Hand me that saw," the major said without looking up. "This leg has to come off."

The lieutenant seemed dazed. He had received his commission less than a month before and, strange as it might have seemed for an aspiring young physician, he had seen few dead men before his arrival at Gettysburg. Now he had seen thousands. But the dead were the lesser of his problems. As far back as his memory reached, he had dreamed of becoming a doctor, but his dreams had never included *this*. It seemed impossible that such agonizingly mangled men could still live.

The army had provided nothing to prepare him for what he would encounter. He'd had a year of medical training left when an army medical officer had inquired if he wished to complete his training in the army. The army needed doctors, the medical officer had told him; there simply were too few to go around. The lieutenant had eagerly responded to the opportunity. That had been in late May. Now his senses were numb, his mind refusing to adjust to the horrors he had seen since the Confederate bombardment had started shortly after one that afternoon.

"Goddamnit! Hand me the saw, Lieutenant."

The young officer snapped from his daze. "Which one?" he asked as he looked in bewilderment at the instrument table.

"The large one, you idiot. That's the one I need to saw off this leg."

The lieutenant handed the doctor the bloody instrument. He watched as the major cut through the tattered muscle with the Catlins amputating knife and exposed the bone. "Here, hold this flesh back so I can see what I'm do-ing." He began to carve the muscle away from the bone.

Forcing himself to watch, the lieutenant gasped in an effort to catch his breath. He wiped his hand on a rag and pressed upward on the raw flesh. The major began to saw. Thank God the man is unconscious, thought the lieutenant. "Will he live, sir?"

"Probably not," the doctor replied, "but we have to try. He's young and strong—probably a coal miner, judging from the grime and calluses on his hands. He has a better chance than most." The doctor wiped his brow with his upper arm. "Keep that muscle pulled back." The bone broke free. He cut through the underlayer of flesh, and an aide removed the leg and carried it to a pile of severed limbs stacked behind the tent. "Okay, you can sew him up, Lieutenant." The surgeon stepped back and wiped his brow again. "I have to get some air. Have the next one brought in."

"Begging your pardon, sir," said the lieutenant, "I almost forgot. There's a woman outside who says she'd like to help. She wants to talk to you."

The major appeared haggard, obviously worn by the day's gruesome labor. He peered into the darkness at the barely visible form, a middle-aged female standing about ten yards away. "Is that her?" he asked, pointing.

"Yes, sir, over by the tree."

The doctor walked into the warm evening air. He wiped his bloody right hand on his trouser leg before touching his sweaty brow with his forefinger. "May I be of service, ma'am?"

"Are you the surgeon?" she asked.

"Yes, ma'am, and I'm quite busy just now."

She noticed the insignia of rank on his shoulder. "I can see that, Major. My name is Caroline Healy. I live on a farm just north of town. My father was a doctor, and I know a little about medicine. I feel I must do something to help." Her attention shifted to the mass of wounded men stretching down to Rock Creek, nearly two hundred yards to the east. "May I be of assistance, sir?" she asked, almost pleading.

"What can you do?" asked the major. His eyes slowly traversed the acre of suffering, prostrate humanity extending out of sight into the darkness. He was personally opposed to women's involvement in the practice of medicine. They become too agitated at the sight of torn flesh and excrement, he thought. Still, so much needed doing with too few hands for the task.

"Well," she replied thoughtfully, "I've helped with a few amputations—resulting from hunting accidents mostly. I've helped treat bullet wounds, but only a few." She hesitated. "I'm not a squeamish woman, Doctor. I just want to help." Her eyes drifted slowly over the mob of wounded men. "And it certainly looks like you can use some."

He balanced the options in his mind. "Oh, I need you, ma'am. Right now I need someone to help sort out the more seriously wounded from those who can wait a few hours. Do you think you can do that?"

"I believe so, sir."

"Good. I'll assign a couple of corpsmen to assist you. Don't worry about the gut shot—pardon me, ma'am—the ones with abdominal wounds. I want men I have some chance of saving."

"I understand, Doctor."

"Now, if you'll pardon me . . . " He turned and moved hastily toward the tent.

As Caroline threaded her way through row upon row of wounded men, holding a lantern at arm's length, her mind began functioning on two distinct levels. The carnage before her was worse than she thought possible. Nothing could have prepared her—or anyone—for the experience. She knew what to look for: signs of vitality, of conscious awareness by the soldiers of their own distress. They pleaded with their eyes for assistance. Others, accepting death, waited only for the moment to arrive and end their suffering. One could see it in their eyes. Many had the vacant stare impossible for a living being to imitate. She pulled a blanket over those faces and moved on to the next.

As minutes turned into hours, the agonizing task became more mechanical than consciously reasoned. "Quickly, take this man to the doctor," she would direct the corpsmen. "Tell the doctor this one has a good chance if he gets prompt attention." At the sight of others she simply shook her head and offered comforting words before moving on. She had the sensation of playing God, deciding who might live and determining irrevocably who would die.

This she did on the conscious level. Subconsciously, her mind drifted to the past. She had lost contact with Samuel, her son. For all she knew, his would be the next face illuminated by her lantern. On the day before the battle began, she had received a telegram from him, informing her of his promotion to lieutenant colonel and of his hope of being given command of a regiment. If that regiment was a part of General Meade's Army of the Potomac, her son had a one-in-four chance of being a casualty at this moment. When morning arrived, when the direction of the battle became more clear, she intended to inquire about her son. She did, after all, have influence.

Six hours had passed since Caroline arrived on the field. Every muscle in her body seemed to ache. She had helped triage more than four hundred soldiers in that time. Dawn was less than an hour away.

"Mrs. Healy," said a distant voice.

She turned at the sound of her name.

"Mrs. Healy, please come here," the doctor said urgently. "I need some assistance."

She made her way through the prostrate forms. "What do you need, Doctor?"

"My assistants are too exhausted to help me with this delicate procedure, ma'am, and I think I can save this young man if I can just stop the bleeding." He dipped his hand in a bucket of water turned red with blood, then splashed his face. "Will you assist?"

Caroline nodded as she moved into the light. She followed the doctor into the tent and looked dispassionately at the young, bare-chested soldier, his legs covered with a blanket. She moved closer and looked at his face, the features largely obscured by dried blood. Looking more closely, she turned suddenly cold as her hand sprang to her mouth. "My God!" she exclaimed, "It's my son, Samuel."

The doctor turned. He seemed surprised. "Is your son in the Confederate army?" he asked.

"No," she replied, tears flowing down her cheeks. A pale, still soldier lay on the wooden slab before her. Only the slow, shallow movement of his chest offered the slightest sign of life. "My son's a lieutenant colonel in the Union army," she added.

"Well, Mrs. Healy, this man is a Confederate officer, and he needs our help or he will be a dead Confederate by sunup."

As he spoke, Caroline noticed a patch of gray trouser leg barely protruding from the blanket. She moved closer. "Simon, can you hear me?" she asked. "It's your Aunt Caroline."

The young man made no response.

She looked up. "I was mistaken. He's my twin sister's son. What can I do to help, Doctor?"

The doctor shook his head. What a war, he thought. "I have to probe for the bullet in his side. I need your help in controlling the bleeding and removing the bullet. It's a deep wound. The process will be difficult. Can you do that?"

"I'll do whatever you say, Doctor, only hurry!"

Her nephew had two wounds. Caroline cringed as she stared at a deep, open gash that extended downward from the top center of his head to near the hairline. A large, irregularly shaped black bruise surrounded the laceration. The wound was matted with crusty dried blood.

The doctor paid no attention to the head wound. The abdominal wound was the immediate threat. A bullet had penetrated Simon's lower left side, just above the hip, and was deeply embedded somewhere in his body. The gross abdominal swelling and discoloration left no doubt there was serious internal damage. Simon's clammy skin, ashen face, and nearly white lips revealed that he had sunk deep into shock. His pulse was faint and rapid.

Luck had kept him alive this long. The stretcher bearers had placed him in the only available open place near the tent, laying him on the side of a depression, his head at the lowest point. There he had remained, all but unnoticed in the darkness, for nearly six hours. Even if someone *had* noticed, his chances may have been no better. As a Confederate, he was on his own while the doctors struggled to salvage as many Union lives as possible. The wounded man twitched mechanically as the doctor inserted the Nelaton's Probe, a piece of flexible wire with a porcelain tip, into the inflamed, swollen hole. Otherwise, Simon remained immobile and unaware.

Caroline saw hardly any bleeding to control. Simon's system had nearly shut down, rationing the blood that remained for distribution to vital organs. Twice he seemed to stop breathing, only to gasp for air after a few seconds when the doctor pressed against a nerve.

"The bullet caused considerable damage. The flesh inside seems to have closed around the minié," said the doctor. He leaned forward, placing his ear close to the point where he was probing. He smiled faintly when he felt firm resistance to the probe. "There. I think I feel it," he said haltingly. He hesitated a moment. "I think it missed the intestine. That's good news." The doctor stiffened slightly, holding his breath as perspiration dropped from his nose onto the man's exposed flesh. "Yes." He kept his hand firmly in place as he turned his eyes upward. "Ma'am, if I let my hand slip, I'm afraid I'll lose contact with the bullet. I need your help here."

"What do you want me to do?" she asked anxiously.

"See that instrument there, the one that looks like a large tweezers? It's called a forceps."

"I know," Caroline replied impatiently. "I told you I've done this before."

"Take it and insert it in the hole in his side; then slide it gently down the edge of the probe. When you reach the bullet, try to clamp it and pull it out. Due to the swelling, you'll need to apply considerable pressure to hold it."

Caroline picked up the forceps and slid it into the hole more than three inches before striking the porcelain bulb on the end of the probe. She wiped her brow with her shoulder, then took a deep breath and moved the forceps forward until she felt it press against the flat end of the bullet. She had to force the air from her lungs; then she gulped in another breath. She spread the forceps and moved it forward. The swelling flesh resisted her effort. She pushed harder. The forceps turned slightly, and she pushed it slowly forward a fourth of an inch. She pressed hard on the handle, felt the resistance of metal, and squeezed with both hands. "I have a good hold," she said through gritted teeth.

"Listen carefully, ma'am," said the doctor. "I want you to turn the forceps about a quarter turn. If you can feel any resistance, it means you've clamped tissue between the end of the instrument and the bullet. You're very close to the gut. If the tissue tears open, he'll die for certain, so turn the forceps slowly."

Caroline nodded and sucked in more air. She began to turn, loosened her grip slightly, then clamped down again. She felt no resistance, but how could she know for certain? "It feels like I'm on solid metal, Doctor."

"Good. Now clamp it down and we'll change places." He reached over with his left hand and grasped the instrument as her right hand slid to the probe; then he began to pull. The forceps moved slowly outward for two inches; then the bullet gave way with a loud, sucking pop. The soldier's right leg kicked reflexively upward, and he screamed. A good sign, thought the doctor. He released the forceps, and the bullet dropped with a dull clunk into a small tin bowl sitting on a nearby camp table. The doctor extended his leg and kicked the thigh of the medic sitting upright in a folding camp chair, sound asleep, near the side of the tent. The medic jumped, then rubbed his eyes.

"You've had enough sleep for one night," the doctor said gruffly. "Bandage this man's abdomen and clean up his head wound, then bring in the next one."

The doctor walked into the warming morning air as the first glimmer of sunlight filtered through the trees lining both sides of the creek. A sergeant and a private sat drinking coffee next to the dying embers of a fire. "Sergeant, move the man inside into the open and help the orderly carry in the next patient."

"I'll take him, Doctor," said Caroline Healy, "if I may?"

"Take him where?" the doctor asked.

"To my home, north of Gettysburg. He'll surely die without constant care."

"Sorry, ma'am, but he's a rebel officer. I can't let you just take him away from here."

"Who's to know, Doctor? He certainly isn't going anywhere on his own for a long time."

"Sorry, ma'am."

She saw no point in arguing. "Who can grant me such authority?" she asked.

"The army commander can, Mrs. Healy."

"That would be General Meade, am I right?"

"Yes, ma'am, but . . ."

She had already turned and begun walking up the hill toward Meade's headquarters. Her legs ached from so many hours without the slightest rest. Although the grade was slight, she wearily struggled to lift her feet over even the smallest obstacle. She gasped for air as she approached the headquarters area.

"I wish to speak to General Meade," Caroline said breathlessly to a lieutenant pulling earnestly on a stiff piece of jerky.

"Sorry, ma'am, the general's busy."

She brushed past the officer and peered into the tent. Meade was sitting on the edge of a cot, holding a boot in his right hand and his head in his left. "Sorry to disturb you, General Meade," she said.

The general turned wearily at the sound of his name. The sight of a woman caught him by surprise. "What in God's name are you doing here, ma'am?"

"I'm Col. David Healy's wife, sir. I own a nearby farm."

As she spoke the lieutenant grabbed her arm. He had been instructed not to let anyone see the general without the adjutant's approval. Caroline stiffened, then turned and looked at him sternly. His features softened and his eyes dropped. She felt his grip loosen. She relaxed, smiled, then nodded slightly. "I need just a moment, General Meade. My nephew is a gravely wounded Confederate officer. He's near death, sir. I wish to take him to my home and try to keep him alive—if I can. I've been told I need your approval." She paused. "I'll be forever in your debt, General. His name is Simon Thornton, sir. Lieutenant Colonel Simon Thornton, my sister's only son."

Meade sighed as he examined her haggard appearance—her dress covered with dried blood and streaked with dirt, her face pale and drawn, her hair in disarray. Her red, swollen eyes revealed her fatigue. "How long have you been here, ma'am?"

"By *here,* General, do you mean here on this hill?"

"Yes, Mrs. Healy." He slipped on his boot, stood, and walked into the early morning light.

"I arrived last evening, about nine."

"And what have you been doing since?"

She crossed her arms tightly across her chest as she faced downhill toward the tormented men. "I've been assisting the doctors with the wounded, General. Why do you ask?"

"So that *was* you I saw in the lantern light about midnight last night."

She nodded. "I suppose so, General." She patted her hair; then, realizing how hopeless she must look, she decided to seek an additional favor. "May I also inquire, sir, if it would be too much trouble to send one of your men to Gettysburg to secure a horse and wagon from a friend? I'd fetch it myself, but I'm so tired."

He reached out and touched her arm, then smiled. "You shall have your nephew and your wagon, Mrs. Healy."

She nodded. "Thank you, General. I'm in your debt."

"No, madam. Quite the contrary. Where shall I have the vehicle sent?"

"To that cluster of hospital tents, down by the creek," she said, pointing. "I'll be waiting with him there."

The general touched his bare forehead in respect, then turned and motioned to an aide. Caroline wearily lifted her skirt and tramped ponderously back toward the tents. Meade turned and watched her unsteady movement down the ravaged hillside. The refuse of war cluttered the landscape. This, the far side of the hill from the battlefield, had taken a frightful pounding during the Confederate bombardment the previous afternoon. The first few rounds had crashed solidly on target, slamming into the pickets and packed ranks of infantry soldiers waiting on the crest of the ridge. Then the shells began to arc slightly higher, their elevated flight carrying them farther and farther beyond the crest to the slope behind. As a result, most of the men killed and wounded during the hour of relentless shelling had been noncombatants: cooks, medical personnel, ammunition carriers, staff officers—and, to no one's irritation, a fair number of shirkers who normally found any available excuse to abandon their posts before battles began.

Meade shook his head, asked his aide for paper and pen, and scribbled out an order authorizing the release of one Lt. Col. Simon Thornton, CSA, to Caroline Healy. "Get a wagon and two horses, Lieutenant, and bring them to Mrs. Healy at the field hospital. Take a couple of enlisted men with you." He handed the lieutenant the slip of paper. "This is your order to assist her. Make a copy and leave it with my aide."

The young officer saluted. "Yes, General. Where am I going?"

"She will direct you, Lieutenant."

Caroline squatted next to the fire sipping at a tin cup of dark coffee. Her thoughts had drifted eight hundred miles distant and twenty-four years back into the past as the doctor ambled unenergetically toward the fire. "You did a superb job last night, ma'am. On behalf of the wounded men, please accept my grateful appreciation." Caroline simply smiled, then blew on the coffee.

The doctor squatted next to her and lifted the large pot. "There's more to you than meets the eye, isn't there?" He poured the steaming liquid into his cup.

"I'm exactly what you see, Doctor, a worn-out woman with much on her mind."

"I think there's more than that, ma'am."

She looked at him questioningly. "Why do you think that, sir?"

"Several things. First, there is this woman of obvious culture, crouched here by a campfire sipping on a tin cup of coffee. Few women I know have the self-confidence to forget themselves and act so natural."

She smiled. "I've never had the time to learn how to be pretentious, Doctor. I've been on my own far too long."

"Yes, your self-reliance is obvious. But while I know a few women who might squat by a fire to drink their coffee, I know none who would boldly walk up that hill and ask the army commander to release an enemy soldier into her custody. My guess is that the general approved your request. Am I right?"

She placed a hand on the dew-covered grass behind her and settled her tired frame to the ground. "Yes, General Meade approved my request—for all the good it may do. It will be a miracle if my nephew lives."

"Indeed, madam. But there's one other thing: it seems strange that you should suddenly materialize on the same battlefield on which your nephew, a lieutenant colonel in the enemy's army, fell. How do you account for that?"

"It's a long story, Doctor."

"I've got the time to listen. Ten doctors recently arrived from Washington, and I'm too overwrought for sleep just now. Perhaps a good story will ease my mind."

Caroline lifted her eyes toward the churning sky, then closed them in pensive reflection. She sighed wearily as she wiped her brow with her forearm. "Well, Doctor, nearly twenty-five years have passed since I arrived here from Illinois.

My father willed my identical twin sister, Victoria, and me a farm just north of town. We were hardly more than girls when Victoria met a wealthy plantation owner. She was elated by the idea of living on a large plantation, so she married him and moved to Alabama. The day she left was the loneliest of my life.

"A few months later, I married a young lawyer. I moved here when the marriage failed." She shook her head and sighed deeply. God, such a long time ago, she thought. She turned and looked deep into the doctor's eyes. Her throat tightened, and she set the cup on the rocky ground. She pulled her knees closer to her chest, then leaned forward and placed her chin on her knees as she locked her arms around her legs. Tears ran down her pale cheeks.

"Mrs. Healy, this is obviously distressing you," said the doctor. "Please pardon me for intruding into your private life."

"You're right, Doctor. It is distressful. It's the dark side of a woman's life that's better not brought to light." Caroline took a deep breath. "It's sufficient to say that Victoria came for a visit four years after she had gone to Alabama. She arrived at a time when my husband was away. Victoria was with child—a fact confirmed by my doctor two days after her arrival. That same night, two men broke into the house. They planned to rob and kill me. A slave whom my sister brought with her—his name was Jefferson Petree—was in the barn. He heard the scuffle in the dark house and rushed inside. He'd had the presence of mind to arm himself with a pitchfork. He drove the pitchfork through one of the attackers, killing him, and then he disabled the other.

"After the attack, Victoria felt too ill to return to Alabama. She remained in Illinois under my care. She eventually gave birth to triplets—identical twin boys and a girl. One of the boys had a large birthmark on his head—about here." She placed her hand on the side of her head. "The doctor told Victoria she'd be unable to care for all three infants. She might have found a way to deal with that problem, but it terrified her to think how her husband would react when he saw the large spot on the side of the boy's head." Caroline wiped the tears from her face and turned toward the doctor. "As we talked about it, one thing led to another, and she finally asked me to take the child for my own. It didn't take much convincing, since by that time my marriage had been annulled.

"Victoria left for Alabama in early summer. I didn't see her again for more than twenty years. A day after she left, I struck out for Gettysburg." She paused and looked toward the horizon. "I raised Samuel—that's my son's name; his identical twin is Simon—less than a dozen miles from here. Several months after we arrived, I met a man who needed money to start a small shoe factory. I had some money to invest, so I took a foolish chance. One thing led to another, and now I have more money than I'll ever be able to spend. You see, Doctor, the army needed shoes for its men, and I had the means of making shoes—lots of shoes.

"I remarried a short time ago. My husband is a colonel." She placed her palms against the ground and pushed herself back to a squatting position, then rose to her aching feet. "As you can see, this war is anything but risk-free for me. I must confess, Doctor, that I think my son and husband are both here, somewhere. Whether they are alive or dead, I have no way of knowing. I simply had to find out. I never suspected I'd find my son's twin. That's why seeing him shocked me so. But neither my son nor my husband are among the wounded—at least not here." Her attention shifted toward the crest of the hill. "One or both may be among those being buried, but for now I have a task to keep me from going mad thinking about it."

The sound of creaking wheels behind her caused Caroline to turn. "That must be my wagon coming now. Doctor, will you ask someone to help me load up my nephew?"

As the first spray of light filtered through the windblown gaps among the branches, Lt. Col. Samuel Wade lifted his head and propped it on his up-turned palm. Despite feeling mildly refreshed, he doubted he had slept much during the night. The delicious aroma of boiling coffee filled his nostrils. Then he smelled another, less pleasant odor. Himself. He had last washed shortly before leaving Washington on June 30. It was July 4—Independence Day—1863.

He flinched. The discomfort gnawing at him lacked a specific definition—had no point of beginning, no end. He felt it everyplace—and no place—a sensation more of pressure than hurt. Strange, he thought. The distress seemed to have emanated from some deep, inner recess of his mind more than from any location on his body. Still, separate from the more troubling areas of sensitivity, his side had a throbbing sensation. He flinched again as an image took shape in his mind. It was a vivid, three-dimensional picture of the angle in a rock wall. His eyes squinted as he tried to focus on the mental image. Then it disappeared, and with it the pain. He took a deep breath and relaxed as the tension flowed slowly away.

His bones creaked as he turned and rested his forearms on his bent knees. In the half-light of the dawn, he noticed a dark figure squatting next to the fire a few feet from the tree-lined bank of Rock Creek. Only the dimly out-lined profile of the man's face had any definition in the pale light, just enough for him to recognize the silhouette of Maj. James Clinton. Wade pulled on his boots, rolled slightly to one side, and rose stiffly to a half-crouched position. He straightened himself awkwardly, acutely aware of every muscle involved in the process.

Although his normally firm body had lost some of its hardness as a result of his captivity, he felt less frail than he appeared. His five-day growth of beard and slightly stooped shoulders, which made him look shorter than his above average height, added to his wan appearance. His sparkling blue-green eyes and smooth, nearly flawless skin, narrow nose, and mouth that turned mischievously upward at the corners when he smiled were complemented by a congenial manner that masked the tough-minded courage surging through his veins. Yet there was no sense denying that the rigors of two years of war had taken a toll.

He dragged his fingers through his long blond hair to loosen the tangled mats. He winced as he rubbed against the knot caused by a musket that had dropped on his head. Feeling much older than his twenty-four years, he moved down the hill, gliding silently with a caution now firmly ingrained in his manner. After so many months in the Confederate ranks, the feeling that he was on the verge of detection remained with him still. Perhaps it's just a natural part of having been a spy, he thought. Although that time had passed—for the duration, he hoped—the unrelenting strain had sharpened his senses.

Jim Clinton seemed unaware of Wade's approaching footsteps. The major's thoughts were lost in the smoldering embers that he absently stirred with a green willow stick. Wisps of smoke and sparks rose and swirled in the morning breeze that had started to rise only moments before. Clinton glanced up at the eastern sky. Clouds were exploding out of nothing, fading, then billowing again. The weather's changin', he thought. Maybe rain will keep old man Lee from attackin' again.

"That coffee sure smells good, Jim," said Wade.

Clinton flinched at the realization that someone had approached him from behind. "Does, doesn't it? Want a cup?" He didn't look up. It failed to occur to him that his commanding officer had just addressed him. Nor had it occurred to Wade. They were equals. The two men had shared too much of life—and death—to think of each other as anything else. During the previous year they had confronted and lived through the worst that war had to offer. Armed conflict defines experiences and relationships clearly, even without words. But if any particular word mattered, it was *trust*. Neither man would let the other die if it was humanly possible to prevent it.

Clinton, a willowy twenty-two-year-old from Georgia, became a Union private shortly after the war began. He might just as easily have been one of those butternut-clad rebels who had advanced across that field the afternoon before. His outspoken rejection of slavery, in both thought and deed, set him apart from his fellow Southerners. But more than that, on a personal level, he loved his country and the simple idea of union. In that, he had a covenant with President Abraham Lincoln. As a result, he never gave a thought to which army he would join, expressing no ambivalence at all when asked if a Southern boy such as he might have made a wrong turn someplace on his way to the war. Clinton had the accent to prove his heritage—a condition that, on occasion, had resulted in misunderstandings. Despite his drawl, his demonstrated courage under fire had earned him the gold major's leaves he wore on his shoulders. That latest distinction, although a brevet promotion, had been bestowed less than a week before.

At the moment, though, Clinton's thoughts were on the previous day's events. For reasons that defied satisfactory explanation, even to himself, he kept remembering the marvelous demonstration of bravery he had witnessed. But for the grace of God, he told himself . . .

"Is something troubling you, Jim?" Wade asked.

"Naw, Sam, not so much troublin' me as I can't put it out'ta my mind." He let his rump settle to the ground, then looked up at Wade. "What'd y'think of it, Colonel, the way those men came 'cross that field? I never seen anythin' like it."

Wade's throat tightened and his head dropped. He had to say something. Before him sat the only person remotely capable of understanding what he felt. He sighed deeply. "I can't be sure, Jim, but I think I killed my twin brother yesterday. If I didn't, I sure meant to. That's the same thing, isn't it?" He felt the pain again. His eye twitched in nervous reaction to a sudden, onrushing sensation of guilt. He clutched his side. Why is there pain there? he wondered.

"We didn't make this world, Sam, and we sure didn't make this war. I don't know what t'tell ya 'bout your brother—I'm no philosopher—but he's what he is an' you're what you are. Flesh ain't everythin'. Sometimes we have ta 'cept that our ideas are more important. But I do know this. I wouldn't of recognized my own father in that fracas, so how can y'be sure y'saw him?"

"It was at the rock wall, Jim," Wade said softly, fearing that someone might hear, "sure as sin. I'll admit to being charged up. Anyone would have had difficulty making sense of that chaos, but I saw enough to recognize him clearly. When we charged into them, I kept firing my pistol until it emptied. Then I stumbled, and a rifle butt hit me in the head and knocked me flat. Everything started spinning. I managed to climb over the wall just as this group of Rebs came charging forward through smoke so thick they seemed to spring out of a fog. There was nothing one moment, then they were on top of me the next. Thinking wasn't a part of what happened next." The words rushed out. He had to explain, expel the self-condemnation that threatened to engulf him.

"I acted out of instinct more than anything. I lunged with my saber at this rebel colonel. Several moments passed before I realized that another man, Emerson Pollard, a man I knew from West Point, had thrown himself between me and the Reb officer I meant to stab. You remember me telling you about Pollard, don't you? God, Jim, I felt I had been drawn into a terrible dream. Nothing about it seemed real. Still doesn't."

Wade poured another cup of coffee and took a sip before continuing. "I didn't recognize the man I'd tried to stab until after I cleared the blood from my eyes, Jim. You don't mistake something like that." He sniffed and wiped his eyes with his sleeve. "Goddamnit, Jim, can you imagine what it's like seeing yourself die?" He pressed his eyes against his forearm and sobbed. He felt Clinton's hand squeeze his shoulder, and he shook his head to clear it. "Mustn't let the men see me bawling like a baby," he added, wiping the tears from his face.

"Hell, Colonel," Clinton replied, "the only thing these men care 'bout is that y'led 'em into the jaws of hell yesterday, an' they lived to tell 'bout it. Ain't none of 'em gonna say nothin' 'bout your catchin' a spark and wettin' down your eyes a little."

Wade lifted his face toward the swirling morning sky and sighed. "S'pose not," he replied. He looked at his friend. "Jim," he said solemnly, "I couldn't tell if my sword stuck Simon or if he'd been shot, but there was no mistaking the patch of fresh blood on his jacket. I never saw such pain in a man's eyes. He tried to get up and then just crumpled to the ground and stopped breathing. I must have passed out right after that. I came to an hour later in a field hospital. Everything had turned quiet again. It was nearly dark by the time I convinced the doctor I'd be all right. I walked to the crest of the hill and tried to make myself go down to the wall. I just couldn't get my legs to move. I felt as though I'd somehow be better off if I didn't know for sure. So I just stood there, looking down at that wall."

He rose and walked to a nearby tree, leaned against the trunk with outstretched arms, and let his shoulders sag. "Hell, Jim, I only saw him three times before in my whole life—not more than a total of ten minutes altogether." He laughed at the absurdity of it all. "Said—what?—maybe twenty words to him in those three times. Yet it's like a large chunk has been ripped from my guts." He paused and turned. "Or my soul." He clutched at his side as a faint whimper escaped his lips. The pain had become more intense. It seemed deeper inside his gut. It's probably this lousy food, he thought.

The shrill notes of a bugle blaring in the distance brought the camp to life. Wade returned to the fire and placed his hand on Clinton's shoulder. "Better wake up the men," he directed. "No telling what old man Lee has in mind for us today. We did well yesterday, didn't we, Jim?"

Clinton emptied his coffee cup on the fire. "Yessir. We lost twenty-two men all tol'. Eight dead an' fourteen wounded—five seriously. The report's in your tent." He turned and strode away to find the company commanders.

# CHAPTER

# 3

An hour after sunrise, Gen. Robert E. Lee stood in the tree line on the opposite ridge, looking east. He moved his binoculars to the right, toward the Round Tops, then back toward the ridge leading to the cemetery on the hill to the northeast. Beyond that lay the small, war-ravaged town of Gettysburg. Lee saw plenty of movement on that ridge, but nothing that resembled preparation for an attack. Brigadier General John Imboden stood to the right and slightly behind Lee. Twenty feet to his right, Lt. Gen. James Longstreet leaned against a tree with one foot propped against the trunk.

A reflection attracted Lee's attention. He turned his field glasses toward the brick arch leading to the cemetery. There he saw a group of Union officers looking back at him. He wondered if one of them was General Meade. He would have given a regiment of men to know the Union commander's thoughts. Never had Lee been more vulnerable. He stood deep in enemy territory with no hope of support if disaster approached. What had occurred the preceding afternoon on the ground before him came as close as he cared to disaster.

As Lee watched, a wagon moved across the crest of the ridge. The driver guided the two-horse team at a slight angle down the hill toward the gathered officers. A woman sat beside the driver, and two more men followed on horseback. The wagon pulled to a stop. Lee saw the officer tip his hat and talk to the woman for a moment. After that, the officer turned to another man, who promptly saluted and ran to where a troop of cavalrymen held their horses about fifty yards up the hill. He shouted at the group, and two of the troopers mounted up and rode down the hill. The two troopers tied their horses to the back of the wagon and climbed on. The driver cracked the whip and the wagon moved north. When it reached the crest of the hill, it veered east and disappeared.

Lee observed all of this without comment.

"What are you thinking, General?" asked Imboden.

"I'm thinking we have to leave here," Lee replied.

"We never should have come north in the first place," General Longstreet said under his breath.

Lee ignored the comment and looked at the sky. "It's going to rain, I think. That will help cover the sound of our retreat." He looked at Imboden. "I want you to see to preparations for moving the wagons out this afternoon. Send the wounded through the pass at South Mountain. I want you to head toward Williamsport. The army will move out after dark and cover your left flank. We'll cross the Potomac at Falling Waters." Lee thought for a moment. Back when Stonewall Jackson served as Lee's chief lieutenant, loose verbal instructions would have been sufficient. No more. General Jackson died in May after being wounded at Chancellorsville. Nothing had gone as planned since then. "I'll issue formal orders with full instructions," Lee added. He motioned to his aide.

Imboden saluted and moved into the trees.

Longstreet walked to Lee's side. "Do you think Meade will attack?" Longstreet asked.

Lee moved his field glasses from right to left. "No. I think he will be content to see us leave." He lowered the glasses and let his head drop. The brim of his hat shaded his eyes from the bright morning sun. "I intend to oblige him," he added softly. He sighed, then looked up at the swirling clouds. "I hope it rains. It will soften the road for the wagons carrying the wounded." The injured were foremost on his mind. The army had the resources to care for itself. But the wounded . . .

Shortly after one in the afternoon it began to rain—a warm summer drizzle at first, then harder, then as if a heavenly dam had given way. Two enlisted men were just lifting the wounded Confederate colonel from the back of the wagon when the first drops fell.

"Hurry, men," Caroline urged. "The last thing he needs is to catch a chill. Put him in the front bedroom." She raced ahead and opened the door. The house smelled musty. She had left late last fall, planning to be gone a month. More than seven had passed, and a lifetime of misery filled the void. "Place him on the bed and bring in the supplies," she instructed. "Then you may return to your camp."

By the morning of July 5, a steady downpour had been in progress for eighteen hours. Word had reached Meade's headquarters at dawn that Union cavalry had spotted a long wagon train moving toward the southwest. An hour later, another shadowing troop of cavalry reported seeing the Confederate army moving south toward Emmitsburg. Lee had started his retreat. But was he quitting? Or was it a trap? Meade, fearing the latter, sent a telegram to the War Department informing General Halleck of what he knew. He reported that he had sent his cavalry to follow Lee's retreat and inflict such punishment as possible—from a distance. He planned to follow with the main body of the army as soon as he got the reinforcements situated and everything organized—perhaps as early as the next day, but almost certainly within forty-eight hours. Meade had no way of knowing the consternation this delay caused in Washington. Lee was escaping.

Shortly after one o'clock on the fifth, with the steady downpour now twenty-four hours along, a courier arrived with a telegram addressed to General Meade, commander of the Army of the Potomac. Meade read the message, then turned to an aide. "Have the adjutant find Lt. Col. Samuel Wade and fetch him here, Lieutenant."

"Yes, sir." The lieutenant saluted and pulled his raincoat over his shoulders.

An hour later an assistant adjutant reported to Meade. "This is Lieutenant Colonel Wade, General. Will there be anything else?"

"Not for the present, Captain." Meade looked at Wade. "I remember you," he said with nodding surprise. "You're the one who brought me the message outlining Lee's troop strength."

"Yes, sir," Wade replied.

"And you were right about Jeb Stuart's cavalry, too. He didn't arrive until the afternoon of the second. That proved to be very helpful information, Colonel. Well done."

After Meade's great success in the just-concluded battle, he seemed to have forgotten that he had placed almost no faith in the information brought to him by Wade—and had said so at the time. Blessed are those with perfect hindsight, thought Wade.

"Thank you, sir. Is that what the general wanted to tell me?"

"No, Colonel." Meade handed Wade the telegram. "Read this."

Wade read it quickly. General Halleck had sent the message on behalf of Brig. Gen. Cadwalader Washburn. "Damnit, sir, they want Major Clinton and me to report to Washington immediately. What about my regiment, General? If both Major Clinton and I leave, who'll lead my regiment? There won't be an officer above the rank of captain left to command it," Wade protested.

"Orders must be followed, Colonel. Your regiment will be taken care of. You'd best get on your way."

"Yes, sir. I'll get Major Clinton and go to the nearest railhead." He hesitated. "Sir, my men?"

"I'll take care of it, Colonel," Meade said sharply. He handed Wade a note from his order pad. "Here, you'll need this if you're stopped. I'll send someone with you to bring back your horses. We may have need of mounts when we set out after General Lee."

Wade saluted. "Yes, sir." He stuffed the order and the telegram into his pocket, mounted his horse, and half rode, half slid down the rain-soaked hill toward the creek. He drew up in front of Clinton's tent and dismounted. The horse snorted as his hooves began to settle out of sight into the mud.

Clinton came to the opening. "What'd the ol' goggle-eyed turtle want, Sam?"

"Get your things together, Jim," Wade said sharply. "We're going to Washington."

"Washington? What for?"

Wade withdrew the telegram and handed it to Clinton. As he read, his shoulders sagged. "Does this mean what I think it means, Sam?"

Wade took the note and walked toward his tent. "I don't rightly know, Jim," Wade said over his shoulder, "but I doubt that Colonel Thompson would pull us out of here in the middle of a battle unless he had something important on his mind." He entered the tent. Five minutes later, with saddlebags in hand and wearing his only other uniform, he stood at the entrance. He slipped on his raincoat and buttoned all of the buttons. Sighing, he moved into the open.

A corporal, rain dripping from his soggy, broad-brimmed hat, sat waiting on his horse. He made a halfhearted attempt at a salute. "Are you Colonel Wade?" the soldier asked.

"I am," Wade replied, returning the salute.

"I'm to ride with you to the train and return with the horses, sir." The soldier's expression conveyed his displeasure with his assignment.

The general probably pulled him away from a poker game, Wade thought. He nodded as he grasped his horse's reins and swung into the saddle.

A train loaded with wounded soldiers moved slowly across the stormy countryside. Seriously wounded men lay packed shoulder to shoulder on rickety flatcars. Rain spattered in their faces. Those with the energy to do something for themselves covered their eyes with a forearm. Most lacked sufficient interest in life to care. A few rode sitting up. All were hurting. The less seriously wounded would make the trip to Washington or Baltimore by wagon, probably arriving in worse condition than when they left Gettysburg.

Wade and Clinton, who had managed to squeeze aboard the train at the last minute, stood most of the way, clinging to the iron rail around the back platform of the only enclosed car other than the caboose. The train screeched to a stop under the canopy fronting the Washington train station at twenty past two in the morning. The rain had stopped. Gaslights glowed along both sides of the street. The city never seemed to sleep, especially in the aftermath of major battles. None of them, not Shiloh nor Antietam, not even Fredericksburg, had surpassed Gettysburg for wanton savagery and butchery.

Even before the train stopped, men rushed trackside and began climbing onto the cars. Sergeants screamed orders as officers stood watching. Soldiers

lowered the men on stretchers to waiting hands below. Colored tags identified the type and seriousness of the wounds. For some, the time of urgency
had passed. The long, bumpy train ride had taken its toll. Once the bodies were
examined by a doctor, soldiers moved them to a vacant lot across from the
station house. Other soldiers lifted those still alive into wagons, which took
them to the waiting hospitals.

Wade and Clinton stepped down onto the shiny brick platform. They slapped
at their clothing, trying to dislodge some of the soot. The effort mostly failed.

"Well, now that we're here, where do we go?" Clinton asked. "It's the
middle of the night."

"I suppose the warehouse is as good as anyplace," Wade replied. "If Colonel
Thompson isn't there, at least we can get some sleep and meet with him in
the morning."

They both knew Col. Jason Thompson well. When Thompson was a major, he had recruited Clinton and several others to accompany him behind
enemy lines back in the fall of 1862. They had captured a rebel colonel and
brought him back to Washington, then taken him to where only God and
Thompson knew. The abduction set in motion a chain of events that was still
evolving. Although that first mission had been successful, it ended tragically
for one of the men in the party. In a careless moment, Capt. Timothy Bottoms, Thompson's second in command, had suffered a fatal wound inflicted
by friendly troops. At Harper's Ferry, only minutes from safety, a frightened
Union sentry had shot him through the heart. His death hit both Thompson
and Clinton hard.

Bottoms was another Southern boy who chose to stay with the Union when
the war began. During the infrequent quiet times, when Clinton had a moment to dwell on the distress caused by the war, he still thought of that terrible moment. It made no real sense, but Bottoms deserved to be remembered—
and thinking about him made Clinton feel better. Bottoms had recommended
Clinton's promotion from private to corporal, just after Bull Run. They had
known each other since childhood. Perhaps that explained Clinton's affection for Wade. Bottoms and Wade were alike in many ways. They even looked
somewhat alike, with the same slender build and unruly blond hair. Neither
knew the meaning of fear—or if they did, they feared only failure in performing their duty. Such men were good to have nearby in emergencies. Clinton
had been powerless to save Bottoms, but if there was a way to keep Sam
Wade alive, Clinton meant to do it.

Thompson had sent Clinton with Wade when Wade replaced his twin brother,
Maj. Simon Thornton, on Stonewall Jackson's staff. Thompson had carefully
planned the switch. In the plan's original form, Clinton posed as a Confederate courier from Richmond who had stumbled on Wade, who was posing as
Thornton—injured and dazed by an exploding cannon shell. In the meantime,

the real Thornton was well on his way to seclusion in some faraway northern military prison. The ruse had worked—almost too well. The idea had been for Clinton to fade away as soon as Wade had settled in. Clinton finally did leave—three months later. Until then, the two of them went everywhere Jackson went, usually where shot and shell were the heaviest. Later, while Wade recovered from wounds in a Richmond hospital, Clinton staged what appeared to be his own death and returned to Washington. Wade's later action, which led to Jackson's death at Chancellorsville, subsequently resulted in Wade's capture and trial as a spy. The court-martial sentenced him to death. Then, just days before his scheduled execution, the Union and Confederate governments became involved. Practically on the eve of the battle at Gettysburg, Wade had been part of a prisoner exchange.

And now this.

Clinton knew without asking why Wade was so upset when they were ordered to return to Washington. If captured again, Wade would, once identified, be executed. Clinton figured that if Thompson had called them back to Washington, it must be important. Thompson, after all, had gotten Wade his regiment. Thompson, more than anyone, knew what Wade faced if he went on another mission behind Confederate lines.

The young private buttoned his jacket as he ran across the street and up the long walk to the White House. He clutched several sheets of paper in his sweaty hand. He knocked. A doorman opened the door. The soldier bowed slightly and handed the Negro the sheets of paper. The doorman turned to a captain leaning against the stair rail in the hallway and handed him the stack of papers. The officer raced up the stairs and stopped outside the president's study. He knocked.

"Come in," said Lincoln.

"A message from the telegraph office," the captain said. "It's from Gettysburg."

"Place it on the table, Captain, and thank you."

"Would you like something from the kitchen, sir?"

"I don't want to trouble you, Captain."

"No trouble, sir. There's still some roast beef."

"That would be nice," Lincoln replied. "How about you, Stanton, do you want some beef? It's quite tasty."

"I'll join you, Mr. President," he said. The secretary of war turned to the aide and added, "and a glass of milk, too, Captain."

The officer saluted crisply and hustled down the hall.

After hastily devouring supper at the Willard's Hotel—the bar and dining room were open except on Sunday night—Wade and Clinton walked silently the eight blocks to the huge wooden warehouse. They entered the building at just after three in the morning. Conditions had changed in the past week. Nearly a third of the building had been emptied, with the vacated space now used as a temporary hospital for some of the less seriously wounded. With as many as thirty thousand injured soldiers being moved to Washington, every possible space had to be used. But there were far fewer than thirty thousand hospital beds. The men mostly lay on pallets on the floors. Transshipment of the wounded would begin as soon as their conditions had stabilized and they had healed enough to travel without seriously aggravating their wounds. A narrow aisle had been left through the middle of the warehouse, which Wade followed in the direction of Colonel Thompson's office.

Thompson had his back to the door. He sat reading what appeared to be a battle report. Sensing a presence, he looked up and saw Wade's solemn reflection in the window. Thompson spun the chair around and smiled. Wade and Clinton returned the gesture and entered the room. Wade removed the glove from his right hand as Thompson rose and extended his own hand across the desk.

"Am I ever glad to see you two," Thompson said. "I didn't expect you here until sometime tomorrow."

"Why not, Colonel?" Wade replied. "When the commanding general of the Army of the Potomac ordered us to get here as soon as possible—well, I just figured we needed to act."

"I see your point," Thompson said with a nod. "So, Sam, Jim, how was it up there? Rough?"

"Bloody, sir," Clinton replied. "I never saw anything like that last rebel charge. They ran 'cross that field right into a curtain of canister an' massed musket fire. God, if it wasn't somethin' t'see. Those Southern boys know how t'die well, Colonel."

"You saw that, huh?" Thompson asked. He wanted nothing more than to go into battle. The war seemed to be passing him by. Being good at one's job in the military frequently prevented promotion. Thompson was unsurpassed at his job—so good, in fact, that no other job like it existed in the Union army.

"More than saw it, Colonel," Wade said. "We were right in the middle of it. The center of the last assault hit just below our position." His exuberance faded as sadness darkened his eyes. "Simon was there, too. He's dead, sir. I saw him die."

"I'm sorry, Sam," Thompson said softly. "I truly am. I got to know him fairly well when we held him prisoner. I noticed an eerie similarity between you two—much more profound than your physical features. You would have liked him."

"Yeah," Wade replied, "but there's this damned war." He looked at Thompson. "Colonel, are we close to winning this thing?"

Thompson shook his head. "I'm afraid we're no closer to winning than we were when the first shell hit Fort Sumter. We might have been, if Meade had pressed his advantage. But two full days have passed since Gettysburg, and he still hasn't moved. Now Lee and his army are thirty miles south—which brings me to why you were called here."

"Don't think we haven't given that some thought, Colonel," Wade interrupted.

Thompson walked to the coat tree and removed his cap. "I can imagine, Sam. Perhaps it won't be as bad as you think. Let's take a walk. We'll talk on the way."

"Are we going someplace special, sir, or just taking a stroll? It's been a long day. We could use a couple hours of sleep."

"We're going to the White House, Sam."

"For God's sake, Colonel, the White House?"

Thompson smiled. "Don't worry about it, Sam. The president is generally quite placid at this time of morning—unless we have to wake him."

"I knowed I wasn't gonna like this a'tall," Clinton said, dropping all pretense of disguising his accent.

They arrived at the White House at 3:45 A.M. sharp. The doorman motioned them in.

The large mansion, dingy and dimly lit, resembled a battered old plantation house. They entered and a captain sleepily waved at them to follow. The four men moved quietly up the staircase and walked down the hall to the living quarters. The captain knocked softly on the study door. "Colonel Thompson and two other officers to see you, sir."

"Come in, Colonel," Lincoln said.

Thompson stepped into the room. He stood at attention, his cap tucked under his arm. "Mr. President, I have Lieutenant Colonel Wade and Major Clinton with me."

The president shifted his weight and looked around the high back of the chair. "So these are the two men," Lincoln said, nodding his approval. He laid a thick stack of papers on the coffee table to his front, then rose, moved toward the three officers, and extended his hand to Wade. "It's a pleasure to meet you, Colonel. Indeed it is."

Wade shook the president's hand. The strength of his grip startled Wade. "Thank you, sir. I'm honored."

Lincoln turned toward Clinton. "And you, Major Clinton, *you* are what this struggle is all about."

"Sir?" he asked, astonished.

"I understand you are a Southerner—from Georgia, they tell me."

"Yessir, that's right." Clinton seemed confused, as if there had been something in the brief exchange that had slipped by him.

But the president declined to elaborate. "Have a seat, gentlemen," Lincoln instructed. "We have some matters to discuss."

The three visitors squeezed themselves onto a horsehair couch that was pushed against the wall across the small room.

"Excuse my manners, gentlemen. Permit me to introduce Secretary of War Stanton."

Clinton and Wade rose, shook Stanton's hand, and returned to the couch.

"Colonel Wade, I'm pleased that your twin brother survived the recent battle," Lincoln said offhandedly.

"What, sir!" Wade exclaimed. How could he know about my brother? he thought. He, like Clinton, was growing more confused. "Sir," Wade said solemnly, "my brother died at Gettysburg."

"Not according to this report, Colonel." Lincoln flipped to the second page. "This is the first listing of ranking Confederate officers captured during the battle. It reached me less than an hour ago." He squinted to read the handwritten list in the dim light. "Seeing your brother's name caught my attention. Here it is—Lt. Col. Simon Thornton." He hesitated. "The notation says he was seriously wounded." He handed the list to Wade.

Wade smiled as his finger stopped at Thornton's name. For God's sake! he thought. He turned to Clinton. "Do you suppose it's true, Jim?"

Clinton shrugged.

"I thought his wound was fatal," Wade said as tears gathered in his eyes. He sniffed and wiped at them. "I appreciate your concern, Mr. President. After all, he is the enemy."

Lincoln bristled. "No," he replied sharply. "He's an American." Accepting the list from Wade, Lincoln limply settled his lanky frame into a cushioned chair. For a moment he seemed withdrawn, almost inside himself. "All those men who died in that tragic debacle this week are Americans," he said. "If I let myself forget that for even a moment, I doubt I could endure."

Startled, Clinton stiffened as he considered Lincoln's words. The president's earlier comment now made sense. The underlying meaning of the war suddenly became clear. More than the slavery issue, even more than the abstraction of union, the war was about people. In a larger sense, it was about *a* people— who, for better or worse, were inseparably bound by the common yet troubled heritage that had driven them to armed conflict.

Clinton now realized the abysmal, ironic tragedy of the war, of any civil war. Without realizing it, the nation had engaged in an unrelenting struggle to transform itself—provided it managed to avoid exterminating itself in the process. Nobody had expected the conflict; no one wanted it. Now no power on earth could stop it, save victory for one side and defeat for the other. The truculent issues that divided them were narrow but beyond reconciliation. Something had to yield, or the people themselves, as much as the nation, would be ripped apart. Providence had ordained that Lincoln, and Lincoln alone, would be the guardian of the people and the nation until a new national shape emerged. That explained the pain in the president's eyes; it explained the daunting irony behind the all-consuming event of the time. Every fiber of Lincoln's being had been at work to end the war. But to end it, he had to direct, even enthusiastically promote, the killing and maiming of a substantial portion of the people he devoutly sought to reunite.

Clinton glanced at Thompson. The colonel's thoughts seemed far away, as if he had heard nothing of interest in Lincoln's statement. Or had the comment passed over him, gone unrecorded because his thoughts were on something with potentially more immediate impact?

Lincoln reached into his pocket and withdrew a folded telegram. He handed it to Wade. "What do you make of this, Colonel Wade?"

Wade read the paper. "This is a copy of General Meade's July Fourth comments to the army, sir. Every brigade commander read them to his men."

"Does anything strike you as strange about that message, Colonel?"

Wade thought for a moment. "No, sir. It had no particular effect on the men, but the words eased my own concerns."

Lincoln rose and walked to Wade's side. He looked at the paper for a moment, then pointed. "What does this say?" he asked.

Wade read it again, shrugged, then repeated what he had read. "It says that Meade thinks his men 'should exert still greater effort to drive from our soil every vestige of the presence of the invader.' "

Now for the test, Lincoln thought. "Exactly where does *our* soil end, Colonel?"

Wade's brow furrowed with surprise. Nothing about this meeting had gone as he had expected. "Why, in the South, sir. Virginia, the Carolinas, Georgia—"

Lincoln raised his hand to still Wade. "I'm sure General Meade would say the same thing. That's the problem." Lincoln slumped and closed his eyes for a moment. His long, lanky shadow, created by the backlight of the lantern on the desk, stretched along the floor and up the wall.

"Colonel Wade, what the president is saying is that this is all one country," explained Stanton. "No South, no North. Just Union—all Union. Lee is simply trying to leave one part of the Union and go to another. Does that make any sense to you, Colonel?"

Wade thought for a moment. "Yes, sir, when you put it like that. But if that is so, then up to now everything about this war has been wrong. We've been trying to protect Washington and capture Richmond. The target should be General Lee's army."

Lincoln's eyes brightened as he returned to his chair. He sat on the edge. "See, Stanton," he said, shaking a finger at the secretary of war, "it's so easy to understand." Then his mood changed without warning. As if suddenly confronted by an enigmatic riddle, his eyes opened wide, expressing the torment that had plagued him throughout the war. "So why do my generals have such difficulty grasping that fact? Why won't General Meade go after Lee and destroy him?" As the president's personal agitation became more intense with each unanswerable question, the pitch of his voice elevated. "Lee's trapped on the north side of the Potomac. He couldn't be better placed for defeat if we had planned the maneuver for a year. General Meade has twice as many men as Lee." Lincoln flung his arms wide to emphasize the difference, then dropped his chin to his chest. Lincoln sighed as he shifted his weight to the other side of the chair. "So why can't I get General Meade to move?" he asked again, emphasizing each word. He shook his head slowly. "My God!" he exclaimed after a prolonged silence, lifting his hands high above his head as if to beseech the Almighty's assistance. "Why can't they see it?" He propped his elbow on the arm of the chair before resting his cheek in his hand. "Nothing has changed since I relieved McClellan"—he thought for a moment—"except that a quarter million more men are dead and wounded."

Stanton leaned forward in his chair, his legs spread wide, his arms fully extended between his legs, his short, puffy fingers interlocked just above the carpeted floor. Lincoln agonized for the nation; Stanton agonized for Lincoln.

Wade looked at the disheartened Stanton, then rolled his eyes slowly toward Lincoln. Considering the twin victories at Gettysburg and Vicksburg, Wade had expected unrestrained exuberance, but gradually he came to understand the reason for the deep despair in this cramped, dark room. Victory in battle meant nothing so long as Lee's army roamed freely about the countryside, able to strike at will. And Lee *would* strike again, Wade knew, as soon as his supply and ammunition wagons were filled and the horses were fed and rested. Yet Meade hung back, hesitant, loath to risk all to preserve all. Lincoln had reluctantly reached a point where he more preferred defeat born from aggressiveness than the pretense of success resulting from defensive timidity. As with Clinton, but for different reasons, Wade's perspective on the war changed radically as he contemplated the context of the strain manifest in the president's sad expression.

Lincoln's weathered face fascinated Wade. The eyes offered glimpses of the trepidation that gripped his soul. The large folds of skin beneath his sockets blended with the deep wrinkles of his cheeks and forehead, intensifying the suffering projected by his dark, deep-set eyes. To Wade, the man's broad shoulders seemed to have been formed for this critical moment in time—to absorb the weight of this war—and his face sculpted to express the suffering that had resulted.

For the moment, the president appeared to have departed—at least in spirit and mind—the despairing eyes fixed on some distant, dreadful abyss. Wade's own fear, brought on earlier by thoughts of what this audience might mean, melted away as he pondered the extreme burden that Providence had placed on his commander in chief.

The president had not sought war. To the contrary: he had done everything within his power to ease the fears expressed within the South. But that knowledge gave no solace to Lincoln now.

"Well, Colonel Wade, I suppose you need some rest," Lincoln finally said, breaking the long silence. He walked to his desk and opened the middle drawer. He removed a small map and spread it on the desktop, then turned up the lamp. "Come here, gentlemen," Lincoln directed. "Colonel Thompson, please inform Colonel Wade and Major Clinton what it is we need."

"Yes, sir." Thompson leaned one hand on the edge of the desk and motioned with the other. "As of six o'clock last evening, Lee's engineers were digging fortifications here, at Williamsport, at this loop in the Potomac." He traced with his finger as he talked. "As of that hour, the lead elements of Lee's army were just filing into those trenches. It will be the eighth or ninth of the month before his army can concentrate. We know he's short of supplies, especially artillery ammunition. Wagon trains loaded with what he needs are already en route to where Lee plans to stop to lick his wounds after crossing the river." Thompson tapped his finger on the map. "The river is his problem, gentlemen. The river has risen more than five feet in the past twelve hours. Union cavalry destroyed the bridge Lee had built downriver, so he's trapped for the foreseeable future.

"But here's the other side of the coin. Yesterday, Meade had a council of war with his generals. They voted five to two against pursuing Lee. That means there will be no attack. If we read between the lines of Meade's message to his men, we must conclude that he's content to let Lee cross the river and march back into Virginia."

Thompson looked at Wade, then at Clinton. "This is where you men come in. What we want is for you to drift into this area north and west of Winchester and find out anything you can. We are uncertain of Lee's current strength, and we don't know if reinforcements are on the way—although it's likely no effort will be spared to replace his losses. Lee's fate, and the fate of the Confederacy, are inseparably linked." He lifted his shoulders. "Your job is to get in and get out—without raising suspicion if possible—and then get back with the information. When you do, report directly to me."

Wade rubbed his neck just as the first morning light entered the window. "Sir, is there any chance of us getting a few hours' sleep before we leave?"

Thompson smiled. Sam's accepting this with unusual grace, he thought, especially since only a week earlier he had assured Wade that there would be no future assignments behind Confederate lines. But Thompson had no one else. In his mind, Wade and Clinton made the perfect team. More important, he had unbounded confidence in them. Wade, with his extensive military training, knew the significance of what he saw, or even what he failed to see. Clinton, born and raised in the South, knew the culture, the language, and the attitudes.

Thompson also knew himself—his own strengths and weaknesses. He knew he would keep sending them out indefinitely, until one or both failed to return. If they had to die, better it be doing something they wanted. When this mission ended, he had to remove both from his reach. Wade would have his regiment, and Clinton would serve under him. He would send them to the West.

# CHAPTER

# 4

From the diary of Caroline Wade-Healy

*July 9, 1863*
*5:00 A.M.*
*The sun's coming up. I cannot think, I cannot sleep. God help me! I am so tired. But I must keep Simon alive. He is the flesh of my beloved sister, and his life is in my hands. But I feel I am losing the struggle. His pulse remains weak, his color is only slightly improved. He remains unconscious. In fact, he has remained still since I placed him in the bed. I sent for old Doctor Underwood, but he refused to administer to a rebel. I've sent Washington back to tell the doctor that he will roast in Hell if he could have helped my nephew and Simon dies.*

*8:30 P.M. (continued)*
*God bless Doctor Underwood—I think. I don't know why it worked, or even if it made any difference, but Simon spoke a few words two hours ago. The doctor told me to put Simon in a tub of cold water and let him soak. I sent Washington to the icehouse to fetch the last of the ice. We placed Simon in the tub for more than an hour. Nothing happened. An hour after we got him back in bed he began to groan and move his head. The doctor said he couldn't explain it; he'd just seen it done once before on a man in Simon's condition and it had worked. I have new hope.*

*July 10, 1863*
*3:00 P.M.*
*All is less than I hoped it might be. Simon has been awake since noon, and his strength seems to be returning. But he remembers nothing. He*

looks at me as if I am a stranger. I could understand his having no memory of me—if it weren't for the fact that I look exactly like his mother. Surely he would remember her face. He doesn't seem to know who he is or why he might be here. It must be the blow to his head. It's a terrible wound, worse than I first thought. His head is all swollen and dark around the deep gash. The wound in his abdomen looks much better to-day. It still seeps at times, but it's beginning to heal. I think I hear the doctor's carriage coming down the road.

5:00 P.M.
I have no strength to move. Simon is asleep again. Doctor Underwood just left. He, too, believes that the head wound has caused Simon's memory loss. He thinks his memory will return in time, but when? He would not hazard a guess. Otherwise, Simon grows stronger by the hour. He is still too weak to walk, or even to get out of bed by himself to use the toilet. He's embarrassed that a woman has to help him. I told him that I had taken care of him for days while he was unconscious, but that doesn't help.

As I look at Simon, the irony of his head wound cannot be ignored. The large, dark bruise looks very much like Samuel's birthmark, only much worse. They are in about the same place. Doctor Underwood shaved the hair around the wound to aid healing. He insists that it looks worse than it is.

The doctor met a military courier on the road. Since Doctor Underwood was riding here anyway, the courier gave him a telegram to deliver to me. I'm afraid I don't understand its meaning. It's from Colonel Thompson in Washington City. He'll be here day after tomorrow to visit with me. There is nothing more—no explanation for the visit. I've met the colonel only briefly, at our wedding when he escorted David's daughter, Ellen, but Samuel has favorably mentioned him several times. Still, David has mixed feelings about the colonel. David says the colonel somehow forced him back into the army, but that's all he'll say. I pray the colonel's visit is not bad news about Samuel—or David. God, David and I have had so little time together since our wedding.

One bit of good news. A letter sent to me three months ago but held at the post office finally arrived. The shoe factories are producing day and night, six days a week. Profits are averaging $20,000 a week. About a month ago my net worth passed $2,000,000. I never dreamed there was so much money in the world. I suspect there will be many rich men—and one rich woman—looking for something to do with that money when this war ends.

Think I will take a nap.

The weather had returned to normal for mid-July—hot, humid, hardly a breeze stirring the air. Caroline sat peeling potatoes, waiting for Colonel Thompson. He had neglected to say in his telegram when he would arrive. It's past four in the afternoon, she thought, and still no sign of him. She looked up and smiled at Simon. Endeavoring to give his legs some exercise, she had assisted him on the short, unsteady walk to the table. He sat, looking impassively at the movement of the knife in her hand. Simon had made remarkable progress in the past nine days. Some of the color had returned to his cheeks; the wound in his abdomen had started to heal. Even the swelling in the head wound had subsided. But his memory remained shadowy, as if shrouded in a dense fog, and he was so weak that the short walk from the bedroom to the table exhausted him. Good nourishment would correct the latter; what to do about the memory loss was more problematic.

In truth, she knew little about her nephew's past. There had been a smattering in Victoria's letters during the twenty years of their correspondence. Most of it had been so trivial that Caroline doubted she knew anything that could have really shaped Simon's life. Other events—what had happened to him during the war, for instance—she learned firsthand or from Samuel.

It seemed that the more Caroline told Simon about his past, the more confused he became, with each discussion ending with a flat, vacant look in his eyes. He had memory flashes about the slope of a ridge and a large number of men shooting and screaming. He remembered an explosion nearby, then a sharp pain in his side. He remembered nothing of what happened after that. He knew about the war and that he had been a part of it, but none of the details were clear. Nor could he recall his name or anything about his family.

How do I break through the fog? Caroline wondered as she looked at Simon across the table.

She heard horse hooves clopping against the hard dirt road. Several riders were approaching the house. Simon paid no attention. Caroline rose and walked to the window. It was Colonel Thompson and a small cavalry escort. She lifted her skirt slightly and moved toward the front door. Glancing in the mirror, she patted her hair before opening the screen door and stepping onto the porch.

From the corner of her eye she saw Washington—a lean, round-faced Negro youth—running across the field. The seventeen-year-old—nearly eighteen and every part a man, he said when the subject arose—always came to inspect and quiz visitors, especially army visitors. He talked often of joining the army, but Caroline doubted that the opportunity would arise. Even in the North there were few chances for Negro boys to demonstrate their talents. Washington had many abilities, and they were varied. He knew as much about farming as any youth his age, yet that was of little use in the army.

But he had expert carpentry skills and knew his way around a blacksmith shop. Although he had received no formal education, he read well—his father had insisted on it—and now he kept all the farm records for his mother. As for common sense, Caroline knew of no peer his age.

Caroline stood on the edge of the porch, shading her eyes against the late afternoon sun.

Colonel Thompson pulled on the horse's reins. "Hello, Mrs. Healy," he said, offering a courtesy salute.

Caroline curtsied and nodded slightly. "How are you, Colonel?"

Thompson swung his leg over the horse and stepped to the ground. "Hot," he replied. He turned toward the young lieutenant and six enlisted men who had ridden up with him. "May my men take a drink from your well?" Thompson asked.

"Of course. It's behind the house. Help yourselves, gentlemen," Caroline replied with a sweep of her arm.

The soldiers tipped their hats and dismounted. The lieutenant led the way, taking his horse by the reins and instructing his men to do the same.

Caroline watched them disappear around the corner of the house before turning to face Thompson. "Welcome, sir. I can't tell you how surprised I am to see you." She felt more at ease. Thompson showed no evidence of distress, as she might have expected if he had brought bad news. He had made the journey for some other reason.

"I beg your pardon, ma'am, but didn't you receive my telegram informing you of my arrival?"

"Oh, yes, I received it, Colonel, but that did nothing to alleviate my surprise. It's a long trip from Washington. I'm sure you have more in mind than a little chat."

She had offered two possible areas of response. He chose the benign one. "Not so long a trip, ma'am. Five hours by rail and a two-hour ride on horseback."

"You'll stay for supper, of course?" she asked.

"That would be too much trouble, ma'am. There are eight of us."

"Don't give it another thought. I'll just peel a few more potatoes. There's plenty of pot roast. I even baked a couple of peach pies. We'll make it stretch."

Thompson appeared surprised. He knew of Caroline's reputation, hard as nails and capable of holding her own with any man in a business transaction. Her confrontation with a quartermaster colonel more than a year before in Philadelphia had become legend. He somehow had never pictured her in a kitchen.

"I cook quite well, Colonel," she said, adding a broad smile.

Thompson blushed. She reads minds, too, he thought. "I'm sorry, Mrs. Healy.

We get a picture of someone in our mind's eye and think that's how it is. And please, call me Jason."

"All right—Jason. I've spent my entire life living on a farm—by choice. As you'll observe, I have no servants."

"Then who is this young fellow?" Thompson asked, pointing at Washington.

"That's Washington Petree. His mother owns about six hundred acres just past that house over there." She pointed. After thinking for a moment she added, "Surely you remember her—Molly Petree, the bridesmaid at my wedding?"

Thompson smiled. Anyone who attended that wedding remembered the Petree woman. For a white woman to have a Negro serve such an important function—well, even in the North there were conventions. Some things simply were not done. He suspected that had prompted her to do it. No one said a word—that he heard—but the frowns were unmistakable when Caroline turned into view and began walking down the aisle with a black woman leading the way. "So he's her son," Thompson said. "How are you doing, boy? Will you fetch me a cup of water?"

Caroline stiffened and her fists clenched as she struggled to rein in her anger. Washington's father, Jefferson, had been the closest thing to a father Samuel had known. No one would ever speak badly of him, or any member of his family, and fail to know her feelings. But there would be a better time for that—not here in front of Washington—so she choked down the words.

"I'm doing fine, Colonel," Washington replied politely. He moved from the shadow of the porch and approached Thompson. "Perhaps you misjudged my age, sir. I'm nearly eighteen. Around here I'm thought of as a man."

Thompson's jaw dropped. Caroline smiled.

"And, sir," Washington continued, "I'd be most pleased to get you a cup of water when I'm in the army—which is where I want to be. I'd take any order you gave me—if I was in the army."

Caroline laughed. "Washington, would you do me a favor?"

"If it's within my power, Mrs. Healy."

"Go tell your mother that I would be honored if she and you would join us for supper. Tell her we'll eat in about an hour. We'll have a picnic, out under the oak tree. Ask her to bring a couple of those lattice-back folding chairs with her."

Washington cocked his head and squinted. He looked at Thompson, then back at Caroline. "Are you sure, ma'am?" he asked skeptically.

"Of course. And tell her I'd like to borrow some milk."

Washington nodded, then ran toward his house. He stopped and turned. "Colonel," he yelled.

Thompson looked in his direction.

"I'm goin' to get you that drink, because I want to, and because you look thirsty. Someday I may ask you to return the favor." With that he disappeared behind the house.

Caroline turned back to Thompson and smiled. She waited for him to say something. It does him good to squirm, she thought. Knocks some of that arrogance out of him.

Thompson cleared his throat. "Am I correct in assuming that I've just been put in my place, ma'am?"

"How perceptive you are, Colonel, and how quickly you learn to judge others with less haste"—she looked at him, expressing wonder with her eyes—"I think. Now, won't you please come into the house? We can talk as I prepare supper."

Washington rounded the corner of the house carrying a dipper. He handed it to Thompson and waited. Thompson emptied the dipper, then extended his arm to return it. "Much obliged, young man." He smiled. Washington grinned back and nodded. They had silently reached an understanding.

Caroline motioned for Thompson to enter the kitchen. She followed. "You've met my nephew, Simon," Caroline said evenly, waiting to see how Thompson would respond.

"Of course," he replied blandly. He kept his eyes on Thornton, who, even with all of the excitement, had remained seated at the table. Simon looked dispassionately at the Union colonel, who showed no surprise at seeing the young man in the house. The colonel should have expressed something, she thought, if not surprise perhaps anger at seeing a known rebel here.

In the silence that followed, their thoughts traversed parallel paths, both remembering an unpleasant past.

Thompson had plotted Simon's abduction in early December 1862 and had arranged for Sam Wade to replace him on Lt. Gen. Stonewall Jackson's staff—a substitution that the general never suspected. Only months later did Simon learn what had happened. Perhaps he had even figured out why, but by then the drama had reached its conclusion.

Caroline painfully remembered the four of them—gaunt and ragged, disillusioned after months of hostile confinement—plodding down a rain-soaked lane between Union and Confederate lines. Simon and Nancy Caroline, his triplet sister, had been part of the prisoner exchange, swapped like so many head of livestock for her and Samuel. That fleeting moment, a bizarre family affair, had been the brief nexus of their common experience of war.

Although Caroline did not know it, no record existed of the exchange, or the stories behind it. Wade, at Thompson's direction, had prepared a report, but Lincoln himself had pitched it into the fire. Thompson and Secretary of War Stanton had been the only witnesses to its demise.

"Let's drop the pretenses, Colonel. You and I both know that you held Simon captive from early last December until last month." She turned and began quartering the potatoes and plunking them in the pot to boil. "How well I remember that day," she added without turning to gauge his reaction.

"Mrs. Healy—"

"Oh, don't worry, Jason—and please call me Caroline—I don't blame you for what happened. I'm not naive. I'm well aware of the human cost of war. I've seen it firsthand. But you'll excuse me if I get a bit emotional about all of this." She turned sharply and looked sternly at Thompson. Tears glistened in her eyes. "I just want you to remember that Simon is my son's brother. They are identical in every way save one." She spoke the words with a truculent firmness, her tone a warning far more poignant than the precise meaning of the statement. "Do you have any idea what that means?" She did not expect an answer to the rhetorical question. She expected comprehension.

Thompson lowered his eyes. He recognized the veiled threat. He had hoped for a more relaxing, uneventful visit. It had been neither since he climbed down from his horse. He had said nothing about Thornton, one way or the other—except to blandly acknowledge his presence—yet she had instinctively grasped that he had something planned for the pathetic-looking figure seated before him. He looked at Caroline, her back now turned as she opened the iron door of the stove and stuffed a wedge of wood into the fuel chamber.

How many women would have survived seven months in isolated confinement, he wondered, held by enemy soldiers who had no respect at all for her? He resisted even imagining what she had endured. Now that he had observed firsthand her character and spirit, he suspected that her temptation to resist her captors would have been overwhelming. Despite the absence of specific information to the contrary, he instinctively knew she had yielded to the physical degradation. If she had fought back, she would have paid with her life. She had proved herself a survivor. It was evidence of remarkable self-will. More important to him, he now knew where Samuel Wade got the qualities that elevated him above the temptation toward submission that marked lesser men. Her son had learned from a master the art of self-determination.

Despite how Caroline's ill judgment made him feel—a condition made more uncomfortable by the correctness of her assessment—Thompson now knew that stock in his evolving plan for her nephew had increased in value. That the rebel must suffer, perhaps worse—well, Caroline Healy had expressed it plainly: she had seen firsthand the human cost of war.

They talked very little about Thornton and his condition. A visual assessment answered the most important questions. In a couple of weeks the man would recover enough for travel. A month or so later he would be sufficiently recovered physically for a mission that he would never suspect. Thompson set as his immediate task Thornton's removal from Caroline's custody. If she kept talking with him, feeding him information, he might regain his memory. That had to be delayed as long as possible.

A warm breeze rustled the leaves on the large oak tree that shaded the picnic area. One of the enlisted men took out his harmonica and began blowing a soft ballad as the others hummed. Caroline, her eyes closed, smiled as she swayed gently with the tune. Thompson sat smoking a pipe, watching her face. This war, with no end in sight, had wrecked so many lives. This remarkable woman had suffered more than most. But he saw reason for hope. He looked at Mrs. Petree, raised as a slave, seated next to Caroline in unquestioned equality. If it could happen here, what could prevent it from happening everywhere? Thompson watched as Caroline unthinkingly slid her hand toward Mrs. Petree's arm and gently around the dark flesh.

The song ended and Mrs. Petree, a serene glow in her eyes, turned toward Caroline and smiled.

Thompson lifted his legs over the bench and rose to his feet. "You set a grand table, Caroline."

"Thank you, Jason." She smiled but remained seated. She wanted to ask him straight out what this visit was about. Thompson never let on, but she suspected the call had served its purpose. She decided to keep her questions to herself. She did not trust him. Or perhaps she trusted what she knew about him too much—and what she knew frightened her. She knew from Samuel's comments that she was dealing with an officer whose influence far exceeded the level of his rank. His late-night visits to the White House—she had learned about them through discreet inquiry—were common knowledge around Washington. She had concluded that he was a man people knew *about* even if they did not know him personally. But she had to consider her son; she knew the high regard he had for Colonel Thompson.

Thompson patted his stomach. "It's time my men and I got back to Gettysburg. I have to be in Washington by tomorrow afternoon, and the train leaves at seven o'clock sharp." He lifted his cup and drank the last swallow of coffee. "Mrs. Petree," he said, "do you think I might talk to Washington for a moment?"

What about? she thought. "As you wish."

"Thank you, again, Mrs. Healy. I'll instruct the men to get ready and we'll be leaving soon." He turned. "Lieutenant, boots and saddles in five minutes."

The lieutenant saluted.

Thompson walked to the well where the young black man sat easily on the circular rock containment.

"Son, I couldn't leave without asking you to accept my apology for my earlier rudeness."

Washington turned and smiled. "I'd already forgotten it, Colonel."

"What do you think of Mrs. Healy?" Thompson asked.

"Best person I know"—he hesitated—"'cept for my own mother."

"And Colonel Wade, what do you think of him?"

"He's the bravest man I know."

Thompson waited for a qualifier. None followed. "Well—" He shifted his weight to turn away.

"Colonel, I meant what I said earlier," Washington stated seriously.

"What was that, son?"

"The army, sir. I want to join the army. I understand they are letting men of my race enlist now, that colored regiments are being formed."

"Yes, but—"

"*Please,* sir." Washington snapped to attention. "I want that more than anything in the world." The smile disappeared, replaced by a stern, military demeanor.

Thompson nodded. "I see. I think that can be arranged—if it's what you want. The 45th U.S. Colored Infantry Regiment is forming now, in Washington. But what would your mother say?"

"My mother?" He thought for a moment. "She would say, 'Washington, this is your country, too, and you have to defend it—with your life if necessary.' "

Thompson smiled and nodded. "Your mother does have strong feelings, doesn't she?"

"Yes, sir, she sure does. But ask her yourself if you don't believe me."

"I think I will. You seem well educated for a colored, Washington."

"For a *colored,* Colonel? I'm well educated for anyone. Now that I think about it, the only man I ever knew who was smarter than me was my pa—and Colonel Wade. He's from West Point, you know. I can't match that"—he smiled—"yet."

Thompson laughed. "You're something, young man. I sure can see Colonel Wade's influence in you."

"I keep the books for the farm." He moved his arm in a half circle. "As you can plainly see, we aren't broke yet."

"No, as I can plainly see. But who helps with all the farm work? There has to be more than you and the two women."

"Ten more men, Colonel. You can't see them from here, but there are places for the workers to stay beyond that grove of trees. Four of the men have families. The other six are single. If we hire a married man and there's no house for him, we provide the material and he provides the labor to build it. The others usually pitch in, so it doesn't take more than a couple of weeks. If a man stays three years, he gets to keep the house and the acre plot it's built on."

"That's an incentive to stay," said Thompson.

"It is at that. We last hired a man about six years ago, I'd say."

"And who supervises them, Washington?"

"I do, now. Pa did until he died. Then Ma took over—until I grew up."

Thompson noticed a large Negro pitching hay from the loft of the barn. "Is he one of your workers?" he asked, pointing.

"That's Ned," Washington replied. "He's been here about fifteen years."

"Are the others colored?" asked Thompson.

"Half and half. That's Miss Caroline's idea. Ma calls them the salt and pepper gang." He laughed.

The young man's answers had satisfied Thompson. The time had come for Washington to serve his country. Thompson felt that the country would get the best of the bargain. "Call your mother for me, Washington."

Washington ran to his mother. "Colonel Thompson wants to speak with you, Ma."

She wiped her hands on her apron and turned. "What about, Colonel?" she asked as she approached.

"About this son of yours, ma'am. He wants to join the army, and I think he would make a fine soldier. What do *you* think?"

She smiled, her white teeth gleaming against her black face, as she looked up at her anxious son. She placed a hand firmly on his shoulder. "The colonel thinks it's time for you to pay your debt to your country and your namesake, son. Your pa'd be proud." She looked back at the colonel. "When do you want him, sir?"

"If he'll raise his right hand, I'll swear him in right now."

She flinched, her expression suddenly more serious. "So soon? He hasn't had time to pack."

"From now on the army will clothe and feed him, Mrs. Petree."

She thought for a moment, then nodded. "God bless you, Colonel."

# CHAPTER

# 5

Catherine Blair—Cathy to her friends—stood at the edge of the rain-swept porch. She lifted her arm and pressed her palm against the weathered corner post as she gazed forlornly up at the steel gray sky. Windblown rain washed down her face; her soggy print dress dripped a circle about her bare, muddy feet. Her right arm hung limply at her side. Her straight hair, resembling a matted brown rag, clung to her glistening, rain-soaked back.

She had slept fitfully, her slumber frequently interrupted by the pelting raindrops that beat incessantly against the roof of the antebellum plantation home. But more than that, there had been the grinding, aching loneliness. She never fully removed the fear from her thoughts that Noah, her husband, might never again place his strong, loving arms around her and gently kiss her forehead as he crawled into bed. She ached to hear his soft whisper: "I love you," he would say. "Make a spoon." She yearned for the feel of his firm body pressing hard against her backside.

She had lost track of her husband since she last saw him in late April. Lee's army had fought two major battles after that brief visit. The most recent, at Gettysburg, had concluded nearly two weeks before. She had heard plenty of rumors during the few days before the rain settled in, although nothing had been confirmed. But the consistency of the rumors convinced her that Gettysburg had been a terrible affair, perhaps the worst of the war.

The fate of the Confederacy rested in Lee's hands. Everyone, North and South, knew that. If the Yankees captured him, the cause would wither and die in a month. She repressed her guilt as she silently wished the white-haired old man the worst—not because she hated Lee or objected to what he fought for, but simply because she wanted the war to end.

A clap of thunder had driven her from bed at first light. After slipping her dress over her naked, weary frame, she had splashed her way to the barn to gather eggs, feed the chickens, and milk the cows. After pitching several forks of hay to the cows and throwing some scraggly ears of corn into the pigpen, she sloshed wearily back to the house to wait for the weather to clear. Sandy, her two-year-old daughter, would awaken before long and demand her breakfast.

The weather had turned unseasonably cool. The rain, alternating between drizzle and blinding downpour, had thoroughly drenched the farm. What had once been plowed fields covered by three-foot-tall corn now shimmered in the dull light reflecting from three inches of standing water. Most of the corn had been irretrievably lost. The limp stalks lay prostrate, as if a knife had cut them off at ground level. The rain had been pouring down, off and on, for more than a week—since July 5, if she remembered correctly. It was now the fourteenth. Even if the rain stopped immediately, several days would pass before the fields dried. Then, with luck, she might have time to squeeze out another crop of something before the first frost. But it wouldn't be easy, not since the slaves had fled north. And the rain and cool weather would only make the weeds worse. She hated hoeing.

Before the war, when life had been beautiful and full of promise, her older brother, Pervis, her younger brother, James, and her half brother, Frank, had raised some of the best tobacco and cotton in Georgia. But it had been different then. Slaves had done the heavy work. Now James was dead, killed in the Wilderness in early May when General Jackson's soldiers had flanked General Hooker's right wing. Pervis had been seriously wounded at some obscure crossroads skirmish in September 1862. Nothing had been heard from him since. Frank, the eldest, born of her father's first marriage—his first wife had died of smallpox when the boy was only one—was serving with General Pemberton at Vicksburg. Although his fate remained unknown, it seemed likely he had become a Yankee prisoner when the Mississippi fortress fell.

To the undying disgrace of her father, Pervis had cast his lot with the North. He simply rode from the plantation the day Georgia seceded from the Union. He never left so much as a note or said good-bye. She had expected it. Neither was she certain he had been wrong. Grandpa Bowman had forbidden Pervis's name to be spoken in his presence. Frank, James, and her husband, Noah, had chosen the Confederacy. Long ago, she had decided not to give a damn one way or the other—so long as the war ended soon, Noah survived, and she and her family again knew something of a normal life. If the rumors were true, that might be sooner than she dared hope.

The thunder rumbled to the northeast. It now had a more menacing sound, a lower pitch. It continued without pause, varying only with sporadic louder bursts before settling again into a dull, growling roar. Perhaps it isn't thunder at all, she thought. Perhaps it's the roar of cannon! If so, that means Lee has somehow escaped and retreated up the Shenandoah Valley. Might Noah be that near? she wondered. Might he find a way to see me, if only for a sweet hour or so? She smiled dreamily at the thought and sighed as she unconsciously wiped the rain from her face.

She turned anxiously toward the faint sound of Sandy's whimper, then smiled as she moved toward the door. As she reached for the lever, she flinched in response to a distant sound—a gunshot, or something quite similar, she thought apprehensively. The noise of the rain made it difficult to know. She tried to filter the sounds in her mind. Nothing out of the ordinary, she concluded. She relaxed. She lifted the latch and had one foot inside the house when she heard the noise again. This time there was no doubt. She recognized the popping— more like a pistol than a rifle, which had a deeper, more resonating sound. She knew her weapons. But where had it come from? Somewhere behind me, she thought. Perhaps from the woods.

The rain had settled to a gentle drizzle. Cathy squinted, straining to peer into the misty darkness of the tree line a quarter mile west of the house. She thought she saw something move, then it faded. A horse, she thought—no, two horses—weaving through the trees. She turned and rushed inside. She reached the crib and lifted Sandy into her arms. Soggy clear through, she discovered, just like me. She moved back to the window. "There they are!" she said in a whisper. Two of them—Confederate officers. She stepped back into the shadows. Strangely, she felt no fear, or even anxiety. Just concern. One never knew, and her a woman alone . . .

The two men drew up just inside the protective tree line. The man in front looked to his right, then to his left, then over his shoulder. The second man leaned over the horse's neck. He seemed unsteady; his limp right arm hung at his side. He began weaving in slowly expanding circles. Spurring his horse backward, the other man extended an arm in support, then took the reins of the slumping man's horse. He checked to the right and left again before moving slowly into the clearing. He appeared to say something to the other man before nudging his horse forward.

The two horses moved uneasily on the slick turf toward the barn. Careful to stay in the shadows, Cathy moved to another window. She patted the child's back in an effort to keep her from crying. When the men reached the barn, the one leading the other horse dropped its reins, dismounted, and looked around. He opened the barn door and leaned inside. Then he stepped back and helped the other man dismount and half carried him into the barn. The first man emerged a moment later and led the horses inside. Moments later he extended an arm from the shadows and pulled the door shut.

Cathy took a deep breath and exhaled slowly. What were these two doing on her farm? They were obviously running from someone reason told her there were others nearby, chasing them. She needed time to think. She decided to change the baby. The task finished, she set Sandy on the bedroom floor and returned to the window. Her attention shifted to the woods. She had been right; there were others: it was a column of Union cavalry.

The soldiers walked their horses to the tree line and halted briefly before fanning out to cross the field. She counted nine of them—an officer and eight enlisted men. Cathy waited. They seemed reluctant to come into the open. As the others held their position, the officer moved uneasily into the clearing. His apprehension was evident, even at this distance. She watched him stop and examine the terrain before raising his arm and motioning the others forward. They moved at a walk, the horses' breath misting in the cool summer air. One of the enlisted men advanced to the officer's side. As the group moved cautiously forward, the man next to the officer leaned from side to side, his attention directed at the ground. He stopped abruptly and pointed at something. The officer signaled the others to stop. The man who had been examining the ground dismounted and squatted on a slight rise. He lifted his head and said something to the officer, who nodded; then the man mounted his horse and pointed toward the barn. The officer nodded again.

The men swung their horses into a column behind the officer. They circled left toward the barn, carefully maintaining a reasonably safe distance. The officer again signaled a halt, dismounted, lifted his raincoat, and drew out his pistol.

Cathy opened the door and moved noisily onto the porch. "Is something wrong?" she shouted.

The young officer spun around and dropped into a crouch. The other men vaulted from their horses. Within seconds, nine weapons pointed ominously toward her chest.

She instinctively raised her hands. "Don't shoot," Cathy screamed. "I'm alone, except for my baby daughter." She cautiously sidestepped and pressed herself against the front corner of the house.

The officer relaxed and lowered his weapon. "Just who are you, ma'am?" he asked.

"My name is Cathy Blair. I live here."

"And you say you're alone?" asked the officer, looking cautiously from side to side, demonstrating the persistent alertness characteristic of a survivor of war.

"Yes, my husband's a major in Lee's army."

The officer began walking toward the house. "When did you last see him?" he asked.

"Last month," she lied. It had been nearly three months since he had been home.

The officer moved closer. He ran his eyes up and down Cathy's slender frame. Even in the muted light, he could see the outline of her legs through

the thin print dress. He forced the image from his mind. "Did you see anyone ride past here?" the officer asked as he approached the porch.

They must have found a hoofprint in the mud, she thought. "I think so. I
was changing the baby and through the window I thought I saw someone ride
by. It was raining hard then and difficult to see." She moved to the edge of
the porch, close enough to reach out and touch the officer. Best to seem unafraid,
she thought.

By now, his attention had been thoroughly diverted from his mission. He
looked at the form alluringly silhouetted by her wet, clinging dress.

"It's let up now," she continued, extending her hand beyond the roof of
the porch. She pointed north. "I think they rode that way."

"They? How many?"

"Two, I think—but I couldn't be sure."

"Have you been to the barn lately?"

"I went out early this morning," she replied. "I had to feed the livestock
and milk the cows."

"What's in the barn?" he demanded.

"Several cows, two plow horses, a mule, and some chickens and pigs."
She hesitated. "The mule's been poorly of late. Do you know anything about
mules? I'd appreciate some advice on what's wrong with him."

"I'm from New York, ma'am. I don't know anything about horses—including the one I'm riding."

"Mules aren't the same as horses," she said.

The young lieutenant looked ashamed. "I *know* that."

"You're welcome to look around," Cathy said casually, placing her hands
on her hips. "Just take off your boots if you go into the house—and don't
frighten the baby." She was playing a dangerous game, and she knew it.

The officer started to turn, then hesitated. The men still had their carbines
propped on their saddles. He waved and they elevated the barrels of their
weapons. "You said north, huh?"

"That's right—off toward that road."

"Did one of them seem hurt?" he asked.

She pursed her lips and pretended to think. "I really didn't get a very close
look—so many soldiers come this way that I don't pay much attention anymore. I counted five Confederate patrols yesterday afternoon alone—and that
with it raining like sin." She shrugged. "It's hard to say."

The lieutenant waved his arm. "Bring my horse, Corporal. The rest of you,
mount up and prepare to move out. We're heading north." He turned and tipped
his hat, then awarded himself a long, last glance at Cathy. Perhaps in a more
peaceful time, he thought. "Thank you, ma'am. You've been most helpful."

"Anytime, Captain."

"It's lieutenant, ma'am. Lieutenant Dwight Beason."

She smiled. It never hurt to flatter. "I don't see many Union soldiers, Lieutenant. The place is overrun with Confederates most of the time."

"I see," he replied. He placed his pistol back in its holster. "Let's go, men," he said as he swung into the saddle.

Cathy hurried into the house to check on her daughter. The child had dozed off on a rug. Cathy stood by the front window and waited until the Union soldiers had ridden out of sight before rushing out the back door and sloshing her way toward the barn.

She stopped at the barn door. She felt eyes looking at her menacingly. Her heart beat loudly. She drew in a deep breath, pushed it out, and drew another. "I'm coming in," she said calmly but firmly. "I'm alone." They undoubtedly know that, she thought. She lifted the latch and opened the door a crack. "I'm alone," she repeated, then opened the door far enough to step inside. She slipped into the dark building. The only light came from the door, which she had left ajar, and what filtered through the cracks between the boards. She knew someone had been moving around to her left. Dust particles still swirled in the narrow beams of light nearest the door. She waited a moment for her eyes to adjust to the darkness. A figure gradually came into focus. A man lay facedown on a bed of hay. "Is he badly hurt?" she asked the second man, whom she sensed was close by.

"What'd y'say t'them soldiers?" said a voice from the shadows.

A Southern voice, she thought, Georgia or Alabama. Not Virginia or the Carolinas. They have a different inflection. "I told them you rode north."

"It sure took y'long enough t'tell 'em," the man said accusingly.

"If they're still around, you're as good as dead, so why discuss the matter? I told you what I said. Now, do you want me to look at your friend, or do you prefer that he die?" She heard the rustle of feet moving across the straw-covered floor.

Cathy turned. A pistol pointed at her chest came into view first. The man remained in the shadows. "I don't concentrate well with someone aiming a gun at me," she said firmly.

The figure moved from the shadows. "I don't think it's that bad of a wound," the man said.

"I'll take a look," she replied, then walked toward the man lying on the hay. "Light that lantern and bring it over here," she directed, pointing at a support beam. The officer reached up and removed the lantern from a nail. He tried several times to light it, but all of his matches were wet.

"There's some matches in the tin can on the shelf," she told him. "Try one of those."

The first one caught. He lit the lantern and carried it to her.

"Hold it so I can see," she directed. Cathy rolled the prostrate figure face up. He was conscious, looking up at her through expressionless eyes.

He feels no pain yet, she thought. "There's blood on the front of your jacket," she said in a soft, low voice as she peered into the blue eyes of the blond-haired young man. Too handsome, she thought, to have to die so young. "The bullet went all the way through. You're lucky."

"It's all in how you look at it," the man replied, wincing for the first time from the pain. "If I'd *really* been lucky, I wouldn't be lying here bleeding on your hay."

She smiled more broadly. "I suppose you're right." She turned to the other man. He had lowered the pistol, letting it hang at his side. "Now that it's clearing up, there are likely to be more soldiers riding by. There's a small toolroom in the back of the barn. He'll be safe there."

"Just patch him up," the standing man said. "We'll be ridin' out after dark."

"It's fine with me—if your plan is to kill him. He'll bleed to death in an hour if he rides a horse."

"She's right, Jim," said the wounded man. "You go back. I'll be all right here. I'll make it back when I'm able to ride again."

Cathy examined the standing man's uniform. It bore the insignia of a captain. She recognized the insignia of the man lying on the hay as that of a Confederate lieutenant colonel.

"I won't leave y'here, Sam," said the man. "No, sir. We ride back together or we stay here together."

The colonel sighed. "We can argue about it, Jim, or you can get going now and save a lot of time. Either way—"

"Y'don't even know this woman's name," Jim interrupted.

"What's your name?" the colonel asked.

"Cathy," she replied as she ripped open his tunic.

Sam Wade flinched with pain. "There," he said with a start, "now do you feel better?"

"Y'know what I meant, Sam."

"Jim, I've never *ordered* you to do anything since I've known you. Must I start now?"

Clinton slid his pistol into its holster and set the lamp on the ground. He leaned forward and, taking the woman's shoulders in his hands, forced her to face him. "I'll say this plain, lady. I'm leavin' for now, but I'll be back. Y'won't know when, but I'll be back. If the colonel's gone, or if anythin' a'tall happens t'him, I won't ask no questions. I'll just shoot ya an' be done with it." He kept his voice even and calm, with no expression of anger. He wanted her to believe that he was wholly sincere—that he would fulfill his threat without a second thought. "Is that clear?" He rose, stooped to pick up the lantern, and hung it on a nail protruding from a stall's corner post.

"Very," Cathy replied, otherwise ignoring him as she wiped the blood from around the wound with Sam's shirt. "Do you want some breakfast before you leave?"

She's a cool one, Clinton thought. He looked at Wade, who managed a smile.

"She has no fear of you, Jim," said Wade. "That's obvious."

"Ain't necessary," Clinton replied, "so long as she believes me. Thank ya, ma'am. I think I'll take ya up on that—soon's y'bind his wounds."

Clinton rode out shortly before ten—after carrying Wade into the toolroom and laying him on a bed made of hay and blankets. The bleeding had stopped, but Wade felt light-headed and a bit nauseated. He had difficulty remaining alert.

"Will you be all right?" Cathy asked. "I have a two-year-old in the house. She doesn't take too well to being left alone."

"Go tend to your child, ma'am. I'll be just fine," said Wade.

She rose and started to leave.

"Ma'am," he said softly, "don't tell anyone I'm here."

"*Anyone?*" she asked, surprised. "What if a Confederate patrol rides by?"

"*Anyone,*" he repeated.

She thought for a moment, then shrugged and nodded.

# CHAPTER

# 6

From the diary of Caroline Wade-Healy

*July 17, 1863*
*My God! 50,000! The story in the paper reports there may have been*
*as many as 50,000 casualties at Gettysburg—Union and Confederate.*
*Our losses were half of that. How are we to sustain this horror with no*
*lasting result? The cost of this war is like nothing before seen on this*
*fragile land.*

*General Meade took command of the army less than three weeks ago*
*and already there are demands for his resignation. He had a chance to*
*end it, if only he had pursued General Lee's broken army. But he held*
*back, and Lee made good his escape into Virginia once the waters of the*
*Potomac receded. Now there is nothing to do but wait for the next battle,*
*and, I fear, the next, and the next, . . .*

*I met a man at the hotel day before yesterday. The encounter nearly*
*broke my heart. He had taken the train down from Philadelphia and*
*arrived the day before. He looked at me with red, swollen eyes, his features*
*drawn and haggard. I asked if he was in pain. He replied he had never*
*felt such anguish. His son, his only child, was killed on the second day*
*of the battle and he had come to take the young lad's body home for burial,*
*but he had not found him and doubted he would. I spent the remainder*
*of the day helping him search. Toward sundown, we found a sergeant*
*who remembered seeing the boy go down. The records confirmed the site*
*of the burial, in a mass grave with nearly a hundred more who perished*
*on the ridge north of Little Round Top. In the end, the man decided to*
*leave the boy here. He said that nothing seemed more appropriate than*
*to let the boy rest with the men who had fought at his side.*

*Simon grows stronger each day, but still no word from Samuel. At least he was not listed among the casualties.*

*I received a letter from David yesterday. He wrote that the morale of the army is surprisingly good, but says the men wish we could have ended the war here, at Gettysburg. They sense that the worst remains ahead. Now the army must pursue Lee into Virginia, where he is sure to surface again—reinforced and resupplied.*

*This war has turned into a killing frenzy, with talk of victory and defeat pointless. It seems that nothing will stop the carnage until one army or the other has no more men left to fight.*

*Simon is standing at the window, watching the sun go down. I must stop now and prepare supper.*

---

Colonel Thompson slammed his fist against his desk. He never would have thought it of Clinton. "How could you leave him there, Major?" Thompson demanded. "I thought you two were friends. How could you just leave him there, helpless—and in the hands of a rebel, no less?"

Clinton stood at rigid attention, looking straight ahead. "I had no choice, sir."

"What do you mean you had no choice? Of course you had a choice."

"But the information, sir. I had t'get back an' report. We was all expectin' a risky mission, Colonel. The Shenandoah's in Confederate hands—has been for most of the war."

No one was disputing that. The broad, fertile valley was both a rebel sanctuary and a year-round source of provisions for Lee's army and livestock. The inability of Union forces to gain control of the valley had caused unending irritation to Lincoln and the War Department. But that had changed nothing. Most of the people in the valley were Southern sympathizers. Those who sided with the Yankees were wise to keep it to themselves. Lee had used that route to elude Union forces on his way to Gettysburg. His control of the valley had become so complete that Union forces were unaware that Lee had passed that way until he broke free of the mountain screen thirty miles west of the Pennsylvania town. Now he hoped to escape the same way.

"All the more reason to get Sam out of there. You know what'll happen if he's caught," snapped Thompson.

The remark irritated Clinton. Of course he knew! It had been Thompson who had promised never to send Wade behind enemy lines again. But the colonel had sent him anyway. "No one knew that better'n Colonel Wade, sir."

Brigadier General Cadwalader Washburn, Thompson's immediate superior, stood in the corner of the room, his back to the two officers, his hands clasped behind him. So far, he had said nothing, only listened. He knew the cause of Thompson's irritation, probably better than Thompson himself knew. Thompson felt guilty about sending Wade on this mission. Best to let him work through it, thought Washburn, then we can plan our next move.

Thompson relaxed and let himself sink into his chair. He supported his head in his hand, his elbow resting on the desktop. "This is a difficult problem you've presented me with, Major. We have reliable information that Lee has crossed the Potomac and is moving into camp at Bunker Hill, Virginia."

"I can confirm that, Colonel," said Clinton. "I rode through the area early yesterday. They was constructin' defensive positions, an' supply trains was movin' in an' out with regularity—an' there was reinforcements by the thousands. Lee'll be back to his former strength within a week."

Thompson's anger subsided. "How sure are you of the accuracy of your information, Jim?"

"Positive, sir. None of Lee's retreatin' infantry was there when I passed through, but I stopped an' had coffee with an advance troop from Stuart's cavalry. They said they was expectin' the lead elements of Lee's infantry by nightfall. He got away, Colonel. General Meade let Lee get away."

Washburn turned. "Then we must begin to think about what's next, gentlemen. What would you say that is, Major?"

"Gettin' Colonel Wade out, sir."

"How do you propose doing that, Jim?" asked Thompson.

"The same way we got there in the first place, Colonel. I only come back t'make my report. I'll leave tonight."

"But there will be sixty thousand Confederates in the area by the time you get there!" Thompson exclaimed.

"That's right, sir. But I owe it t'Sam. We both knew the importance of our mission. He took a hell of a risk orderin' me back."

"I see." Thompson regretted his earlier display of hostility. How could he have fairly judged the circumstances? He hadn't been there. That's what galled him. He was never there, wherever *there* might be. He saw the war passing him by. He felt trapped. He was a facilitator, never a *doer*. "How much trouble will it be to get him out, Jim?"

"It should be easy enough t'get lost in the crowd," Clinton replied with a grin. "Assumin' the general thinks it's the thing t'do."

Washburn cleared his throat. "And if I don't?"

"Then I request a week's leave, sir."

"So you can go back without orders, Major?"

Clinton confined his answer to a sideways glance.

"At ease, Major," the general said. "Tell me more about the woman."

Clinton relaxed. "There isn't much t'tell, General. 'Bout twenty-five, pretty, an' she didn't scare worth a damn. She had a small child in the house. While we was in the barn, she sent a Union patrol ridin' in the wrong direction, sir. They was prob'ly the same ones that chased us an' shot Colonel Wade."

That information startled Washburn and Thompson. "*Union* troops shot him?" queried the general.

"Yes, sir. We'd stopped t'try an' get a couple of hours' sleep. We was under a rock ledge in a ravine an' couldn't tell if they was rebels or Yankees in the dark. We barely got away."

"Why didn't you just tell them who you were?" Thompson asked.

"Remember Cap'n Bottoms, Colonel? We told 'em who we was then, an' look what happened." He needed to say no more.

"Do you think this woman will turn Sam over to the Rebs?"

"Not as a spy, sir," replied Clinton. "She seemed convinced we was Confederates, so she'll prob'ly hail the first Reb patrol that passes by. If that happens, well . . ."

The urgency for prompt action pressed on them all. Thompson rose and walked to the front of his desk. "How long before Sam can ride a horse?"

"I'm no doctor, sir, but knowin' Sam, I reckon he'll be ready t'get out'ta there by the time I get back."

"Are you tired?" asked the general.

"Not really, sir. My blood's up."

"How long will it take you to get to him?"

Clinton measured the distance in his mind. "Well, sir, as the crow flies— an' I ain't no crow, General—it's 'bout forty miles. I reckon it'll take 'til after nightfall tomorrow, maybe longer."

The general walked to the door. "We can get you about halfway there by train, Major. We control everything to within about twenty miles of Winchester."

"That'd help, sir. I could make it by sometime late tomorrow mornin'."

Washburn turned toward Thompson. "See to it, Jason. Do what you must."

The monotonous clank of the wheels against the seams of the track beat against Clinton's brain. He had given up even trying to think about his mission; the repetitive noise shattered his thoughts—not that he wanted to think, except perhaps about home.

Nearly three years had passed since he left his family's farm near Rome, Georgia. His father had been feeling poorly at the time, and his mother had asked him to stay and help. But there comes a time when every young man must go out into the world and try to make his fortune. He'd seen no future on the hundred-acre patch of Georgia red clay. Few opportunities were available in the South unless one had a substantial financial stake. He had scarcely enough money for the trip north.

Clinton smiled inwardly as he recalled his youth and the enjoyable hours spent in his private cave. A fresh, natural spring bubbled to the surface near the edge of the farm. To the casual observer, the water seemed to come from nowhere, just popping to the surface out of the layered rock that formed the base of a twenty-foot-high bluff. He'd known better. At the base of the bluff, about thirty feet from the source of the spring, he had found a small opening the size of a rabbit hole. He would rest next to the hole during the heat of summer and let the cool breeze that gushed from it flow over his body. In time, curiosity had gotten the best of him, and he had reamed out the hole and crawled inside. Fifteen feet down was an opening as large as a house. There he had found a gently flowing stream. The large room had two trails that led farther downward, into the darkness. He had never explored them much, but he had imagined the cave extending deep under the hills.

Strange what you remember, he thought as the train labored up a steep grade at ten miles an hour.

As far as Clinton knew, his sister still lived at home. She'd be about what, he wondered, nineteen now? Probably thinking about marriage—if anyone remained at home to marry. Jake, his little brother, had recently turned sixteen. Many of the bodies that littered the field at Gettysburg were those of men—boys—as young or younger. Jim's heart ached at the thought. He'd always thought of Jake as the type who would live forever. The experience of war had changed that.

When Clinton left Thompson's office, he had gone to the quartermaster's warehouse. The colonel had given him a blank requisition: "Get what you need," he had said, "and then bring Sam back." He had emphasized the word *back*. The more Clinton considered his prospects of success, the more improbable they seemed. He had selected a worn and tattered Confederate major's uniform, a red checkered shirt, a general's dress cape—to give the uniform some flavor—a belt and holster, a canteen, cavalry boots, three revolvers, and fifty extra rounds of ammunition. He doubted he'd have time to reload if he encountered trouble. He then had walked the mile to the National Hotel and eaten a leisurely but heavy lunch. He left the hotel shortly after three and stepped into the stifling midday heat and humidity. White spots had flashed before his eyes as the fatigue finally reached its limit and began playing tricks with his mind. He hadn't slept at all the night before, and very little the night before that. He had leaned against a building and nearly fallen asleep standing up. The queasiness had passed in time, but the fatigue remained. He needed rest.

Thompson told Clinton to arrive at the depot no later than six. The train would leave without him if he was late. He arrived at 3:50 P.M., just as the engine backed up to the station. A line of flatcars waited idly along a sidetrack, every square inch loaded with equipment going to a depot where supplies were being stockpiled on the eastern fringe of the Shenandoah Valley.

General Meade would march that way soon in a plodding, futile attempt to bring some imagined disaster to Lee's army from a dozen miles' distance. Meade's opportunity had passed, as Lincoln had known it would. Clinton thought it more likely that the Union army was unwittingly transporting the supplies for use by Lee's army.

Clinton had mounted the engine and persuaded the engineer to let him sleep there until they headed west. It's an uncomfortable place for a nap, he recalled thinking, but if he left the train he might miss the ride. He planned to get a horse and other gear at the railhead. He remembered nothing from the moment his head touched the engine's floor until the engineer nudged him with a boot.

Clinton pulled out his watch. It was past eight. Only a faint shimmer of light lingered in the clear evening sky. The train hadn't traveled ten miles, yet it had already stopped three times to pick up additional cars and passengers. Tents were set up in rows that were four deep on both sides of the tracks, and thousands of men moved listlessly about, as if there were no war. A second engine had chugged from a siding at the third stop and hooked up to a caboose to help push the growing load. Could have made better time on my horse, Clinton muttered to himself, but he knew better.

His mind begged for more sleep, but the train's clanking and rocking on the hastily laid track—coupled with his anxiety—kept him awake. He had no illusions about his mission; he expected it to be dangerous. When had his life in the army been anything else? One gets conditioned over time, he tried to assure himself. No, his agitation had another source; he feared failure more than death. He had already made up his mind: if Sam wasn't at the farm, he would track him down if it took until the end of the war. He certainly had no intention of going back to Thompson without Wade in tow.

The woman—what was her name? Cathy?—troubled him more than anything. It seemed only logical for her to hail the first Confederates she saw and get Sam to a hospital. Surely Lee had established permanent patrols with orders to protect his flank. More than eighty-five hours had passed since Clinton had begun his circular route to Washington and back. What were the chances of Wade remaining undetected for that long? Remote. Clinton's sense of urgency bordered on panic.

A thought flashed in his mind, then disappeared just as quickly. Had he seen Cathy somewhere before? He covered his face with his arms and squeezed his eyes shut to protect them from the soot. Had he known her years before, during their youth? The faint memory seemed incomplete—disjointed and out of focus. The rattle of the wheels made coherent thinking difficult. He concluded that her identity was of no importance. Nothing mattered except one thing: she was married to a Confederate officer.

Suddenly, all his hope vanished. He'd never find Sam—not at the farm or anywhere around it. He had told Cathy he would kill her if anything happened to Wade. Clinton forced that thought from his mind. Where war went, madness usually followed.

Hoping to trade the cinders in his eyes for a measure of silence, he stuck his fingers in his ears in a futile attempt to shut out the engine's roar. It only made him more aware of the vibrations. He sat up and hooked his elbow around a caisson wheel, then looked upward toward the dark, moonless sky filled with stars. As nights go, he thought disconnectedly, there have been worse ones on which to die.

# CHAPTER

# 7

Sam Wade had managed to fall asleep in midafternoon. The heat had made him drowsy and dulled his preoccupation with the pain. Must have slept about four hours, he thought as he observed the sun's position when he awoke. The slight movement had stimulated the pain with a vengeance. He shivered as a stiff breeze began to blow through the cracks of the barn. The woman had invited him to sleep in the house at the end of the first day, but he had decided against it. I'd be too vulnerable there, he had reasoned. He had no way of knowing what thoughts she kept hidden behind those alert, black eyes. At least in the barn he could hear her approaching. He had considered the possibility that she simply intended to wait patiently until the next rebel patrol passed by, then turn him over. If that happened, the barn offered only the illusion of protection.

It had been strangely quiet since Clinton left. That afternoon Wade had heard the sound of sporadic rifle fire in the distance—cavalry skirmishes, he figured—but the fire had died down quickly, and his thoughts kept returning to the woman. She seemed kind enough, but she remained aloof, detached. She never smiled, but neither did she frown. She moved through the day without much attention to anything other than her routine. Wade had simply become a part of that routine. She came by at mealtimes and again just before she went to bed. She usually said only a few words as she inspected his bandage and changed it when necessary.

Christ! he thought. I'm feeling sorry for myself. I have no right to expect anything else from her. She risked her life to keep those Union troopers from finding me.

It had been four full days since he had been shot during the encounter with the Union patrol. In his run-down condition, he had hardly begun the healing process. His shoulder still ached, especially when he tried to move.

Two days had passed before the bleeding had fully stopped. She has been an attentive nurse, he thought—giving her just due—and she was a darned good cook.

He strained to sit up without moving his shoulder, then paused to catch his breath. He placed a blanket behind his head and leaned against the rough wall. As he started to doze, he heard the distant sound of a leisurely galloping horse. It came nearer, moving toward the house. He pressed his left eye against a crack. He saw a single rider, a Confederate officer. Looks like a major or lieutenant colonel, he thought, but it was difficult to determine which in the fading light. Wade slid up the wall to a standing position. He bit his lip to keep from crying out in pain. Have to get to the other side of the barn, he thought—try to find a place to hide. He stuck his pistol in his belt. Pressing his extended hand outward to keep from falling, he leaned his good shoulder against the wall and peeked through a knothole. He was drenched with sweat. He placed his hand against his forehead. I'm burning up, he thought. He took a deep breath, trying to clear his head with the rapidly cooling evening air.

The officer seemed almost formal as he stiffly walked up the porch steps and strode to the front door. From Wade's vantage point, the man seemed more a shadow than real. The soldier straightened his tunic, then knocked. The light in the house grew brighter. He saw the woman's form pass by the window. The soldier stepped back as she opened the door. He removed his hat and bowed stiffly, then came to parade rest. Wade doubted that the visit had anything to do with him. They would have sent more than one man. But that could change with one short phrase from her.

The soldier remained on the porch, stiff and formal, as he spoke to the woman. He did most of the talking, his words too soft and far away for Wade to understand the substance of his message. He never looked toward the barn, never expressed with motion or tone any sign of alarm. As Wade relaxed, a wave of exhaustion rolled over him. Perhaps if I get more exercise I'll sleep better, he thought, almost forgetting the danger just sixty paces away. He let himself drop to his knees before rolling onto his side. His eyes rolled back in his head and he lost consciousness.

"What are you doing out here?" Cathy Blair asked admonishingly. "If you insist on moving around, you'll only open the wound." For the first time, she had the toddler with her.

Wade shaded his eyes from the lantern light and tried to focus on her. "I heard a noise and came out to investigate," he answered, rubbing his eyes. "I guess I didn't make it."

"Let me help you back to the toolroom," Cathy said, kneeling at his side. She lifted as he struggled to pull himself up on unsteady legs. Once in the small room, he dropped to his knees before shifting around and falling back on the blanket. "I hate being a cripple," he said under his breath.

Cathy placed the sleeping child in a nearby pile of hay before setting the lantern on a nail keg. She kneeled at Wade's side. He watched her face as she lifted the bandage to examine the wound. He sensed her discomfort as she consciously avoided looking at his eyes. The wound had bled a little; nothing to worry about, she assured him. She leaned back on her heels and folded her arms tightly across her chest, then slowly lifted her face toward the ceiling. As he watched her in the flickering, muted light, he saw her chin begin to quiver and tears form in the corners of her eyes.

Wade shifted his weight slightly and placed a hand on her arm. He felt her turn limp as she let her eyes drift slowly toward his. Her bottom lip quivered; then she broke into unrestrained sobbing. Wade knew that he should say something, but he was overwhelmed by the feeling that suddenly stirred within him. Cathy buried her face in her hands and let her head drift downward toward his chest. She began to rock rhythmically on her knees as he placed his hand on the back of her neck and ran his fingers through her hair. For the first time in four days, the persistent pain in his shoulder faded from his thoughts.

As her sobbing subsided, Cathy slowly lifted her head and reached up to wipe the tears from her cheeks. She sniffed and turned her head away from the lamplight. "That noise you heard outside—it was an officer from my husband's brigade. He rode out to inform me that a shell fragment struck Noah down at Gettysburg." She lifted her right hand and rubbed the back of her neck. She sighed. "They had to bury him where he fell. It was too hot to transport his body home." She looked up at Wade. "You've been in battle; how bad is it?"

He hesitated before answering. Anything he said was likely to raise more questions. "Do you think it would make you feel better if you knew?"

Cathy closed her eyes and shook her head. What she needed was to feel a soothing hand, hear a sympathetic voice, know that someone cared.

She slid her knees outward and reclined on her side. Her cheek pressed warmly on his abdomen, head rising and sinking in time with his slow, rhythmic breathing. "I'm so lonely," she said finally. "Do you mind if we spend the night here with you?"

She let the gentle flow of his fingers through her hair answer the question. For a brief moment she forgot her suffering and smiled inwardly before she fell asleep.

All had hushed. The irregular shapes of the barn boards swayed in time with the flickering, yellow-white lantern light. Somewhere in the next room a rodent scurried about in the hay. Now that the pain in his shoulder had subsided to a dull ache and he could think clearly, Wade risked a speculative glimpse into his future. This war would end, as all wars must; life would return to normal or be redefined as normal in some other sense. But how many wounds, physical and emotional, must he suffer? How many friends must die before the killing ended? What has fate devised for me? he wondered. The plan surely included more than killing or being killed.

As he let his fingers drift through Cathy's silken hair, the heat of her soft body merging with his, he found it only natural to think thoughts of the future, perhaps with Cathy. But now was the wrong time to act on them. They both were in distress—his physical, hers of the heart. But most wounds heal with time. She would need a man to be a father to her child. He would need a woman because—well, because the time had come. Was it wrong to think of those things?

Her breathing was slow and steady; she had escaped into sleep. He gently untangled his fingers from her hair and placed his hand delicately on her still-moist cheek. She moaned faintly, then, seeming more to sob than exhale as she nudged closer, she pulled into a knot. Their paths had crossed at a desperate time; events beyond their control would drive them apart soon enough.

He suddenly felt old, aged by the rigors of emotional turmoil and physical distress. He frequently ached for something unimagined, beyond his vision, something he had expected least of all to find in a weather-beaten old barn far behind enemy lines. But a new reality lay on the ground beside him. Because of what he felt for Cathy, he shared in her pain. She needed a man to take her dead husband's place. It wasn't fair—to either of them—that it had developed this way, but he saw nothing of fairness in what he had experienced during the past two years. Already the war had made countless young widows and taken from so many young women their lovers and kin. The nation was experiencing its rebirth in sorrow and pain. War had become the midwife. Perhaps it was futile to try to understand the deeper meaning of the churning in his mind, but he understood what he felt for the woman lying beside him.

The dull, orange light began to flicker, casting unearthly shadows from the irregular shapes within the cramped room. The kerosene lamp was empty. All that remained was the oily residue in the wick to fuel the tiny flame straining to light the darkness. His eyelids drooped as his stiff shoulder settled gently into the hay and he drifted into sleep.

Lucius Bowman sat impassively in the wicker chair, gazing straight ahead. Two slaves—boys of eight or so—stood on either side and slightly to the rear of the old man, fanning him, their motion synchronized so that one fan moved up when the other went down. A steady line of carriages rolled down the lane toward the mansion. Each stopped at the base of the veranda, and the driver of the next vehicle in line drew up and waited his turn, fifty or so feet behind. Thus the ritual progressed.

Two young Negroes, properly dressed in red vests and white waistcoats with tails, black shoes dusty but shined to a glare, would rush obediently forward, one to each side of the coach, and extend an arm to help the passengers as they stepped down to the gravel drive. Never did a passenger acknowledge the assistance. Each male passenger walked stiffly around the back of the coach and extended an arm as he approached the waiting lady, and the two marched up the eight steps to where the old man sat. Each gentleman tipped his hat as he made a few meaningless comments and wished the old man a happy birthday. Each lady nodded, just so, before the couple moved imperiously toward the main entrance.

The old man said nothing to anyone, nodded to a favored few, and never removed his eyes from some object of his attention far in the distance. There were more than twenty carriages neatly aligned on the manicured grassy knoll next to the stately mansion; a dozen more were strung out down the lane for several hundred yards, their occupants patiently awaiting their turn to wish the local patriarch many happy returns.

The old man's birthday—July 24—had been, as far back as anyone could remember, the glowing social event of the summer season. This year's gathering, marking his seventy-fifth year, lacked the proper elegance of better times. Few of the grand carriages sparkled as they had in the past. Some of the leather carriage seats had begun to crack and fray. The flower beds that lined the lane to the mansion were less well tended than in the past, and occasional tufts of grass marred the normally well-hoed turf between the rows. Bare spots on the pillars and the front facade of the huge dwelling suggested that the time had long passed for a fresh coat of paint. The rustling satin and taffeta dresses worn by the ladies were faded in spots. But no one noticed, or at least they pretended not to.

It wasn't that hard to do. A cool breeze carried the mingled scents of magnolia, pine, and mint. The color-streaked, late-evening sky blended perfectly with the soft greens of the gently swaying limbs of century-old trees. Nothing of war had marred the tranquil homeland of these people who had brought the war on in the first place.

But some things had to be endured in silence. No man under the age of twenty-five stepped down from any of the elegantly appointed carriages. Here and there, an unescorted lady or two rode with a couple who graciously had consented to provide passage. The ladies' husbands had long since departed to defend a way of life built on the suffering of another race, a suffering that many of those with less pigment in their skin believed to be ordained by God.

Some of the young men would never return. The old man's placid expression masked the turbulence within him, for he had concluded that, unless vigorously committed men acted soon, the genteel, unchanging way of life that had endured in his homeland for more than two centuries would disappear forever.

Fifteen days had passed since the first sketchy reports of the twin disasters at Vicksburg and Gettysburg had appeared in the Rome, Georgia, newspaper. Since that time more details had become available, and with them came mass public depression. People now dared to speak, if only in whispers, of the cause being lost. The strategic extent of the twin defeats exceeded imagination, and the local impact defied speculation. No one dared even to dwell on the human cost. An entire regiment from the surrounding area served in Longstreet's corps of Lee's Army of Northern Virginia. The paper reported that a Mississippi regiment of six hundred men, mustered into service in mid-1861, had experienced 99 percent casualties: by the late afternoon of the first day of the Gettysburg battle, all but three soldiers in the regiment had been killed, wounded, or otherwise lost to service. All of the men were from one county.

Two men stood quietly talking near one end of the porch. The old man had directed his attention more to them than the approaching guests.

"Do you believe it?" one asked. "The most recent report suggests that the casualty count at Gettysburg exceeds twenty thousand. My God! That's nearly a third of Lee's entire force." Everyone assumed that, if the reported casualties were that high, the true extent of the losses must be worse.

The other man nodded. "And we don't seem to be able to get any word on the fate of our own 18th Georgia." No one knew. Details were days, perhaps weeks, from being accurately published. "At last report," he added, "Lee's army was dug in, trapped on the north side of the Potomac, and General Meade's army was approaching their trenches."

One of the old man's grandsons had been at Vicksburg. His granddaughter's husband, a regimental staff officer in Hood's division of Longstreet's corps, was with Lee at Gettysburg. Another grandson was thought to be somewhere in western Tennessee, a staff officer with Union forces in the Chattanooga area. The old man had forbade even the mention of his name after he had ridden north to fight for the Federals. James, the youngest of his grandchildren, had died at Chancellorsville.

This evening's gathering had three purposes. In addition to the birthday celebration, tradition called for the old man to pass on the leadership of the family. At precisely midnight, the honor and all the responsibility that went with being patriarch of the Bowman clan would pass to Arthur, Lucius's eldest son. This approaching event had caused mixed emotions for the old man. He liked the power, the control, the idea of his word being law. He thought of himself as a latter-day Solomon. By common agreement, whenever a dispute reached an impasse, the old man would weigh the facts, measure the most good for the most people, and render a judgment. He questioned his son's ability to command the respect necessary to exercise such unquestionable authority. But he also knew that his own father had expressed similar doubts when his time had come.

The third reason for the gathering involved the impending arrival of a special guest. The man had been sent on a secret mission. But Lucius knew the reason—and he had yet to decide precisely how he felt about it, at least part of it. The idea of assassinating Abraham Lincoln bothered him less than did the thought of swatting a fly. He smiled inwardly. Thinking about the other part of the mission—the end justifying the means—evoked conflicting feelings. The old man had always prided himself on never compromising his basic values. That, more than anything, had elevated his wisdom in the eyes of the others, giving it a special quality that all could respect without question. Now, at this late stage in his life, the thought of compromising those values troubled him more than ever. But he saw one compensation: he would be out of it, at least out of the forefront, and that made it easier to release to his son the reins of authority. But then, he thought, his son knew nothing of the grand design. How would he respond? What chances would he take to carve a new future for the South?

The special guest planned to spend the night. He would discuss his ideas only in the most general terms with the male guests. A full disclosure of the grand design would follow later. Lucius would measure reactions and identify those men needed to help develop the details. The real work would begin later. Only the worthy—the truly committed—would receive invitations.

The last carriage stopped and the couple inside it emerged and moved gracefully up the steps. Lucius sighed as Arthur and his wife approached. "It's time to begin, Father," Arthur Bowman said, stooping to touch the old man's arm. "Everyone is here, waiting to make the annual toast."

"Hmmph," said the old man. "A damned good excuse for them to get a free meal and drink my liquor."

"Come now, Father," said Arthur's wife, Pearl. "You know they all love you."

"Love me, Pearl? Poppycock! Respect? Maybe. Fear? Definitely. But never love."

The guests held up their glasses as the old man shuffled into the ballroom.

Lucius nodded and smiled. As the guests drank a toast, Arthur turned and kissed his father on the cheek. The elder Bowman wrapped his arms around his son. "This is all yours now," he whispered. "No matter what happens, preserve it for your grandchildren." His father had said the same thing to him twenty-five years earlier, and now it was his turn to step aside.

The sound of heavy boots moving down the hall interrupted the old man's reverie. Three men stopped under the broad arch of the doorway. All were Confederate officers, but the dust on their uniforms made identifying their rank difficult. "Ladies and gentlemen," said Lucius, smiling in recognition, "it is my pleasure to present a special guest: Maj. Gen. Henry Thornton, commander of the Alabama militia."

# CHAPTER

# 8

Two miles short of the farm where Clinton had left Wade, a cavalry patrol came into sight. Clinton detected no urgency in their pace; they rode along at a canter so slow that the animals had difficulty moving forward at a balanced pace. Clinton slowed his horse to an easy gallop, barely closing the gap, to give himself time to think. He counted eleven men in all. As he drew closer, he stiffened in the saddle and slowed the horse. There were eleven, all right, ten in the patrol—and Sam Wade. Clinton easily recognized his friend. Wade wore his shirt draped over his back with his right arm in a sling tied around his neck. His long blond hair flowed in the breeze. Five men rode in front of Wade, one rode at his side, and four brought up the rear. Except for the cavalryman at Wade's side, they all seemed relaxed enough. The sergeant at Wade's left had his pistol drawn. By the time Clinton had observed all of this, he had closed to within thirty yards.

Clinton concluded that he had two choices: he could ride up friendly-like, try to gain their confidence, and then wait for an opportunity to escape with Wade, or he could ride in hard, guns blazing, and trust to surprise and luck. As Clinton closed to within twenty yards, a soldier at the end of the line turned and saw him approaching. The soldier hesitated for a moment, his hand suspended above the carbine slung from his saddle. Clinton's anxiety dictated his choice of actions. If he hoped to surprise them . . .

Clinton waved with his left hand to distract the man and reached casually with his right for a pistol stuck in his belt. He simultaneously drew the weapon and spurred his horse to a run. He leaned forward, arm extended, took aim, and began firing. What followed appeared to Clinton as though in slow motion.

His first shot caught the soldier in the arm, causing him to drop his carbine. Clinton's unconscious glance revealed that the man had no other weapon. By the time he recorded the observation, his aim shifted and his finger sent a second bullet hurtling toward the next man in line. It caught him at an angle, in the back of his neck as he made a quarter turn. The man continued to rotate slowly before dropping in a fluid motion to the ground, mortally wounded.

Clinton's third shot slammed into the left hip of the rider in the left rear position, knocking him from his horse. His fourth bullet missed, and the fifth pull on the trigger resulted in a misfire. The soldier who had been riding with his weapon drawn rotated halfway around in his saddle and brought his pistol unsteadily to shoulder level. Clinton's last bullet entered the man's left eye, exited through his left temple, and tumbled on in its deflected course before striking the horse of the startled young officer leading the group. The horse and both men hit the ground in rapid succession.

Clinton dropped the empty pistol to the ground and drew another from the holster on his right hip. He had approached to within five yards of Wade. Clinton fired again, nicking the right ear of the only man still behind Wade and causing the man to jerk on his horse's reins. The animal reared skyward and toppled its rider backward from the saddle. The soldier slid down the mare's hind section toward the road, landed on his feet, and ran into the woods.

Clinton's last two shots were on target as well. One clipped the spine of a corporal, and the other crashed into the chest of a cavalryman who had turned halfway around in his saddle. Clinton was close enough to see clearly the man's expression. After looking down at the hole in his jacket, the man peered curiously at Clinton, his eyes squinting and his brow furrowed, apparently bewildered by the conclusion that a Confederate major had just killed him. The muddled expression froze on his face as he slumped in his saddle before sliding limply to the ground.

The remaining three men still in the saddle—one shot through the arm and two unhurt—flung their arms into the air as Clinton's momentum carried him past the head of the column. Clinton pulled to a stop and yanked hard on his horse's reins to turn him around. The officer, by this time recovered from his tumble and surprise, frantically tried to draw his pistol. Clinton calmly extended his arm and aimed his weapon at the young lieutenant's chest. The rebel officer froze, the pistol half in and half out of its holster. His other arm drifted slowly over his head.

The encounter had lasted less than fifteen seconds from start to finish.

"Y'all have somethin' I want," Clinton said calmly to the officer.

"What's that, sir?" asked the young officer.

The lieutenant's mannerly response amused Clinton. It must be the Confederate uniform, he thought, smiling to himself. These're sure well-disciplined soldiers. "That man with his arm in a sling," Clinton said, pointing at Wade. "And if you don't mind, I'll take your horses and side arms."

The officer made no response.

"Throw that pistol on the ground 'fore I blow your head off, Lieutenant." The weapon dropped free before Clinton finished speaking.

"How y'all doin', Colonel?" Clinton said in his thickest Southern drawl. "Y'almost got away from me this time." The remark was intended to convey concern to his friend while adding to the Confederate lieutenant's confusion.

The glazed expression in Wade's eyes concerned Clinton. The bandage had a dark red stain—the wound had obviously reopened with all the activity—and he seemed barely able to hold himself upright in the saddle. Clinton immediately concluded that Wade had no chance of making an unassisted, forty-mile dash to safety. They might make a mile, two if necessary for immediate safety, but no more. Wade's condition forced Clinton to think of an alternative.

Clinton motioned for the three men still astride their horses to dismount. "Drop your guns," he said calmly. He flung his saddlebags at the lieutenant's feet. "Put 'em all in here and return the bag t'me." Once the men were disarmed, Clinton moved from one horse to the next and grasped the reins. When he had them all in tow, he looked down at the lieutenant and smiled, then motioned with his pistol. "Lieutenant, are you up to a short ride?"

The young officer shrugged.

"Get on that horse with the colonel. It 'pears he'll need a bit of steadyin'." The lieutenant looked defiantly at Wade and remained still. Clinton cocked his pistol and stared down the barrel at the man. It was all the incentive the young officer needed. He demonstrated superb horsemanship as he ran forward and vaulted up and over the animal's hindquarters. He wrapped his arms around Wade and took the reins.

Clinton smiled at the other Confederates. "Y'all have a nice day, now. Get movin', Lieutenant. You go ahead of me. We have a far piece t'ride."

Although Clinton had no intention of stopping at the Blair farm, he ordered the lieutenant to ride in that direction. He planned to turn east soon, after riding a mile or so, and move cross-country without stopping, back toward Union lines. They would switch horses every five miles or so. With luck, they could cover the twenty-five miles to the railhead before dawn the next day.

By the time Clinton ordered the turn, Wade had lost consciousness, forcing the rebel to hold him in place. Sam needs to hole up for a while, Clinton thought. But it's too late to worry about that now. Within an hour, two at most, Wade's former escorts would contact a larger force. Then the hunt would commence in earnest. If there was to be any chance of making it to safety, they had to move fast.

"Where y'from?" Clinton asked the lieutenant as they waited in a shallow stream for the horses to drink.

"Virginia, west of Harper's Ferry," the man replied. That section of Virginia had become the new state of West Virginia, but the South still claimed the land. Clinton, knowing this, avoided the temptation to rub salt in a wound.

"What's your name?"

"Atchison. Jesse Atchison."

"How long y'been in the army?"

"Almost since the beginnin'. I joined in May of '61." The lieutenant turned in the saddle and looked at Clinton. He understood nothing that had happened to him and his men. One thing he did understand: these two were not what they seemed. It made no sense. The major spoke with an unmistakable Southern accent and he wore a Confederate uniform. He had easy, soft-spoken Southern mannerisms. But he had virtually wiped out Atchison's patrol. The major and the man Atchison supported both were his enemies. Why should he care about either of them? But he had to admit, if only to himself, that he had begun to question the war's purpose. Both of his parents strongly supported the Union. And he had seen the misery caused by the irregulars who operated with moral impunity in the Shenandoah and its environs, taking what they wanted, killing anyone who resisted. His favorite uncle had been a victim, as had a cousin—a boy of only thirteen—who had hurled a stone at one of the bandits. The war clearly had gotten out of hand. Beyond that, it said something about a man who would place himself in so much jeopardy by attacking ten times his number to rescue someone. It took something more than military orders to make a man take such a risk. Atchison doubted he would have done the same—for any reason. Sitting there looking at Clinton, the lieutenant realized he faced a difficult choice. Before making it, he would examine the current situation a bit more thoroughly. "What's this man to you?" he asked.

"He's my best friend."

"Too bad," said Atchison casually. "He probably ain't gonna make it."

"You a doctor or somethin'?" Clinton asked.

Atchison extended a dripping, bloody palm toward Clinton. "Nope. Don't have to be, Major."

He's right, thought Clinton. Sam'll bleed to death if I don't do something soon. But what? Surrender? He might die if we keep going, but the Confederates will certainly kill him if they get their hands on him. "I'll give it some thought, Atchison. Let's get goin'."

Clinton pushed hard. By six that evening they were on their third set of mounts. That left one spare each—and they still had at least fifteen miles to ride. They had avoided several rebel patrols earlier in the afternoon. Now, as they rode closer to the Union lines, there was little activity. Wade's condition grew worse by the minute. His breathing was shallow, and Atchison was having a hard time keeping him in the saddle. They had to stop frequently to tend the wound and allow Atchison some rest. With each passing hour, Clinton's apprehension increased. Wade was losing too much blood. They had to stop soon.

A high bank of clouds began forming at the horizon, then rolled menacingly east. Darkness settled quickly as the storm rumbled over them. They had moved into hill country and had avoided the roads. Clinton began to look for shelter but there were no buildings in sight. Then it started to rain, gently at first, then with large, pelting drops. Then the clouds exploded into a torrential downpour.

"We have to get out of this," Atchison screamed over the roar of the wind. "Your friend will be dead in an hour if we don't."

Clinton nodded. He rode to Atchison's side. "There're some rocky cliffs over there." He pointed. "Head that way."

They spurred the horses to a trot. Lightning flashed overhead and thunder reverberated over them. Although it was dark, the almost constant illumination from the lightning guided them through the trees. "Over there, on the side of that hill," Clinton shouted above the storm. "There's a rock outcroppin'. Let's get under it 'til this lets up."

Atchison nodded. He was exhausted from trying both to control his terrified horse and keep Wade from sliding to the ground.

Clinton rode ahead and tied his mount securely to a log. Just to be safe, he hobbled the animal. "Okay, lower the colonel to me," he said as Atchison pulled to a halt. The lieutenant held Wade's belt as he slid limply into Clinton's arms. "Help me carry him," Clinton directed. Atchison dismounted and lifted Wade's legs. They carried the comatose form to the shelter of the rocks. Lightning flashed and the roar of thunder shattered the air.

Wind had eroded the soft earth and sandstone under the rocky outcropping, creating a cozy shelter. The roof sloped sharply downward toward the back, forcing Clinton and Atchison to stoop low as they carried Wade under the protective overhang. Fortunately, the opening faced northwest, away from the main force of the wind and driving rain. The ground remained dry where they stood. "Lay him here, against the back wall," Clinton said. Wade groaned as they stretched him out. "See if y'can find some dry wood for a fire. I'll tend t'the other horses," Clinton added.

Atchison soon had a fire going, but it offered little more than the comfort of having light. The wind swirled about the opening, first billowing, then nearly extinguishing the flame. There remained nothing to do but keep Wade as comfortable as possible, try to dry out—and wait. As the storm raged, Clinton examined his friend in the flashing and flickering light. He shook his head. "He's losin' too much blood. I don't know what t'do."

"Seal the wound," Atchison said.

Clinton reacted with surprise. "Seal it?"

"Yeah. Cauterize it."

"Y'mean burn him? Fry his skin?"

"He'll keep bleeding if you don't. It probably won't matter by morning. With the chill, and the blood he's already lost, I don't give him more than a 10 percent chance."

"You keep talkin' like a doctor," Clinton observed.

"Veterinarian. My father's a vet. When an animal gets badly injured, like when a bull gores a cow, we press a hot iron to the wound. We don't lose many."

Clinton stared down at Wade. He had been delirious for the past hour and had developed a fever. Blood continued to ooze from the wound. He was dying, and Clinton felt powerless to save him. The time had come for bold action. "Will you do it?"

"If you want. Got a knife?"

Clinton hesitated a moment, then pulled his knife from the scabbard on his belt and passed it handle first to the rebel. Their eyes met. Clinton felt the touch of Atchison's hand as he reached for the knife. Clinton let go of the blade and leaned back.

Atchison had his answer. Having a friend means risking all for him. Few men he knew had that kind of courage. Perhaps none. Atchison grasped the handle and inserted the blade in the flame. He picked up a stick and brushed hot coals around the blade, then leaned down and blew on the coals to make them burn hotter. Several minutes passed before the hard steel glowed red. He rotated the knife and placed the blade on top of the coals. He waited until a flaky, oxidized film formed. "It's ready," he announced.

Clinton opened his mouth to speak, but the words never passed his lips. A bolt of lightning struck the ground thirty feet from the cave's opening. He had a fraction of a second to be dismayed by the sight of fire shooting from the tips of the fingers of his left hand before he was lifted from the ground and slammed against the dirt wall. The impact forced the wind from his lungs, and he crumpled on top of Wade. Clinton felt as though he was clamped in a vise, with the weight of the world pushing against the handle. He screamed in pain. To the front of the shelter, where the lightning had hit, a large maple tree exploded in flame and split with an ear-shattering, ripping sound. Clinton watched helplessly as half of the flaming trunk crashed against the hill just above the overhang. Branches splintered from the impact and flew into the air. One of the largest slammed against Atchison and drove him to the ground.

Clinton clutched at his smoking hand. He grimaced at the stabbing pain. His bare arm brushed against a metal button on his coat and he jerked away from the hot metal. His mind felt numb; nothing around him seemed real.

Stunned into semiconsciousness, he sat motionless, with the full weight of his body pressing down on Wade's legs.

Gradually, Clinton's mind began to clear. He gathered his strength and rolled awkwardly to the left, off of Wade's legs, toward a small open spot between two splintered branches. He looked outside their small shelter and saw Atchison lying prostrate just outside the overhang. Clinton heard him groan and saw a leg move. At least he's alive, he thought. The lieutenant still clung to the knife. The blade sizzled and smoked as raindrops splashed against it.

"How badly are you hurt?" Clinton asked Atchison as his thoughts cleared.

"Can't tell for sure. My arm's broken and my leg is pinned under these branches."

Without really thinking, Clinton gripped the large section of smoldering trunk. "When I lift, you try to pull free." Atchison nodded. "Ready? *Now!*" As Clinton strained to move the limb, he felt the last spark of energy drain from his weary arms. Despite exerting maximum effort, nothing happened. Then he slowly rose to a standing position, bringing with him a quarter-ton chunk of the tree. His muscles vibrated from the strain, and his mind created bizarre images that danced in expanding circles.

"Free!" shouted Atchison.

Clinton needed no further encouragement. He flung his arms outward and his body crumpled to the ground. He lacked the strength to move the small branch that pressed against his throbbing hand. As his body settled into the soothing mud, his mind refused to consider anything more complex than the sensation of driving rain washing the dirt and grime from his face. It was enough to remind him that he was alive.

Without waiting to assess his own condition, Atchison rolled toward the dancing yellow flames and inserted the knife blade back into the few remaining coals. Sheltering the dying flames with his hat, he began to blow.

Several minutes later, Clinton flinched at the piercing sound of a scream. He rolled on his side and saw Atchison pressing the knife's glowing blade against Wade's shoulder. He winced at the sound of sizzling flesh.

Atchison turned toward Clinton. "Help me roll him over before the blade cools. We have to seal the other side."

Clinton lifted his arm and strained to reach for Wade's far leg; Wade rolled smoothly over. Clinton lay flat on his back and waited. He heard the sizzling sound again, followed by a second scream.

"He's waking up," said an orderly. "The fever's broken."

Sunlight from the low window burned directly into Sam Wade's eyes. He lifted his good arm and turned his head away from the glare.

"Can you hear me, Colonel Wade?"

Wade nodded once, barely. He shifted his arm and looked through blurry eyes at the figure bending over him.

"We almost lost you, son," said the doctor. "How do you feel?"

"Weak," Wade said in a raspy whisper, "and very thirsty."

"Orderly, bring the colonel a cup of water." Wade licked his cracked lips in anticipation. The doctor squeezed his arm. "You're dehydrated from the fever. We couldn't get much water down you without your gagging. You had a rough time of it." He took the cup from the orderly and pressed it to Wade's lips.

"Where am I?" Wade asked.

"Washington," said another voice. "You've been out for several days."

Wade smiled. He recognized Clinton's voice. "So you got me back after all, Jim."

"Wasn't that simple," Clinton replied. "Lieutenant Atchison, more or less, got us both back."

"Lieutenant Atchison?"

"Y'don't remember, do ya? He commanded the rebel patrol I rescued y' from."

Clinton's explanation brought Wade fully alert. He rolled his eyes toward Clinton, who was lying on the mattress to his right. A bulky bandage covered much of Clinton's head. His right hand was tightly wrapped, the gauze stained yellow by salve. Both his eyes were black, and his bare chest, devoid of the thick, black hair that Wade remembered, was covered with scratches and large bruises.

Reacting to Wade's quizzical look, Clinton said, "It's a long story, Sam."

"Must be." Wade smiled. "You look like you lost a wrestling match with the devil."

Clinton laughed. "That's one way of puttin' it. Atchison an' I got t'know each other quite well on the ride back. He's an interestin' man—for a Reb. You'd like him, Sam. Hell, some of those boys ain't such bad sorts." He smiled broadly. "Look at me. But it's a long story, Sam, and y'need your rest. I'll tell ya 'bout it later. I'll even take y'to meet Atchison, if y'like. Y'all might want t'tell him thanks. He saved your life."

"Where is he?" Wade asked.

"In a prison hospital. Like me, he's a bit worse for wear. Has a broken arm and assorted other ailments."

"I don't remember any of it," said Wade.

"T'be frank with ya, Sam, y'all are lucky you're here t'remember that y'*don't* remember. You weren't ready for the kind of ridin' I put y'through. Even then, it was a close call. If'n I'd arrived an hour later, you'd be buzzard meat by now."

The thought startled Wade. "You didn't do it, did you, Jim?"

Did I miss something in this conversation? Clinton wondered, totally surprised by Wade's question. "Do what, Sam?"

"Kill the woman at the farm. You said you'd kill her if I wasn't at the farm when you returned."

Clinton relaxed. "Naw. Never had much taste for killin' women. They're too tough. Besides, Atchison told me what happened. She tried t'keep him out of the barn, but he insisted. One of their horses had a loose shoe an' they was lookin' for tools t'nail it back on. When he pushed past her on the way t'the barn, she had t'tell him 'bout you. Atchison had no doubts at all 'bout who y'was. He figured he'd get a promotion for rescuin' a high-rankin' Confederate officer. S'prised the hell out of 'em when I rode up shootin'."

Wade tried to maintain a bland expression but failed. "Thank God! I'm going back after her, Jim—when the time's right. I—we killed her husband at Gettysburg. She'll need help. I owe her that. This war won't last forever."

" S'pose not," Clinton agreed. "I doubt I can stand much more of this excitin' life." He reached across to Wade and placed his hand on his friend's forehead. "Cool as ice. Are y'up t'talkin' t'the colonel?"

"Thompson?" Wade asked.

"Yeah. Go easy on him, Sam. He feels right bad 'bout sendin' ya on this mission—'specially after he said he wouldn't do it no more. He chewed on my ass good when I come back without ya the first time."

"I practically ordered you to leave," Wade countered.

"Didn't matter none t'the colonel," Clinton replied, his lips pursed. "He has this strange idea that we're invincible or somethin'."

"I feel about as invincible as a twig in a flood," Wade replied.

"I know what y'mean, Sam. I'll get Colonel Thompson."

Wade closed his eyes as Clinton moved out of sight. He was extremely tired. What a strange war this is, he thought. Southerners fighting for the north. Southern ladies protecting Yankees disguised in rebel uniforms. Northern soldiers saving Southern soldiers, Southerners dying to save Northerners. It's absurd. Lincoln had sized it up correctly. Americans are no good at killing each other. Strange ideas keep getting in the way. He pushed it from his mind. It was too complex for a man in his condition to sort through.

"He looks asleep to me," said Thompson.

"Just dozing," Wade replied. "Sorry I can't stand, Colonel. I'm a little weak in the limbs just now."

"Would you prefer we talked later, Sam?"

"No, Colonel. What can I do for you, sir?"

"I'm sending you away, Sam."

"Away, sir? Where?"

"West. I have to get you out of here, away from Lee's army—away from me. No telling what I might think up for you to do if you stay here."

"How far west, Colonel?"

"General Rosecrans's army, down near Chattanooga. He and Braxton Bragg's rebels are waltzing about down there in the woods. I'll see to it you get another regiment, Sam. You've earned it for keeps this time."

"Oh, *that West,* sir. I thought you had in mind Colorado, or maybe California."

"You're not that lucky, Sam."

"And Major Clinton, sir?"

Thompson looked at Clinton and smiled. "He'd be useless around here, just getting underfoot and talking Southern all the time. I'm afraid to be near him for fear someone will shoot at him and hit me."

Clinton looked straight ahead. He wasn't sure how much Thompson had softened since he'd brought Wade back.

Wade tried lifting himself up on his good elbow, but failed. The effort drained his strength. He gasped for air as he collapsed on his back.

"You okay, Sam?"

"Fine, Colonel. In a couple of days I'll be ready for a stroll in the park. When do we leave, sir?"

"Not for several weeks. We have to get you all healed up. You lost a bucket of blood. Somewhere after the first of September should be soon enough. Maybe later. It doesn't look like much is going to happen down there any sooner."

General Washburn had been listening from a few feet away. All that had happened with Wade and Clinton had been his doing, with Thompson's assistance, of course, but he had avoided Thompson's personal involvement with the two men. At first he resisted when Thompson sought permission to send Wade to Rosecrans's army, but he had finally yielded. Wade and Clinton had become valuable resources, and he found Thompson's sentiment regarding their safety misplaced. In time of war, a soldier had to take his chances.

Washburn walked to where the men were talking and laughing. He bent down and touched Wade's hand. "How are you doing, son?" the general asked.

Wade saluted and smiled wanly. "I'll be on my feet soon, General. We Wades are hard to kill."

Washburn thought of Wade's mother and her ordeal. "No doubt about that, Colonel. How is your mother doing?"

"Haven't heard from her since before Gettysburg."

Washburn looked sharply at Thompson. Thompson turned away. He had several letters from Wade's mother in the office safe; Wade's eyes would never see them. They were full of information about Wade's twin brother. Thompson had determined he must keep such information from Wade, at least for a while longer. Whatever Thompson's feelings for Wade, he felt nothing for Simon Thornton. He was, after all, one of the enemy, and in such matters Thompson had no room for sentiment.

Washburn harrumphed and bent down to place a sheet of parchment on Wade's chest. "That's your promotion to major in the regular army. You've earned it, Sam."

Wade smiled feebly as he picked up the document and silently read it. Does this make it all worthwhile? he wondered. It certainly helps. His promotion would mean a lot when the army was cut back—as he knew it would be—after the war. He knew generals whose permanent ranks were lower than major. "Thank you, sir."

"You've earned it, son," Washburn repeated. "Now get some rest—you too, Major Clinton. The war will have to wait awhile for you two to get back in it."

Wade nodded as he pressed the parchment to his chest and let his eyelids drop.

From the diary of Caroline Wade-Healy

*July 28, 1863*
*I've been too distressed to write anything for the past day. I received two telegrams yesterday, both with bad news. One informed me that Samuel has been wounded. The message was brief, stating only that the wound wasn't serious and he would be up and around in a few weeks. I don't know where he is. Even if I did know, I'd not leave Simon. If not for Simon, I'd take the train to Washington and find out for myself where Samuel is.*

*Maybe now that Samuel is out of the war for a while, he will have an opportunity to write. Then, at least, I'll know where he is.*

*The second telegram, from the Washington provost marshal's office, informed me that I have to give up Simon to military custody by August 2. What possible danger is he when he can't even remember his own name? They seem to think he might be faking his memory loss. I know better. I'm the one who sees that vacant look in his eyes when I mention events from his past. I must admit that Simon is well on the way to recovery— at least physically. But he still gets very confused about his past. Another month can't hurt anyone. Simon will have all his strength back by then, if not his memory. I am not hopeful. I have sent a letter to General Meade asking him to let me keep Simon here a bit longer. By the time the letter catches up with him, I suspect Simon will be gone.*

*I'm useless here. I can't concentrate anymore. The shoe business takes care of itself. I just receive the notices of deposit from the bank. I fear the country will be flat broke when this war ends. Where does all the money come from?*

*Washington is with a colored regiment that is just forming. He wrote his mother that he recognized the army-issue shoes as ones made in one of my factories. She is so proud of him.*

*It's such a beautiful sunset. I think I'll join Simon and Molly on the porch. I think he likes Molly very much. He doesn't seem to remember his disdain for Negroes. Ironies seem to guide our lives.*

———————

# PART 2
# CHICKAMAUGA

# CHAPTER

# 9

Pelting rain from a dreary gray sky had long since drenched the Confederate prisoners. Mud kicked up by the outriders' mounts splashed on the plodding columns. The men no longer bothered to wipe it off, and the Union cavalry gave no thought to the prisoners' miserable condition.

A more motley, downtrodden procession seemed hard to imagine. Many limped; more than a few had an empty pant leg or coat sleeve. All were demoralized beyond caring. The prisoners strained as they hoisted their mud-caked feet from the clinging soil. Those on crutches had the most arduous task. They frequently lost their balance and crumpled into the sucking clay.

If the Confederates were a grim sight, so too were the columns of Federals who sloshed up the trail toward them. They were a similarly sorry lot, equally worn and haggard and, if possible, carrying even less flesh on their bones. Such conditions were among the anomalies of this war. Neither side had the interest or ability to properly care for prisoners. Using a formula that applied a weighted value for officers and enlisted men, the two governments periodically exchanged their prisoners, an action that decidedly favored the South. The South had fewer men to begin with, and caring for captured Union soldiers placed a burdensome strain on its meager resources. At least a soldier in the field could scrounge for himself. His ability to fire a rifle only added to the advantage. Recognizing this, the Union general in chief, Maj. Gen. Henry Halleck, more than three months earlier had ordered an end to large-scale prisoner exchanges. But as is usual in the army, someone failed to get the word.

Mixed among the rebels staggered a bewildered Lt. Col. Simon Thornton. As poor as his condition might have appeared to a casual observer, the nature of his afflictions placed him in the ranks of the most fortunate of these miserable souls. His abdominal wound had largely healed. The scarred and darkened flesh on the side of his head remained tender to the touch but otherwise had healed. The quarter-inch stubble of patchy blond hair would soon grow in length to cover the damage. His greatest affliction remained invisible. His mind was virtually blank.

When Colonel Thompson first saw Thornton at Caroline Healy's farm, he was convinced that Thornton's brain had become a dark, blank slate upon which new information might be recorded. After Thompson had the Confederate returned to his custody, he soon discovered that the soldier's gray matter resisted even his adulterating efforts, so he had decided to leave well enough alone. Nothing might be better than something that would stir memories best left submerged.

A limp, soggy tag identified Simon Thornton, Lt. Col., CSA; the man himself lacked the competence to confirm or deny the tag's accuracy. If his comrades wanted to know more, they would have to discover it for themselves. Thompson was confident that their confusion and doubt would compel the Confederate high command to think conservatively about this man.

The soldiers at the heads of the two opposing columns halted on cue. Inattentive to anything other than the point where the next step would lead, the men behind them bumped into those ahead, compressing the columns into half their length. All sense of military discipline had faded during their period of hard, humiliating confinement.

Less than a hundred feet separated the opposing columns. Officers dressed in blue and gray rode forward. They met halfway between, under a grove of roadside trees with drooping limbs. Enlisted men moved among the Southern prisoners, distributing to each man two hardtack biscuits and a tin cup half filled with rain-diluted molasses. "Drink it down, men. Toss the cup in the wagon as you march by." The instructions never varied. They needed no urging to consume the spartan rations. None had eaten since the prior evening. It was now four in the afternoon. Their arduous trek had commenced at dawn.

As the delay continued, a few fell from the ranks and stretched out beside the road. They soon fell asleep. If nothing else, the war had taught them the art of enduring misery by taking rest where they found it. Most stood limp, their heads drooping, as they waited for whatever those in charge planned for them. A column of open wagons pulled to the head of the Confederate column. They were crammed with soldiers who had fallen from the ranks along the way. Guards roughly nudged the anxious, stricken figures onto crude stretchers before placing them on the ground. Others selected stronger prisoners and pushed them out of line with none too gentle shoves from musket butts. "Pick up that stretcher, Reb," they ordered, "and be quick about it." Out in front, as the litter bearers waited for orders to move forward, the officers from both sides hotly but inaudibly exchanged words.

The prisoner exchange was about equal: 1,222 Confederates for 1,221 Union prisoners. One of the Union soldiers had attempted to escape. Too weak to fight his way through the mud, he stumbled and began to crawl. An over-zealous rebel had shot him in the knee. The prisoner had slowly bled to death during the journey. Explaining how that had happened was the cause of the hostile exchange among the officers.

Motivated more by anger than common sense, the Union provost captain threatened to remove the highest ranking Confederate from the ranks for return to a Union prison. As he contemplated the paperwork, he persuaded himself of the merits of reconsidering. Simon Thornton never suspected, nor would he have understood, the significance of that decision. Thornton, his thoughts barely troubled by anything other than his immediate discomfort, slouched indifferently while others decided his fate. The discussion among the officers ended abruptly. The men carrying the dead soldier's loosely draped corpse led the procession of enfeebled Union soldiers as they were carried on stretchers past their healthier counterparts, moving in the direction of home. Then the mobile prisoners marched aimlessly from captivity back into the war. With that, the ugly drama concluded.

Back in a Washington hospital, a doctor had bound Samuel Wade's ailing arm to his chest, making movement awkward. Opening the letter he held in his hand was a challenge. Wade shifted his weight clumsily as he labored to settle into a comfortable position. Finally, he found a posture that temporarily eased the strain on his shoulder. Forcing a finger from his good hand under the seal, he opened the letter. He began to read, smiling now and again as he absorbed the words from his friend Bill Healy. They had been closest friends at West Point, and with the marriage of Healy's father to Wade's mother, Bill had become a brother.

Although the letter from his friend had brightened Wade's day, it unleashed a flood of haunting memories. Following the Battle of Chancellorsville, Wade had lost track of Healy. Back in early May, both had been captured on the night that Stonewall Jackson met his fate. In the process of defending an obscure piece of the Wilderness, Wade had been partially immobilized when a rebel jammed a bayonet into his thigh. Later, when an opportunity for escape arose, Healy attempted to make his way back to Union lines. He tried to persuade Wade to come with him—even offered to carry him to safety—but circumstances of war compelled Wade to remain behind. He had a more urgent calling. A Confederate major, another man from Wade's West Point class, had been shot in the neck. The bullet had hit an artery, and as blood spouted from the wound, Wade had instinctively pushed his finger into the hole. Removing it to go with Healy would have meant certain death for his former friend. The major's pleading eyes convinced Wade to remain while Healy crawled to safety and back into the war.

"It's from Bill Healy," Wade said absently to Clinton, who was in the next bed. "You remember me telling you about him? He's been transferred to Rosecrans's army, down in Tennessee. He's on temporary assignment to Colonel Wilder's brigade. Says they just received some of those new repeating rifles, and the men can hardly wait to unload them on General Bragg's Rebs."

When Wade heard no response from Clinton, he looked across at him. He seemed sound asleep. Clinton had healed slowly. One of his fingers—the one next to his little finger—had become gangrenous and had to be amputated. Following that, the stub became infected; then the whole hand and arm had become inflamed. It had been a close call. The surgeon had been only hours away from amputating his arm when the infection began to subside. Now Clinton felt a persistent numbness in his left hand. He still had difficulty holding any but the lightest object. Everything combined had taken its toll.

Wade's condition had improved equally slowly. His wound, too, had become infected. Only now, more than four weeks after the ordeal, did he feel himself returning to normal.

Both men had been moved from the warehouse to a hospital a week after their return from the mission. Thompson had come there frequently during the following ten days. Then his duties became more pressing. Nearly a week had passed since Thompson had stopped by, and then only briefly while on his way to the train station. Now, Wade patiently waited for the doctor to examine his wound.

As the sun set, nurses in stiffly starched dresses with cold, forbidding expressions moved through the open ward lighting lanterns. The sickening stench of death and unwashed bodies hung in the air. Hospitals are a fine place to die, Clinton had told Wade at a low moment. Never a day passed that events failed to prove his point.

Wade folded the letter from Healy and placed it on the table beside his bed. He closed his eyes and waited.

At eight o'clock the doctor arrived. "Let's take a look at you fellows," he said as he flipped a chair into the narrow walkway between the single beds. "Nurse, will you please remove this bandage?" He pointed at Wade.

Clinton rolled over and sat on the edge of his bed. "How long do y's'pose it's gonna be 'fore this damnable tinglin' in my hand stops, Doc?"

"Can't say, Major. Little is known about electrical shock—which isn't surprising. Most people struck by lightning don't survive to discuss the experience." He watched as the nurse cut the binding.

"But it didn't strike me direct. It hit at least thirty feet away."

"In a rainstorm?"

"Yessir."

"Might as well have hit you directly. The charge moves right through the water. It's a killer, Major. You're fortunate to be alive." The doctor pulled his spectacles low on his nose. "Now, let me take a look at this shoulder, Colonel. Uh-huh. Looks like it's healing nicely now." He lifted Wade's arm and rotated it while prodding his shoulder joint. "Does that hurt, Colonel?"

"It's more stiff than painful, Doctor."

"It'll be that way for a while." He pressed a finger against the rosy-colored flesh of the wound. "How about that?"

"Hurts some," Wade answered, flinching at the touch.

"I think we'll let you keep it in a sling awhile longer—just to be sure. I'm going to wait a couple of weeks before releasing you for duty, but you're free to take a short medical leave if you want. Do you have a place to go?"

"My home's just north of Gettysburg."

"Gettysburg, huh? I hope we never have another battle like that one." He removed a small pad from his pocket. "Here, let me write you a pass. This will get you home for a week or so. I'll look at you again in about two weeks. Keep the arm in a sling until then. And you, Major, just take it easy for a while."

"Is it all right if he goes with me?" asked Wade.

"I don't want to intrude, Sam," Clinton said.

"It's a big farm, Jim. Besides, I want you to meet my mother. You'll like her. Is it all right, Doctor?"

The physician looked at Clinton. "It's up to you, Major."

The rain had stopped by the time the former prisoners reached Richmond two days after their exchange. Soldiers from the provost company herded them onto a parade ground for sorting and classification according to unit and rank. They grumbled and cussed their saviors no less than they had their captors, but with more enthusiasm. Elements essential for a vibrant life were returning.

Sergeants moved through the ragged formations and directed the men to straighten their ranks, exhorting them to act like soldiers again. The admonitions mostly failed. Acting like soldiers reminded them of the one thing they most wanted to avoid. To a man, their thoughts were of home.

Most had been captives only since the first of the year or later. A few, those in the worst condition, had been prisoners since First Manassas. More than half had been captured during the first two days at Gettysburg. Most had been wounded. None had the physical fitness or mental acuity needed to return to active service.

Three officers—a colonel, a captain, and a lieutenant—stood twenty feet beyond the front rank. They shook their heads as the guards prodded the resisting former prisoners. The trio had the unenviable task of trying to reinstall in these ragged individuals a renewed respect for military discipline and, hopefully, a sense of personal pride. Experience had taught them that new recruits were less difficult to manage. These men had no illusions about their prospects once they were declared fit. No man ever performed the same following release from captivity. When the numbness passed and they realized that their ordeal had ended, they would react in a variety of ways. Some, filled with hate, would be overeager to get back to the task of killing Yankees. Few of these would emerge from their next battle unscathed—if they survived at all. Most would endeavor to do their duty as they saw it—but with increased caution and a firm commitment to avoid capture. A few, those whose experiences had broken their spirits completely, would be unfit for any military service that took them within miles of combat. They would end up as prison guards or stationed at some boring, isolated post or coastal fort. A few would drift into insanity.

Fearing what would happen once they returned to duty, a handful had resisted release. These men had robbed, molested, and even killed their fellow prisoners. One in fifty within the ranks would face a court-martial for his excesses while in captivity. More than a few of these men feared returning to combat, not because of what the Yankees might do to them, but because of what they knew their comrades were certain to do when the bullets began to fly. They realized that in the heat of battle they had no effective defense against a gunshot in the back, a risk compounded by the virtual absence of the threat of punishment for the act.

The colonel limped closer, followed by the two junior officers. "Bring the men to attention, Captain," he said softly.

The captain moved sharply forward. "Regiment, attennn-shun." He waited a moment, then shouted, "Report!"

The sergeant major stepped forward, faced to the left, then marched briskly to where the captain stood at attention. "Nine hundred forty men present for duty, sir," the sergeant major said, saluting. "Two hundred seventy-seven on sick call. Five dead."

The captain returned the salute, executed a snappy about-face, and returned to the colonel's front. "All present or accounted for, sir."

"Very well, Captain. Separate the officers from the others and bring them front and center."

"Yes, sir." He turned. "Puh-rade rest. Officers, front and center." The officers moved listlessly forward and formed a ragged line in front of the enlisted men's ranks. The maneuver required several minutes to complete. Of the forty-six officers present for duty, four had lost a leg and six had only one arm. One had lost both hands.

About average, thought the colonel. The damned Yankees don't want to care for them.

The colonel limped forward. "All right, gentlemen, I know y'all have had a difficult time, but the worst is behind you. I'm Colonel Hatcher. We'll get you some clean clothes, see that you get a bath, and a shave if you want it, and then we'll give you a few days to put some meat back on your bones before you're reassigned." He hesitated, then limped a step closer. "Remember, you're soldiers in the army of the Confederate States of America. Those who're able will be returned to their units. Those with medical problems will be cared for. Enlisted men who have lost three fingers or a thumb, or have lost a limb, will be discharged and sent home. Officers with similar afflictions will have the choice of being discharged or remaining in the army with a staff assignment. The army's short of qualified officers, so I know each will do his duty as he sees it. Sergeant Major Brockman, front and center."

Brockman strode quickly to his post in front of the formation and saluted.

"Sergeant Major, are you prepared to issue new clothing to the enlisted men?" the colonel asked, returning the salute.

"Yessir, and the water's boilin' for their baths, sir." He smiled.

"Very well, Sergeant Major, take charge of the men. Captain Means, bring the officers to the officers' mess tent. I'll meet you there in fifteen minutes."

Later, as the colonel approached the mess tent, Captain Means was forming the officers in a single rank. "All right, Captain, what do we have here?" Hatcher asked.

"Twenty-eight lieutenants, twelve captains, five majors, and a lieutenant colonel, sir."

"The exchange list included a general officer, Captain."

"I know, sir, but Lieutenant Colonel Thornton is the highest ranking officer in the bunch."

"Lieutenant Colonel Thornton?"

"Yes, sir. That's him over there," said Means, pointing.

"Let's have a look, Captain." Hatcher limped slowly toward the end of the line. He stopped and examined Thornton's grimy, bearded face. Then his attention shifted to the raw-looking gash on Thornton's scalp. "You have a nasty wound there, Colonel Thornton." He paused, then turned and whispered to Means, "I remember him, or remember hearing of him." He stared at Thornton. "Weren't you a spy at Chancellorsville, Colonel?"

Thornton made no response.

Hatcher's expression hardened. "Colonel, I expect an answer when I ask a question."

Thornton's eyes connected with the colonel's, but he said nothing.

"What's the matter with this man, Captain?"

"Don't rightly know, sir." He hastily examined the file. "Says here he was shot in the side and head at Gettysburg. He appears to have lost his memory, too."

The colonel nodded. He remembered hearing about the spy incident, but nothing more. He knew none of the details, but he knew someone who might. "Captain, do you know Major Prichard of the provost battalion?"

"No, sir."

"You'll find him somewhere over by the provost headquarters. Go tell him I want to see him."

"Yes, sir." Means saluted and moved out at a trot.

"Stand at ease until the captain returns, gentlemen. Lieutenant Northcroft, see that these gentlemen are fed."

Colonel Hatcher sat at his desk reading through the sketchy files of the returned officers. He looked up as Captain Means entered. "This is Major Prichard, sir. It took some doin' to find him."

"Thank you, Captain. That will be all. Have a seat, Major."

Prichard unfolded a canvas camp stool and seated himself.

"Tell me, Major, weren't you involved last spring in a matter concerning a Lieutenant Colonel Thornton?"

"Yes, sir, I commanded the guard unit assigned to the court-martial. But, sir . . ."

"Yes?"

"The incident actually involved a man named Wade, who was impersonating Colonel Thornton."

"What happened?"

"Well, sir, I didn't pay much attention to the testimony."

"Do your best, Major."

"As I remember it, sir, Wade was a Yankee spy. He impersonated an officer named Thornton who was serving on General Jackson's staff. The Yankees kidnapped the real Thornton and Wade took his place. They said he covered for himself by pretending to have a head wound until he got to know people and how things operated. They said Wade got pretty close to General Jackson. Stonewall even promoted him for valor at Fredericksburg. He headed north after one of our own men shot General Jackson, but we captured him and the Yankee unit he'd joined shortly thereafter. After his capture he saved the life of one of our officers on the last day at Chancellorsville. I don't remember the officer's name, but he testified in Wade's favor."

Prichard stopped for a moment before continuing. "I remember very clearly that General Lee took an intense interest in the matter. He wanted to see Wade hang in the worst way. The court found Wade guilty of spying but never mentioned a thing about General Jackson's death. I only knew about that from private conversations. I heard that the generals wanted the rest kept quiet. They didn't want it known that a Yankee had gotten that close to General Jackson. Even so, the court had more than enough evidence. The court sentenced Wade to death. I heard that the government later included him in a prisoner swap— at President Davis's insistence, I might add, sir. That's about it, sir."

"Describe Wade to me," said Hatcher.

"It's like I said, sir, he looked exactly like Colonel Thornton. He talked like he'd been raised in South Carolina, but they said he grew up in Pennsylvania. He knew his way around our army, Colonel." Prichard thought for a moment. "That's about it, I guess. If you don't mind my asking sir, why is this comin' up now?"

Hatcher ignored the question. "Would you recognize Wade if you saw him again?"

"I think so, sir. I'm sure of it."

"Come with me."

The two officers left the tent and walked to where the former captives were eating breakfast. "Do you see Wade here, Major?"

Prichard moved closer. He wandered slowly among the officers, then stopped at the end of the second table and pointed. "If this isn't Wade, it's his twin brother, Colonel."

Hatcher motioned for Prichard to come closer. "Major," he said softly, "do you think you can get hold of the court-martial records?"

"I think so, sir."

"Do it, Major. And don't mention this to anyone. Do you understand?"

"Yes, sir. No one."

"Thank you, Major. I appreciate this."

Colonel Hatcher turned away and walked into the open. He leaned against a telegraph pole and contemplated the impassive Thornton as he tried to discern in his mind what might be afoot here. Why would the Yankees chance sending Wade where someone would almost certainly recognize him? Or had their intent been to create confusion? Despite the earlier prisoner exchange, the death sentence would still be in force. Had the Union become so desperate for information? Not likely. There had to be more to it than that. And what good would it do to send Wade south disguised as a man who appeared not even to know his name? Perhaps they had returned the real Thornton, and everything else was simply coincidence.

Hatcher smiled as he considered the opportunity opening to him. He had to get out of this dreary, dead-end assignment. He had been a staff officer in Bragg's army at the time of Stones River. A piece of shrapnel had cut through his calf, putting him out of action. He had been sent to Richmond to recover and had drifted into bitterness in the meantime. Were it not for the wound, he would be a general officer. Now that he had recovered, or nearly so, he needed something to bring attention to himself. He was convinced he had found that something. He simply had to be patient and gather the facts, then put them to use. For now, he had to get Thornton—or Wade, as the case may be—cleaned up and thoroughly examined by a doctor.

"Are these men about through with breakfast, Captain?"

"Yes, sir."

"Then get Colonel Thornton a bath and a clean uniform. Bring him to my tent when he's ready."

"Yes, sir. I'll attend to it personally."

Two days later, Colonel Hatcher stood at parade rest in front of Brig. Gen. Daniel Brown's desk. To his left stood Simon Thornton. The general looked first at Hatcher, then at Thornton. "Have a seat," the general said finally. "Tell me, Colonel Hatcher, what is your opinion?"

Hatcher sighed as he looked at Thornton. "This man isn't Thornton, sir. That's what I think."

The general shifted his attention to Thornton. "Colonel—whatever your name is," he said calmly, "it's time to tell the truth. Just who are you?"

"I don't know, sir," Thornton said.

"Do you know where you are?" asked the general.

"Richmond, they tell me, although I've never been here that I remember."

"What happened to your head?"

"They told me that I took a saber blow. I don't remember."

"Who are *they?*"

"My captors, General."

"How long were you unconscious?"

"I don't know, sir. A long time, I guess. I just don't remember."

"Don't you find that a bit too convenient, Colonel?"

"I really can't recall anything, sir. I try, but there's nothing there."

"What do you remember of the time before you were struck with the saber?"

Thornton fidgeted, crossed his legs, then, remembering whom he was with, uncrossed them and straightened up in the chair. He stared at the floor. "I remember—I—I—it was all so confusing, men screaming, guns firing." His voice trailed off and he clenched his fists tightly. "I really don't remember anything after that."

"Where were you when you woke up?"

Thornton looked down again, obviously reluctant to answer.

"I'm waiting, Colonel."

"A farmhouse, sir. I woke up in a farmhouse. That's all I remember." He had enough presence of mind to know that by saying more he might condemn himself. He easily remembered his conversations with the woman who said she was his mother's twin sister. He remembered Colonel Thompson's visit. He remembered everything since he'd awakened at the farmhouse. But he had no specific memory of earlier events and, more important, he had no way of knowing what this general knew. The safest course seemed to be to pretend he knew nothing at all. He shrugged.

"That's all *I've* been able to get out of him," said Hatcher.

"Tell me, Colonel Hatcher," said the general. "Why do you think he's Wade?"

"First, sir, the story about the saber wound is too pat, too convenient. The medical examiner says the wound could have been surgically induced. Then there are the records, or should I say the absence of records. I've questioned nearly twenty of the returned prisoners, including several of the officers. None of them saw this man until the morning of the exchange. Our people have no record of a Colonel Thornton being in any of the Yankee prisons. He just appeared.

"Sir, I think he's faking his memory loss. Look at it this way: if no one had suspected him, just accepted him as Thornton, I think he would have experienced a miraculous recovery and everything would have returned to normal. But if we suspected something—well, sir, those bastards had to know we wouldn't execute a man who can't even remember his name. Most important of all, sir, I've read the court-martial records."

"And?" asked the general.

"This Wade is a crafty son of a bitch, sir. He's a West Point graduate. As such, he has detailed knowledge of military operations. He successfully planted himself on General Jackson's staff and fooled the general for six months—right up until the night he tricked some of our jumpy troops into shooting the general and his guard. The general never suspected Wade. And then there's the matter of Wade's mother. She may also have been a spy. The Union government wanted them both back badly enough to go to elaborate lengths to secure a trade.

"Sir, the real Colonel Thornton fought at Gettysburg. He's been listed as captured or dead. We just don't know which. But remember, none of the men just exchanged saw him in prison, and four men who knew Thornton saw him go down on the third day. None of them saw him alive after the battle. It's interesting that none of those captured from Thornton's regiment were returned in the two prisoner exchanges since Gettysburg. I think Colonel Thornton died at Gettysburg and the Yankees simply thought it was worth trying to plant Wade back down here again." He nodded. "That's what I think, sir. It's the only thing that makes sense."

The general had watched Thornton as the colonel talked. He heard the colonel's words, but the expression, or lack of expression, on Thornton's face sent another message. Although logic told him it was Samuel Wade who now sat before him, the evidence he had heard was all circumstantial. Conjecture, what ifs, maybes, I thinks—nothing he could hold up and say, this is proof positive. Because the evidence was circumstantial, he felt compelled to give serious consideration to the one established fact: the real Thornton's father was a general. If one must err, err on the side of caution—had always been Brown's motto. That seemed to be sound advice for this situation. Since he knew of no way to resurrect a man, it seemed prudent to avoid executing him until his identity was clearly established. The general held up his hand and waved at the door. "Sergeant, will you please remove Colonel Thornton. Keep him under close guard."

"Yes, sir." The noncom took Thornton's hand and said, "Come with me, Colonel."

General Brown waited until the door closed. Then he turned to Hatcher and asked, "What is Wade's relationship to Thornton, Colonel?"

"We're unsure, sir. He could be a relative with a strong resemblance. At his trial, Wade said he didn't know Thornton. Said he'd simply been acting on orders and never knew the particulars. I don't believe that. The Yankees never would have put him in that dangerous a position unless they knew everything possible about Thornton. And I should mention the other incident, General."

"What other incident?"

"Sir, a few weeks before the Yankees kidnapped Thornton and substituted Wade, there was another abduction from General Jackson's staff. At first the adjutant reported it as a desertion. He had tried unsuccessfully to get leave to visit his bride in Maryland. Later, he escaped from the Yankees and made his way back. Seems he'd been held captive and questioned over a long period of time. He said they even let him meet with Thornton."

"Where are you leading, Colonel?"

"Sir, at the time the Yankees were interrogating him, the real Thornton was still on General Jackson's staff. His abduction took place later. The other officer seemed totally convinced of Colonel Thornton's legitimacy, but it had to be Wade. Wade had to know more than he let on at his trial. Otherwise, he never would have been able to convince the man he was Thornton. Sir, there is undisputed evidence of an elaborate plan, a plan carried out over several weeks, to substitute Wade for Thornton so he could serve as a spy in General Jackson's headquarters."

"General Brown, if I had the say-so, I'd hang him today and be done with it."

The general nodded absently. Nothing said so far resolved his present dilemma. Which man had he just sent back to prison? Nothing else mattered if that question remained in doubt. He rose and walked to the window. In the distance, he saw the guards leading Thornton away. What to do? Whatever he decided might be wrong; it might create a national crisis. He had to think it through and be sure.

"You make a convincing case, Colonel. It's evident that this matter is of interest at the highest levels of both governments. You said General Lee himself wanted Wade executed, yet President Davis overrode him." Brown shook his head. "My God, Colonel, there's more to this than either of us knows. It could explode in our faces."

Brown clasped his hands behind his back as he thought. The colonel and he were cut from different cloth. Hatcher was a man of action, a military officer in the traditional sense of the term. Shoot this impostor and let the devil take the consequences, he proposed. Easily said; hard to undo. He, on the other hand, was one of many ambitious men who yielded to the opportunities provided by war. He never would have admitted this, especially to himself, but he was what he was, and political success required caution in the face of uncertainty. War, after all, was nothing more than political action by another means. If he had learned anything, it was not to open a door unless you knew what was on the other side.

There were grave political risks attached to the two most obvious alternatives. On this issue, Lee and Davis stood on either side of a vast gulf. Davis had overruled Lee in the Thornton matter. Common sense suggested that the president had wanted the affair settled, and he had been willing to go against the heartfelt desire of General Lee to settle it. Now, to have the whole sordid mess surface again at a time when the war was going badly . . . well, what would the president think? He just might direct his wrath at the man who had demonstrated the bad judgment to let such a thing happen.

What were his choices, and what were the potential results? If the man *was* Thornton, there would be nothing gained by accepting that at face value. But if he had Wade in his grasp, there could be hell to pay. Politician or not, Brown was a general. Generals were expected to solve problems, not create them. If he moved a step outside this office and announced his uncertainty, he would lose control—and good politicians never let themselves lose control.

All things considered, this was hardly a comfortable situation for a man whose very fiber had been stitched with the belief that when there were conflicting choices with devilish consequences for making the wrong choice, it's best to avoid drawing attention to one's self. Find a middle ground; go with what worked in the past. Do nothing. Push it away. Let someone else take the risks if they wish, but don't *you* bet everything on a single turn of the card. A man's character, after all, is not so easily changed.

Then again, it might be prudent to hedge his bet. He nodded with satisfaction at his reasoning. What would it hurt if he secretly sent a courier to inquire into what General Thornton knew? Nothing. Time would pass and the issue would simmer down. Then, if information leaked, he would have covered himself. That settled it.

Brown smiled as he turned and watched Thornton disappear behind a building. Disappear. All things considered, a prudent solution. He turned back to Hatcher, who had been waiting quietly. "Well, Colonel, no harm has been done—yet.

This man has certainly had no opportunity to gather any secrets. I'm going to send him to Libby Prison while I give the matter some more thought."

Hatcher showed no reaction. He had witnessed the result when others argued with generals. An ugly sight. Instead, he decided to attend to his own needs. "Sir, if I might ask, has a decision been made on my request for transfer?"

The general seemed suddenly alert. "Tell me, Colonel, how is your leg healing?"

Hatcher instinctively placed his hand on the wound and rubbed. It still ached if he stood on it for more than a few minutes. "Fully healed, sir, and I limp less each day."

"Do you think you're up to taking a position in the line?"

Hatcher smiled. "What does the general have in mind?"

"I'm thinking of sending you west, Colonel." Actually, the prudent thing *was* to send the colonel as far away as possible. Hatcher's request for a transfer offered the perfect opportunity. "There's nothing official yet, but there's a possibility that General Longstreet's corps will be sent to support General Bragg in Tennessee. He's still short of qualified brigade commanders."

"I've never been with a combat brigade, sir. If the general thinks I'm qualified, I'll do my duty, sir."

"That settles it then. I'll have the orders prepared at once. One more thing, Colonel. I want you to remove this matter with Colonel Thornton from your mind. Don't speak of it again. That's an order."

"Understood, sir. Thank you for your confidence."

"Don't mention it, Colonel. Now, if you'd be so kind, please instruct Major Prichard to transfer Wade or Thornton or whoever he is to Libby Prison. Tell him the paperwork will catch up in a couple of days. That's all, Colonel."

"Yes, sir." Hatcher saluted and tramped briskly from the office.

Only one thing left to do, Brown thought. I have to send a letter to General Thornton. Brown rose and walked into the outer office. He motioned to his aide. "Come into my office, Major Cooke. I have a task I need you to have performed."

Wade and Clinton stepped from the train at half past noon. The wilting heat and high humidity made breathing difficult. Both men were drenched and hungry; neither of them had the stamina that had sustained them during the arduous ordeal back in late July. The combination of traumatic injury and easy days of hospital life had taken its toll.

Wade half expected his mother to meet them at the station, but he saw her nowhere. She might be away on business, he thought. There had been no response to his telegram informing her of his arrival. Then again, it was a ten-mile ride to the farm, so the telegram's delivery might have been delayed. She often stayed at the rooming house for that reason, to be near enough to a communications link with her business.

Wade walked to the station-house window and tapped on it. The old man inside looked up and smiled. "Gawdallmighty, if it ain't Colonel Sam."

"How you doing, Charley?" Wade asked with a broad grin.

"Oh, my rumatiz has been actin' up some—but you don't want to hear 'bout me. Lawdy me. Does your mama know you're a comin'?"

"Sent her a telegram, Charley, but I don't know if she got it. Will you check?"

"Don't have ta. Now I remember. I sent a boy to the farm with it late yesterday evenin'—but it was the end of the day, so he didn't report back. He ain't come in yet today. If she's home, she got it. One thing for sure, if'n she'd left on the train I'd know 'bout it."

Wade nodded. "She might be at the warehouse, or maybe the rooming house. I'll check those first. Charley, there's someone I want you to meet. This is Maj. Jim Clinton. We've been through a lot together."

The old man stuck his arm through the opening. "Nice t'meet ya, Major. You been takin' good care of my boy here?"

"We been takin' care of each other, Charley. I'm pleased t'meet ya."

Charley leaned forward and spoke in a whisper loud enough for both Wade and Clinton to hear. "Are y'sure he ain't a Reb? Sounds mighty Southern t'me."

Clinton and Wade laughed. "He's from Georgia, Charley," said Wade, "but he's a Yankee at heart."

Charley smiled. "Well, that's good enough for me, Colonel Sam. Hope y'find Mrs. Healy." He shook his head. "I ain't never gonna get used t'callin' her that. She'll always be Mrs. Wade t'me."

"Nice talking to you again, Charley," said Wade. "We'd best be getting on our way."

They checked the rooming house first, without success. As they walked down the boardwalk toward the warehouse, Wade saw a woman sweeping dirt out the door. "Mother, is that you?" he called.

Caroline Healy turned at the sound of the familiar voice and shaded her eyes against the sun. She smiled broadly, dropped her broom, and half ran, half walked toward the two men. "My God, Samuel, why didn't you let me know you were coming?"

"I sent a telegram, Mother. Unfortunately, they delivered it to the farm," he said as he opened his arms and pulled her to him. He had removed the sling to avoid worrying her, but his arm still ached when he moved it too rapidly.

"It feels so good to hold you, Samuel. I never know from one day to the next if you're dead or alive."

"Well, I'm alive today, Mother—thanks to Jim here."

She pulled back and studied Clinton carefully. "So you're Major Clinton. Thank you for taking such good care of Samuel for me."

He grinned and extended his hand. "It's all I can do just t'keep up with him, ma'am. He moves faster an' gets inta more trouble in less time than any man I ever knowed."

She grasped his outstretched hand in both of hers. "I'm so pleased to finally meet you, Major. I feel like I know you; Samuel has written of you so often."

"Jim, ma'am. Just call me Jim."

"How long can you stay?" she asked, looking back at Wade.

"Only a couple of days, Mother."

A frown replaced her smile. "Can't the army spare you for longer than that?" Her features hardened slightly as she placed a palm against his face. "Why haven't you been writing to me, Samuel? I haven't received a letter from you in nearly two months. I had to find out from Colonel Thompson that you were wounded."

"I haven't received a letter from you either, Mother. The last one reached me before the battle here. I've sent at least one letter a week."

"Well, so have I—even more lately. I don't understand it." She hesitated. She had lost faith in Thompson. She judged him to be wholly self-serving. The time had come for a test. "Come in out of the heat. I'm boiling out here." They moved into the small office. "I assume Colonel Thompson told you about Simon."

Wade seemed surprised. "What's there to tell? I heard that Simon had been captured, but the colonel said nothing more."

It was just as Caroline suspected. "Simon spent more than a month with me while he recovered. He nearly died. God kept him alive for some reason, Samuel. I surely had little to do with it. He still couldn't remember a thing when they came for him."

"Who came for him?"

"Some soldiers came and hauled him away in a wagon about a week after Colonel Thompson left here. Took him to a prison camp, I assume. I showed them the letter General Meade gave me, but they had orders from Secretary Stanton."

"Colonel Thompson came here? He said nothing to me about that. And why couldn't Simon remember anything?"

Caroline unleashed a torrent of words on Sam, describing all that had transpired since the night she'd shown up at the field hospital and mistaken Simon for her own son. When she finished, she turned away to hide the tears. "You have to find out what they did with him, Samuel. From what I've heard about our prisons, he won't survive long. I can't penetrate the military bureaucracy." She turned and looked deeply into Wade's eyes. "Perhaps a well-placed bribe or two would get you some information. I'm certain that colonel of yours knows where he is. Just tell me what you need."

Wade was confused. The fact that Thompson had neglected to tell him about Simon meant he had intended to keep it a secret. But why? Thompson never did anything without a reason. No more purposeful man existed. And why no letters? Mail service had deteriorated with the war, but there were trains running between Washington and Gettysburg nearly every day. "I don't understand this, Mother." He looked at Clinton, who shrugged. "Why did Colonel Thompson keep this from me? I'll find Simon, Mother. Don't worry." He hesitated, remembering the unexplainable pain and distress of the early morning following the last day of the battle. He had felt an almost mystical link to something, or someone, and now he knew what it meant. "I think I'll die if he dies," he said softly.

Caroline's hand went to her mouth to restrain the gasp. She had no need to ask her son what he meant. She understood—as only an identical twin could understand. But hearing the words uttered still shocked her.

The sun was setting as Sam Wade and his mother walked leisurely toward the large oak tree behind the house. Sorting through the past several months of their lives had taken all afternoon. Wade held back the worst parts of his difficulties while behind Confederate lines. Caroline refused to offer any details of her time in captivity, shrugging as she dismissed it as a time best forgotten. They had talked about the horror of Gettysburg, the Healy men, and the war in general.

Following supper, Clinton saddled a horse and rode out to inspect the surrounding country. For the first time since their reunion began, Caroline and her son were alone.

"Where are they sending you next?" she asked as they stopped at the well.

"West," he replied.

"West?"

"Yes. To Chattanooga—to the Army of the Cumberland, under General Rosecrans."

"Can't they let you rest for a while? Why so soon?"

"We have to get this damn war over with, Mother. Thousands of officers have been killed and wounded. A serious shortage is developing."

"Nevertheless, it wouldn't hurt them to wait a month or so," she replied sharply. "You've given so much already, Samuel."

"I'm a West Pointer, Mother. It's my duty." He placed an arm around her shoulder and pulled her to him. "By the way, there's *some* good news. I've been promoted to major in the regular army. That's quite an honor for someone my age."

"But you're a lieutenant colonel. I don't understand."

"We all have a permanent rank, Mother. It's the lowest rank we can be demoted to without being removed from the army. When this war ends, many generals will become captains and lieutenants. Few have a permanent rank as high as major."

Caroline nodded absently and began walking toward the large tree. It comforted her to stand under its long, sweeping limbs. Something so large and old had a sense of permanence about it, a security she needed desperately in her own life. West. If he goes out west, she thought, it may be a year or more before I see him again. Maybe never. She hated it when such thoughts crept into her mind.

Since Gettysburg, the war had entered a lull in the East. Both armies had been battered to the point where neither seemed eager to confront the other. But war clouds were boiling in the West. The press clamored for more aggressive action, and the president's patience was known to be near an end. Chattanooga might as well be on the moon as far as it affected her. Even so, she knew she would become more interested in the place—and soon. The signs were clear: two armies would meet there and blood would flow. And Samuel would be in the middle of it.

She looked at her son. He remained at the well, hesitating, reluctant to raise the unspoken subject that neither knew how to address but had been foremost on his mind. He had to know. "Mother," he said.

Caroline avoided his eyes, irrationally terrified given the blissful setting. She resisted answering, for she knew instinctively that the time she had dreaded for more than twenty years had finally arrived. There was something in the tone of his voice, in the way he said that single word, *Mother*. She closed her eyes and sighed. "Yes?" she said quietly.

"I have to know, Mother. I have to know everything about Simon and me."

She let her head drop. "I know." She clasped her hands behind her back. "Come, walk with me to the tree." She waited until he drew alongside. She turned slowly and looked fearfully into his eyes. She touched his cheek and smiled that crooked little smile that she had copied from her twin.

"It's a long story, Samuel"—she drew a deep breath—"and anything but flattering." Her hand drifted from his face to his shoulder. "I have to trust that you'll understand." She turned as a gust of wind blew her hair across her face. She brushed it away, then rested the heels of her hands on her hips. "Where to begin?" She hesitated. "At the beginning, I suppose." She told him first of the endless misery of her life with her husband. Somehow, that part hurt most; it represented in her mind a tormenting failure.

She advanced quickly to the elation she had experienced upon seeing her twin sister riding toward her on that July afternoon in the summer of 1838. She spoke joyfully of how they had spent a leisurely afternoon recalling the rapture and excitement of their childhood. Her mood darkened as she recalled the horror of that life-changing moment when two strangers had violated her sanctuary during the dead of night and tried to rape Victoria and her, how the attackers had boasted that the judge—her husband—had sent them to murder her, and how they had become confused upon learning that her identical twin was in the house. Tears flowed down her cheeks as she recalled her sister's scream when the vile attacker kicked Victoria in the abdomen as she resisted his assault.

Caroline's muscles tensed and her expression hardened as she spoke of the sudden attack by Jefferson, Washington Petree's father, when he charged into the room and saw his mistress prostrate on the floor, writhing in agony, and how the slave had run one of the men through with a pitchfork smeared with manure, leaving him to die. She hesitated before telling him of the incident in the barn, where she had threatened to bury the subdued molester alive if he failed to tell her everything leading up to his intrusion that terrible night.

She explained how she had been a weak person, unable or unwilling to break free of a marriage conceived in hell. But everything about her changed, she assured him, when she realized that she had to deal with her husband in the only way he understood—with raw, unrestrained power. In exchange for keeping his vile deed a secret, she had forced her husband to have their marriage annulled.

She told Samuel about his biological mother's pregnancy, confirmed the day following the assault, and how Victoria's injuries prevented her from returning to Alabama until the babies were born in the sisters' childhood home. Samuel was born with a large birthmark on the side of his head, and Victoria had been afraid that her husband's prejudices would prevent him from accepting an imperfect child. She had pleaded with Caroline to take Samuel and raise him as her own, without Henry Thornton ever knowing of his existence. Victoria went home with her twins, Simon and Nancy Caroline, and Caroline fled to Pennsylvania with Samuel and created a new life there as a lonely but determined widow.

Caroline walked a few steps, afraid to face the judgment she expected to see if she looked into her son's eyes. She prayed for his understanding, but she had long ago prepared herself for a harsher verdict. With her back still turned to him, she added, "To this day, Samuel, your father doesn't know you are his son. He believes you are his nephew." She turned sharply and forced a momentary glance into his glistening eyes. "You should judge your mother no more harshly than you judge me," she said sternly, unwilling to fully abandon the role of mother and protector. "The birthmark served only as an excuse for her immediate need to face a harsh reality, for she had another, stronger reason for leaving you with me, one that meant life or death for one of her infants, and perhaps all three. She had a difficult pregnancy and spent most of that time in bed and in poor health. The doctor told her she would never produce enough milk to feed three infants. And she had yet another reason, one perhaps you will understand now that you feel such a strong attraction to a twin brother whom you don't even know. She knew how much I wanted a child and might never have one. We had shared everything, Samuel, throughout our lives. What she did—what we both did—seemed as natural as breathing. It's no excuse, but we were hardly more than girls.

"But whatever guilt Victoria and I may share, you must come to terms with one fact: your father is blameless. It's unfair to hold him responsible for a transgression for which he bore no responsibility."

As she concluded, she felt an oppressive weight lifted from her soul. The thought that this moment would eventually come had haunted her, at times almost consuming her—and perhaps had destroyed her sister's love for her. Neither of them had found a way to fully adjust to the burden caused by their decisions. But Caroline had to admit—if only to herself—as she looked into her son's eyes: given the alternatives, she would do it all over again and never feel regret.

A tear rolled down her cheek and her lips quivered slightly. Unable to endure her son's silence any longer, she flung her arms around him and wept uncontrollably.

He softly stroked her back and hair. That always relaxed her. He kissed her on the crown of her head. Still, he said nothing. It seemed to him the best response. His mother—he would always think of her as that—was a strong woman. In that regard, despite her harsh judgment of herself, he knew of no woman who placed even a close second. Both would move on, as they had moved past so many difficulties in the past. One thing was certain, however: he had never loved her more than at this moment.

The Confederate captain had been lost for two days. At some point since leaving the train south of Chattanooga, at the last Southern outpost, he had taken a wrong turn and wandered into enemy lines. Now he found himself in the midst of what seemed to be the whole Union army. In all his years he had never fired a shot in anger at anyone, and he considered himself particularly unsuited to his present predicament. He was a staff officer, for God's sake, and staff officers followed orders. They never acted on their own, especially behind enemy lines. A heavy rain had pelted him most of the day. He had eaten the last of his food early in the morning. He was tired and hungry and, most of all, scared.

Something disturbed the leaves on the crest of the narrow ravine eight feet above his head. No sense in going on, he thought. Time to surrender and get it over with. What real difference would it make if he never completed his mission? It wasn't as though the war would be affected one way or the other. He stepped into the open and raised his hands. A single shot cracked, and a look of amazement froze on his face. He died before his bloody head hit the ground.

A Union corporal slid down the wet embankment. "It's a Reb all right, Lieutenant. He has some sort of official-lookin' pouch attached to his belt."

"Well, remove it so we can get on our way," the officer said impatiently. "What's in the pouch?"

The corporal unfastened the buckle and withdrew the contents. He read the letter that accompanied a folder containing a personnel file. "Don't seem of much importance, sir. Just an inquiry from one Reb general to another, askin' him to verify the identity of some lieutenant colonel named Thornton. Looks pretty routine, sir."

"Well, bring it along anyway. I'll look at it closer when we get back to camp."

"What about this Reb?" asked the corporal.

"Don't worry about him, he isn't going anywhere."

"Don't seem Christian, somehow, just leavin' him here all alone ta rot."

"That's every man's destiny, Corporal. Now saddle up and let's get back to camp."

"I'll just cover him with some brush, Lieutenant. It won't take but a minute."

The lieutenant swung out of the saddle. "Better not take longer than it takes me to piss."

The corporal laid the pouch on the ground and began to gather dead limbs. He scattered wet leaves over the dead officer, then dragged the limbs across the body. Satisfied that he had done his Christian duty, he scrambled up the side of the ravine and mounted his horse.

He never gave the pouch another thought until they reached camp an hour later. The lieutenant ordered him to forget about it and get some food. They might attempt to find the pouch the next day—if they had time. Where had that ravine been? One ravine looked much like another in this rugged country. Oh well, what did it matter, really?

# CHAPTER

# 10

From the diary of Caroline Wade-Healy

*September 9, 1863*
*Dear God, it pained me so when Samuel rode away. I would give up my*
*soul this moment to assure his safe return. I wonder how many mothers*
*feel as I do. Tens of thousands, I suppose, North and South.*

*The story of this war is written on the faces of the people. I see it*
*everywhere I go. Locations previously found only on local maps, places*
*that no one ever heard of before, have become monstrous symbols of*
*calamity and sorrow, their tragic aftermaths destined to ravage families*
*and communities from the tip of Maine to far-ranging frontiers. Bull*
*Run, Chancellorsville, Antietam, Shiloh—strange, heretofore meaning-*
*less names now etched on tombstones that mark the graves of a lost*
*generation of our sons, fathers, and husbands.*

*I have fought against the despair caused by this war, but I sense that*
*each day brings me closer to losing the struggle. I shy from reading the*
*newspaper for fear of the tragic news that will confront me. The reports*
*of battle crash down upon us with mind-numbing suddenness, and we*
*are powerless to do anything about it. There is no refuge, no relief—*
*only endurance and grief.*

During the hard days since the *Rome Courier* had confirmed the full extent of the twin disasters at Vicksburg and Gettysburg, the town's collective
despair had gradually turned into numb resignation as its citizens for the first
time sensed the war closing in around them. Nowhere did the gloom seem

more evident than on the border between Floyd and Bartow Counties in northwest Georgia, fifty-odd miles south-southeast of Chattanooga.

Unlike the glacial spread of the reports of earlier defeats—the impact often neutralized by the rapid reporting of succeeding victories—word of the latest disaster had spread like wildfire. One day earlier, September 9, the paper had reported that Union forces were marching unopposed into Chattanooga. A corporal's guard could have captured the city, and in doing so cut rail transportation to a third of the shrinking Confederate enclave. Without being formally implemented, Union Maj. Gen. Winfield Scott's earlier scheme for winning the war, the Anaconda Plan, was unfolding by accident. His idea had been to squeeze the South bit by bit, isolating and neutralizing chunks of territory and commercial hubs, until the restricted supply of manpower and materials forced Southern surrender. Already, Confederate defeats at New Orleans and Vicksburg, and at lesser points in between, had denied the rebels access to territory west of the Mississippi. Compounding the problem since early spring was the increasingly effective federal sea blockade, which had reduced foreign trade by 60 percent compared to the start of the war. In 1861, Union blockade ships were able to prevent only one in ten blockade runners from reaching port. In 1862, one out of eight was stopped. By 1863, the ratio had risen to one in four, with one in three the standard during the last two months. The trend had become irreversible. After more than two years of war, serious shortages of a variety of materials were commonplace. Only locally produced necessities were in ready supply, and luxuries were the stuff of fading dreams.

A lacy fog rolled over the summerhouse nestled among the trees behind the Bowman mansion. The flickering lanterns cast haunting, muted reflections on the dew settling on the foot-tall grass that covered the spacious grounds. With his legs crossed and his head reclined against the back of his favorite wicker chair, Lucius Bowman sat with eyes half closed as he listened indifferently to the whispered conversations of several small clusters of men gathered about the building. His son Arthur remained cloistered in the main house. Arthur, General Thornton, and another man—a Northerner whom no one knew— had been in secluded conference since late afternoon. The old man had declined an invitation to participate in the discussion. He had made an irrevocable decision: he would offer such moral assistance as might be necessary to dispose of the satan Lincoln, but he vowed never to participate directly in any activity that had as its assumption the demise of his beloved South. Defeat might be destined, but he refused to hurry it along.

A hundred yards away, candlelight flickered in the windows and through the cracks of weathered, crumbling shacks. Here, in the tranquil evening hours before dark, the plantation slaves took relief from their toil. Shadowy figures sat on many of the stoops, their presence revealed in the enveloping darkness only by occasional red glows from handmade pipes. Shortly they would drift inside for a few hours of sleep before beginning another tedious, backbreaking day of harvesting the cotton crop that no longer had a market. The men in the summerhouse, their view screened by the thickening fog, gave no thought to their presence.

Cathy Blair, dressed entirely in black, moved silently across the brick floor and set a pitcher of lemonade on the table. With the easy grace of a lifetime of attentive Southern rearing, she moved from one cluster of men to the next, making small talk and offering encouragement for success in a war she secretly hoped would end before Christmas—no matter the outcome. Once she disposed of the social amenities, she walked to the old man's side and leaned down to speak softly in his ear. "How are you feeling this evening, Grandpa?" she asked caringly. She truly loved the old man, and he returned her affection.

He smiled and lifted a wrinkled hand, placing it behind her head and pulling her face around so he could look into her eyes. "The sight of you is enough to give an old man hope," he said. "I'm sorry about Noah. Such a fine young man."

She smiled and nodded. "Thank you, Grandpa. There are so many widows in our desperate country. I don't know how we'll endure."

"We'll all endure, child—because we must. The Yankees give us no choice."

She knelt on the floor and rested her head on the old man's arm. "What'll happen now that General Bragg has abandoned Chattanooga?"

Lucius sighed. "I suppose he'll try to recapture it. If he doesn't, the Yankees'll move on Atlanta. That would be worse than the loss of Richmond."

Cathy turned her head and looked into her grandfather's eyes. "We're losing the war, aren't we, Grandpa?"

The old man let his head drift toward the back of the chair. "It looks none too good, child. The loss of Vicksburg has been a terrible blow, perhaps the worst of the war."

"Then why do we continue?" she asked. She wanted to add, "sacrificing so many of our young men," but the words would have sounded like she was condemning the sacrifices already made.

He patted her head without response. He had no answer. As autumn drew near, with winter close behind, the war would grind to a halt for a few months. That would provide time to think and plan. In the minds of those who knew the South's desperate condition, the objective had become time rather than victory. Prolong the war and wear down the North, the planters were saying. Make the North pay and pay dearly, until the death and suffering overwhelm them and they throw out Lincoln. Increase the casualty count; make them pay in blood for every inch of Southern soil. The difficulty with this theory was that the war also drained the blood from the best of Southern manhood.

Deserters were already dribbling from the fringes of the army. In time, as supplies dwindled and the hardships and loneliness pressed more intently upon them, the dribble would become a flood, leaving only the best and the bravest to stop the Yankees' bullets. If the South purchased time with the lives of the planters' sons, who would remain to lift the nation from its ashes? This had become the old man's secret anguish, for he knew the answer. Northerners. Northern money would flood into the South. The man in the house with his son and General Thornton was a harbinger of things to come. Before long the Yankees would own everything of value, including—most abominable of all—much of the South's prime soil. To anyone who cared to look beyond the end of summer, the future was clear.

Every day the North became stronger and the South weaker. For every Northern soldier who fell, two immigrants stepped ashore or two young men came of age on a western farm. Time favored the Yankees, so Lincoln saw no need for compromise. Conditions had moved beyond an impasse. An impossible dilemma confronted the South, and Lucius had abandoned his search for a way out of it.

Aware now of the old man's even breathing, Cathy looked up at his face. He had fallen asleep. She gently lifted his hand from her head and placed it in his lap, then rose silently and walked to the far corner of the spacious building. As she looked out the screen-covered window, she thought of the similarity in what she saw and in her own life. She had the freedom to move, but she had no idea where her next step would take her. As with the gently rolling terrain outside, all of her dreams had become fogbound; she had become a speck of life adrift in a . . . She saw no point in speculating about an uncertain future. The present was bad enough. Her husband was dead; her daughter had no father. She wondered why she had come home. Had it been simply to listen to aging men plot irrationally while their sons sacrificed their lives in a lost cause? It made no sense. They ought to make the men who start wars shoulder the rifles. If they did, there would be no more war.

Cathy had acted on impulse. Unable to endure another lonesome day on her farm, she had thrown together a few treasured possessions and enough clothing for the journey and driven the buckboard to Winchester. In the three hours before the stage departed, she had sold, sight unseen to the purchasers, everything of value on the farm. She had received barely thirty cents on the dollar. Then she contacted an agent and told him to get the best price possible for the farm itself. Carrying her young daughter in one arm and dragging a trunk with the other, she had stepped off the train four days later in Chattanooga with eighty dollars in gold and five hundred dollars in Confederate bills. From there, with a broken-down horse and a battered wagon she had purchased from a desperate farmer who needed money to feed his family, she drove the sixty miles to Rome. She arrived in the nearly deserted city late the next day.

By 1861, Rome, located in the heart of the Coosa Valley, had become the commercial center of Floyd County. The city boasted a population of just over four thousand souls—nineteen hundred of whom were slaves—and a thriving commercial center stimulated by its fortunate location at the confluence of the Oostanaula and Etowah Rivers. Four flat-bottomed, shallow-draft stern-wheelers were homeported in Rome. A railroad spur tied the city to Atlanta.

Broad Street, the city's main thoroughfare, was lined with numerous stores. Larger business enterprises and manufacturing establishments rimmed the city. Shade trees lined the boardwalk on either side of Broad Street, and recently installed gaslights, the pride of the city dwellers, lit their way at night. At the east end of Broad Street stood Rome Female College, where Cathy Blair had been a member of the first graduating class just before her marriage. The *Rome Courier,* published by a transplanted Vermont Yankee named Dwinell, tied together the social structure of the city and the surrounding county.

Rome's small size belied its commercial importance. The city had a prosperous ironworks, with the capacity to manufacture virtually any implement or commercial engine. The first railroad engine constructed entirely in the South—made from locally provided raw materials—was built here. A number of grain and cotton mills, along with a large cabinet and furniture factory, added to the town's importance. The stern-wheelers transported much of the raw material needed for the community's industrial base.

Added to all this was the value of another important commodity: the largest slave population in northwest Georgia. At the start of the war, the nearly six thousand slaves in Floyd County had an average value of $651.70.

The residents of Rome—Romans, they called themselves—and the surrounding county had much to lose if the war ended badly. It was understandable, therefore, that they were willing to support any effort designed to prevent that from happening. As a result, despite all of the other forces—including a strong religious base—politics controlled events and attitudes in the region.

But after more than two years of war, the people in Rome and its environs had fallen on hard times. When the slaves heard that the Yankees were only fifty miles north, more than a hundred of them snuck away during the night in search of freedom. The thought of freedom drew them like a siren call, yet few had the slightest idea of its meaning—or its responsibilities.

As Cathy Blair had driven at dusk down nearly deserted Broad Street, the absurdity of everything had overwhelmed her. She had abandoned one uncertain world only to step into another, this one even more depressing. The bustling town that had been her anchor, the greatest source of her childhood happiness, was another casualty of the war. She was appalled at the sight of weather-beaten storefronts, crumbling cotton mills, and untended gardens. After tying her horse to a tree, she had walked to where the Oostanaula and Etowah Rivers merged to form the Coosa and sat on the bank. That had been her favorite place of solitude as a child. Later, she had wept uncontrollably as she whipped the horse into a trot to escape the sights that confirmed, more than anything in her experience, that the South was losing the war. She and her daughter had spent that first night at a friend's house. Then, at dawn, they had driven west on Kingston Road toward home, arriving at the Bowman plantation about noon.

The sound of approaching footsteps drew her back to the present. The squeaking door opened. Her father entered first, followed by a nattily dressed civilian, and finally by a Confederate major general. The general's handsome features startled her. She sensed she had seen him someplace before, but that seemed unlikely. She searched her memory but no name came to mind. Their eyes met across thirty feet of space, and he smiled and nodded. She returned the gestures.

"I believe everyone has met General Thornton," said Arthur Bowman.

Cathy stepped into the light. "I haven't, Father."

"Oh, I'm sorry, my dear. I didn't know you were here. General Henry Thornton, may I introduce my daughter, Cathy Blair. She only recently returned from Virginia. We were all distressed to learn that her husband was killed at Gettysburg."

The general flinched. "Gettysburg?" He moved toward her. "What do you know of that battle, young lady?"

She stepped back, startled by his sudden approach. "Why, almost nothing, sir. I was told my husband was killed on the last day."

Thornton's shoulders slumped. "I'm sorry," he said. "My only son, Simon, was there. We've heard nothing of him since. I've tried everything, but without success, to learn his fate."

For a moment, Cathy thought she might ease her pain by sharing Thornton's, but she understood that polite words offered no comfort. She started to reach out to touch him, then drew back. Why do I feel so drawn to him? she wondered. "I'm sorry to hear that, General," she answered, smiling uneasily. "Perhaps he has been captured and is safe."

"Perhaps," Thornton said wistfully. "Perhaps." His spirits lifted as he reached into his breast pocket. He pulled out a leather wallet, removed a picture, and handed it to her. "We had this made when he came home on leave last year."

She glanced at the photograph and recoiled. Impossible! she thought. It can't be the same man. The man in the picture has a beard, but other than that . . . "It's difficult to see what he looks like, General, but I'd say his features very much resemble yours. He's quite handsome, I might add."

"Thank you, ma'am. Some say there's a strong resemblance, but I think he looks more like his mother."

She looked at the picture again, then at the general, then back at the picture. They both had the same almond eyes, the same deep bridge of the nose. Different hair, but the same as . . . "When did you see him last?" she asked, returning the picture.

"In late June." Thornton took one last look at the photograph before returning it to his wallet. "It's a long story. Perhaps we can talk later."

"I'll look forward to it, General. Now, gentlemen, if you'll excuse me, I'll let you get on with your business." She nodded. "General."

Thornton bowed stiffly. "Ma'am. I regret that I failed to properly express concern for your grief. It's just that . . ."

She placed her hand softly on his arm and looked deeply into his sad eyes. She smiled knowingly. "No regrets are necessary, sir. I quite understand."

As twilight approached, Sam Wade and James Clinton stood outside the entrance leading from Judiciary Square Hospital. Wade absentmindedly rotated his arm to assure himself that movement had returned to normal. The memory of the bullet ripping through his shoulder still lingered, but the doctor had just pronounced both of them fit for duty. They were heading back into the war, but first, Wade had a painful task to perform.

They walked nearly a mile before they found a cab. "Warehouse Number Four, driver. Do you know where that is?"

"Yes, sir," the man replied without hesitation.

When they arrived at twenty minutes before nine, the building was almost dark. None of the wounded remained. The building had been returned to its former use. Wade meant to ask Thompson someday why he and General Washburn kept their offices in the drafty old barn of a building, cold in winter, scorching in summer, hardly a breath of fresh air at any time. With their connections, they could have requested and received accommodations of their choosing.

Clinton preceded Wade from the cab. "I think I'll just disappear awhile, Colonel—if'n it's all the same t'you. Ya need your privacy."

Wade had confided everything in Clinton. He'd had to share his feelings with someone, and who better than Jim? It had helped, talking about it, but Wade still felt sufficiently hostile toward Thompson that he knew he would have to keep a tight rein on himself. "You're right, of course. I'll meet you back at the hotel. I may be late."

"Think I'll commence t'get myself a beer or two. It's likely t'be a while 'fore the next one." Clinton struck a match on the side of the building and lit his pipe, then let the smoke drift lazily from his mouth into the still evening air. "Good luck, Sam. I'll be awake—just in case y'want t'talk when it's over."

Wade sucked in a deep breath before entering the building. He removed his cap and walked briskly down the nearly dark aisle. Two lanterns—one sitting on a box near the entrance, another at the far end of the building—provided the only light. His footsteps echoed as he moved toward the far light. As he approached, he saw Thompson and Washburn leaning over a table constructed from boards laid between two sawhorses. Maps covered the make-shift table.

Washburn and Thompson stood erect when Wade stopped and saluted. "You're a bit formal this evening," said the general as he and Thompson returned the gesture.

"Begging the general's pardon, sir, but I would appreciate an opportunity to speak with Colonel Thompson in private."

"Say what you have to say, Sam," answered Thompson.

"I doubt that would be appropriate, sir. You may be offended if I say what I'm thinking."

"We've known each other a long time, Sam. I can't imagine anything you'd have to say being inappropriate."

"Very well, Colonel, may I speak frankly?"

"Of course, Sam."

Wade cleared his throat. "Sir, it's about my brother."

"Oh?" said Thompson.

"The doctor gave me a pass, and I went to see my mother."

"And how is Mrs. Healy?" asked Washburn.

"Depends, sir. She's most unhappy about what happened to Simon."

"That was a military necessity, Sam," said Thompson. "There's a war on."

Wade stiffened. "I can't accept that, sir." He hesitated. "The colonel said I had permission to speak frankly?"

Thompson nodded. "Continue, Sam."

"According to my mother, Simon was in no condition to be moved any-where. What's worse, he had no memory of the time before Gettysburg. He represented no immediate threat to anyone, let alone the country."

"There *are* regulations," said General Washburn.

"Yes, sir. I know that. But regulations were being violated all the time he was there. She had General Meade's permission. You could have assigned a guard if security was an issue. God knows my mother had earned the right to that small concession."

"It *is* a security matter, Sam," said Thompson. "We can't discuss it."

"Can't discuss it, Colonel? My God, sir. I've operated half my army life behind enemy lines. I know as much about the enemy as any Northerner alive. I know some of the deepest, darkest secrets of this war, and you say we can't discuss it? This is my twin brother we're talking about, sir. He's hardly just another rebel."

Washburn sighed. "What do you want to know, Sam?"

"Sir," warned Thompson, shaking his head.

"Sam's going to find out for himself, no matter what we do here tonight," Washburn stated flatly. "I'd just as soon he hear it from us."

Thompson let his eyes close and his shoulders droop. "I think it's a mistake, General, but if you say so."

"I do, Colonel."

Thompson shifted his weight and turned to face Wade. "Ask your questions, Sam."

"Where is Simon, sir?"

Thompson hesitated. "I honestly don't know."

Wade's temper flared. "What? You don't know where he is? What have you done, Colonel?"

"We sent him south about two weeks ago along with a thousand others. He was involved in a"—he placed his hands on the table and looked away from Wade—"prisoner exchange. We don't know where they took him."

"I know how you think," Wade said in carefully measured tones. "You had a reason for all of this. I want to know that reason, Colonel."

"We did it to perhaps save your life, Sam."

"That makes no sense, Colonel," said Wade.

"Because we're sending you back to a combat unit, we hoped to remove attention from you. As reckless as you are, there's a good chance you'll be captured again. I say that in a positive way, Sam. You're one of the best officers in the army. It makes sense, if you think about it. In Simon's condition, there is virtually no chance that he will ever see combat duty again. Only two things are possible. They will conclude he is himself and send him home—"

"Or?" said Wade.

"Or they will conclude he is *you* and put him in prison."

"Or they'll hang him!" Wade exclaimed.

"We considered that possibility," said Washburn, "and feel it's unlikely."

"Begging your pardon, sir, but did you ever consider that the rebels don't think quite like we do? That's why we're at war." Wade stepped closer. "Sir, do you know where your brother, Congressman Washburn, is right now?" Wade was beginning to lose control.

"He's probably in his room asleep. Why do you ask?"

Wade pulled his pistol. "Because," he said placidly, "I'm going to put a bullet in his head." He had become irrational with anger, risking everything to ease the hurt inside. Tears began brimming in his eyes.

Washburn stiffened as Thompson moved quickly forward. "Goddamnit, Sam, that's enough!" Thompson shouted. He extended his hand. "Give me your gun. That's an order."

Wade stepped aside and glared at Washburn. "How does that make *you* feel, General? He's just a normal brother to you. What's a bullet in the head among brothers? It happens all the time in war. Simon is my twin, sir, my identical twin. He's me and I'm him." Tears began rolling down his cheeks. "I know you'll never understand what that means, but that's the best I know how to explain it. I went through a living hell when I thought I'd seen him die right before my eyes. Then Mr. Lincoln told me he had survived. Since then, I've had an obsession to uncover the truth, General. Can you understand that?"

Washburn relaxed. "Leave him alone, Jason."

"But sir—"

"Leave him alone, I said," Washburn snapped. He looked at Wade and his tone softened. "Put the gun away, Sam." They all stood silently for a long moment, awash in the dim glow of the single lantern, then Washburn turned and headed toward his office. "Come with me, gentlemen," he ordered. Wade hesitated, then he slipped the pistol back into its holster and stepped in front of Thompson, who followed.

"Take a seat, gentlemen. I have something to tell you," Washburn said as he sat behind his desk, swiveled his chair, and opened a small cabinet. He withdrew a bottle of whiskey and three glasses. He poured, then handed glasses to Wade and Thompson. "When I was twelve and my sister was ten, we went down to the riverbank. She was the most beautiful child on God's earth." He sighed, then added softly, "I wish they had been able to make photographs at that time. Her face has almost faded from my memory. We were always teasing each other—you know how siblings are. She said something"—he shook his head slowly—"I can't remember exactly what, and I gave her a shove. She stumbled and fell into the river. It had risen from a recent rain. She never surfaced. Just like that she disappeared forever, leaving nothing behind except the sound of her scream as she fell."

He gulped down the whiskey and poured some more. "I never told anyone what really happened—no one, including my parents. I just told them she slipped and fell into the water and the current pulled her under. Hardly a day goes by that I don't think about it, and it has been that way for forty years. I sometimes think the incident is suspended in time and I'm doomed to repeat it over and over in my mind." He leaned forward and looked into Wade's watery eyes. "Yes, Sam, I think I know something of what you feel. This war has put a cloak over our humanity. The ends we seek have come to justify the means. It's a dangerous situation we find ourselves in. Don't you agree?" He looked at Thompson. "So what do we do about it, Jason?"

Thompson lowered his eyes and shook his head. "I don't know, sir. I just don't know."

"Well," said Washburn, "it pains me to say this, but you're the smartest man I know. I trust you to figure out something." He turned back to Wade.

"It's the truth, son. We don't know where they've taken your brother. If you had to speculate, Jason, where would you say he is now?"

"Well, sir, we know they took the whole bunch to Richmond. We know that the individual in charge of getting their returned prisoners fit for duty is a Colonel Ingram Hatcher. He's a West Pointer. Graduated in the upper third of his class. Served as a staff officer before being wounded last winter. I counted on him to outthink himself and conclude that Colonel Thornton was really Colonel Wade. There were clues that would lead a thinking man to suspect something was afoot."

"You haven't answered my question," said Washburn.

"Probably Libby Prison, General, but that's a wild guess. I counted on the Rebs doing nothing serious if Colonel Thornton's loss of memory seemed convincing. Under the circumstances, he couldn't be anything *but* convincing."

"General," said Wade, "I'd like to request an immediate, indefinite leave."

"To do what, Sam? Get yourself killed—and your brother, too? No, there has to be another answer."

"What's so special about Libby Prison?" asked Wade.

"It's the worst they have," said Thompson. "It's for officers only and it's right in the heart of Richmond. It's a four-story warehouse next to the James River. It was a ship chandler's warehouse before the war. I saw it once. It's built like a fort."

"I'll figure a way to get Simon out," said Wade.

"This needs some planning, Sam," said Washburn. "I'm sure you know your way around down there, but this is different. We can't go breaking men out of every prison until we find your brother. I'm sure you can see that." He emptied his glass again. Wade and Thompson followed suit. "Sam, I'm going to suggest something. I know you won't like it, but I think it's best. You go on down to Chattanooga. I'll put Jason to work on a plan. If—when—he comes up with something, we'll send for you. Major Clinton, too, if you wish."

"Sir, if Simon's condition is as bad as my mother described it, he's like a small bird in the jaws of a cat."

"I know, Sam, but as you so eloquently pointed out, he's your twin brother, flesh of your flesh. My guess is he's a survivor—like you. We have time to do this the right way. I promise you, we'll find a way."

Wade shook his head. "Sir, what if he recovers his memory and tries to talk his way out? They'll kill him for sure then. Or what if our men begin to suspect he's a plant? They'd kill him in a minute, and I wouldn't blame them."

"We'll have to trust that he'll be smart enough to figure that out and remain quiet," said Thompson, who was beginning to look upon the task of rescuing Thornton as his greatest challenge yet.

"Colonel," responded Wade, "I've experienced rebel prison life. I actually considered death as a release when I thought they were about to execute me. A man will do anything, take any risk, to get out."

"Do you have a better plan?" asked Washburn.

Wade thought for a moment and sighed. "No, sir. Just don't take too long." Without waiting for a reply, he rose and moved slowly toward the door.

# CHAPTER

# 11

From the diary of Caroline Wade-Healy

*September 12, 1863*
*Tonight I am filled with feelings that I must express to someone, if only*
*to myself.*

*We take our pleasure where we find it these days, but it seems there*
*is no escape from the war. Hoping to cheer myself, I accepted an invitation*
*to a small social the other night. The hostess, Mrs. Bonner—her husband,*
*a sergeant major, is missing and presumed captured by the rebels—had*
*asked Terry Hunter to sing a song for us. I must confess that I thought*
*Mrs. Bonner would have chosen something uplifting and airy, something*
*to take our thoughts from the war. It wasn't to be.*

*Terry lost a foot at Chancellorsville, and it brought sadness to our*
*hearts just to see him struggle as he made his way to the piano. A hush*
*settled over the room as he turned toward us with a look that seemed*
*to reach to eternity. We all settled back and Terry began to sing "Tramp,*
*Tramp, Tramp" as Mrs. Bonner played:*

> *In the prison cell I sit, thinking, Mother dear, of you,*
> *And our bright and happy home so far away.*
> *And the tears they fill my eyes, 'spite of all that I can do,*
> *Tho' I try to cheer my comrades and be gay.*

*Everyone was profoundly moved by the time Terry finished the song.*
*There were sobs as his bright tenor voice faded into silence. Except*
*perhaps for "Taps," another haunting tune inspired by this war, no*
*melody so perfectly captures the mood of our time.*

*As this war drags into its third full year, the words to this haunting*
*melody seem to unleash a pent-up wellspring of emotion that has searched*

*in vain for broad expression. With no end to the war in sight, with its beginning fading from our memory, a gnawing melancholy has spread across the land. Something has happened. I think it began after the battle here at Gettysburg, when the appalling casualty totals became known. Now that the rhetoric of war has subsided and we take time to dwell on its human cost, the horror of this war, numbly expressed in the lengthening casualty lists, is only now taking root in the collective mind.*

*All, be they from the North or South, must wonder at what we have unleashed upon ourselves.*

*Limited as we are by the perspective of time, no one quite thought of this conflict in terms of where it has taken us. No review of history could have prepared us for what we have brought upon ourselves. Battles are being fought on an epic scale; armies move over hundreds of thousands of square miles of unsullied wilderness; material costs are growing at a rate that defies comprehension. As summer slips uneasily into a third autumn of war, few have been able to express their distress and agony in words that have meaning. The mournful song we heard the other night expressed our feelings eloquently. This song of physical pain, emotional suffering, and anxious loneliness truly describes the terrible blows the war has brought to nearly every hearth in the land.*

---

After the Battle of Shiloh nearly a year and a half before—two days of the worst fighting ever endured on the continent up to that time—the nation mourned the news of nearly twenty-five thousand casualties. The result had been proclaimed a national catastrophe. Nothing before approached it in the experience of a single living American. More than fourteen months later, over a three-day period at Gettysburg, there were fifty thousand casualties. Following that battle, virtually everyone in the Union high command, including President Lincoln, heatedly expressed disappointment that General Meade had resisted all inducements to pursue General Lee and destroy his battered army. Ignoring every mental and moral restraint, the orchestrators of war were changing their views of the sacrifices required to end it.

Even so, tactical changes came slowly, almost invariably an outgrowth of the prolonged failure of older methods. As a matter of expediency, each new war begins by borrowing the tactics and strategies of the preceding conflict—no matter how great the gap in time. There were few reliable precedents and even fewer individuals who were willing to break with the traditions established during the Napoleonic Wars five decades earlier. Generals of the 1860s had learned slowly that these tactics were ill suited for the weapons of the day. It took considerable time before the combatants fully realized that an officer on horseback was an easy target at two hundred yards, or that tightly packed formations looked grand on the parade ground but left almost nothing to chance for those willing to stand and deliver massed musket fire.

It took time for men to learn how to spend their lives wisely.

Except for the perfection achieved in the rate of killing and maiming, the war had ground on inefficiently. The most appalling example was the treatment of prisoners of war. It made no difference whether soldiers were enlisted men or officers, Union or Confederate. Their chances of survival were about equal. Man for man, soldiers in combat regiments at Shiloh or Gettysburg—or any other battle—were four times less likely to die than a man in prison. Part of the odds were associated with the luck of the draw: where a man was sent following capture, and when his capture occurred. By the fall of 1863, exchanges were becoming a thing of the past. From the beginning, the exchange process had been an impractical procedure, an irrational recycling process that served only to prolong the misery.

Of all the miserable places where men found themselves confined against their will, none save Andersonville had a reputation worse than Libby Prison. Libby was housed in an unremarkable building, 3 stories high, 80 feet wide, and 110 feet in length, constructed before the war by the ship chandlers' firm of Libby and Sons. Richmond city streets surrounded the building on three sides. The building's entrance faced north, fronting on Twelfth Street. A tier of dungeons—formerly an unused storage area—had been constructed under the sidewalk. In the rear and to the west, the land sloped away, exposing the basement and giving the appearance of a fourth floor. Time had discolored the walls; its rough-hewn doors and rusting windows, filled only here and there with an unbroken pane, were draped with cobwebs, making the whole building look bleak and uninviting.

To the east was a small, open field contained by a ten-foot-high wooden fence. Just beyond stood a storage building that masked the field from easy line of sight. A short distance to the south, the James River flowed swift and deep, the sun's reflection from its waters making the prison unbearably hot in summer.

The entrance lobby had been converted into a small guardroom. Beyond a stout oak door, to the left and separated from the guardroom by a thick brick wall, was a room about forty feet wide and fifty feet deep, with scarred brick walls and a splintery plank floor. The room, encompassing nearly half of the first floor, had been used as a kitchen by the prewar tenants. A prominent fireplace covered part of the far wall. A row of tin washbasins and a wooden trough that served as a bathtub were at the other end. A dozen wooden stools and hard-bottomed chairs were scattered about a room otherwise bare of furniture. Here—the only large room in the building not used for sleeping quarters—the prisoners were permitted to roam unguarded during the day.

This room, with five others of similar size and appointments, and a debris-filled basement with an earthen floor constituted the prison in which thousands of the best and bravest men who ever went to war were allowed to rot and starve. Twelve, sometimes thirteen hundred men were amassed within the prison's half-dozen shabby rooms, with a space of only ten feet by two feet allotted to each for all of life's purposes.

Cold or hot in the extreme, depending on the season, the stale air fouled their lungs. Each man's daily ration was no more than two ounces of rancid beef and a scrap of moldy corn bread. A bullet in the head awaited anyone who moved too close to an exit. In such a place, men who upon arrival were serene in their sense of personal well-being had difficulty remaining alive for half a year. What chance had Simon Thornton in his sorry state?

Barely visible in the dim light, a score of men wandered aimlessly or sat against a damp wall with their thighs pulled to their chests, their foreheads pressed against forearms crossed at the knees.

A single man closely examined Thornton, who stood motionless in the middle of the large room. Uncertain, the man approached to within five feet. "Got any tobacco, friend?" asked the man, a Union captain wearing a threadbare uniform.

Thornton made no effort to respond.

The captain shook his head. "Better get used to it, friend," he said. "I've been here since Stones River. It ain't pretty, but it's home. Now, about that tobacco. I'll give you half my evening rations for enough to fill my pipe." He reached inside his pocket, withdrew the darkly stained device, and waited patiently for a response.

Thornton shuffled limply forward, drawing his arms tightly across his chest and grasping his upper arms near the shoulder with trembling hands. His knuckles turned white with the pressure; his mind was aflame with silent, ungovernable fear. He looked slowly upward toward the black ceiling, then downward at the well-worn floor. Finally, he turned his head slowly toward the man standing nearby and, with an almost imperceptible shake of his head, asked, "Why?"

When he received no answer, Thornton's lower lip began to quiver uncontrollably, and a tear etched a path down his filth-encrusted cheek. As his last illusion of hope drained away, he sank wearily to his knees. He might have felt less anxious if he had retained even a kernel of uncertainty about what these few steps into perdition meant for him. But the experience of six months in a Yankee prison, an episode suddenly luminous in his memory, had eroded his capacity for self-deception.

Now, with his facility for self-preservation crumbling, a foreboding image streaked across his tortured mind, a searing vision of a young Negro drooping before him—hands chained to a steel I-bolt driven deep into a post, dark blood streaking down his torn, sweaty back, rage flashing in his eyes. An explosion of awareness inundated Thornton's senses as the recollections of a lifetime erupted into his consciousness.

His memory had returned.

He recognized the transformation as the worst of all conceivable events. He had lost the shelter of delusion. His mind, loath to accept reality, urged him to rush to the guard and tell him of the terrible mistake that had placed him in this hell. But the discipline of a man trained as a soldier stirred a faint scent of caution. Shut out the fear, he thought. Act with reason. Think beyond the agony of this moment.

He blinked. A second scene flashed in his mind. He saw himself lunging headlong through boiling smoke gripping a sword with both hands, its glistening point aimed at his own heart. Impossible! he thought. Just an absurd, idiotic daydream. Then he remembered the rock wall, and it all came together. Now everything made sense. It had been more than a mind weakened by months in prison would accept. Somehow, he had blocked the event from his memory. He had tried to kill his cousin, Samuel Wade. Or was Wade his cousin? The image faded. He squeezed his eyes so tightly shut that they ached.

Think! he commanded himself. Think! Logic told him that he would fail if he tried to reverse his fate and talk his way out, and that death awaited him if he failed to convince Confederate officials of the truth. He had to think, to plan—to survive.

He let his head drop. As he began to sob, the man who had asked Thornton for tobacco shrugged and shuffled off into the darkness.

The trip was long and arduous. A slow supply train transporting Wade, Clinton, and sixty other assorted officers and enlisted men had pulled out of Washington at daybreak on September 11, headed for Baltimore. At eleven in the morning, following a thirty-minute delay, the men had boarded another train and begun the long westward leg of the journey. All that day and throughout the next, they rolled toward Cincinnati, arriving late in the evening on September 13. They continued westward from Cincinnati for a short time, then south to Louisville on a route only marginally secure from rebel raiders. Following three stops for engine repairs and at least two dozen more for wood and water, they arrived in Louisville an hour past midnight on the fifteenth. Travel had been slower than usual through the rugged hills. Rarely was the train on level ground.

Following an eight-hour delay in Louisville, the trip resumed along the last and most dangerous leg of the journey—traveling south, across Kentucky and the full width of Tennessee, first to Nashville, then down toward Chattanooga. The ride seemed rougher over the recently captured narrow-gauge track, but they made good time—until the train made an unscheduled stop.

The engine screeched to a halt. A provost captain ordered everyone off the train and ushered them toward rickety old wagons for a backbreaking ride on a dirt road. They bounced along for the next thirty miles, headed toward a point northeast of Stevenson, Alabama. A few days earlier, leading a thousand-man cavalry contingent, Confederate Maj. Gen. Nathan Bedford Forrest had cut the rail line south of Tullahoma. During a three-hour frenzy, the rebels had ripped up nearly ten miles of track and burned the main bridge across the Tennessee River. All along the way, Union soldiers worked frantically trying to repair the lifeline to the sixty-thousand-man army maneuvering south of Chattanooga. Workers had just completed a new trunk line leading from a point ten miles west of the convergence of the Tennessee-Alabama-Georgia borders. At 12:30 A.M. on the eighteenth, the weary travelers boarded a waiting string of flatcars. From there, it was a straight, uneventful run into Chattanooga.

Wade had never seen such country before. He had read reports about the difficulties encountered by General Rosecrans's Army of the Cumberland as it tried to regain contact with General Bragg's Army of Tennessee. Even so, like most Northerners, Wade had trouble understanding how it could be *that* big a problem.

Even at 3:00 A.M. the town was alive with activity. "No point trying to get any sleep with all this noise," Wade said to Clinton. "Let's find army headquarters." A young lieutenant stood in front of a squad of soldiers. Wade approached. "Excuse me, Lieutenant, I need some directions."

The lieutenant snapped to attention and saluted. "If I may be of service, Colonel."

"Will you direct me to army headquarters?"

"That's easy, sir." He pointed. "It's in that hotel in the middle of the block."

"Thank you, Lieutenant." Wade motioned for Clinton to follow and they walked across the street and toward the hotel. A sergeant sat at what had been the front desk, reading a newspaper.

"Sergeant, we just arrived from Washington," Wade said. "Here are our orders. Will you direct me to someone who can give us our assignments?"

The sergeant silently examined the papers, then stood and said, "Follow me, gentlemen."

They climbed the staircase to the second-floor ballroom. "Do these people never sleep?" asked Clinton as he entered the spacious room.

"Yes, sir, but we've been working 'round the clock these past few days. At last report, less than three miles separate the Confederates from our forces."

"How far is that from here, Sergeant?" asked Wade.

"A short distance, sir. No more'n a dozen miles or so—down near Chickamauga Creek."

Strange name, thought Wade. Must be Indian.

The sergeant stopped in front of a desk. "Sir, this is Lieutenant Colonel Wade and Major Clinton. They just arrived from Washington." He turned to Wade. "The lieutenant will take care of you, sir."

"Thank you, Sergeant."

"Samuel Wade?" asked the lieutenant, looking at a sheaf of papers he'd extracted from a pile on the desk.

"That's right, I'm here with Maj. James Clinton."

"Are you both from Pennsylvania?"

"I am," said Wade. "The major's not."

"Well, Colonel, you've been assigned to the 77th Pennsylvania. The regiment's commanded by Col. Thomas Rose. That's in Col. Joe Dodge's brigade in XX Corps. And you, Major, you're assigned to brigade headquarters."

Wade shook his head. "There must be a mistake. They assured me in Washington that I'd have a regiment, with Major Clinton assigned as my exec."

The lieutenant looked through the pages. "Sorry, Colonel." He pointed to the orders. "It says right here, clear as day, 'On temporary assignment to Army of the Cumberland, Maj. Gen. William S. Rosecrans, commanding. Duty Assignment: 77th Pennsylvania Volunteers, 2d Brigade, 2d Division, XX Corps.' See? Here's General Rosecrans's initials. Don't get more official than that."

"What exactly does *temporary* mean in General Rosecrans's army?" asked Wade.

"Generally means that a reassignment is in the works, Colonel. But nothin's come in yet." He extended the papers for Wade and Clinton to examine. "I'd hurry," added the lieutenant, "or take it easy, according to your preference. I'd be surprised if this army isn't in a fight by sun-up tomorrow. We've been ordered to be ready to pull out on two hours' notice."

"Sounds like someone's a bit short of confidence," replied Clinton.

"Well, sir, 'Old Rosey' ain't one to take chances."

"Is there someplace quiet where we can get a few hours' sleep?" asked Wade.

"You might find some space on the third floor, sir, but it ain't fancy."

"Thanks, Lieutenant. Where's the QM warehouse?"

"Block south and three west, down toward the river. Can't miss it, Colonel."

At 2:00 P.M. on September 18, Wade and Clinton were galloping easily down a curving, dusty road bordered on both sides by towering trees. A supply captain going to a field quartermaster company had asked to tag along. To their right rose the craggy west face of Lookout Mountain, an eight-hundred-foot-high rocky monolith that dominated the antediluvian river valley. To their rear was a horseshoe bend in the broad, placid Tennessee River. Across the valley to the west, dulled by a dense, gray cloak of a thick morning mist, protruded the wispy outline of Missionary Ridge. Only the top third of the ridge was visible through breaks in the forest.

Surprisingly little traffic moved down the narrow road. Nearly all of the combat brigades had moved south during the previous few days as the army's units were brought together for the anticipated clash with Braxton Bragg's Confederate Army of Tennessee. Wade and his companions rode around a slow-moving string of wagons transporting musket ammunition and medical supplies. No one doubted that a major battle was about to occur. Only the time and place remained in question.

A few miles south, the road turned west. Just beyond lay Missionary Ridge, now clearly visible through the thinning tree line. By early evening they had located the lead elements of Maj. Gen. Alexander M. McCook's XX Corps, which was strung out along the road extending south from Pond Springs. The smell of wood smoke and coffee filled their nostrils. Cooking fires crackled along both sides of the road as the three men passed through the bivouacked divisions. The men seemed relaxed, almost uncaring, as they prepared their evening meal. The damp undergrowth and thick canopy of leaves held the sound close to the ground. The men talked in low, almost whispered tones, as if unwilling to disturb the solitude that their presence violated. Vibrating notes of harmonicas and guitars drifted through the dense woods. Wade detected no sense of urgency—hardly what he expected knowing that a major battle was imminent.

Five hundred yards farther along, Wade asked for directions. "Corporal, where can I find Colonel Dodge's headquarters?"

The corporal pointed north. "Y'passed it 'bout three-quarters of a mile back the way y'came, Colonel. It's on the west side of the trail."

At twenty past seven they rode into Dodge's headquarters area, dismounted, and strode toward a large tent. Flies swarmed about a plate of half-eaten beans setting near the edge of a table. A major sat working on reports. "Major, will you direct me to the adjutant?" Wade asked.

"You're speakin' to him," the major said in a stout Tennessee accent without looking up.

Wade cleared his throat, and the major lifted his eyes. Seeing that Wade was a lieutenant colonel, he straightened in his chair but remained seated. Wade handed him their orders.

"Welcome to Colonel Dodge's brigade of Brig. Gen. Richard Johnson's division, gentlemen." The major paused and spat a stream of tobacco juice. "Major Clinton'll be movin' on through, sir. We're full up on majors."

"Damn!" exclaimed Wade. "Look, how far are the Rebs from here?"

"Just over yonder," the adjutant replied casually, pointing northwest.

"It's about to bust loose, isn't it?" asked Clinton.

"Sometime today, I'd say," replied the major, "tomorrow for sure. You'll be needin' t'get movin'."

"Well, Jim, I suppose we'll meet again when this is over," Wade said as they stood a few minutes later leaning on the side of Clinton's horse. An uneasiness gnawed at Wade. He'd tried to get the orders changed, to keep Clinton at least in the same brigade. But orders were orders, said the adjutant. Clinton had been reassigned to Col. Bernard Laiboldt's 2d Brigade in Maj. Gen. Philip H. Sheridan's 3d Division, posted a half mile south of the road. It would have been better, Wade thought, if they were at least in the same division. He regretted that Colonel Thompson's tentacles of influence had limits after all.

"Don't worry none, Sam. We'll get it sorted out in a couple of days," replied Clinton. "I have confidence in Colonel Thompson. It'll just take some time." He stepped into the stirrup and swung his other leg over the horse. "Good luck, Sam." He saluted.

"Good luck to you, Jim," Wade replied, returning the salute.

The rattle of distant musket fire turned heads. There followed a few moments of silence as the tension mounted and attention turned northeast toward the sound. A second burst of fire followed. Skirmishers, thought Wade, about a company in size. With experience, one could tell the size of the forces engaged. The rebels had momentarily touched down near West Chickamauga Creek, and sparks had flashed. But that evidently ended it—for the moment.

Soldiers resumed their quiet conversations as they returned to their cooking. It never varies, thought Wade. The soldiers knew that the time for battle was drawing near. The numbing thought that men would soon be dying had a settling effect. The rowdy, profane behavior so typical of men in less stressful times nearly always disappeared before a battle. No one wanted to go to his maker with blasphemy on his tongue or anger in his heart. Nearby, a lieutenant sat solemnly, flipping pebbles with his thumb. A few feet away, a corporal of about eighteen years whittled on a stick, a grim yet determined expression on his face. Wade guessed that the young soldier was steeling himself for the ordeal ahead. Off to the right, next to a circle of stones that contained a bed of dying coals, the charred remains of a deck of cards littered the ground. Wade smiled inwardly. The owner of the deck had probably decided to eliminate the chance of his body being sent home with the sinful game still in his possession.

Everywhere Wade looked he saw the same thing: men gathered together, yet each alone—isolated with his fears of death or, even more dreadful, a terrible wound—fighting against the horrifying dread that, overcome by the stress of battle, he would fail to perform his duty. Someone began playing a lively tune on a harmonica, accompanied by Jew's harp and guitar. False confidence, thought Wade as he turned his horse and moved at a walk through the trees, looking for Colonel Dodge's tent.

Ten minutes later, Wade dismounted. Finding the place in the woods had been difficult in the gathering dusk. A colonel, immersed in deep thought, sat before a map table with his chin propped in his upturned hand. A half-dozen other field-grade officers stood in a loose semicircle around the table. Wade waited for a break in the conversation. "I'm looking for Colonel Dodge," Wade said, saluting.

"I'm Dodge," replied the early-middle-aged colonel as he leaned back in his canvas chair.

"Lieutenant Colonel Samuel Wade, sir, reporting for duty." He extended an envelope.

"Ah, yes, Colonel. I've been expecting you." Dodge accepted the envelope and removed a folder containing Wade's personnel file. He flipped through the pages, skimming them hurriedly. "Impressive, Colonel. Very impressive." He looked at Wade and smiled. "You've had a busy war so far, young man." He handed the file to Col. Thomas E. Rose, a heavyset man with a full beard and piercing, deep-set eyes. "Colonel Rose, it seems you and Colonel Wade are both from Pennsylvania. Welcome to the brigade, Colonel Wade. We'll try not to make your stay too hot—but I can't make promises for the rebels."

Dodge removed his glove and shook Wade's hand, then Rose reached out. "Welcome, Colonel Wade. Come with me for a moment." He went to the fire, poured a cup of coffee, and handed it to Wade. "It's hot, Colonel. I seem to remember that name, Wade, from someplace. Your family is in the mercantile business—or is it shoes?"

"My mother is in the shoe business, Colonel. To be honest with you, sir, I don't pay much attention to her dealings. What with my time at West Point and the war, I haven't seen much of her in the past seven years."

"Well, Colonel, welcome to the 77th. Everyone in the regiment is from Pennsylvania."

Wade smiled. "Glad to be here, sir."

Rose nodded as he examined Wade's file. He shook his head unconsciously as he read in amused detachment. "I see you recently worked with Jason Thompson. Colonel Thompson and I go back a long way." He momentarily looked up at Wade. "Interesting record, Colonel. Have you known Colonel Thompson long?"

Wade grinned. "We've had an intense if brief history, the colonel and I. I've known him about a year, sir."

Rose continued thumbing through the record. Then he paused. "Is this an error, Colonel? It says here you hold the regular army rank of major."

"That's correct, sir."

"Well, Colonel, there must be more to you than's in your file." Rose continued to nod absently as he read on. Finished, he closed the folder and looked at Wade. "We'll talk more later." He placed a hand on Wade's shoulder. "Come, let me introduce the other officers."

With the formalities concluded, the officers returned to their review of the crudely scaled maps. Fifteen minutes later Rose and Wade rode into the deep woods, toward the regiment's camp. From the distance came yet another brief clatter of musketry, followed by a few single reports. Then the noise stopped. Men from the opposing armies were searching for each other with lead fingers. So far, they had avoided close contact and no one had been hurt.

General Daniel Brown was sitting at his desk reviewing a stack of files still in need of action in one form or another when he came to the Thornton file. Brown had almost forgotten the matter. Weeks earlier, he had sent a courier to Alabama with a message addressed to General Thornton. The message outlined what Brown had learned during his inquiry into the matter of the man who claimed to be Lt. Col. Simon Thornton. Brown had heard nothing from the courier and wondered what had happened.

After Brown finished stacking the files in a neat pile, he rose from his chair. At that moment, he moaned and grimaced, then reached for his head and tumbled to the floor.

Hearing a loud thump, the sergeant in the outer office rushed in, knelt at the general's side, and shook him by the shoulders. "General Brown! What's the matter?" Brown's eyes were open, but they seemed focused on another time and place.

"What's the matter here, Sergeant?" asked Brown's aide, who had also heard the noise.

"I don't know, sir. Something has happened to General Brown."

The aide leaned over Brown. A thin trail of foam flowed from the general's mouth. His right arm and leg jerked convulsively. His left side was rigid and unresponsive. "Get the doctor, Sergeant, and be quick about it."

Five minutes later, the physician entered the room. "What's the problem here, Captain?"

"It's General Brown, sir. He's had some sort of attack."

"Let me have a look, Captain." The doctor bent close and took hold of Brown's wrist. There's hardly any pulse, he noted. He spread Brown's eyelids. "Do you have a match, Captain?" he asked. The officer handed him a match. The physician struck it and passed the flame close to the general's eyes. "Just as I thought," said the doctor. "I think this man has suffered a stroke. It doesn't look good. Find a couple of men and help me get him to the hospital."

Thirty minutes later, General Brown was dead. His last conscious thought had been to dismiss the idea of sending a telegram to General Thornton to see if the courier had gotten to him. He had decided that with Wade or Thornton or whoever it was he had sent to Libby Prison, that act might draw undue attention, opening one of those doors that he feared might be hiding something better left hidden. Now Brown would never learn the truth—and no one else would think to ask.

# CHAPTER

# 12

Cathy Blair had spent a wakeful, uneasy night. The cloud of desperation that hung over the plantation was sapping her will to endure. She had never believed in the war. Honor and the purity of the cause put no food in a soldier's belly or clothes on his back. Considerable time had passed before that reality sank into the heads of the more stubborn Southern patriots, but now even that rare breed of doggedly irrational diehards saw no hope except through desperate action.

At first, conversations had diminished to whispers whenever Cathy approached. Clusters of men, ever changing in composition and demeanor, moved about the plantation, plotting and planning, acting as if their efforts made a difference. During the past week, she had observed them indifferently. They grew increasingly bold as their mood shifted from grim resignation to near euphoric conviction that they would emerge from the present disaster with everything preserved, their property and their honor restored to antebellum refinement. Buoyed by artificially instilled confidence, they discussed their plans openly, even boisterously, to the point of ignoring the slaves who occasionally drifted within earshot. Only slowly had Cathy grown to realize their seriousness.

But now it was quiet as she walked toward the giant oak on the knoll. She shook a blanket into the air and let it settle onto the tall grass. After setting her daughter in the middle, she let herself settle limply onto the nearby swing. Cathy pushed with both feet and set the squeaky contraption in motion, then leaned her head back and let the cool breeze wash over her.

"Mrs. Blair?"

She blinked her eyes and turned her head toward the sound of the voice. "Oh, General Thornton. I thought you'd left for Alabama."

"Please, call me Henry. May I join you?"

Cathy slid to one side. "Please do. We never did have our talk."

Thornton sat beside her and looked into her eyes. "You always seem so sad," he said finally, his concern genuine.

"I've found precious little to be happy about these past months, General."

"You must have faith, Mrs. Blair. Conditions are improving. I've never felt more confident that we're going to win. We just have to hang on until the next election up north. All the signs are there. The North is growing weary. They'll vote Lincoln out and embrace an offer of peace."

"I doubt it, General—Henry. They'd have to be blind to miss seeing that we're hanging on by our fingernails."

"Perhaps we are, but some fifty miles from here a great battle is about to begin." He paused and looked skyward. "If we can hold on here in the West, General Lee will never be defeated in the East. Tenacity is our strength."

"Perhaps," Cathy said quietly, "but from what I've heard around here, Lee's men will need much more than hope. I hear that half their horses are too weak to pull a load, and that we can't replace half the men who fall in battle. On top of that, winter is coming."

"I admit it'll be difficult, but we have to think of winning politically rather than militarily. The army will have to buy the time."

"And what happens if Lincoln wins *next* year? Where will we be then?"

"We're already planning for that. There are many men up north, powerful men, who have even less use for Lincoln than we do in the South. They tell us that pressure is building to open up the West so they can begin building railroads. They are losing interest in the South. They just want us to go away. We're finally convincing them that we never wanted anything more than that in the first place. We have to concentrate on altering the political structure up there. I'm convinced that, with careful planning and patience, we'll succeed."

Delusion, Cathy thought. An impossible dream. She placed a hand on his cheek. "I know, General." Her voice softened. "Ah, Henry. You and my father are so alike. You're clinging to the past. Can't you see that it's gone? *Gone.*" She stood and turned. "Look at this place." She swung her arm in an arc. "Weeds growing in the fields. No livestock. And you're talking about holding on for another year!"

She had touched a nerve. "Women should not worry their pretty heads over such matters," he said finally, knowing *he* intended to worry about it a lot.

Her anger flared. "General, I've given my husband to this war. I've lost a brother. I've earned the right to an opinion."

"I didn't mean . . ." There's no sense arguing with a woman, he thought. They just don't understand—not that it matters. Events are in motion. There is no turning back. Ever chivalrous, he rose, walked to her side, and touched her arm. "I appreciate your feelings, Mrs. Blair, but we're fighting for our existence. We have to try everything, even if every man over sixteen has to wear a uniform." His thoughts flashed back three years, to a confrontation with his sister-in-law, Caroline Wade. What was it he'd told her? The South would raise a million men if need be to preserve its way of life. Back then, those had been just words. Now the prophecy had been nearly fulfilled, perhaps exceeded. She had told him that they would lose their sons; she had screamed it, in fact. Had she been right? A chill ran down his spine as a brisk gust of wind blew against his sweat-soaked jacket. Please, God, let Simon be alive.

"I have to leave, Mrs. Blair. I sent orders today to move two brigades of the Alabama militia to the eastern border. I have to see to their arrival. If General Bragg loses, he'll need all the reserves we can muster. The next seventy-two hours are critical for the South."

"I wish you the best, General. I truly mean that."

Thornton touched the brim of his hat. "Thank you, ma'am. Now, if you'll excuse me." He hesitated, then touched her cheek and smiled before turning and leaving her alone with her fears.

Cathy waited until Thornton had disappeared from sight before stooping to lift her daughter. She walked into the summerhouse and sat in her grandfather's favorite chair. The child snuggled against her breast, sighed, and quickly drifted into sleep. Through mist-filled eyes, Cathy noticed a large, framed map leaning against the table a few feet away. Square-cornered tracts of land had been marked with different colors, forming an unbroken line from Charleston west, across the heartland of the South, then across the Mississippi and on into Texas and beyond, to the far edge of the map, ending at Santa Fe, in the New Mexico Territory. Shorter lines of colored squares extended from the longer line, ending at the southern coast or extending into Yankee territory.

At various times during the past two days, she had observed small groups of men looking at the map, but she had paid no attention to them. Two strangers— one with an odd appearance and a New England accent, the other quite handsome and with a midwestern inflection in his voice—had arrived from Rome by carriage three days earlier. One of them had brought the map and asked that it be framed. The two men were in the house now, talking with her father.

Pretty, colored maps and boisterous chatter are no substitute for bread and gunpowder, she thought as she stretched out her legs and closed her eyes.

Sam Wade walked to where a corporal turned a quarter section of beef over a glowing bed of coals. Drawing his knife, Sam sliced an ample portion for himself. Then he cut a second slice and let it fall onto Rose's plate. He scooped a ladle full of beans onto each tin plate and topped the meat with generous portions of sourdough bread before walking to where Rose sat working on reports in the firelight. The rattle of distant musket fire had kept everyone uneasy for the past twenty minutes. Forward elements of the two armies had moved within clear sight of each other for the first time. Wade set the tin plate on the colonel's small table. "Better eat something, sir. That firing seems to be drawing closer."

Rose leaned back, then looked up and smiled. "Thanks, Sam." He stood and placed his hands in the small of his back. Then he stretched and strode to the edge of their campfire. "I expect we'll be well into it by this time tomorrow," he said as he squatted by the small fire and poured a cup of coffee. "Want some, Sam?"

"Thank you, sir." Wade squatted beside Rose and held out his cup. "This is a hell of a place for a big battle, Colonel. They can hide whole divisions in this forest."

"Unlike Gettysburg, I suppose," said Rose.

Wade nodded. "There are more trees within a stone's throw of here than on all of the Gettysburg battlefield. God had a bird's-eye view of the devil's work during those three days."

Rose smiled. "I understand you led a countercharge against Pickett's men. That must've been something."

"Set my blood to racing a bit, sir. But it was nearly over by then. It sure taught me something about those Rebs, though. They know how to die. Half of them can't read their own name, but there's not a lick of fear in a whole regiment of them."

"I've noticed that myself. Many of my men haven't seen any serious action. Most are replacements for those who were killed and wounded at Stones River. I have to wonder how they'll hold up when they hear that damnable rebel yell."

"They tend to hold up about as well as they're led, Colonel. That's been my experience."

Rose looked into Wade's eyes and smiled. "I wonder how *I'll* hold up? This is my first battle commanding a regiment."

"I wouldn't worry about it, Colonel. It's not as though you haven't been in battle."

"Yes, but I'm not a professional soldier like you, Sam. I'll need all the help I can get." He placed a hand on Wade's knee. "In fact, Colonel, I'm *ordering* you to tell me if I've overlooked anything."

"I'm here to serve, Colonel."

Rose blew on his coffee. "You have any brothers or sisters, Sam?"

Wade hesitated. No one had asked him that question since his mother had told him the truth. "Sort of, sir."

"Sort of, Sam? How does one 'sort of' have brothers and sisters?"

They ate as Wade gave Rose a shortened version of how he learned of the existence of his triplet siblings. He was still struggling to resolve in his own mind the right and wrong of it. He had never thought that his mother could hide something so important from him. But who was he to judge? There were more than a few things that he had seen and done that he would never think of telling his own son—if he had a son. Rose settled on his rump and chewed slowly as the story unfolded. All the while, to the south, the ripping sound of musket fire grew more intense.

"That's a hell of a story," said Rose when Wade finished. "Where's your brother now?"

"I wish I knew. Colonel Thompson promised me he'd do everything possible to find him. But there's been no word yet. All I know is, I won't have another peaceful night's sleep until I find him."

"Do you two look alike?" asked Rose.

"Exactly," replied Wade. He removed his hat. "Except I have this birthmark on the side of my head and he doesn't."

"Beggin' the colonel's pardon," interrupted a stout sergeant who had approached quietly from the side. "The men are feelin' a bit jittery tonight, sir, what with the shootin' and all. Would the colonel care to join us in a song? The men'd sure appreciate it, sir. Then maybe the colonel would say a few words before we turn in. I think it'd ease their minds some, sir."

Rose shifted his weight and stood. "It'd be my pleasure, Sergeant Hennesee. Care to join us, Sam?"

Wade smiled. "Don't mind if I do, sir. I'm feeling a bit jittery myself."

The sergeant grinned. I like this new colonel, he thought. The word had spread quickly through the ranks that Wade had been wounded at Gettysburg. Soldiers found comfort in knowing that their leaders had seen the elephant and lived to report the results.

Rose, too, had done his share in the war. He'd entered the army as a private in April 1861, and the men had elected him to be their captain four months later. Fifteen months after that, following the battle of Stones River, he had been promoted to colonel. At thirty-three he was younger than a quarter of the men in the regiment. But they trusted him. It was difficult to say more for a man who held other men's lives in his palm.

The men had reason to be afraid. They had been maneuvering in the woods north and south of Chattanooga for more than two months, secure in the knowledge that Rosecrans's army outnumbered the Confederates by as many as five thousand men. But that had changed, or was in the process of changing. The capture of a lieutenant the night before gave rise to rumors that Gen. James Longstreet's corps had been dispatched from Lee's Army of Northern Virginia to reinforce Bragg's forces. General Rosecrans, however, refused to believe that the rebels would send so large a force nearly eight hundred miles and leave Lee's army so vulnerable to attack. Rosecrans's refusal to at least consider how to adjust for the presence of as many as ten thousand additional enemy soldiers left many of his subordinates wondering if Rosecrans knew his business. Longstreet's reputation was sufficient in itself. The possibility of his presence was enough to send a wave of anxiety through the Union ranks.

With nothing visible but shadows, the clatter of musketry gradually subsided. A low, clinging fog slid effortlessly among the trees and settled in the eroded brushy gullies and depressions. A single shot rang out in the darkness as the eighteenth day of September 1863 drew to a close. Then one more shot. Then silence.

The day's work had concluded and, insofar as was possible, each army had fixed the location of the other. Neither had any intention of moving. Scattered here and there in the forest were small log cabins standing lonely sentinel over fields cleared years before through the sweat and tears of desperate pioneer farmers. They never would have believed that their efforts set the stage for unspeakable horrors and carnage. War had come to their primeval forest. No power on earth could hold it back. Along a ten-mile front, men sat in silence by dying fires, dwelling on their mortality. Some wrote letters home. Others, more practical, cleaned their rifles and arranged the minié balls in their cartridge cases. An eerie silence filled the void as the smoke blended with the fog.

An unseasonably sharp chill sent a shiver down Sam Wade's back. He kneaded his shoulder, trying to ease the ache that seemed never ending, as he scooted closer to the embers. Hands cupped behind his head, he gazed at the crisp white stars through a break in the trees and smiled faintly as his eyes slowly closed. His last conscious thought was of a sobbing woman pressing her warm cheek against his bare chest. Strange that I should think of her now, he mused. His muscles flinched as he tried to hold onto the fleeting vision in his mind. The effort failed, and he yielded to fatigue.

# CHAPTER

# 13

A place prepared for battle has an eerie quality at night, this one more than most. Dotting the all but impenetrable darkness were the pinpoint flickers of five thousand dying fires. The fleecy, smoky-smelling fog clung so close to the ground that a moving man appeared to be floating ghostlike through the mist as he wound his way circuitously through the dense growth. Under the canopy of trees, a two-inch-thick bed of leaves held in an enduring dampness that kept the temperature unnaturally cool and muffled every sound. West Chickamauga Creek flowed through forest broken by small, irregularly shaped fields, few larger than eighty acres. The creek meandered from the southwest to the northeast through a small, rugged valley, cutting a snakelike path nearly hidden from above by tall trees. A craggy, dense growth of clinging vines and prickly bushes obscured the waterway at ground level. Within the confines of an area eight miles deep and five miles wide, the creek flowed lazily along a twisting course covering nearly thirty miles. The deep but narrow waterway had been around for a while. Over the eons, the grinding force of rampaging spring floods had carved deeply into the modestly soft loam and sandstone, leaving the creek banks rugged, steep, and high. Except at a couple of fords, a traveler needed an urgent reason before making the effort to cross from one side to the other.

The receding end of Missionary Ridge—virtually impassable except for two narrow passes in this region—bordered the western edge of the area. Pigeon Mountain—not really a mountain, but a rise that bisects two narrow bands of relatively level, low-lying ground—served as the area's ill-defined southern boundary. A labyrinth of narrow roads and trails—the most important of these was La Fayette Road—crisscrossed the area, following the generally irregular lay of the ground. West Chickamauga Creek defined the eastern boundary of the field and marked the location where the struggle began.

At three o'clock in the morning on September 19, a sergeant shook Wade from his sleep. "A staff officer just rode in, Colonel," said the sergeant. "General Rosecrans has ordered the division to move north. Colonel Rose wants the regiment ready to move in thirty minutes."

Wade rubbed the sleep from his eyes. He squinted and vigorously shook his head, trying to clear his thoughts. "Did Colonel Rose say where we're going?"

"No, sir. Must be north somewhere. It looks like most of the army is moving in that direction. Somethin' must be up to bring on a night march through these woods. There's a little coffee left, sir. Want a cup?"

"Thank you, Sergeant. Can you get me one in the dark?"

"Got it right here, Colonel." He handed the cupful of steaming liquid to Wade. "It's hot, sir. Watch your tongue. Beggin' your pardon, sir, but I've got to move on." The sergeant turned and faded into the darkness.

Wade saw Rose in the dim light of the fire, snapping his suspenders into place. "Where are we going, sir?" asked Wade.

"Damned if I know for sure, Sam. We've been ordered to be ready to move out at three-thirty. Can't see a damned thing."

"What would you like me to do, sir?"

"Just keep the men calm and ready to move out on a moment's notice."

Rose sat on his camp stool and pulled on a boot. The damp ground had aggravated the chronic gout in his other foot. He rubbed the bad foot gently, trying to stimulate the circulation before pulling on his boot.

Daylight arrived, then midmorning. Dodge's brigade remained immobile. The 2d Division's other two brigades had moved out at dawn, and the tension felt by the men of Dodge's brigade grew as the morning wore on. The rattle of musketry had begun in earnest at about half past seven, off to the northwest. The immediate area remained serenely quiet. At eight, Colonel Dodge gave orders to stand down from the alert and cook breakfast. The men needed no encouragement. The morning dragged on.

Shortly before eleven, a rider rode up on a lathered horse. "General Johnson's compliments, Colonel Dodge. You are ordered to follow this route, sir, as fast as possible." He handed the colonel a roughly drawn map. "You are to march to the location of the other two brigades and form on the right. That will be on the south, sir, next to General Willich's brigade." The staff officer saluted, turned his horse, and galloped back down the road.

The men marched without stopping until nearly one in the afternoon, growing ever more nervous at the sound of cannon and musket fire less than a mile to their right. Immediately upon stopping, the men were ordered to load their rifles. Dodge summoned the regimental commanders and ordered them to form their regiments along the edge of the road, then gave the order to move across a long, narrow field fronting the woods. They had moved about a hundred yards past the clearing when a lieutenant rode up to Dodge and said, "General Johnson's compliments, Colonel Dodge. You are to move to your right and form to the rear of General Hazen's brigade. Once there, you are to relieve him, as his men are growing short of ammunition. Be on the alert, sir. These woods are full of Rebs."

"Thank you, Lieutenant. Where is General Johnson's headquarters?"

The lieutenant pointed. "About five hundred yards to the northwest, Colonel." He saluted and wound cautiously through the trees. By shortly after one, Dodge's brigade had moved into position, and Hazen's men marched behind them and left the field. Dodge met with the regimental commanders and told them to be on the alert, then gave orders to move by the right flank.

Dodge, riding out front and near the right corner of the 29th Indiana, had his eye on the smoke drifting toward his brigade from the front when a staff lieutenant ran toward him. "Colonel Rose's compliments, sir. He ordered me to report that the enemy is concentrated in force to our front, and the brigade to our right is currently engaged."

"Thank you, Lieutenant." Dodge spurred his mount and rode in the direction of the firing. Across the clearing he could see the rebels, their right flank no more than fifty yards ahead, the main line oblique to the line of march of his brigade. By now, the nearest enemy soldiers had noticed Dodge's men moving through the woods. Several of the rebels turned and fired into the front rank of the 77th Pennsylvania. A few of Rose's men were hit, and the others scrambled for any available cover.

Dodge rode up as Rose was trying to restore order to his shaken regiment. "What's your situation?" Dodge inquired.

"I don't know for sure, sir. We came under fire, but I'm not certain how many of the enemy are to our front."

"Well, we can't stay here. We're too exposed. Get your men organized. I'll send word to the other regimental commanders. We'll change front to face the enemy and attack on my order."

"Yes, sir. We'll be ready." Rose turned to Wade. "Order the men to fix bayonets, Sam. Form the men in company line facing the enemy. We'll move forward on Colonel Dodge's command."

"Yes, sir." Wade turned and ran along the line, informing the company commanders.

Tension mounted as the men waited for the order to charge. Holding position when bullets were zipping through the trees and bushes, occasionally finding flesh, was among the most difficult of all orders to follow. Officers moved among the men, speaking softly, trying to calm their nerves. They waited.

"Front rank . . . advance." All along the brigade front, officers gave the order and the men moved cautiously forward. When the front rank had advanced ten yards in front of the second rank, Dodge rose in his stirrups and waved his sword. "At the double time . . . *charge!*" Regimental and company commanders echoed the order, and the men burst through the underbrush and charged toward the startled Confederates. The rebels, seeing that they were outnumbered, fired a quick volley; then, almost as one, they turned and bolted through the forest, away from the screaming Yankees.

Dodge's men pursued the rebels for a mile before their energy began to wane. Here and there, the Union soldiers slowed to a walk, then stopped altogether. By now there were no recognizable lines; for all practical purposes, company commanders had lost control of their men. Dodge ordered the brigade to halt in place. Gradually the companies and regiments drifted back into a reasonable semblance of an organized formation. Dodge rode along the line, praising their gallant effort.

Rose was leaning against a tree trying to catch his breath when Wade found him. "What did you think of *that,* Sam?" asked Rose with a self-satisfied smile.

"As fine a charge as I've ever seen, Colonel." They shook hands.

Rose walked a few paces to his front and turned as he placed his pistol in its holster. "Get the men organized, Sam. I'll report to Colonel Dodge for orders. Send out skirmishers—and tell them to be alert. There's no way to know what's a hundred yards to our front."

"Yes, sir. I'll see to it right away." Wade saluted and disappeared into the thickets as Rose moved to his left. It was midafternoon and the men were hungry. There had been no time for lunch. Far to their right they heard the movement of Union troops advancing through the forest.

An hour later, with the shadows growing longer, the men of Dodge's brigade again advanced cautiously through the woods. They could hear the sound of musket fire in the distance, but to their front and on either side, it was quiet. Keeping order in the ranks was difficult, as seldom was there more than a few feet between trees. Officers and sergeants moved among them, giving directions to control the rate of advance. Progress was slow, and they could barely see the skirmishers fifty yards ahead. If there were rebels out there, the skirmishers would know it first.

At five, Dodge gave the order to stop and post pickets. The men, exhausted from a hard afternoon of fighting and marching, settled immediately to the damp ground. Uncertain of what might lie ahead, and wary of drawing attention to themselves in this unguarded pause, the Union soldiers crouched behind trees and any other available cover. Some gathered in small clusters and talked solemnly about the men lost earlier to rebel fire. They munched on crackers and anything else they had in their packs. As they waited for orders, they lit pipes or cigars. They had done a good day's work, and they knew it. They deserved a rest, and they meant to take it now, for as long as Colonel Dodge agreed.

As the sun settled, a brisk, chilling wind began to blow through the trees. Above, the branches swayed and squirrels scampered for cover. The weather had changed suddenly and the wind swung around from the north. A few of the men shifted position, searching for one of the few rays of sunlight that broke through the canopy of leaves.

In the fading twilight, fifteen minutes past sunset, visibility had dropped to a hundred yards. A sergeant ran back toward the huddled men. The skirmisher reported to Colonel Dodge, who was conducting a meeting with his field officers. A few minutes later, Dodge spoke to the clustered officers. They seemed uncertain; then a 2d Division staff officer rode up. The men watched as he leaned forward and talked to Dodge. The staff officer ordered Dodge to move his brigade two hundred yards to the north, to the edge of a small clearing, and close up on General Willich's right flank. Dodge relayed the command to his subordinates and sent them back to their regiments.

"Pass the word, Sam. Officers' call," Rose shouted to Wade as he ran up. "One minute, right here."

The officers formed a half circle around their commander. Rose talked to them, gesturing now and again, then turned and studied the ground to his front in the quickly fading light. According to the division staff officer, there was supposed to be an open field out there somewhere. I'll be damned if I see it, thought Rose.

"Rebels are moving through the woods to our front and right," the line officers told their men. "Be alert. We're moving ahead about two hundred yards, to the edge of a small clearing. See to your weapons. Get ready to move on command. Be alert, men." The tension grew.

The thick carpet of leaves muffled all but the most undisciplined movement of troops. The leaves rustled gently in the chilling breeze. The men fingered their triggers as they moved uneasily forward, listening for the slightest sound ahead. As they threaded through the woods, they came in sight of a crumbling shack owned by a man named Winfrey. Winfrey, of course, had fled the area by that time. A hundred yards north of the house was Winfrey's field, the clearing mentioned by the division staff officer.

Ten minutes later the first men reached the edge of the clearing—if one could call it that. The area was mostly covered with scrub trees, brush, and tall grass, and hadn't felt a plow for years. As the men in Dodge's regiments approached, they spread along the tree line, the 77th Pennsylvania on the extreme right. Rose set up his headquarters near the regiment's left flank; Wade moved to the far right. To Wade's right there was nothing but empty woods.

The men had become accustomed to the woods. The thought of crossing even so narrow an opening as lay before them caused anxiety. Muscles taut, nerves on edge, every sense alert, they nestled into the bushes and tried to fade from sight. Tension grew as the minutes passed. They waited.

This defined the position of Dodge's brigade at six in the evening on September 19.

Only a faint red glow remained above the ridge when the rebels moved uneasily from the wooded cover into the narrow clearing. The command fell dully on the Union soldiers' ears: *"Fire!"* The first volley caught the Confederates unaware. A dozen or more dropped, and many more limped or crawled back to cover. The column sank back into the forest as rapidly as it had appeared.

"Steady, men," Wade said as he walked along the line, his saber tip cutting a narrow path in the covering of leaves. "Reload quickly. They'll come again in a moment."

The words had barely left his lips when the rebels boiled out of the woods at a dead run. It had turned totally dark. The sky was overcast; not even a star lit their way. The shadowy outlines of the approaching enemy were barely visible as the men of the 77th Pennsylvania leveled their muskets and fired. A streak of light flashed along the length of the front rank. The nearest rebels recoiled from the impact as the second rank charged around them, dodging obstacles as they lunged forward, bayonets slicing an invisible path through the cold, damp air. All along the line, soldiers in blue and gray slammed together. In less than a minute, three rebel regiments had driven a deep wedge between Rose's regiment and the others in Dodge's brigade. Bayonets crossed in frantic bursts of hand-to-hand combat as the Confederates catapulted from the darkness into the ranks of the outnumbered Union defenders.

In the brief flashes of gunfire, Wade saw a solid body of enemy soldiers moving to encircle Rose and the other staff officers. "You men," Wade yelled during a lull at his end of the line, "Colonel Rose is in trouble. Follow me." Twenty men followed Wade toward the center of the collapsing formation. They had covered less than half the distance when rebels poured through a break in the Union line and cut them off. A rebel soldier materialized in the darkness, his bayonet aimed at Wade's chest. A Union corporal lunged forward and knocked the enemy soldier to the ground. Wade fired his pistol point-blank into the soldier's chest. "We can't do nothin' more here, sir," the corporal shouted.

Wade hesitated, unwilling to move, unable to grasp the reality that confronted him. He felt strangely unafraid. He had seen men flee from battle, hundreds of them, at Bull Run, during the Seven Days, in the Wilderness, and at Gettysburg. He had never considered any motivation for their action other than fear. Yet he had never been more afraid than when he charged down the rock wall at Gettysburg, straight into the blazing chaos of battle. Now, for the first time, he realized that there were other reasons for running. Here, he felt only futility. In the flash of musketry he saw his newfound friend, Colonel Rose, raise his hands in surrender, along with most of the other officers.

Thirty yards away, as other Union soldiers recognized the futility of further resistance, the struggle ended as quickly as it had begun. One after another, the men raised their hands. Am I to join them, Wade asked himself, or should I run? Other than sacrificing himself for no purpose, running seemed the only choice.

He pressed his back against a tree and looked down at the corporal's pleading eyes. "Let's get the hell out of here," Wade whispered.

The corporal sprang into motion at the words, with Wade and a half-dozen others close behind. They plunged into the darkness, into the safety of the forest. Lead balls cut through the branches overhead. Within ten strides, the woods closed in around them, providing an impenetrable shield against the bullets fired by men too weary to care if a few Yankees got away.

They ran until exhaustion forced them to stop. Without a word, they melted into a gully and pressed against the bank, their gasping for breath the only sound.

Overhead, unseen in the darkness, the clouds pushed forward by a weather front boiled and churned. A stiff, cold wind whistled through the trees, drowning out the sound of their labored breathing. The temperature dropped several degrees as their breathing returned to normal.

"What we gonna do, Colonel?" asked a soldier who had joined the race to freedom.

"Nothing," Wade replied. "If we move, we're as likely to be shot by our own men as by the rebels. We stay here for the night and move out at first light." Wade lifted himself upright and looked over the lip of the gully. No fires in sight, he thought, and no sign of life. It seemed as if everything had gone into a state of suspended animation as the men of the two armies settled in and waited for daylight to begin the killing again. Then, in the distance, a man lit a match and immediately attracted an angry swarm of bullets. A mournful groan followed. His light had been permanently extinguished.

At a quarter past eight, Cathy Blair opened the library door and entered the spacious room. Polished oak beams supported the high ceiling. The man sitting at the corner desk looked up and smiled. He rose and bowed politely.

"Good evening, Mrs. Blair," the man said softly. "Won't you please come in?"

"I think I will, sir, if you don't mind." I'll go wherever I please in this house, she thought sardonically.

"We've never been properly introduced, Mrs. Blair. My name is Jeremy Wagner."

"You're a Yankee, sir." She immediately regretted the note of contempt in her voice.

Wagner flinched. The woman makes it sound like a fatal disease, he thought. "Why, yes, ma'am, I believe I am."

"Might I ask, sir, what a Yankee is doing in Georgia?"

"There's nothing mysterious about my presence, Mrs. Blair. I'm here at your father's invitation—and General Thornton's kind request."

"That's hardly what I meant, Mr. Wagner. What are you *doing* here?"

Wagner cleared his throat as he walked from behind the desk. He pulled a chair from under a large table in the middle of the room. "Won't you please be seated, Mrs. Blair?"

She hesitated as she appraised the man. She had seen men such as him up north, outwardly gentle, polite to a fault, always in control—never quite honest yet never lying outright. One never noticed them in a crowd. This man had the habit of wrinkling his brow and looking over the rim of his glasses when he listened. The annoying mannerism distracted her, so she avoided looking directly at him. She guessed that he was an accountant rather than an executive. If so, that meant he had traveled south on behalf of someone, or some group, who preferred to remain anonymous. She moved toward the chair.

He walked to the far side of the table and sat down. "I'm here on business," he said abruptly. "It's very boring. I doubt it is anything you'd want to concern yourself with."

"Oh, but I am concerned, sir. I'm concerned anytime there's a Yankee within a hundred miles of my home. What business could you possibly have with my father that won't put him in danger?"

Impudent bitch, he thought. "I recommend you ask your father that question."

"I have."

"And what did he say?" Wagner demanded.

"The same thing he usually does," Cathy replied sarcastically. "Business is men's work. Women should concern themselves with more gentle pursuits, like knitting and canning. Is that what you mean?"

"Well, there you have it, Mrs. Blair. You should trust your father's instincts in such matters."

She sighed, then rose and walked toward the door. She pushed it shut. "No, Mr. Wagner. You see, I don't trust *you.*" She walked back to the table. "If I'm to trust you, then I must know your purpose here."

"If I told you that, I'd be betraying your father's courtesy." His smile was strained. "I'm a guest, Mrs. Blair. I mustn't be discourteous."

She leaned forward, placing both hands on the table, and looked him in the eye. "Then let me tell *you,* sir. Your business is railroads, isn't it? You're here to buy up Southern land."

He leaned back and smiled broadly. "If that's what you think, then why bother asking me about it?"

"Because I believe you are trying to lure my father into something that will bring him misfortune. I also believe that before that happens, you will be long gone and conveniently remember nothing about your stay here."

"My, you have a sinister view of me, Mrs. Blair. I mean your father no harm. I mean no one any harm."

"I've seen the map, Mr. Wagner."

He blinked. "I'm afraid I don't understand, ma'am."

"The map you left in the summerhouse last night. It's gone now, but I saw the colored parcels of land. The path of those squares leads from Charleston to Atlanta, then right through the heart of this plantation to Chattanooga. There's another line of squares, squares of a different color, running across Alabama. I know the South, sir. It can mean only one thing. Railroads."

He feigned indifference. "Do you have something against them, Mrs. Blair? Railroads mean prosperity, especially for those fortunate enough to own property along their path. I would think that would please you—assuming the map is about railroads, of course."

"Why would a Yankee be interested in the railroads in this area, Mr. Wagner?"

"Because the war won't last forever, that's why. Two years from now we'll be fellow countrymen again. The South must be rebuilt when the war ends. I represent interests that want to assist in that endeavor." He sighed. "There, I've done it. I let you drag it out of me." He reached into a coat pocket and withdrew a cigar. "May I?" he asked.

"As you please, sir. But there's more to it than railroads, isn't there?"

He wagged a finger in her direction. "Oh no you don't. I've said too much already. Trust me, Mrs. Blair. I'm here to help your father *and* the South. You must believe that. I'm your friend, not your enemy."

"You're here to make money, sir, at the South's expense. I've read your newspapers. Your government is spending millions every day to run its war. That means there will be many rich men when it ends—all of them Yankees." Wagner smiled tightly, drawing occasionally on the cigar, casually blowing a stream of smoke through pursed lips. She waited for a response. In the uncomfortable lull, he finally shrugged and tugged at his vest as he shifted his position.

Cathy rose and walked to the map hanging on the library wall. She traced a path with her finger. "It's this line that is most curious, Mr. Wagner, a line that leads in the direction of Birmingham, then to the west. There's no railroad along that line, or anywhere close. Such a line would serve General Thornton's interests, don't you agree?" She paused again but still heard no reply. "I suppose we'll have to leave it at that—for now. We'll talk again, Mr. Wagner."

"I'm afraid that will be impossible, Mrs. Blair. I'm leaving for Mobile tomorrow, then for the Continent."

"England?"

"Among other places. Have you ever been there? It's beautiful this time of year. All the flowers remind me of the South."

"I've never been to Europe, sir, nor do I have any interest in going there." She rose and walked to the door. As she opened it she turned and added, "Have a safe trip, Mr. Wagner." And may your ship sink in a hurricane, she thought.

Caroline Healy sat at a corner table. She looked at the clock. A quarter past eight. She had eaten too much and her eyes were growing heavy. She sipped on a glass of wine as she thought about her conversation with Colonel Thompson. It had been an uncomfortable hour for both of them. He had avoided looking her in the eyes whenever possible. No wonder, after what he had done to her nephew! She grew tense every time she thought about it. She had learned during the conversation that her husband had been in the city for two days. Thompson knew everything about everybody. The colonel had sent a message on her behalf, asking if David would meet her at Willard's Hotel at eight. She waited for his arrival as she contemplated the wisdom of her recent decision.

David Healy Sr. entered the dining room, scanned the surroundings, then smiled when he caught sight of Caroline. He walked briskly to her table and leaned down, kissing her on the forehead.

"Is that all I get?" she asked, looking mildly hurt.

He leaned down and kissed her on the mouth. "Is that better?"

"Much." She smiled.

"Why didn't you tell me you were coming?" he asked as he pulled up a chair.

"I didn't know myself until the night before last," said Caroline. "Besides, I didn't know you were here."

"I arrived on Thursday. We're having some supply problems. I'm here to untangle the paperwork. It's a frustrating business. Have you taken a room?"

"Yes. You'll be able to spend the night, I hope."

"Are you serious?" he exclaimed. Heads turned. "I haven't seen you in nearly two months, my dear," he continued in a whisper. He placed a hand on hers. "Shall we go?"

Caroline smiled to herself as they lay silently in the dark room, her head resting on his arm, her fingers twirling the hairs on his naked chest. She felt like a schoolgirl every time she was with him, and those times were all too infrequent. She turned and pressed her bare breasts against the side of his chest and sighed. "You've heard about Chattanooga, of course."

"Yes. It's going to be one of the biggest battles of the war."

"I know." She hesitated. "Samuel is there. Did you know that?"

He rolled his head and looked at her. She shifted and looked into his eyes. "You didn't mention it in your last letter," he said. "It seems we both have sons in harm's way." They sighed. "Bill's with Colonel Wilder's brigade," he continued. "That man thinks he's immortal. I've been frightened half out of my mind ever since I learned of Bill's assignment."

"When's this war going to end, David?"

"We may know better by tomorrow evening. If Rosecrans whips Bragg, I don't see how the South can hang on much longer. Every day now we're getting twenty or more deserters from Lee's army. They say more would come but they're afraid to take the chance. The Confederacy is coming apart."

"I'm going south, David." She regretted saying it that way, that bluntly. But she had settled the question.

He bolted to a sitting position. "After what you went through, I can't believe you'd even *think* that, let alone do it."

"I got a letter through to my sister with some difficulty. I wrote and asked her about Simon, just to see how she would respond. Judging from the date, she wrote back immediately, but the letter took weeks to get here. I received it day before yesterday. She's frantic with worry. She says she has heard nothing since being informed that he'd been listed as a possible Union prisoner. But Simon was sent back south nearly a month ago, in the last prisoner exchange. Colonel Thompson confirmed that to me today. She should have learned of Simon's return by now. Something is terribly wrong. I have to find out what it is and do something."

"Why didn't you just tell her about his release in your letter?"

"Because if I had, I might have compromised either or both of our sons." Pulling the pillow upward against the headboard, she slid to a half-sitting position. "Something is wrong, David," she said again. "I'm not sure what, but she *is* my twin sister. Maybe Henry can find out what has happened. But he must have someplace to start. I have to tell her what happened, that I took care of Simon for all those weeks when he was in ill health. I can't chance the harm I may do by writing such things."

"Yes, of course. But even so, Caroline, you mustn't go there. They'll hang you for sure. You're still considered a spy."

"I've asked Colonel Thompson to work on a plan. He has connections. Did you know that his father and Jefferson Davis were friends before the war? I've done some checking on our Colonel Thompson. Did you also know that he's a very wealthy man?"

"Not nearly as wealthy as his father," said David. "The old man was in the shipping business before the war. That's no secret."

"Well, it's all Jason's now. His father lost his mind some time back, and Jason had him placed in a *very* private sanitarium back in Illinois. He died about a month ago. Jason went to see him when he learned of the old man's deteriorating physical condition. He pretended the trip was for military reasons. He obviously didn't want anyone to know the truth."

"How did you learn all this?" asked David.

"I have connections. I did some checking, and one thing led to another."

"I don't see that it matters."

"Neither do I. Colonel Thompson isn't even aware that I know. But I'm sure of one thing: if Jason Thompson wants something to happen, it usually happens. If anyone can get me safely into the South, he can."

"Caroline, this is absurd, and you know it. In time of war there is no such thing as safe passage into a belligerent country." He paused and playfully pushed a finger into her belly button. "Of late, I've been giving considerable thought to growing old with you."

She smiled and placed her arms around his neck. "I feel eighteen just now, sir." She pulled him to her and kissed him on the nose. "I'm not ready to grow old."

"Well, I didn't mean this very moment." As he lowered her to the pillow, her hair spread in a fan. He kissed her hard on the lips, then lifted his head and looked deeply into her eyes. "If you're serious about this, I'm sending someone with you."

"Who?"

"David."

"But he's just a boy, David."

"Far from it. I never told you this, but he came with me when I went south to convince General Thornton to set you free. When that didn't work out, David Jr. went off on his own—at Jason's prompting, of course. He went to the Thornton plantation to rescue you. He thought you were still there at the time. When he learned you had been taken away, he took Nancy Caroline instead. He acted on a whim. But the important thing is, he faced a difficult choice and wasn't afraid to act. It seems I raised that boy better than I thought. Anyway, he made it all the way north with her—a remarkable accomplishment in itself."

Caroline was speechless. She had been so relieved at being set free that she had never really given any thought to how her niece became a prisoner. So much had happened so quickly afterward that it had never occurred to her to ask. She placed a hand on her husband's cheek. "You and I are going to have to sit down some evening and have a long conversation. I'd like to find out what else I don't know about that family of yours."

He leaned down and kissed her.

"But not this evening," she said softly in his ear as she pulled him to her.

# CHAPTER

# 14

Morning broke over a landscape crowded with tense, wide-eyed survivors of the first day's action. They had huddled collectively throughout the long night, anticipating that any sudden, imprudent move would arouse a swarm of bone-jarring lead projectiles. Nine hours earlier, the men had settled uneasily to the dank earth, shielded only by the cavelike darkness that blotted out all things living and inert. They were mingled together, blue and gray, with no way of knowing the color of the uniform worn by an unseen warrior ten yards away. Now, as the first pink streaks of sunlight highlighted the boiling clouds, an unspoken truce prevailed as they scurried through the underbrush, searching for the remnants of their regiments.

Sam Wade rubbed his shoulder, trying to restore circulation as he scanned the terrain surrounding the gully where he and five others had found sanctuary. A few feet away, with his back pressed against the rotting carcass of a long-fallen tree, sat a Confederate soldier trying unsuccessfully to tie a tourniquet around his limp arm. Too much of his life already had drained onto the leafy carpet for him to fulfill the task. He sank back, exhausted by the small effort, gasping for breath.

"Do you need some help?" Wade asked softly.

The rebel bolted upright, his senses momentarily alerted by the unknown voice from the shadows. "Who's there?" he asked uneasily, looking right and left. He rubbed his eyes and squinted, straining to see in the pale light. He instinctively grasped the stock of his musket but lacked the energy to bring it to bear.

Wade crawled over the rim of the gully and moved on knees and elbows toward the stricken, bleary-eyed man. "Here, let me help you," he said as he drew close. "That's a nasty wound. You've lost a lot of blood." He looked at the man's ashen face and doubted he would survive. Wade leaned across the man's chest and tied the tourniquet. "Where's your regiment?" Wade inquired.

"Can't rightly say," said the young rebel. "Off to the east a bit, I reckon." His head began wobbling uneasily on his slumping shoulders.

"You need medical attention. What's your regiment?"

"Thirteenth Tennessee," the man replied, straining to say the words.

"Hello out there," Wade yelled. "Anyone from the 13th Tennessee?"

A long silence followed, then a cautious voice called out. "Who wants to know?"

"What's your name?" Wade asked of the wounded man.

"Kirk," he replied. "Kirk McGee."

"Kirk McGee," Wade hollered.

"That you, Kirk? We figgered y'd bought it for sure. Where are ya?"

"Over here," Wade replied. "Wounded in the arm. I need help."

As Wade heard the rustling in the bushes, he eased himself to the other side of the tree trunk. He pulled his pistol and waited. Two rebels, crawling low to the ground, slowly stuck their heads through the gnarly branches of a nearby bush. "By God," one of them said, "y'don't look so good, Kirk ol' boy." They moved across the small clearing to McGee's side. "Hey, wait a minute. He's unconscious," said the older of the two.

Wade cocked his pistol and pressed it against the younger man's head. Both men froze at the sound. "You better get him some help soon, or he's sure to die."

"Hey, y'all are the one who yelled out, ain't ya?" The soldier turned his head slowly and looked at Wade through side-cast eyes.

"That's right," said Wade. "I didn't know what else to do."

"Why y'helpin' him?" asked the older of the two.

"Don't worry about it," Wade replied. He eased the hammer forward. "Now get this man to an aid station."

The older rebel leaned back against the log. "Where y'all from, Colonel?" he asked casually.

"Gettysburg," Wade replied. "And you?"

"Just a hoot an' a holler from here, thirty miles acrost the Tennessee border. My brother an' I sharecrop a small piece of bottomland."

"Well, Johnny Reb, you keep your head low today. I suspect things will get hot before long."

"Yessir, I reckon they will."

The three men eyed each other silently. Then the older rebel turned and shouted, "We got us a wounded man and we're bringin' him in. Hold your fire. Y'all hear?" The man looked back at Wade. "Go on now, Colonel. Y'better skedaddle. No one's gonna bother y'none."

Wade grasped the man's shoulder and squeezed. "Thanks. Maybe some-day I'll have an opportunity to return the favor." With that he crawled away.

"Let's get out of here," Wade said quietly as he dropped below the rim of the gully. "Stay low and keep moving, no matter what." Wade led the way, heading west in a crouch, through the clinging undergrowth. They moved slowly and tediously through a section of the woods without another blue uniform in sight. They worked their way around several enemy camps. For-tunately, the rebels were too cold to pay attention to anything other than their own misery.

Nearly an hour passed before they reached a clearing on the west edge of La Fayette Road. Four shivering Union privates and a corporal huddled on picket duty, crouched in a small grove of scrub oaks. Wade pressed himself against the ground, ordering his followers to do the same. He took a deep breath. "Colonel Wade, 77th Pennsylvania, coming in. Don't shoot, men."

The pickets bolted to a standing position, pressing the stocks of their rifles against the trees. "Come in easy, Colonel, else you're a dead man."

Wade lifted his arms in the air as he cautiously rose from behind a bush. "There's six of us. Just take it easy, men. Don't do anything foolish."

Wade's companions rose and walked apprehensively behind him toward the clearing. The pickets lowered their muskets.

Wade breathed easier. "You men know where the 77th Pennsylvania might be? It's part of Dodge's brigade in Johnson's division."

One picket looked at another. They both shrugged. "I think they fell back last night, up north, somewhere in the woods. Heard they got shot up pretty bad."

"What unit are you men with?" Wade asked.

"General Wood's division, Colonel," replied the corporal. "Fifty-seventh Indiana."

"Are those our men on the other side of this clearing?" Wade asked, pointing.

"Yessir. That's the picket company. There's no one wearin' blue east of here. I'm s'prised y'made it this far. Most folks fell back last night when the fightin' stopped."

"So we noticed, Corporal. Thank you for your assistance. Where might I find General Wood's headquarters?"

"Over yonder somewheres." The corporal waved toward the tree line across the way.

Wade tipped the brim of his hat and ran in a crouch across the mist-cov-ered field. The others followed. Secure amid friendly uniforms, Wade and his small band moved quickly. The sun had just cleared the edge of the trees when they found the headquarters clearing. Wade, seeing a brigadier gen-eral talking with a major, approached and saluted. He introduced himself and identified his unit. "We were cut off last night, General. We had to crawl through a fair portion of the rebel army to get here."

"You came from due east of here, Colonel?"

"Yes, sir."

"Did you see anything of Longstreet's corps?"

"Couldn't tell, General. We weren't that interested in getting close enough to identify units."

The sound of musketry broke the tranquillity. A battery of cannon fired. Everyone moved faster. "Sir, I need to get a message to my brigade commander, Colonel Dodge. Do you have anyone riding in his direction?"

"Maybe later, Colonel. You better stay here. Sounds like things are heating up." Wood raised his field glasses and looked east. "Can't see a damned thing through those infernal trees." He lowered the glasses. "Yes, you better stay here for now, Colonel. There's been a major battle going on up north. You'd only be in the way there now. I have a senior captain commanding a regiment right over there. Would you mind giving him a hand until I can find a qualified officer to relieve you?"

"If the general so orders. Might I request something in writing, sir? I don't want to be charged with desertion."

Wood extended his arm, and the major handed him his orders book. He scribbled a brief note and gave it to Wade. "This should do, Colonel. It's the 65th Ohio. Report to Colonel Harker, the brigade commander. I'll relieve you later this morning. That'll be all."

"Might I get a horse anywhere around here, General?"

"Major, help the colonel find a horse," said Wood.

Wade saluted.

An hour later, after replenishing their ammunition, eating a quick breakfast, and reporting to the brigade commander, Wade and his followers joined up with the 65th Ohio. Wade had just introduced himself to Captain Shead, the acting commander, and assumed command when the clatter of musketry arose from across the road. Shortly, a dozen pickets scurried through the brambles, rushing for the security of the trees.

"Rebels comin'!" one of them screamed.

"Order the men to their positions, Captain," Wade said calmly.

The men rushed forward, fading into the brush just beyond the lip of a small hill. During the night they had piled up trees and rocks, making long, low breastworks that extended from north to south. Wade approved of their initiative. Even in the dark, they had fashioned a formidable defensive position. Muskets at the ready, the soldiers crouched and waited. Nothing much happened unless someone exposed himself. The Confederates seemed interested mostly in holding the Union troops in place. They sent a steady peppering of lead into the trees but failed to advance. Wade took advantage of the relative calm to introduce himself to the regimental officers. They waited as the sun moved slowly overhead.

At a quarter to eleven, a rider rode up to Wade. "General Wood's compliments, sir. The division has been ordered to move north and close up on General Reynolds."

Wade flinched in surprise. "But that will leave a wide gap here," he replied. "There's nothing between us and General Sheridan's northern flank."

"Them's the orders, Colonel. Be ready to move in five minutes."

This is idiotic, thought Wade. We're engaged with the enemy and being ordered to move by the left flank across their front! "Captain, we've been ordered to move by the left flank in five minutes. Inform the company commanders that we'll form on the right of the 3d Kentucky."

"But, sir—"

"Those are the orders, Captain. Alert the men."

"Yes, sir."

The men had moved about three hundred yards, Wade's regiment in the right rear, when a volley crashed into the brigade's flank. Nine men dropped, three of them dead. A second volley sent twenty more men pitching forward. The others instinctively slumped to a crouch and spun toward their tormentors. As if from nowhere, a thousand men wearing butternut uniforms boiled from the woods, crashing through the forest and driving straight toward the Union flank and rear. The rebels surged unrestrained into the gap left by the withdrawal of Wood's division. Within minutes a great gray hemorrhage spilled over everything in sight, five divisions in all, nearly eleven thousand men. Two and a half months earlier, at Gettysburg, many of those same men had charged across an open field toward a far different fate. Many must have thought of that as they pumped volley after volley into the backs of the retreating Yankees.

Overwhelming panic gripped the Union soldiers. Each Federal soldier who had a clear view of the onslaught had a variation of the same thought—that every one of those eleven thousand was coming straight toward him, with sharp steel at the end of his musket and malice in his heart. A few instinctively fired a quick shot before turning and fleeing. Many dropped their rifles to lighten their load. Only the tightly packed trees prevented a massacre. In less than a minute, Wade's entire brigade had joined in a wild, scrambling rout, many of the officers racing ahead on their mounts.

As the Confederate shock wave crashed forward, slamming into each successive brigade, it sent ripples ahead, alerting the men beyond that something apocalyptic had been unleashed in their rear. In minutes, far faster than the men could run forward to affirm the message, the alarm spread throughout

Wood's division. Even before the rebels came into sight, the men in the trailing units looked over their shoulders. Seeing the mass of their blue-clad comrades swarming toward them, they, too, began running. A few officers unaffected by the panic tried valiantly to stem the tide. They soon learned that the time for reasoning had passed. A man in the rear who so much as stumbled was quickly trampled and subdued, then sent on his way to a rebel prison. Only the sheer mass of terror-stricken soldiers fusing together, scrambling and falling, restrained their forward movement.

Wade, hearing the sound before realizing the cause, turned in his saddle. For a moment he sat mesmerized by the spectacle of the massed Confederate formations storming toward him. Then a bullet drilled into his horse's left flank, followed almost immediately by a second minié in the animal's head, just behind its ear. The mare staggered momentarily, screamed, then crashed to the ground. Wade flung himself to one side, trying to avoid the animal's crushing weight. He rolled, trying to minimize the force of the impact. Unhurt, he sprang to his feet, then stood paralyzed for a moment as he pondered the sheer irony of his dilemma. West Pointers were expected to resist all pressure to run from danger. Die? If need be. Submit to capture? When overwhelmed and subdued, or when wounded and incapacitated. But run? Never. Now, for the second time in twenty hours, he found himself confronted with that humiliating act as his only rational option.

Slowly, as a result of the onrushing rebels' long charge across rugged ground, their energy began to drain. As they fanned out to the right and left, they slowed to a trot, then to a fast walk. Most had fired their weapons as they broke from the seclusion of the forest and came in sight of the massed and unaware Union troops. A few knelt and reloaded, but most simply moved forward or drifted right or left.

Wade quickly reasoned that there was less immediate danger than the numbers confronting him might suggest. He pulled his pistol and, with pandemonium closing from every direction, ran. As he scrambled through the trees, he decided to use his pistol as a defensive weapon, firing only when it was necessary. His immediate goal had become personal security. Killing rebels and winning the war would have to wait their turn.

Only with luck would there be a Union army remaining by nightfall. Small groups of Union and Confederate soldiers slammed together and made their own small war. Few of these confrontations lasted more than a minute or two. The urge to keep moving simply overwhelmed the outnumbered Union troops. And the euphoria caused by the sight of all those running Yankees seemed strangely to have sapped the Confederates' zest for a sustained fight. If a man dropped his rifle and surrendered, the rebels gobbled him up and sent him to the rear, but other than that, they settled into a leisurely stroll.

Wade continued westward at a steady jog, picking up other fleeing Yankees as they staggered through the trees and clinging underbrush, their movement largely masked by the smoke and natural haze.

In time, the small cluster following Wade had outrun all but the most ardent of their pursuers. Wade realized that if things were bad in the mass of the army, they must be worse with Sheridan's troops, totally isolated on the cut-off southern flank. Wade's thoughts turned to Clinton, who was neither a coward nor a fool. Unless killed outright, he would apply his indomitable resourcefulness and find a means of escape. He had spoken often of the special hardships he would face as a Confederate prisoner—given his Southern heritage.

Wade began edging southward, circling around and avoiding the isolated bands of Confederates in the area. Their advantage had waned in proportion to their declining mass. The woods were more dense here, and the ground was more rugged. No longer buoyed by the mass that earlier had fueled their courage, the rebels moved cautiously as they eased deeper into the forest. A man could lose himself within five feet of a foe, or lie in ambush and send lead plunging into the flesh of an imprudent pursuer. Wade slid down the bank of a deep gully and stopped. The others followed him and clustered around.

"Men," Wade said breathlessly, "I won't order you to place your lives in jeopardy." He reloaded his pistol as he talked. "You're free to try to make it back to your units." He motioned south with a nod of his head. "Off in that direction is Sheridan's division. As soon as I rest for a few moments, that's where I'm heading. Any of you who chooses is welcome to tag along. If you think your chances are better going some other way, well, keep low and good luck."

"What if Sheridan's men ran, too?" asked a sergeant.

"I suspect they did," replied Wade. "About as fast as everyone else. But I have a friend over there somewhere, and I mean to find him if I can. Failing that, I'll concentrate on staying alive." Streams of sweat flowed down his grimy, unshaven cheeks. He stood and unbuttoned his jacket. "Who's coming with me?" he asked. Five men raised their hands. The rest, including a lieutenant, chose to strike out on their own. To the east, they heard muffled voices and the rustle of footsteps in the leaves. All turned. "Someone's coming," Wade said quietly. "Time to get moving."

He moved south in a crouch. As he stumbled over the rough terrain, he wished he had asked about Clinton's unit. He had heard the adjutant mention the name Laiboldt, but Wade hadn't recognized it. He had little knowledge of the commanders serving in the Army of the Cumberland. He decided to go with what he knew and work down from there. That meant finding some element of Sheridan's division, no matter how small, and thus narrow his search. In front, he saw nothing but dense woods.

Ten minutes later they saw a handful of Union soldiers, one of whom fired wildly as Wade drew near. "Hold your fire," Wade said in a loud whisper. "We're Federals."

"Come on slowly," one of the men warned.

"I'm looking for Maj. James Clinton," Wade stated as he approached. "He's assigned to Colonel Laiboldt's brigade. Anyone know where it might be?"

"That'd be 2d Brigade."

"Any of you from that outfit?" asked Wade.

"No, sir. We're all from Colonel Lytle's brigade. Best we know, Colonel Laiboldt's men skedaddled when the Rebs broke through. Ain't seen nothin' of 'em since."

"Which way did they go?"

"Did y'come from the north?" asked one.

"Yes, along the base of that ridge."

"Well, y'prob'ly passed right through the tail end of 'em. Y'can't see much in those trees."

"Thank you, men. We're going back in that direction. You're welcome to come along if you wish. There's safety in numbers."

"There's safety in hidin', Colonel, if'n it's all the same t'you."

"Then I'd keep my voice down if I were you. We heard you from thirty yards away. Good luck." Wade turned and trotted at an angle up the shallow grade. Shortly, he found some stragglers from Laiboldt's brigade boiling coffee over a small fire. They said that most of the men had moved west, heading toward the pass through Missionary Ridge. As Wade and his men moved along, they encountered more and more of the anxious Union soldiers. More than an hour passed before they met a captain who remembered Major Clinton. He had ridden in the day before, the captain said, and been assigned to brigade staff. The captain remembered because he had passed close enough to hear Clinton talking. The man's thick Southern accent had attracted his attention. That's all he remembered. Wade continued his search.

In the two hours that had passed since the breakthrough, the panic had subsided. The men's immediate concern was assuaging their hunger. Soldiers from the various regiments had mixed together and were sharing their rations. At the second such gathering Wade came upon, he again narrowed his search.

"Yeah, I saw him about an hour ago," said a lieutenant. "He was with some men from the 55th Illinois. Find them and you'll probably find your major." He pointed to the northwest. "Try off in that direction."

Wade soon found an officer who had seen Clinton just ten minutes earlier at a temporary brigade headquarters that had been established in a clearing. Wade made his way through the trees to the clearing. His search ended at a quarter after one. "How's the war going, Jim?" Wade asked calmly.

Clinton turned. A huge smile split his face. "By God, Sam. Ya lost?" He walked toward Wade with his arms extended. They hugged each other and laughed. Clinton stood back, his hands resting on Wade's shoulders. "Can ya believe it, Sam? They sent us all this way just t'see us run. Never figgered I'd do that."

"Me neither," replied Wade, nodding. "But it doesn't seem so bad when there's thousands of men running alongside you."

"Yeah, we sure got whipped good, didn't we? There's goin' t'be hell t'pay for this. I'd hate t'be a general in this army. Have y'had anythin' t'eat? We didn't get away with much, but we salvaged a wagon full of hardtack an' a few boxes of ammunition."

"Hardtack sounds better than nothing," said Wade. "I brought five other men with me. Can you handle them, too?"

"Sure, Sam, there's plenty t'go 'round."

As they walked toward the wagon to secure their rations, a battery of cannon opened fire to the northwest, followed by the rapid, muffled clatter of musket fire. "Someone's still fighting this war," said Wade as he shaded his eyes from a sudden burst of sunlight.

"That's General Thomas," Clinton observed. "I heard from some stragglers that he's pullin' everyone within range to a rise called Snodgrass Hill."

"Then that's where we ought to be," Wade said, thinking that the time had come to redeem himself.

"Colonel," said a staff officer, "there must be ten thousand rebels between here and where Thomas is fighting."

"That may be, Captain. But if the army is holding together over there, they probably need all the help we can give them. I don't have the authority to order any of you to come with me, but as soon as I get some coffee and biscuits in me, I'm heading out. Unless I miss my guess, what's left of my brigade is in that fight. By now they must be badly mauled."

# CHAPTER

# 15

The Washington newspapers reported the catastrophe before President Lincoln received the telegram from Assistant Secretary of War Charles Dana, the government official sent down earlier to monitor events. The report in the late afternoon paper gave few of the details, stating only that the Confederates had broken the Union lines and sent much of Rosecrans's army into panicked retreat. No one knew the whole story. The only good news was that General Thomas had formed a defensive line on a prominent hill and was protecting the retreating army's rear.

Although specific events would become known and their impact clarified within a few days, it would be months—perhaps years—before the story behind the story became known. For now it mattered only that the Union had lost another major battle and the war would continue indefinitely. The immediate effect of the Southern victory at Chickamauga was to give rise to new hope in the South and increase frustration in the North.

Whatever the effect might have been on the armies and the governments, for Caroline Healy the event served only to increase her personal sense of urgency. She had convinced herself that she held the fate of her nephew in her hands. Although she lacked the power to control that fate herself, she believed she had knowledge that, once known by others, would make it possible for them to save him. She saw no shame in failing, only in failing to try. She said as much when she met with Colonel Thompson on the afternoon of September 20.

"I realize what I told you yesterday, Mrs. Healy, but it's out of the question. More so now than ever," said Thompson.

"I fail to understand your reasoning," Caroline answered calmly.

"It's really quite simple," replied Thompson. "Forty-eight hours ago, many in the South were convinced, or were capable of being convinced, that the war would end by spring or before. Those people would have been eager to show their goodwill, to build a bridge to the future, a bridge to peace. People who were considered forward thinkers the day before yesterday will be viewed as traitors for those same views today. I don't think you appreciate the magnitude of what has happened at Chickamauga."

"I fully appreciate it, Jason. Like you, I, too, think the war will continue for a long time, certainly until next summer. But you fail to see that as being precisely *why* my mission is so urgent. If my nephew's life was in short-term danger, the end of the war might have found him alive. Now that hope has faded."

"I simply don't think you have anything on which to base that assumption, Mrs. Healy. What is so urgent?"

"Colonel, may we go for a short carriage ride?"

"Mrs. Healy—"

"Indulge me, Jason. Please. And call me Caroline."

He sighed, then reached for his cap. Once outside, he hailed a cab, then assisted her into the passenger compartment.

"Driver, go to Judiciary Square Hospital," she instructed.

After a fifteen-minute ride, they reached their destination. Thompson helped Caroline from the cab and they walked toward the building. As they approached the main entrance, Caroline tugged at the colonel's sleeve. "This way, Jason. I want you to see what's in the rear." She led him around the sprawling structure.

Among some trees, in back of the hospital, the army had constructed a small stockade. Locked inside were perhaps two hundred wounded Confederate prisoners, cramped into a space inadequate for a quarter of their number. Thompson had never seen the place. When Caroline first saw it, while looking down from a second-story window some time before, she had asked a few questions. The answers provided the basis for her fear. She led Thompson to the only gate leading into the barricaded compound. Approaching the guard, a corporal, she asked to be admitted.

"You don't want to go in there, ma'am. It ain't a fittin' place for a lady."

"That's precisely why I want to go in, young man. Now open the gate."

"I can't do that without an officer sayin' it's okay."

"Corporal," snapped Thompson, "open the gate and let us in." He turned back to Caroline.

"Mrs. Healy—Caroline—I don't see what this is going to solve."

"Take a look, Jason; then I'll explain."

When the corporal opened the gate, Thompson took Caroline's arm and led her into the compound. The gate closed behind them. Even in the open, with a stiff breeze blowing, the smell nearly overpowered them. Caroline coughed. Thompson held his palm to his nose.

"Tell me, Jason, what do you see here?"

He turned his head from right to left. "I see too many men crammed into too small a space. I see terrible unsanitary conditions. I see men who are sick and wounded—nearly all of them. I see half-starved men who have inadequate clothing."

"And?"

"I see a graveyard."

"I've done some checking, Jason. What you really see is the *best* prison currently in operation in this country, North *or* South. There's a hospital less than a hundred yards away—one of the newest and best in the nation. There's a warehouse filled with clothing, and every other imaginable human need, no more than five hundred yards from here. The hospital discards more and better food each evening than these men are allowed to eat in a week, and you can see as well as I that the men are undernourished. It's evident we don't care what happens to them. They aren't men anymore, they are the enemy. We treat them this way because we choose to, not because we must."

"I'll concede your cause for concern, Caroline, but what's your point? I'm hardly in a position to reform the prisoner of war system."

"Oh, I think if you set your mind to it you could, Jason. But you're right, that's not the point. The point is, *I* think Simon is in a military prison like this, only worse. I think he will die in that prison, and no one will ever know or care." She turned and walked back toward the gate. Thompson followed. He knocked. As they waited, Caroline took Thompson by the arm and turned him toward her. "I think you've known where Simon is all along, Jason. I think you sent him to the South *expecting* them to place him in a Confederate prison."

Thompson feigned shock. "What an incredible thing to say! I have no such power."

The gate opened and they walked into the open. "Have you ever noticed lately how frequently you mention how little power you have? I'll make you a wager, Jason. Let's go back to your office. When we get there, I want you to make a casual request of General Washburn on a matter of great difficulty. My guess is it will be granted without question."

"And what are you willing to wager on this absurdity?"

Caroline thought for a moment. "I'll wager my pass to go south against a promise never to bother you again. I'll leave my son in your hands, without question, as long as this war continues."

Remember never to get into a poker game with this woman, thought Thompson. "Answer me one question, Caroline. What possible motive would I have for sending Simon south—just to have him put in a Southern prison? If I had really wanted him imprisoned, I could have sent him to any one of a dozen here in the North."

"Your motive eluded me at first, Jason. Then this morning I remembered something you said yesterday. At the time, it seemed unimportant. Over breakfast I began thinking about everything that has happened, and then I thought of something my husband told me last night. It was also a couple of things Samuel said—and something you did. All of this seemed unrelated—until I considered everything in total. Then it all came together, as clear as a bell on a winter's night."

"You've lost me, madam."

"Until my husband told me last night, I never knew how Nancy Caroline became our hostage. When he told me that story, it reminded me of something Samuel said earlier: that you never did anything important without having a reason and, where necessary, an alternate plan in place, a plan seemingly unrelated to other plans but related nonetheless. He said you create illusions and distractions, with no one other than you knowing the whole story. This morning, I thought of that, which brings me to what you did."

"And what was that?"

"You came to my home when Simon was there."

"Hardly a grand strategy, Caroline."

"True, but aside from the considerable effort involved in the trip, two things were obvious as a result of that visit. First, you had not traveled there to see me—which I knew all along. You were there to investigate firsthand my nephew's condition. I know we never discussed it directly, but I saw how you looked at him. You were obviously making an effort to not talk about him. I know now that you had heard about his capture and that he was badly hurt before you came to Gettysburg. When Samuel came for a visit a short time ago, he told me how he heard of Simon's capture. He said the two of you learned of it within forty-eight hours after the last day of the battle—from President Lincoln, of all people. Your visit with the president, and the circumstances surrounding it, convinced me of the extent of your power. But that's simply incidental to everything else.

"You couldn't have learned about Simon's head wound and loss of memory until you arrived at my farm. You were so distracted by his condition that you hardly paid attention to me, yet you never asked any questions about Simon—not one. You examined him as though he was one of those reports you study so carefully. You know more about people than they themselves know.

"But all of that would have meant nothing except for what you said yesterday, almost as an aside. When I expressed concern about Samuel and his friend Major Clinton being ordered back to a fighting regiment and being vulnerable to capture, you said I shouldn't worry, that precautions had been taken to divert attention from them no matter what happened. The more I thought about that, the more sense it all made. You plan to have Samuel go into the South on one of your damnable secret missions.

"Which brings me back to Simon. You sent him South knowing, or at least hoping, that the Confederates would think he was Samuel. Even if they couldn't be sure of his identity, common sense suggests that they'd be unwilling to gamble on being wrong. Everything had been put in place to create that illusion—and thus the distraction. The head wound, the fact that he had no memory and couldn't defend himself, the exchange of prisoners after General Halleck had ordered that such exchanges be stopped, the likelihood that someone who knew about Samuel would eventually see Simon and think he was Samuel—everything had been neatly attended to. It's all too complex to have happened by accident.

"Now, with everything going according to plan, here you are, calm as you please, pulling the strings from a thousand miles away. My son is in the middle of a defeated army. The army has been routed, and almost anything can happen—nearly all of it bad. You know better than most that Samuel won't let himself or Major Clinton be captured. He knows what will happen if they fall into Confederate hands. But if Samuel survives, everything is in place. He's on the doorstep of the Deep South. Yes, Simon is rotting in some Southern prison for no other reason than to distract attention from his twin brother." She hesitated as they continued their stroll. "Now, Jason, tell me it isn't true—or take me up on my wager."

Thompson stopped and placed his hands behind his back. He turned and looked at her, not knowing what to do or say. Nothing important happens by accident, he thought. We make things happen or we prevent them from happening. If we are better than the other fellow, we win. Otherwise, we lose. We plan for the unplanned, for the incalculable. Just when everything seems to have worked out in the end, that's when it's most likely to fall apart, when one's guard is down.

Moisture gathered in his eyes as he remembered the death of Captain Bottoms. Thompson knew that he had made a mistake in judgment, and a man—a friend—had died as a result. That event, more than any other, had shaped his subsequent approach to carrying out his duties.

As Thompson thought about his options, he had to admit one thing to himself: on a personal level, he didn't give a damn what happened to Simon Thornton. He was an enemy soldier, and Thompson's job was to eliminate Confederates from the war—in any way possible. But everything had become incredibly complex and interconnected. Wade had replaced Captain Bottoms in Thompson's personal hierarchy of important people. He would use Wade because winning the war demanded it. But Thompson had vowed to provide Wade with every possible advantage necessary for being successful and remaining alive. And that created a dilemma. If Wade became distracted by his emotional concern for his brother, his performance could be impeded. As a matter of simple practicality, Simon's safety had unexpectedly emerged as an important consideration. There had to be at least the appearance that something was being done.

"I'll be truthful with you, Caroline, I really don't know where Simon is. I've told Samuel as much. I've been unsuccessful in my efforts to find him. I don't even know where to start looking. Since he hasn't surfaced in more than a month, there are several possibilities. One of them—perhaps the most favorable, all things considered—is that he has been imprisoned. I told Samuel that, too. I did nothing directly that would have led to that action, but I admit that I counted on a combination of natural circumstances leading someone to suspect that all was not what it seemed. The conclusions were theirs to make.

"As a Union officer in time of war, I make no apology for what I've done. I'm convinced that I have successfully promoted the war effort. I will address my conscience after the war ends. And as for General Washburn, he probably will honor any request I make—not because I have some malevolent power over him, but because he knows I would never ask for something without a sound reason. There *is* a difference, even if it's not obvious to you."

"And everything I said earlier, Jason. What about that?"

"In the main, you were correct. But it was a plan that evolved more than something contrived to place Simon in danger. Shortly before your son left for Chattanooga, I made a promise to him that I would do everything possible to find his brother. If there's anything I can do to ensure Simon's safety, I'll do it. But consider this: I must be careful to avoid attracting more attention to him. Otherwise, they may simply execute him and be done with it. Likewise, if *you* go down there, people will naturally ask why. A misplaced phrase may put your nephew in more danger than he presently faces and cause the very thing you seek to prevent. If Simon *is* in prison, your son is the most qualified person alive to work out a plan for freeing him. That much I believe. Sam is the best soldier I know." Thompson placed his hands on her shoulders. "Caroline, you must not go into the South."

Conditions on Snodgrass Hill grew increasingly desperate as the afternoon wore on. Wade and his mixed band of Union soldiers followed the sounds of battle to where the fighting raged. They were drawn by the dull roar of cannon and the staccato clamor of musketry that always seemed across the next draw, beyond the next thicket of trees, just beyond reach.

As best he could, Wade had assessed the situation by piecing together information from the stragglers of Clinton's brigade. The evidence suggested that, with the exception of Thomas's depleted XIV Corps, the rout of the Army of the Cumberland had been complete. Someone reported that General Rosecrans and his staff had abandoned the field and were last seen riding at full gallop back toward Chattanooga. Before striking out through the trees, Wade and his men had gathered as much musket ammunition as they could carry. These volunteers from two shattered divisions were soon joined in their effort to reach the beleaguered defenders less than a thousand yards away. Included were men from the 2d and 15th Missouri and the 73d Illinois—all regiments of Laiboldt's 2d Brigade. The remnants of a company of the 42d Illinois, another outfit from Sheridan's division, reluctantly agreed to help attempt the breakthrough. During their odyssey through the forest, a few more stragglers from yet another division attached themselves to the makeshift regiment. Even so, Wade could count fewer than a hundred men under his command.

As the sun moved lower and they seemed to be making no progress in their search for a gap in the Confederate forces, a hail of bullets zipped through the trees from behind. Everyone dived for the ground, then scampered for the nearest cover. In anxious anticipation, almost afraid to draw a breath, they waited as smoke from the volley drifted lazily through the leaves. Nothing else happened. Five minutes passed before Wade decided to act. He crawled to a large tree and slid his back up the trunk. Thirty yards to his front, he saw what appeared to be a secluded wash. Feeling alone and frustrated, he had reached a reluctant decision: they weren't going to get through. If he forced the effort, he'd only ensure their death or capture. And for what? For all he knew, the men in Thomas's corps were surrounded. With night fast approaching, if Wade and his followers hadn't been overrun by then, they would have no choice but to retreat or surrender. Wade nodded to himself in acceptance. He had tried, and he had failed.

"There's a draw about thirty yards to my front," Wade whispered loudly to the nearest small knot of men. "Pass the word. Follow me, and stay low." Slowly, the men rose to a crouch and scampered toward the draw. As the last of them rushed through the bushes and scurried below the rim, Wade signaled for his followers to gather around. As they pulled into a tight knot, each sensed what the colonel planned to say to them.

"Men," Wade said solemnly, "there are just too many of the enemy for us to find a safe way through to General Thomas. It'll be dark soon, and Thomas's men will have to retreat anyway. Anything we could do now wouldn't amount to much. We have to turn back. I have only a rough idea where we are. I'd recommend going northwest. We'll have a better chance if we break up and travel in smaller groups. You'll find a road not far over there. Turn west on it and head for McFarland's Gap. Once you're on the other side of Missionary Ridge, head north. With the bulk of the army scattered to hell and gone, that seems like your best bet for getting to Chattanooga."

"Colonel?" said a young soldier.

"What is it, Corporal?"

"I feel better, sir. At least we tried. Thanks for givin' us back our pride." The others added a quiet chorus of agreement.

Wade smiled. "I know what you mean, men. This has been one of the worst days of the war. But we'll fight again—and next time we'll whip them good."

Wade looked at Clinton, who was crouched to his right. Clinton shrugged.

"Well, men, I pray that God will see you all safely through this war. Now, get out of here."

In groups of ten or so, the men headed cautiously toward the road. Wade's small contingent included Clinton, a young captain named George Post, and six enlisted men from Laiboldt's brigade.

They had moved only a few yards when they heard the movement of a large body of troops. Wade froze. Ahead, moving in ragged formation, was a company of rebels weaving through the trees. If the Confederates continued on their present course, they would cross the path where Wade stood. He motioned with his hand as he began running in a crouch back in the direction from whence he had come.

"Blue-bellies," a rebel yelled. "Sergeant Jackson, take a squad and go after 'em. We'll wait here for you."

Wade heard the clank of their metal utensils as the Confederates rushed through the woods after them. He drew his pistol and ducked behind a tree. "Keep running, men. I'll try to slow them down. I'll catch up." The others rushed on as Wade propped his pistol against a tree and waited. He fired at the first man who came within range. The soldier clutched at his shoulder and dropped to the ground. The others stopped, knelt, and fired a volley in the direction of Wade's tree. Wade fired two more shots before crouching and running through the thick underbrush. His pursuers, unsure of how many men confronted them, hesitated and reloaded their weapons. The delay provided Wade time to fade into the thickets.

Wade found the others fifteen minutes later. "I don't think they're following anymore," he said. "Let's keep moving." He surveyed the situation to his front. In their headlong scramble through the woods, they had closed the distance to where General Thomas had formed his defensive line atop Snodgrass Hill. With our numbers reduced, he thought, it might be possible to reach the hill unseen. It seemed worth a try. "Let's work to the left, around the Confederate flank," he said in a whisper. "We'll try to get up the back of the hill." The others nodded.

They darted through the thick underbrush, dodging branches as they ran. At times they passed so close to the rebel line that they heard the enemy talking. Wade led his men north, quickening the pace as the noise grew louder and the smoke thickened. His blood raced as the call to duty pulled him ever closer to the battle. Finally, they passed beyond the fringe of the Confederate line. Ahead and to the right, Wade heard the booming sound of cannon. He halted to catch his breath. "I'm going to join Thomas's men," he said firmly. "I suspect they need every man."

The others seemed hesitant. They would be moving in harm's way, with no idea of what lay over the crest of that hill. But there was the safety of numbers ahead; they knew nothing of what might have closed in behind. They faced an uncertain proposition whichever direction they moved, so they placed their trust in the colonel. Wade ran forward. Clinton followed closely behind, with the others strung out behind him. The sound of battle grew louder with each step. The heavy smoke clawed at their lungs. Just beyond the crest, they stumbled into a small clearing and saw the backs of Union soldiers who were firing frantically down the slope of the hill. Wade observed through the smoke that they held a solid if hastily devised defensive position, with piled logs and rock that reinforced the natural cover provided by a saddle between two hills.

At four in the afternoon, Wade led his meager force through the gully leading down the battle-scarred slope.

A startled lieutenant turned and pointed his pistol at the noise behind him, then relaxed when he recognized the blue uniforms. "Where'd you men come from?" he yelled.

"Up the back of the hill," Wade replied. "We were cut off on our retreat to Chattanooga."

"Well, I'm glad to see you, Colonel, but this is the last place I'd have come if I had a choice. Did you bring any spare ammunition with you? We're running out fast."

"We may have a thousand rounds among us," Wade replied. "I told the men to fill their pockets before we came this way. I'll have them distribute it among your men."

"Thanks, Colonel."

"Who's in command?" Wade asked.

The lieutenant looked around. "Damned if I know, sir."

"What unit is this, Lieutenant?"

"Company C, 9th Ohio, sir. That's the 35th Ohio to our left, the last regiment in the line."

Wade shook his head. "It's not a very good situation, Lieutenant."

"No, sir, it isn't. We just beat back our second attack. It's the same all along the line. The Rebs would run over us for sure if they knew how few of us there are."

"How few are there, Lieutenant?"

"Hard to say for certain. Parts of five divisions, but the Rebs outnumber us at least two to one. We're almost out of ammunition," he emphasized again. "The immediate concerns are the flanks—and our rear. There may be a couple hundred men to our left, no more. Beyond them is a battery of four guns, with nothing but uncovered ground beyond that. We're hanging in the air, Colonel." He looked over his shoulder. "Are reinforcements following you in, sir?"

"I saw no signs of reinforcement, Lieutenant, but the woods are fairly thick in that direction." Wade saw no sin in offering a dim ray of hope. "You can't see more than ten yards in any direction."

A lull settled in the immediate vicinity as exhausted men paused to catch their breath. As the smoke began to thin, Wade climbed back up the hill in hopes of finding a place for a clearer view of the troop dispositions to the west. Clinton followed close behind. When they reached a small clearing, Wade shaded his eyes with his hand and peered to the west. Nothing more than an impression could be formed, with the trees and brush being so dense. The Union forces were deployed in a shallow semicircle that dipped in the middle down the face of a hill, then bent back to the northwest about a quarter of a mile. By classic military standards, it was a strong defensive position, with uneven ground covered with trees and numerous small gullies punctuated by occasional knobs. Such ground made an attacker cautious, as no one knew what waited ten yards ahead or to either side.

"A formidable line," Wade said as he turned to Clinton, "but if the other regiments are as short of ammunition as this one, we'll have to withdraw before long. Another assault will about do it."

The clatter of muskets rose to the left. "That may be about now," Clinton answered. A volley slammed into the low breastworks to their front. Stray bullets kicked up puffs of dirt near where they lay. Below, men slumped to the ground with hardly a sound as bullets bit into flesh.

How the war has changed since First Bull Run, Wade thought. There, whole regiments had wilted and run when the initial volleys jolted their ranks. It had been the same on both sides—men advancing shoulder to shoulder in neatly formed lines, only to witness for the first time gaping holes blown in their formations by massed fire from cannons and muskets. The shock of seeing a man come apart was something never far from consciousness. Here at Chickamauga, the men fought almost independently, crouching behind logs and rocks, indifferent to the commands and exhortations of officers, as they took deliberate aim at an enemy scrambling up the slopes in twos and threes and larger groups. On they advanced, often toward an unseen foe, until they closed the range and the withering fire became almost more than flesh and bone could endure. Still they struggled onward, leaning into the screaming hot lead as they might against a pelting hailstorm. Finally, formations staggered to a halt, as if restrained by an invisible barrier. Each man reminded himself of the slim chance of survival if he took another step, then reversed course and faded back down the hill, loading and firing as he expanded the distance between himself and eternal rest.

It always seemed the same. Wade dreaded, as would any rational man, the prospect of battle. But once engaged, he clung to it almost passionately, as if its passing would mean the last breath of life. Battle was a marvel of spectacular beauty and unparalleled horror, blended with an incomprehensible willingness of men to die for nothing more substantial than a vague idea of personal honor. Wade had never tried to understand in others, much less in himself, man's willingness to confront death so openly, but he had felt the exhilaration, the powerful emotion that gripped the soul of every man, blue and gray, as they slammed one against the other, as if the salvation of the world depended on their unflinching courage and indomitable determination. It seemed senseless to the inexperienced; no one who had lived through it required an explanation.

The same occurred all along the line, as regiments moved in undulating waves across the wooded slopes. Butternut-clad soldiers would penetrate the line, then stop to cheer themselves for their hard-won but momentary success. Then someone on the other side would rush reinforcements forward, and the tired rebels would fire a defiant volley before yielding to the rolling tide of fresh troops.

Men too tired to stand and run would coolly load their weapons, then aim and fire. The goal had become individual survival, with overall victory or defeat nothing more than a by-product of collective courage or the yielding to overwhelming fear. The process transcended bravery and cowardice. Just being there and hanging onto the piece of craggy ground where one lay was the ultimate in personal courage, with acts of extraordinary commitment in earlier, forgotten battles now so commonplace that no one noticed.

Behind him, at the crest of Snodgrass Hill, Wade saw the flutter of flags that marked General Thomas's headquarters. The general had no choice other than to compel his troops to defend this small island in a sea of trees. He was buying time with lives, time necessary for the bulk of the army to retreat and secure a defensive line near Chattanooga. What must the general be thinking now? He certainly understood that his men had to keep up their fire to discourage an all-out rebel attack, knowing that, at the same time, each shot fired brought the time for forced retreat a second closer. It was the ultimate dilemma of fighting to hold onto the ground for the near term and realize all the while that the very act doomed the effort to failure.

Clinton tapped Wade on the shoulder. "I hate t'interrupt your daydream, Sam, but look down there."

"It's a rebel brigade," said Wade coldly. The Confederates were forming a battle line on the far side of a field that began near the base of Snodgrass Hill and extended some two hundred yards to the west. Two regiments were in double-filed ranks in front, and a third was to the rear in reserve—about a thousand men in all, Wade judged. A second brigade formed to the left of the first. "They're coming this way." Wade smiled nervously as he brushed the grass from his knees. "Time to go to work, Jim."

"Looks like it, Sam," Clinton answered.

As Wade and his followers slid down the hill toward the cover of the trees, the rebel drummers began a steady march cadence. "There's hell to pay now," said a soldier as he cocked his weapon and took a bead.

"Hold your fire," said Wade. "Let them close to a hundred yards."

The soldier turned and stared sternly at Wade, obviously annoyed that an officer had presumed to instruct him in his task. He had survived this long, had he not? "Yes, sir," he replied dryly as he wet the musket sight. "One of them Rebs is already dead, 'cept he don't know it yet."

"It's your company," said Wade, turning to the young lieutenant in command. "You give the order when it's time to fire."

The lieutenant wiped the sweat from his brow and licked his parched lips. "There's so many of them, sir. Do you think we should retreat?"

"And let them roll up our flank, Lieutenant?"

The lieutenant nodded. "I guess we fight, sir." He hesitated, then stood and leaned against a tree. "Steady, men. Make every shot count. Steady. Let them advance another ten yards. Ready, men . . . *fire!*"

A hail of lead poured down the hill, followed by a bank of boiling smoke. "Fire at will!" screamed the young officer. In his mind he had to know that the thin line would break if the rebels kept coming. There were so many of them, more even than his men had bullets. He knew they had to hold fast for as long as possible. The regiment had to buy enough time for others to close ranks and secure the flank. "Fix bayonets!" he screamed. A brief clatter of steel against steel followed the command.

Across the way, the regiments kept step with the rolling beat of the drums, marching earnestly forward with the single-minded objective of reaching the crest of Horseshoe Ridge and the frail position held by the 35th Ohio. When the front ranks reached the bottom of the hill, they were sixty yards from where two battered Union regiments clung to the extreme end of the line. On command, the rebels charged up the hill and swarmed over the Union defenders. Muskets became clubs, as no one had time to reload. Steel clashed against steel as four hundred personal battles raged along the crest of the ridge. A fresh Union regiment charged into the boiling cauldron, but it only added to the growing pile of dead. There were too many for the Union force to contain, so the men gradually gave ground, retreating slowly up the face of the hill.

Not again! Wade thought. I mustn't run again.

Clinton slammed to the ground at Wade's side, followed shortly by Post and three enlisted men. "I know what you're thinkin', Sam," said Clinton, "but there's no honor in bein' captured. We did our duty by comin' back when most in the army ran t'Chattanooga. Capture's certain if we stay here much longer."

Wade looked up the hill to where rebels were filling the gap between his position and the bulk of the retreating Union forces. He sighed as he finished reloading his pistol. "Well, Jim, it's now or never. Let's stay inside the woods and try to work our way east and south." He forced air into his lungs before bolting into the open.

Three rebels immediately opened fire. One of the Union soldiers fell backward into the gully. Wade and the others raced forward, distancing themselves from the struggle.

For nearly an hour they threaded their way through the brambles, moving farther from their ultimate objective with each step. The woods were thick with Confederates. Wade's small group careened like a billiard ball off a cushion, bouncing from one potential danger to the next. Finally, they found shelter next to the La Fayette Road and waited until it cleared of traffic. Then they rushed across and dived into the bushes. Three hundred yards beyond the road they came within sight of Hall's Ford. They had only seen a few live Union soldiers since leaving Snodgrass Hill. They were isolated, on their own again. Wade had been informed earlier that in this vicinity the narrow ford provided the only easy crossing of West Chickamauga Creek. A Confederate cavalry sergeant and six soldiers guarded the crossing. Wade turned to Clinton. "What do you think?" he whispered.

"I say we take 'em! Then we'll have us some transportation." Clinton pointed in the direction of some horses hobbled near the creek.

Wade looked toward the others. He, Clinton, and Post had pistols. Three of the men had muskets. The other men they had picked up along the way had lost their weapons. "Okay, here's what we'll do," Wade whispered. "I'll take two of you men with muskets. We'll move about twenty yards north to those bushes. Jim, you move through the bushes here. Get as close as you can and still see the bushes where I'll be. When I drop my arm, we'll fire and then rush them. We should take them by surprise."

"Sounds like it's worth a try," Clinton said, nodding.

"Give me a few minutes to get into position," Wade instructed.

Several minutes later, six shots rang out. Three of the cavalrymen dropped dead. The burly sergeant clutched at his leg and tried to run but stumbled and rolled into the creek. The others dropped their weapons and raised their hands as their tormentors sloshed through the shallow water toward them. Wade grabbed the rebel sergeant and pulled him from the water. "What's your unit?" he demanded. The sergeant clenched his jaw. "I'm too tired to argue, Sergeant. I'll just kill you and we'll take our chances."

"We're with Forrest," the sergeant said.

"Where they at?"

"Up the creek 'bout two hundred yards."

"How many?"

"Two companies."

"What's their mission?"

"We're securin' the rear."

"Are there any infantry in this area?"

"I don't know. The generals don't consult me none," the sergeant replied sarcastically.

"Find something to tie them up," Wade told Clinton. "Take off their uniforms first. We may need them later."

Ten minutes later they were ready to move. "We'll have to ride double until we find some more mounts." Wade pulled out his watch. "It's five to six. The sun will set soon. Darkness will improve our chances. Let's get out of here before someone comes to investigate the shooting."

They had barely mounted when a troop of cavalry crashed through the underbrush, carbines cracking. One of Wade's men crumpled to the ground. Wade drove his heels into his mount's flank. The horse flinched, then broke into a gallop. The others rode close behind. The sun had already set as they darted through the forest into the gathering gloom. Bullets buzzed like angry hornets as they twisted and turned to avoid the low-hanging limbs. They broke into a plowed clearing, where a dozen rebels were languishing around a fire cooking supper. Wade fired twice. The men scattered. Brandishing his saber, Wade leaned low against the mare's neck and dashed across the field, directly through the middle of the startled foot soldiers. Ten seconds later, he and his remaining followers disappeared into the trees on the far side of the field.

For the next hour they dodged the trees and moved deeper into the never-ending forest. In their rear, they heard the persistent clatter and shouts of angry Confederates who sought to bring them to bay. A sliver of moon provided the only light. The sounds behind them grew more distant, then faded altogether. They continued south by southeast, edging ever deeper into the rugged Georgia countryside, toward the heart of Dixie.

From the diary of Caroline Wade-Healy

*September 20, 1863*
*10:00 P.M.*
*What shall I do? Colonel Thompson's arguments were very convincing. It comes down to a matter of trust. Will he really do everything possible to find Simon? Will he get the information to Samuel if he finds Simon? I just don't know.*

*Word of events at Chickamauga has cast a pall over Washington. There will be no rest in the White House this night. I pray for an end to the suffering, but God seems intent on punishing us for our sins. Do we deserve less? I doubt it.*

*David has returned to his brigade. I didn't have an opportunity to inform him that Colonel Thompson denied my request for a pass.*

*I've lost count of the times I've made this train ride. I see out the window the same houses that I passed by before the war began. How different must be the lives of those inside after more than two years of war!*

*Oh, Samuel! Be safe. Despite the sins of your mother, remember that you are your brother's keeper. Find him. Take him home.*

# PART 3
# LIBBY PRISON

# CHAPTER

# 16

"Christ," said General Washburn as he walked with Colonel Thompson down the narrow hall, "will we never learn?" Washburn had just returned from New York City, and as they rode in the carriage from the train station, Thompson had briefed the general on the disaster at Chickamauga. The general turned through the doorway leading into his office. "Have you heard anything of Colonel Wade?" asked Washburn. He flung his hat in the direction of the coatrack. The hat spun off a peg and settled on the floor.

"Not a word," replied Thompson, shaking his head as he settled wearily into the chair beside Washburn's desk. "Frankly, General, I'm worried."

The general swiveled his chair and sat, then stood anxiously. The war had been wearing seriously on his nerves. He seldom relaxed anymore, and he too frequently sought solace from a whiskey bottle. "I regret that my delayed return from New York caused me to miss the briefing at the White House today. What's it like down there, Jason, really?"

"Only one word applies, sir. Chaos. General Rosecrans is in a fog. His senior officers are fermenting rebellion and want him replaced by General Thomas. But they don't like Thomas much better. It's essential that the government find a means to stabilize the situation. Assistant Secretary Dana reported that even a halfhearted effort by Bragg's Confederates will most likely push our army out of Chattanooga and all the way to Knoxville. If that happens, the result will be the disintegration of our army out west, perhaps literally." He leaned forward and gingerly removed his boot, groaning faintly as his foot slipped free. The growing corn on his right little toe had nearly disabled him a week earlier. The surgeon had removed the growth, but it ached constantly when he wore the boot. "It's amazing, sir, but the rebels appear to have settled in for a siege. Since there's no evidence that they're preparing for an attack, it can only mean that we must have hurt them worse than we thought—or that Bragg has lost his nerve. They're building fortifications on two prominent heights near Chattanooga—Lookout Mountain and a long, hogback protrusion called Missionary Ridge."

"Has Lincoln expressed an opinion on replacing Rosecrans?" asked Washburn as he lit a cigar.

"He's wavering. One minute he's ready to court-martial him; the next minute he says we must be patient. The man's in a lot of distress right now."

"Aren't we all. What do you think about sacking Rosecrans?"

"Sometimes, as you know, sir, the worst thing one can do is replace a commanding general immediately following a defeat. Things need to settle down, be sorted out. Something happened that allowed Longstreet to break through. You can bet there's plenty of blame to be passed around."

"Did you express those views to the president?"

"No, sir, but I told Secretary Stanton what I thought. He agrees—I think. He's often difficult to read, unless he wants you to know what he's thinking."

Washburn bent and retrieved his hat. "So, Jason, what do we do about Colonel Wade?"

"I don't know, sir. He's been listed as missing. The Rebs either killed or captured all of the other field-grade officers in his regiment—including Colonel Rose, the commander. He's a prisoner. That's been confirmed."

"That doesn't sound promising for Colonel Wade."

"Yes and no, sir. The attack came just at dark. Many of the men in the regiment escaped into the woods. One of them reported being with Colonel Wade for about thirty minutes before they were separated. And, General—" He stopped in midsentence.

Washburn tapped his fingers as he waited. "Well, Jason, what were you about to say?"

"There's a curious circumstance in all of this, sir. Major Clinton is also missing."

"Has that been confirmed?" asked Washburn, his eyebrows raised.

"Frankly, sir, it'll be several days before we can confirm much of anything. Twenty-four hours after the battle ended, stragglers were still making their way back into Chattanooga, wandering in by the dozens each hour. It looks as though the casualty count won't be as bad as first estimated, but it's bad enough."

"Do you have any ideas on Wade?"

"None, sir, short of going down there myself and sorting it out."

The general thought for a moment. He turned toward the cabinet behind him and withdrew a bottle of whiskey and two glasses. He poured, then handed Thompson a glass. "No, Jason," he replied, shaking his head. "The situation is too unstable. I think it best you remain in Washington. Communications are better here."

Their attention shifted toward the office window, toward the sound of approaching footsteps. A young lieutenant attired in dress uniform stopped at the office door and saluted.

"Yes, Lieutenant, what may I do for you?" asked Washburn.

"Sorry if I'm disturbing you, General. My father instructed me to report to Colonel Thompson for instructions."

"You have the advantage of me, Lieutenant," Thompson said, his brow furrowed.

"It's the beard, sir. We met once before, for a short time. I'm David Healy Jr., sir."

"Ah, yes. Did your father say why I wanted to speak with you?"

"He didn't give me many details, sir."

Washburn took another glass from the cabinet. "Care for a touch of sour mash, Lieutenant?"

"If the general doesn't mind, I think I will, sir."

"General," said Thompson, "this is the young man who went into Alabama and brought back Colonel Wade's sister. A remarkable accomplishment, all things considered."

"Indeed it was. Where are you assigned now, Lieutenant?"

"Dullest job in the army, General. They've got me working for the treasury secretary, processing bonds."

Thompson leaned over and patted Healy on the shoulder. "You don't like that much, is that what you're telling us, Lieutenant?"

"No, sir, I don't like it. I'm a certified accountant, Colonel. If I wanted to process bonds, I'd do it in my father's bank for ten times the pay. There's a war raging out there, sir, and I'd just as soon do something besides waste away in a dingy office."

Thompson set his empty glass on the desk. "Well, Lieutenant, it just so happens that another problem has arisen. How would you like to take a trip to Chattanooga?"

Healy's eyes sparkled. "You mean that, sir? They just fought a big battle there. Does that mean I'll get to see some action, sir?"

Thompson looked at Washburn questioningly. The general nodded. Nothing needed saying. "Perhaps, Lieutenant," replied Thompson, "but not in the conventional sense. Are you off duty, young man?"

"Yes, sir. I went to the officers' ball this evening, but I wasn't much interested in dancing."

"Drink up, Lieutenant, and relax. Let me outline a problem that you may be able to help us solve."

Four days had passed since the battle's conclusion. Wade's small band of soldiers had dwindled to five: Clinton, Post, and three privates. Three times they had attempted to go west, searching for a safe route back to Chattanooga. Each time, the rebels had cut them off, forcing them to turn south to escape.

Now, the six hungry fugitives lay prostrate, hiding in the underbrush, waiting for darkness. As the sun set, they detected a small cavalry patrol settling into evening camp. They counted eleven rebels altogether: a captain and ten enlisted men. They watched quietly from the seclusion of the trees as the soldiers prepared the evening meal. Off in the shadows, almost hidden in the trees and unable to see the camp, two men leisurely groomed the horses.

"Here's my plan," said Wade. "We need fresh horses and food. We'll do this by the book. We'll wait until they've settled in for the night. Major Clinton and Private Jameson will crawl unseen over to the picket line. Private Sanders, you go with them. There most likely will be guards. Jim, you dispose of the guards. Do it quietly and permanently. Private Jameson, you and Private Sanders select the six best horses and lead them out of sight back to this side of the road. Major Clinton and Private Edwards will join Captain Post and me in arranging a surprise for the sleeping rebels. We'll act when we're sure they're asleep. If possible, I want this done without firing a shot. We've got to create a diversion, but to make it work we have to delay them as long as possible."

After Jameson and Sanders led the horses around to the near side of the road, they crouched and scampered across. Wade then crept to the side of the sleeping rebel captain, placed his pistol to the man's head, and cocked it. The captain's eyes opened with a start. He looked around frantically before seeing Wade, who had a finger pressed against his lips. Wade motioned for the officer to rise and precede him into the woods. When they were clear of the camp, Wade quietly explained what he expected of the captain. Circumstances convinced the rebel of the need to cooperate. Wade ordered the officer to head back, then he followed him. Weapons at the ready, Wade's men were stationed at strategic points around the camp's perimeter. Once inside, Wade whispered, "OK, Captain, wake your men. If you make a mistake, your men will be dead before they can untangle themselves from their blankets."

The captain nodded. "Men, listen to me," he said in a loud voice.

The Confederates stirred, then lifted their heads. "It seems we've been captured. Don't do anything foolish an' go gettin' yourselves killed needlessly."

The rebels grew suddenly alert. They turned their heads from one side to the other, straining their eyes in the dim moonlight.

"Here's the situation, men," said Wade. "You're surrounded. We mean to take your horses and supplies. If you cause us no trouble, we'll tie you up and leave you here. Someone should be along by morning to set you free. We'll also take your uniforms. We don't want you going anywhere too fast. Gather 'round the fire and take them off. Private Jameson, get their pistols and ammunition belts and put them in that sack." He turned to Post. "Captain, collect their carbines." Post nodded. Wade picked up a pair of field glasses and handed them to Clinton. "These may come in handy, Jim."

Within thirty minutes, Wade and the others had secured the rebels and placed them just inside the tree line. "All right, men," Wade told his followers, "we're riding up that road as fast as possible." He pointed north, speaking loudly enough for the rebels to hear. "One way or another, we've got to make it back to Chattanooga by day after tomorrow." The Union soldiers knew differently. They had already decided that moving south offered the only reasonable chance for escape. All evidence indicated that the rebels had besieged Chattanooga.

They mounted and galloped north for a half mile before turning into the woods well short of a dozen or more campfires flickering along the side of the road and among the trees. A quarter moon lit their way as they wove through the forest. Five hundred yards inside the tree line they veered south. They rode all night, dodging patrols and isolated assemblies of soldiers, taking rest finally in a deeply wooded gully a short distance from a small spring. They unsaddled their mounts and rubbed them down. Wade motioned to Clinton. "How far is it to Rome?" asked Wade apprehensively.

"How far y's'pose we are from Chattanooga?" countered Clinton.

"Perhaps twenty-five to thirty miles," replied Wade. "Hard to say with all the roundabout trails we've taken."

"I reckon it's maybe another thirty miles then, Sam, give or take a few."

"How far to your folks' place from there?"

"Depends on the route we take. I figger it'd be better if we bypass Rome. We're in for some rugged country. If we cut t'the southeast a ways up ahead, we'll save 'bout a dozen miles an' all the traffic. If we head out at sunset, we may make it 'fore morning. It'll be a hard ride, though."

"That's it, then." Wade patted Clinton on the back. "Get some sleep, men. Cold camp. Can't afford anyone snooping around. We ride south at dusk."

Jeremy Wagner had departed the Bowman plantation on schedule, leaving the morning after his conversation with Cathy Blair. His mysterious companion had lingered on, remaining in seclusion most of the time. The second man had features that attracted instant attention. Most prominent of these were snow-white hair and a near-matching complexion. He always wore a wide-brimmed hat when he left the house during daylight. At first sight, he appeared to be blind. His irises, magnified threefold by thick glasses that he constantly pushed up the bridge of his nose, were nearly as light as the whites of his eyes. From a distance, he looked seventy; up close, he had the features of a man closer to thirty. Even in the warm fall afternoons he wore a heavy jacket buttoned to the neck when he walked the short distance to the summerhouse. An albino must have a difficult time traveling, Cathy thought when she first observed him. She had caught a glimpse of the man sitting in the library with the curtain closed. He had glanced suspiciously at her as she stood in the doorway, then turned his head quickly and covered his eyes with a hand. She had walked away without speaking. They had never spoken in the nearly three weeks he had been there.

This afternoon Cathy drifted listlessly toward the summerhouse. A light drizzle began before she reached it, and she rushed to the door to get inside. Then she fell asleep in the high-backed wicker chair. Her daughter had been ill most of the night, and she had remained at the child's bedside until midmorning, when the fever finally broke.

Cathy opened her eyes at the sound of the screen door swinging open. She sighed deeply as she turned her groggy head. Through an opening in the weave of the chair she saw her father, a local man named John Ward, the albino, and General Thornton enter the summerhouse. None of them noticed her as they walked to a small, secluded alcove off the main room. She leaned back and closed her eyes.

"Has it been confirmed?" asked Arthur Bowman.

Cathy tried to remain indifferent; she wanted only to sleep. She shifted her position sideways, pulled her knees upward into the wicker seat, pressed her cheek against her palm, and pulled the light blanket to her chest. More asleep than awake, her thoughts drifted in and out of awareness.

"Sorry to say, Mr. Bowman," said Thornton. "It's fairly clear that General Bragg has chosen to lay siege rather than attack. I don't understand his passivity."

"The man's a fool," said Ward loudly. "He'll accomplish nothing with a siege. The Union army will emerge from its worst defeat and drive our forces all the way to Atlanta. For God's sake, why doesn't President Davis order him to attack?"

"President Davis is reluctant to override his field commanders—even when he knows they're wrong," replied Thornton. "Besides, Bragg's his close friend. He won't humiliate the general if there's any way to avoid it."

"This is the end, you know," said Bowman, driving a fist into his other palm and nodding pointedly. "We'll look back on this day and say we witnessed the beginning of our end."

"It's hardly *that* bleak," answered Thornton. "Bragg still has a strong army. From what I understand, he has occupied two nearly impregnable positions."

"There's no such thing," replied Ward. "If the Yankees are willing to sacrifice the men, Bragg doesn't have enough soldiers to defend two positions. My VMI training taught me that. Besides, it's defeatist to go on the defensive after such a lopsided victory."

"I had no idea you went to VMI," said Thornton.

"Three years. When my father became ill, I went home. I stayed to run the plantation when he died. Give us your best assessment, General. If the Yankees recover and attack, will Bragg be able to prevail? If not, what will it mean?"

"You're right, of course," replied Thornton, choosing to address an earlier point. "If the Federals are determined to drive him out, they'll gather a force sufficient to accomplish the task. They won't risk a second defeat. My guess is we'll see Grant here within a month. If they drive Bragg back, militarily it's only a matter of time until they move on Atlanta. Their strategy is clear. I agree that failing to destroy their army, while we have the chance, may be the most serious mistake of the war. As for what it does mean, it means we will lose the war. Lee can't survive with his rear exposed and his source of supplies and manpower cut off. It'll be a matter of time—unless . . ."

"Unless what?" inquired the albino.

"Unless we remove our target from the picture. We'll have no trouble holding on through next summer, I believe, probably into the fall. But from everything I've seen, our people are losing their will to endure. That's our most critical problem. If Union forces break into the Deep South, we'll fall apart within months."

"That settles it," said Ward. "We have to put the plan in motion. We have to so totally disrupt their government that the war will be over before they recover."

"I don't know," replied Bowman. "That might be the worst thing for us to do. It might anger the people up north enough that they'll come after us with a vengeance."

"You think so?" replied Ward. "Then perhaps we should assassinate Jefferson Davis and blame it on the damn Yankees," he said, half seriously, half in jest. "Maybe that would make our generals mad enough to fight." The others offered weak, nervous laughter. "Besides, John, we've been all through that. I don't see how things can get much worse. We've just won one of the most lopsided victories since Manassas, and I feel like someone slugged me in the gut."

"Correct me if I'm wrong, John," said Thornton, "but you're the one who's been hesitating. Are you now saying we should move forward?"

"Damn right, Henry. This is going to take some time if it's done right."

"We're talking about assassinating ten men, John—all at once. They'll never all be at the same place at one time. There's a thousand things that can go wrong."

"That's why we must begin planning now," said the albino softly, "so that when the time comes, everyone will be ready to move on a moment's notice." The man never applied pressure. His instructions had been firm: recruit only the willing and give them no cause to mistrust either you or our purpose.

"This will cost a small fortune," said Bowman. They had discussed the obstacles so many times that everyone had lost count. They had the answers, or at least all they would ever receive. The barriers existed only in their minds. Not money, not even personal risk, held them in check. They all left unspoken the dark, double irony of their dilemma. Here they stood, as calmly as if they were eating chicken at a church picnic, plotting the assassination of nearly a dozen high-ranking federal officials—and they felt guilty even as they plotted. Not one man spoke of it to the others, nor dared acknowledge it even to himself, but a cold, perverted sort of patriotism repelled each from an act that smacked of treason. Even after the savage conditioning of more than two years of war, they remained haunted by the nightmare that they, somehow, were plotting the overthrow of their own government rather than striking out at a hated enemy power. And to compound their anguish, a Northerner was leading them into the abyss—a Northerner who represented more Northerners, including among them the wealthiest, most powerful men on the continent.

"Gentlemen," said the albino, "that's the least of our problems. With a single telegram, with the single word *yes,* I will have a million dollars in gold at my disposal within twenty-four hours. But before that word is spoken, I must be assured that my benefactors will reap their fair share of the rewards for engaging in such a risky venture."

"Just who in hell are these benefactors?" asked Thornton. He had asked that question many times before, always with the same response.

"You know I can't answer that, General. That was one of their conditions."

"And the others?" asked Ward.

"The only other thing they seek is extreme latitude in making their investment once the war is over."

"You really don't care which side wins, do you, sir?" replied Ward.

"*My* desires are unimportant, Mr. Ward. Think of me simply as a messenger. And think of my sponsors as businessmen, nothing more. The opportunities will be the same regardless of which side wins—provided that certain people are unable to interfere when that time comes. One thing is certain: they'll do nothing unless they're sure they can't be linked to the conspiracy. Protecting their identity is *my* problem. *You* have only to decide if the plan is to proceed."

"Why is it, sir," asked Thornton, "that I feel like a prostitute?"

"I bear no responsibility for how anyone feels, General. If forced to address your concerns, I guess I'd say that, as with prostitutes, they ease their guilt with the rewards they receive. In this case, the reward will be a fifty-million-dollar investment and a South that is strong again. A fair portion of that money will line *your* pockets, gentlemen. If you're looking for something more, perhaps a noble purpose to justify your involvement, tell me now and I'll be on my way." Carrot and stick, carrot and stick—a simple formula, applied from an array of perspectives. Subtle but nonetheless effective, if patiently applied.

A long silence followed. With trembling hand, Thornton quaffed a jigger of whiskey. Ward idly shuffled a deck of cards. Bowman questioned his own sanity for getting involved in this scheme.

"What will it be, gentlemen?" asked the albino, growing impatient.

"What other choice is there?" replied Thornton with a shrug as he slammed his glass against the bar. Despite the forceful response, his answer avoided the albino's question.

"On one condition," said Bowman. "I don't want to know *any* of the details. Then there won't be a possibility of my leaking information."

"Agreed," said the albino.

"Same with me," added Ward. "Just do what you must and keep my name out of it."

"Then it's settled," said the albino. "Will you inform the others?"

"I'll take care of that," replied Bowman with an abating sigh, not unlike a man's final release of life. "They'll be pleased that it's finally settled."

"I have only one more question, sir," said Thornton. "What if something happens to Mr. Wagner and you? Since we don't know those who will be supplying the money, we'd be left out in the cold."

"A fair question," replied the albino. "You will be contacted, that I can assure you. Someone will hand you a silver dollar and ask, 'How is the weather in Rome?' You will reply, 'Sunny all day long,' to which he will reply, 'Then it's time to build a railroad.' "

"Gentlemen," said Bowman, "I have a bottle of forty-year-old whiskey in the library. Will you join me in a drink?"

Cathy Blair opened her eyes as the screen door slammed shut. As the sound of footsteps faded, she clenched her fists. Had it been a dream? she asked herself, or had she just heard her father agree to a plot to kill President Lincoln? There had been no mention of the president by name, only that nearly a dozen were marked for death. But common sense removed all doubt. If they were to fatally disrupt the Union government, Lincoln had to be among the targets.

The storm had been raging for nearly two hours. Afraid to move, yet more afraid of waiting until their pursuers sprang the trap, the four men huddled in the darkness just inside the tree line at the edge of a freshly plowed field. Clinton lay on his chest, his head upturned, as he looked through field glasses, his attention directed past the field to the rugged, mist-clouded terrain beyond. So close and yet so far, he thought as he aimed the glasses toward the base of the hill he knew so well. Only a faint outline glistened through the wind-driven rain, but the mass etched in his mind seemed solid enough to touch.

Wade sat nearby, his back pressed against a tree. He rocked gently as he cradled Captain Post's feverish head in his lap. He gently pressed his fingers against the captain's mouth, only half successful at muffling the man's moans.

Post's horse had stumbled, throwing the young officer to the ground. The resulting break in his arm was as bad as any Wade had seen. Even in the darkness Wade could tell that the arm was bent the wrong way, and the jagged, ivory edge of the radius protruded through Post's sleeve. Drenched and hungry, near the point of hopelessness, Wade shivered and closed his eyes, hoping to catch a moment of rest.

Wade had expected an uneventful ride south, moving easily across the lightly guarded backwoods of the war. Instead, it had evolved into a journey into hell. The woods were riddled with patrols. They were searching every ravine and crevice of the rugged Appalachian foothills. Twice within three hours following their nighttime departure from the secluded gully, pursuing cavalry patrols had forced them to ride for their lives. The second encounter ended with Private Edwards toppling from his horse, killed instantly by a bullet in the back of his head. Their rebel uniforms had attracted more attention than they repelled, but no one made the connection. By midmorning, with their mounts near exhaustion and bleeding from the wild flight through the underbrush, they again had sought sanctuary in a shallow wash near a stream.

During the next three hours, patrols beating their way noisily through the underbrush forced them to strike camp and melt into the woods. In midafternoon, exhausted and hungry, with two of the horses going lame, they had stopped again to wait for darkness, the only effective cover. As dusk settled, they were wearily saddling their mounts when a Confederate cavalry patrol passed less than fifty yards to the west. They pressed close to the gully wall and held their horses silent. Seventy-five yards beyond, the rebels had dismounted. To the rebels' right, a spring dribbled down the rocky face of a small cliff. Four of the Confederates fed and watered their animals as the others prepared a fire.

Twenty minutes passed, then ten more. As the tension mounted, Wade and Post had crept to within hearing distance. They were desperate for information, anything that might assist in their escape. What they heard only added to their apprehension. As the soldiers had led the horses back toward the camp, a lieutenant and a sergeant strolled in Wade's direction.

"Lieutenant," said the rebel sergeant, "this is a wild-goose chase, and you know it."

The officer stuffed and lit his pipe. "I just follow orders, Sergeant. We'll keep lookin' 'til ordered otherwise."

As they discussed their concerns, a lone rider entered the clearing, the major's insignia on his collar barely distinguishable in the fading light. "Have you seen anything?" asked the major.

"Nothin' out'ta the ordinary, sir," said the lieutenant, saluting. "What's this all about, Major?"

"Infiltrators, Lieutenant. Murdering Yankee spies."

"Can you give us somethin' more to go on, sir? The woods are full of our men. We're chasin' each other most of the time. Now that it's nearly dark, I'm afraid we'll shoot some of our own troopers."

The major rode closer and dismounted. "I'll tell you what I know. Last night, five or six Yankees ambushed one of our cavalry patrols while they slept. They cut the throats of two of our men and tied up the others after taking their weapons and clothes."

"But, Major, what if they made it back north?" asked a corporal.

"Colonel Poindexter's convinced that they were sent out in the confusion after the battle, probably to gather information about our defenses between here and Atlanta. Your orders are to stop every small group you see, even if they're wearing gray. If they act suspicious or try avoiding you, shoot first and ask questions later." He turned and walked the horse forward a few feet, then stopped and looked over his shoulder. "Lieutenant, this is priority. There'll likely be promotions all around for those who run them down." He swung into the saddle. "Report back to regiment at sunup. Good luck, men." The staff officer spurred his mount and disappeared into the trees.

As Wade and Post crawled back to their companions, the rebels stamped out the fire before mounting up and riding west.

"Well, Jim, it looks like they're on to us," Wade said as he finished telling Clinton about the encounter. "How far to that farm of yours?"

"Ten miles, Sam, maybe a dozen. These woods all look the same t'me." Lightning flashed through the trees to the south, too distant to hear the thunder. "All we need now is a storm." He had intended it as a negative comment.

"Perhaps a storm would be a blessing in disguise, Jim," said Wade. "It might provide us the cover we need to escape. It appears they're beating the bushes looking for us." More lightning flashed. "Do you think Captain Post's horse will hold up?"

"Looks doubtful, Sam, but he may have a few miles left in him."

"Let's mount up, then. We're moving south," Wade announced.

That had been nine hours earlier. Now only four of the men remained. Private Sanders, an eighteen-year-old farmer's son, had crashed into a low-hanging limb and snapped his neck. Wade regretted that none of them had asked him his first name. They knew only that he had grown up someplace in Iowa. They had put Post on the man's horse after they covered Sanders's body with some dead brush. Now, with dawn fast approaching, two rebel cavalry patrols were pressing in around them. An hour earlier, Wade and his companions had careened off one patrol and bounced into another. Ever since, they had been thrashing about, searching for an escape route. Even with the wind and rain, they could hear the noise as the rebels narrowed the distance between them. Wade estimated from the sound that the rebels would reach the field in five minutes or less.

Wade lowered Post's head to the ground. He shoved with his legs and slid wearily up the tree trunk to a standing position. "What are our chances of reaching it, Jim?"

"I can make out the general location from here, Colonel, but it's a good hunnert an' fifty yards 'cross that field. The horses'll bog down in that mud for sure. Then it's another thirty yards t'the base of the hill." He pushed himself to his knees and rose to his feet. "We'll have t'carry the captain."

"Yeah," replied Wade, "and he'll scream with every step."

"We can't leave him here, Sam. You heard what they said they'd do if'n they caught us."

"No sense talking about it any longer. You lead the way, Jim. Private Jameson and I will carry Post. Slap the horses and send them running through the trees. The distraction may buy us a minute or two."

"Cap'n," said a rebel voice from the dark, "there's some broken branches. They must've went through here. The prints haven't even been washed away. Can't've been long."

"Over this way, men," shouted another rebel in response. "I think we finally have the bastards cornered."

"Let's go, Jim," whispered Wade. He untied the mounts and gave them a sharp slap on their flanks. The horses galloped through the trees.

The men sank to their ankles with each step as they struggled across the recently plowed field. Post's weight nearly pulled them to their knees as they tried to hold him up. Their leg muscles were trembling by the time they reached the middle of the field. A lightning flash danced overhead.

A shot rang out. "There they is," yelled a rebel. "They's crossin' the field." Three more shots followed.

Clinton struggled back toward the others.

Private Jameson fell to his knees, gasping for air. "We ain't gonna make it this way, sir," he said. "You and the major take the captain and give me your pistols. I'll slow 'em down."

Wade turned and looked at Clinton. Clinton had to go; only he knew the way. And Wade, who was larger than the young soldier, had the strength to move faster carrying a heavy load. Clinton nodded as he withdrew his pistol. Lightning flashed again. He pointed. "See that small stand of pines?" he yelled above the wind. "About twenty yards west of 'em is the base of a hill. If—when—y'reach there, jus' turn south an' hug the rocks. Stay low. I'll pull y'ta safety."

Wade handed Jameson his pistol. He lifted under Post's arms as Clinton slid his arms under the captain's knees. As the two men staggered into the darkness,

Jameson lay prostrate in a furrow, facing the approaching enemy. He waited nervously as the crouching rebels drew closer. When the lightning flashed, he fired six shots in rapid succession. The Confederates dived into the mud. Taking advantage of their confusion, Jameson edged backward, shortening the distance to the far edge of the field. A few yards might make all the difference.

Terror threatened to explode in Jameson's chest. The fear in his mind told him to run and keep running until he reached the next county. Common sense warned that he would take no more than a half-dozen steps before a hail of bullets found him.

The dimly silhouetted forms rose cautiously from the mud. Jameson fired two more shots before edging backward again. He looked over his shoulder. Wade and Clinton were nearing the edge of the field. He turned and fired twice more before scrambling on hands and knees toward the trees.

A volley from twenty muskets spewed sparks and lead into the air. The bullets kicked up small splashes of muddy water all around. One ripped part of the heel from Jameson's boot; a second slammed into his cartridge bag. He lost his balance and tumbled face first into the mud. It's like falling on a pillow, he thought as he spit the dirt from his mouth. He looked up. Wade and Clinton had finally disappeared behind the trees. Time to get the hell out of here, thought Jameson. He sprang to his feet and drove his legs forward, his enemy no more than forty yards behind. Jameson stumbled onto firmer ground and dashed toward the small stand of trees. Now reasonably secure within the shelter of the tree line, he stopped for a moment and sucked in huge gulps of air.

I'm dead, Jameson thought as the first of the rebels cleared the field. He knelt, took careful aim, and squeezed the trigger. The blurry form crumpled to the ground with a loud groan. I've got just one bullet left, Jameson thought. With only a vague idea of the proper path—the major had said to go south, along the base of the hill—Jameson crouched and stumbled through the bushes. As he edged forward in the darkness, along the base of the cliff, he felt a hand grasp his ankle. He pitched forward on his face. The impact knocked the air from his lungs.

"Crawl t'my voice," said Clinton in a loud whisper. "Stay low. Don't let 'em see ya."

Jameson saw nothing. Gasping for air, he rolled in the direction of the voice. Two hands pulled on his jacket, and he slithered headfirst through the narrow hole into total darkness. Inside, he heard the sound of trickling water.

A torrential downpour washed over the field and adjoining hills. Within minutes, the rain would wash away all traces of human passage. Somewhere in the darkness, Captain Post moaned. The sound floated eerily through the large enclosure. But the noise no longer mattered; no enemy would hear him through ten feet of rock and soil.

Clinton slid a large, round rock over the opening. "Anyone have a dry match?" he asked casually. "There're some candles in here someplace."

Wade pulled a folded piece of waxed paper from his pocket. He opened it and withdrew a match, which he struck against the rough side of his boot. He extended the flickering match at arm's length, until the twinkling luminescence reflected against the water droplets clinging to Jameson's skin. With his weight supported on his elbows, the young man leaned backward. Wade held the withering matchstick closer. Jameson's eyes sparkled, and he smiled at Wade, then flicked his head slightly, as if to say, "It's been a rough day."

The train ride from Knoxville had been numbingly tiresome. At least the last forty miles on horseback had kept him alert. Lieutenant David Healy Jr. still sat uneasily on a horse. He had ridden the back way into Chattanooga, winding along the last leg of the Cracker Line—as the men had christened the route used to supply the soldiers, now in a state of semientrapment, along the banks of the Tennessee River. Nothing except their refusal to leave really held them in place, unless one counted a direct presidential order. As a result of that order, Rosecrans had consigned them to a siege in name only.

With its warm, sunny days and cool nights, Indian summer had settled across the valley. The trees blazed with color. Birds chirped in the trees, and squirrels scurried across the trail Healy rode on, carrying acorns for winter storage. Occasionally, large deer, often seen watching alertly from the shadows, ventured from the sheltering forest to take advantage of the last few weeks of abundant meadow forage.

The surrounding countryside contrasted starkly with that in Chattanooga.

This army has been soundly whipped, Healy thought as he dismounted into a sea of sour-smelling mud. He slapped some dried dirt from his blue officer's jacket. The brightness of his attire evidenced his recent arrival in this city of despondency. The army had become a mass of faded and worn uniforms that hung misshapen on withering, undernourished frames. The quartermaster had reduced rations to a quarter of normal, yet hardly enough food arrived each day to satisfy even that meager demand.

Fortunately, the army escaped the Chickamauga battlefield with most of its weapons. As the Union soldiers ran for their lives, they had abandoned the wagons that contained much of their ammunition. Resupply to a safe level had been a priority during the two weeks after the siege began. Only the modest quartermaster reserve had been available to keep Bragg and his army at bay during this stressful period. Fortunately for Rosecrans, Bragg neglected even a probing follow-up to his September 20 victory. Natural defensive positions had been fortified first; then, as the shock of the defeat wore off, the men went to work with spade and pick. Trenches gradually appeared in a jagged, irregular path, snaking along the riverbank to the north, then stretching to the tip of Moccasin Point Crossing to the south. Within three weeks, the faint glow of pride and resolve began reappearing on mud-caked Yankee faces. The men might be incapable of driving Bragg from their front, but, more important, any chance for a successful Confederate assault had passed.

An hour later, Healy found the headquarters of the 77th Pennsylvania, now under the command of its senior captain.

"No officer above the rank of captain escaped that night assault," Capt. Orville Bussey told Healy. "They hit us just at dark on the nineteenth. There followed about as wild a twenty minutes as I ever experienced. They came at us with most of a brigade, boiling out of the darkness, unseen until they were nearly upon us. We lost nearly eighty men in all. The remainder sprinted into the woods and through the bushes. Most managed to rejoin the brigade later that night."

"Did you see Colonel Wade following the battle?" asked Healy.

"No. I saw him trying to lead a rescue party to where Colonel Rose and the others were being overrun. A company of rebels rolled through the front line and cut off Wade and his men. I didn't see him after that. My guess is they captured him."

"No, he got away," said Healy. "A straggler from Wade's group later reported being with the colonel for a short time."

"That'd be Private Patterson. He sometimes gets confused. I'd be skeptical of anything he says."

"I see. Well, thank you, Captain."

Another hour passed before Healy found Colonel Dodge's headquarters, where he was directed to the newly appointed adjutant, Major Kemper.

"Major Kemper, I'm Lieutenant Healy. I'm looking for some information."

"I'll help if I can, Lieutenant," Kemper replied.

"I've been sent from Washington to look for Lt. Col. Samuel Wade."

Kemper nodded. "Yes, I saw him around. He replaced Lieutenant Colonel Wherry as exec of the 77th Pennsylvania. I was a company commander in another of Colonel Dodge's regiments when Wade arrived. I never got to know him. Things were pretty confused that first day of the battle. I heard he was captured."

"That's a possibility, Major. Have you heard of a major named James Clinton? He would have arrived about the time the battle began."

"Yeah. He arrived with Colonel Wade but was sent to Sheridan's division."

"Do you know where he is?"

"My guess is dead or captured. I heard he was assigned to Colonel Laiboldt's brigade. Reports had it that Clinton established a temporary brigade headquarters after Longstreet broke through. Colonel Laiboldt never showed up and later was relieved of his command. A captain later told me that Major Clinton headed out with about a hundred men to go searching for General

Thomas. Say, come to think of it, the captain said Clinton had a lieutenant colonel with him when he left, someone the captain didn't recognize."

Healy grinned. "That most likely was Colonel Wade. You say Clinton went looking for General Thomas?"

"That's right, but I'm sure he didn't get to him."

Healy flinched involuntarily. "How do you know that?"

"By that time, about ten thousand of Longstreet's men had moved between them and Thomas's corps. After we pulled ourselves together, we headed back to Chattanooga. There's a sergeant who went with Clinton's group. He staggered in the next morning. He said they tried for hours to find an opening to Thomas but never made it. Along toward evening, they were ordered to break into small groups and try to make it back on their own. He barely escaped with one of the last groups to leave. He remembered seeing Captain Post with Major Clinton when he lit out. Captain Post was a company commander in this brigade."

"Was?"

"That's right. He never reported in, nor did any of those in his group."

"Is there anything else, Major? Anything at all?"

"Not that I remember, Lieutenant. Feel free to talk to that sergeant if you like."

Healy saluted. "Thank you, Major. You've been a big help. Where will I find the sergeant, and what's his name?"

"Harrison, I believe. You might find him down by the river. Big man, about six foot two and two hundred pounds. He has a long beard and two fingers missing from his left hand."

Sergeant Harrison confirmed the major's account, adding three additional bits of information: he described Wade, confirming his presence; he stated that Wade's group was to have been the last to attempt to break out and head back to Chattanooga; and he had talked to a corporal who saw Clinton on the left flank of Snodgrass Hill, then saw him with a small group heading south when the rebels overran it. None from Wade's group ever returned. Even so, it meant that Wade and Clinton had been alive near sundown, almost a day after the capture of Colonel Rose and the other officers. But how had Wade found Clinton in the midst of such chaos? It made no difference, however, for something had happened during the late evening of September 20 that prevented Wade from reaching the relative safety of Chattanooga.

Healy went to the telegraph office and addressed a telegram to General Washburn in Washington. He wrote a simple message:

WADE AND CLINTON WERE LAST SEEN ALIVE AND WELL ON THE EVENING OF SEPT 20 STOP THEY MAY HAVE BEEN ON SNODGRASS HILL AND ESCAPED TO THE SOUTH STOP

NEITHER MADE IT BACK TO CHATTANOOGA STOP WILL
CONTINUE SEARCH STOP

The next morning, General Washburn opened the seal on the telegraph flimsy
sent by Lieutenant Healy. He smiled as he opened the bottom drawer of his
desk and removed Clinton's personnel file. He flipped through it as he made
the short jaunt to Thompson's office. Thompson nodded approvingly as he
read the message. He handed Washburn another message that a clerk had placed
on his desk. The message read:

SOMETHING IS GOING ON STOP REBS IN A TIZZY STOP IT IS
RUMORED THAT HALF A REBEL CAVALRY BRIGADE IS OUT
LOOKING FOR SMALL PARTY OF MEN ASSUMED TO BE
FEDERAL SPIES LAST SEEN HEADING IN DIRECTION OF
ROME GEORGIA STOP WAR GETTING INTERESTING STOP
WILL KEEP YOU INFORMED STOP

Washburn laid Clinton's file on Thompson's desk and pointed to Clinton's
listed home address. "With Clinton being from Rome, do you suppose . . . ?"
asked Washburn.

Thompson rose and went to examine the large map on the side wall of
his office. He tapped his finger on the name of the small northwest Georgia
town and smiled broadly as he turned to face Washburn. "Not a doubt in my
mind, General. Not a doubt in my mind."

# CHAPTER
# 17

Pushing a cloth grain sack in front of him, Clinton crawled through the narrow hole leading into the cavern. Once inside, he rose and brushed the dust from his uniform before walking slowly toward a dark corner. He lowered himself to the upward sloping floor, leaned back, and closed his eyes. He had nearly fallen asleep when he heard feet shuffling at his side. He opened his eyes, turned his head, and saw Wade looking down at him. Clinton sighed and turned away.

"Something wrong?" Wade asked.

"They weren't there." Five days had passed since they had crawled, mud covered and soaking wet, into the cavern. For the past two days there had been no sign of Confederate soldiers in the area. Clinton, who had not seen his family in three years, decided to chance a brief excursion into the open. "The cabin's gone, burned t'the ground." He rolled to his other side as Wade lowered himself to the powdery earthen floor. "Out back I found a grave with my pa's name on a wooden marker."

"I'm sorry, Jim. Any idea what happened?"

"No," he said weakly. "It looked as if it burned down some time ago. Ma could be almost anyplace. She has a sister down in southern Alabama. I'm worried 'bout my brother. He's 'bout of age for the army."

"Do you want to scout around and try to find out what happened?" asked Wade.

"No. I don't think that'd be too smart. This may be political. Any snoopin' would prob'ly stir up trouble."

"Why do you think it might be political?"

"Pa was always opposed t'slavery. He never kept his feelings to himself. Then, with me away, servin' in the Union army, well, almost anythin' could've happened. It's just goin' t'have t'wait 'til the war's over." He rolled away from Wade and sniffed. "I knew pa's health wasn't the best, but it's still kind of a shock t'see your pa's grave when y'didn't even know he'd passed on."

Wade stretched out. He placed his hand on Clinton's shoulder.

The faint light reflected from the teary path down Clinton's face leading into his whiskers. Clinton brought his forearm up and covered his eyes. "How's Captain Post?" he asked.

"He'll die if we don't get him some medical help soon. He still has a fever. Doesn't know his own name half the time. Won't eat. Do you have any suggestions?"

"Yeah. I s'pose it's time I went inta Rome an' scouted 'round some. I'll make my way along the river. If I can steal a horse, the trip'll take only a day or so. I don't see any other choice. Can't let Post die without tryin' somethin'."

"Do you have any idea where to get a horse?" asked Wade.

"The Bowman plantation's 'bout two miles from here. They prob'ly have enough that one wouldn't be missed for a while. I'll leave an hour 'fore dawn."

Private Jameson spoke up. "I've been thinkin' some, Colonel. I'm just a farm boy from Illinois. I'm not cut out for a life behind enemy lines. If it's all the same t'you, sir, I'll go with Major Clinton and find myself a horse. It'll be settled down some by now. I think I can make it back to Chattanooga."

"There are a lot of Rebs between here and there, soldier," Wade replied.

"I know, sir, but they'll be too busy to pay attention to me."

"Without papers you'll have to avoid the provost guards. They'll shoot you if they catch you."

"I'll stay in the woods, sir. That won't be no trouble in this country."

He's probably right, thought Wade. At least it's a chance. "All right. I wish you luck."

"Thank you, sir."

Wade pulled on his watch chain. "It's a quarter to ten now. You both better get some sleep." He patted Clinton's arm. "I'm sorry about your pa, Jim. I know how I'd feel if something happened to my mother. My guess is your mother and brother are fine."

"Prob'ly," Clinton said quietly. "There's some food in the sack. Not much. I went to a nearby farm an' took a few things from their root cellar. They're livin' pretty thin down here."

"Go on and get some sleep, Jim. I'll wake you when it's time to leave."

Wade turned sharply but saw nothing unusual. For the past half hour he had sensed someone watching him. He turned into an alley and leaned against the side of a building. Five days had passed since Clinton and he had crawled into the crisp morning air and carried Captain Post the two hundred yards to the wagon Clinton had confiscated in Rome. Near noon on that day, they had pulled to a stop in front of the newly constructed Bell Hospital and carried Post into the cramped lobby. There had been five hospitals to choose from, all established by the Confederate medical corps to receive the sick and wounded from the western wing of the army. The Confederate army had selected Rome as one of its medical centers because of the city's isolation from the mainstream of the war, and because its railroad and river system linked it with much of the South. The shifting conditions had neutralized the first advantage, but the five hospitals remained and were busier than ever.

Four hours after their arrival, a surgeon had amputated Post's arm just below the elbow. He clung precariously to life. The infection had drained him to the point that he barely possessed the strength to breathe. Wade realized that officials would eventually discover that Post had no records. That would place them all in danger. Looking for a way to provide a degree of deception, Wade had placed his arm in a sling; Clinton had bandaged his hand with the missing finger.

Wade stepped from the shadows outside the hospital. Across the street he noticed a young woman, her head turned slightly to one side. She might have been looking at him from the corner of her eye, or she might simply be window shopping. The stiff hood of her bonnet shaded her face, making it impossible to tell. As soon as Wade moved toward her, she turned and scurried away. When he held back, she stopped and pretended to peer into a store window nearly bare of merchandise. Probably just a coincidence, Wade thought. He turned and paced briskly down an alley leading toward the river, then pulled the collar of his worn coat around his neck and entered a dingy bar next to a foundry. Dusty whiskey jugs lined two sagging shelves divided by a mirror. At the end of one shelf hung a small chalkboard with the faded word *MENU* painted at the top. The words *Sweet Potato Soup* were scrawled at an angle across the center of the board. "Is that all you have?" Wade asked.

"Take it or leave it," said the rough-complected man behind the bar. "Ain't too bad if'n ya hol' your nose an' chase it with a shot of whiskey."

The soup cost a dollar, the whiskey a dime; Wade ordered both. The bartender dipped a large ladle into a simmering pot and poured the contents into a chipped earthenware bowl. He set the soup and a glass of whiskey on the bar before returning to his chores. Wade gagged and closed his eyes at the sight of the grayish orange lump floating in the thick yellow liquid. A few shriveled kernels of corn floated to the surface. He sipped at the whiskey and pushed the bowl aside.

"Food's getting scarce," said a woman from behind him. "That's better than most of our soldiers receive—but of course you know that."

Wade froze for a moment, then lowered the glass to the bar. He looked up and stared at the woman's image in the mirror. "You've been following me," he said emphatically.

"I tried being discreet, but I guess I'm not very good at it." She untied and removed her bonnet. "Perhaps you remember me, Colonel. I'm Cathy Blair."

Wade vacillated between acknowledging their past association or taking a chance and attempting to convince her that she had mistaken him for someone she knew. He gulped the remainder of the whiskey and turned. "You'll have to excuse me, Mrs. Blair, but I never expected to see you in Georgia."

"Nor I you, Colonel." She examined the sling. "I see your arm's still giving you trouble."

He instinctively reached for his shoulder. "It's still weak. It bothers me from time to time. I fell on it and hurt it during the battle. That's why it's back in a sling."

"You fought at Chickamauga?"

"Yes," he replied. He wondered if he had made the wrong choice by expanding the conversation. "What are *you* doing here, if you don't mind my asking?"

"My family owns a plantation about a dozen miles east of here. I saw no reason to stay in Virginia after my husband's death, so I came home."

"Well, you sure traveled a long way to find the war again."

"It seems so, doesn't it—both of us. If you've finished your meal, shall we go for a walk by the river, Colonel?"

"If you like." He placed two Confederate dollar bills on the bar and extended his arm. She placed her gloved hand on his elbow as they departed the shabby establishment. They walked in silence for fifty feet before Wade stopped. His physical and emotional attraction to her remained, only stronger than he had remembered. But this was hardly the time or the place to pursue a relationship. Her attire was clear enough evidence of that. "I see you're still wearing black."

"Only now and then," she said with a smile. "This is the best dress I own, so I wore it to town today. I've adjusted to Noah's death. The South is full of mourners these days. We'd get nothing done if we dwelled on death too long. I didn't know you were in General Longstreet's corps."

"Why do you say that?" he asked, surprised by the sudden shift in the subject.

"Well, I just assumed. The general brought his men down here to assist General Bragg, and here you are."

Better to keep my entanglements as few as possible, Wade thought. "No, I came here on other business and just happened to get swept up in the backwash of the battle. I have a friend who broke his arm, and the surgeons amputated it a few days back. I doubt he'll survive. I thought I would stay around until he's gone or it's clear he'll improve."

"Captain Clinton?" she asked.

His thoughts flashed back to the barn in Virginia. Had Clinton been dressed in a captain's uniform? "It's Major Clinton now. No, not him. It's another man."

"And is *Major* Clinton here with you?"

He resumed walking toward the river. "You ask a lot of questions, Mrs. Blair."

"And you are a mysterious man, Colonel." She stopped and leaned against a tree at the edge of the street. "I feel you have not been entirely truthful with me."

Wade sensed the need for caution. She obviously knew more about him than he knew about her—which amounted to nearly nothing. He feigned surprise. "Why do you say that?"

"When did you see your father last?"

That question surprised him more than the first. More important, he immediately recognized its double meaning. The question had the sound of a test, as if she knew the answer—or thought she did—and had asked the question as a means of probing for his identity. He concluded it would be best to stay as close to the truth as possible. "Shortly before Gettysburg," he answered calmly.

She relaxed. "Then why haven't you written to him since then, Colonel Thornton?"

Wade stiffened. "You have me at a disadvantage, Mrs. Blair. I don't recall mentioning the name Thornton."

"But that *is* your name, isn't it, Colonel?"

"Where did you get that idea?"

"Where else? From your father—General Thornton."

"You know General Thornton—my father?"

"We've had several conversations. He often stays at our home when he's in the area, which is quite frequently these days. You should know, sir, that he's sick with worry about you. I don't understand why men don't take the time to write their families. My brothers hardly ever write, and when they do it's usually only a few sentences."

"I've been busy," he explained uneasily. He extended an arm and leaned against the tree. "How did you learn that the general is my father?"

"He showed me your picture. I didn't recognize you at first"—she glanced upward into his eyes, then turned away—"but I sensed something odd when I first met your father. I thought I knew him, but of course I didn't. You have the same features, except for your eyes. Yours are rounder, softer, more like a deer's eyes." She blushed faintly. "You looked a lot younger in the picture, but I saw something that made me examine it more closely. Even without the whiskers, I recognized it as you."

"I suppose you told the general?" He meant for his comment to be a statement, but it came out as a question.

"Regrettably, I neglected to do that. For all I knew, his worst fears had been realized. I felt it best if he discovered the truth—whatever it might be—for himself."

"His worst fears?"

"He thinks you may be dead. He's heard nothing about you since Gettysburg."

Wade commented without thinking. "Nothing? Not even from the government?" Why would the government keep my brother's release a secret? It made no sense, unless . . . "You said fears—more than one?"

"The best he hopes for is that you are in a Union prison. You must contact him as soon as possible and let him know you are alive and free."

"Where is he now?"

"He's back in Alabama. It's been more than a week since I saw him last."

"Did he say how my mother and sister are faring?"

"I didn't know you had a sister."

Now he could relax. The general apparently had not told her about the prisoner exchange before the battle at Gettysburg. Otherwise, she would have known about Nancy Caroline. "My twin sister. I haven't seen her for a long time."

"Your father called you Simon. You called yourself Samuel when you were hiding in my barn. Why have you been so secretive?"

Hide where she can't get at you, he thought. "It's military business. None of my family knows about it. That's why I haven't written. I mustn't talk about it."

"Surely you could write a short letter, just to say you're alive and well. What would that hurt?"

"Orders," he said sternly. "The army wants my whereabouts kept a secret. The Yankees *did* capture me at Gettysburg, but I escaped with some vital news. When you first saw me—with that Yankee patrol hot on my trail—they were trying to recapture Clinton and me. They'd have done it, too, if the rain hadn't washed out our tracks."

"You ignored my earlier question about Major Clinton. Is he with you?"

Wade sighed. He had to shut her up before she removed all opportunity for retreat. "You ask too many questions, Mrs. Blair. I'll answer this last one and no more. Yes, Major Clinton is with me. He's at the hospital with the wounded man." He turned from her and let his shoulders sag. The time had come to insert some drama into the discussion—all the better that it be true. "I had a dozen men with me when the mission started, but now we're down to three, and one of them lost his arm and is out of the war for good." Let her chew on that for a while, he thought. "Now, no more questions." He placed his fingertips on her cheek. "Fair enough?"

She looked into his eyes and smiled. "Are you going to tell your father that you're alive?"

"When I can, but later—and don't you, either. Is that clear? Now, do we have a bargain?"

"We do," she said, nodding sharply, adding a feigned frown, pretending to accept the sense of mystery he seemed intent on creating. "And I'll respect your wishes." She reached for his arm. "Come, let me show you my favorite spot in all the world. It's ever so much prettier in the summer, but you'll just have to imagine that." She let her hand drop and grasped his firmly as she pulled him toward the river.

They spent the next hour getting reacquainted. As they talked, her soft voice fully rekindled the feeling that had washed over him that last night before the Confederates took him away from her farm. How long had that been? Nearly three months, he thought. It seemed much longer—and shorter.

Until now, they had avoided any discussion of the war, of how the South had fared since Gettysburg. Perhaps the truth had become too obvious to them both. They had only to look around. From all appearances, Rome was a town under siege, yet the nearest Union troops were fifty miles north. The stores had few goods for sale. Food had been scarce for months, and winter was only weeks away. The early frost, on the first day of the battle at Chickamauga, had reduced the fall harvest by nearly 50 percent.

Since then, General Wheeler's men had been systematically confiscating horses and mules. Too few sound animals remained to prepare the fields for fall planting.

If conditions had become this bad without a Union musket being fired within range of the town, how much worse would they become when the Union army broke free of Chattanooga and began moving toward Atlanta? The Romans were expressing their convictions with their feet. The growing exodus confirmed that few were willing to wait for the inevitable onslaught. Wade realized that truly desperate times would eventually arrive. If the Rebs lacked the fortitude to drive the Yankees from the region after the one-sided debacle at Chickamauga, victory would forever elude their grasp. He had learned at least that much during his wanderings about the city. The sagging morale of the soldiers and civilians alike foretold a more malignant disorder, one more debilitating than the material shortages and the steady stream of sick and wounded soldiers. Intangible though that might be, Wade had no difficulty seeing in their eyes—even in Cathy's eyes—that they simply wished the suffering and its cause would end.

"I must return to the hospital," Wade said as he skipped a flat stone along the water's surface. "This is a beautiful spot, Cathy. Perhaps I can come here with you again in summertime, when there is no war."

Her eyes sparkled. "Would you? I'd like that." He turned toward her, but she looked away, hoping to disguise her enthusiasm by avoiding his eyes. She clasped her hands behind her back and swayed gently. "Since you're between assignments right now, perhaps you'd care to spend some time at the plantation?" She turned slowly, trying to gauge his reaction. "Major Clinton is welcome, too. If the other man survives, the guest house will offer a better place for recovery."

Wade ached to say yes. Only the illusion he had built around himself kept him from doing so immediately. For all anyone in the North knew, he had been worm food for nearly three weeks. "I don't know. I'll see what can be worked out." Now that the war had cooled off, he had to think about getting back to the Union army. But there was no need to rush. He suspected they'd have no use for him now, least of all in Chattanooga. If a story he'd read in the most recent edition of the *Rome Courier* had any truth to it, he'd be just another mouth to feed from the dwindling resources. "I may have a task to perform that will take me away for a time. How do I find this plantation of yours?"

"That's easy," she replied airily. "Just take Kingston Road east, out of town. It's two hours by buggy, quicker on horseback. You'll see the house off to the south side of the road."

"I'll see what I can arrange," he repeated, placing his hands on her shoulders. "I have to admit, Cathy, that you have been on my mind."

She looked up and smiled. "Really?"

"Yes. I was thinking about going back to your Virginia farm after the war."

Her smile changed to a frown. "It's clear to me, Colonel Thornton, that you're a man who restrains his passions."

"Right now, Mrs. Blair, the—," he almost said Union government, "the government in Richmond has first claim to my time." He took her hand and strolled in the direction of the hospital.

"And how do you feel about the way the war is progressing, Colonel Thornton?"

Wade shook his head. "I don't concern myself with that. I do my duty and ask as few questions as possible."

"No more than that, Colonel? You don't strike me as a passive man."

"You're correct, but I choose to leave the politics to those who know what they're doing."

Her thoughts were on her father—not to mention the colonel's father—and of politics of a sinister nature. "Without so much as a question? Are there those who truly know what they are doing, or are we simply moving blindly down a darkened road toward catastrophe?"

He ignored the question. "Well, here we are. It's been a great pleasure, Mrs. Blair. I'll give a visit some thought."

"Please do, Colonel Thornton. The table won't be elaborate, but we aren't starving—yet."

He tipped his hat. "Good day, Mrs. Blair. Have a pleasant trip home."

\*        \*        \*

The Confederate guard slammed a musket butt against the small of Col. Tom Rose's back. The colonel groaned as he stumbled forward and fell to one knee. "See if you can break out'ta here, y'Yankee son of a bitch. Jus' so's you'll know, if'n y'tries it, I'll blow your god-damned haid off." The guard laughed. "It's half rations fo' ya the first week—jus' so's y'all will remember what happens t'prisoners what tries t'escape." The guard pulled the door shut behind him as he left the large, ground-floor room of Libby Prison.

Rose winced as he pressed his hand against the swelling knot on his back. As the pain subsided, he slowly examined his desolate surroundings. His eyes locked on the massive, smoke-blackened fireplace. He stood gingerly and dusted himself off before limping toward the large hearth draped with cobwebs. He turned and looked around the room again. This won't be so easy, he thought. He moaned faintly as he pressed his hand against the swelling in the small of his back.

As a nearby prisoner moved toward Rose, the man fumbled to pull something from his pocket. "Got any tobacco, friend?" the man asked as he inserted the stem of a corncob pipe between his teeth.

"Never use the stuff," Rose replied. "How long you been in here, Captain?"

"Lost track a few months back. What day is it, anyway?"

"I'm not certain," Rose answered. "It's somewhere past the middle of October. It's a Thursday, I believe."

"You *sure* you don't have any tobacco?" the man asked again.

"How many men are in this place?" Rose inquired as he walked stiffly toward a window.

"I wouldn't go near them windows if I was you, Colonel. Best way I know to get a bullet through the eye."

Rose stopped. "That seems very unfriendly," Rose said. "How many men did you say?"

"Somewhere 'bout twelve hundred, give or take a hundred. Count's been going up rather steady of late. Where'd they get you?"

"Chickamauga Creek, down near Chattanooga. Anyone else from there been sent here?"

"Can't say for sure. That's a long way off. Why'd they send you clear up here?"

"They didn't, at first. I escaped from the first place they sent me after I was captured. I guess they think this place is more secure."

"No one has ever gotten out of here, Colonel, 'cept in a pine box or through exchange. And there ain't none been exchanged in several months now." The captain clicked his tongue. "Damn. What I wouldn't give for a pipe full of tobacco." His arms hanging limply at his side, his head bowed, he turned and shuffled toward the darkened far wall.

Rose studied the gaunt faces of the men in the room. Hard to see much in here, he mused, though it's easy enough to see that the spirit's been whipped out of these men. Have to do something about that. "Anyone here get captured at Chickamauga?" he shouted. Heads turned, but no one answered. He walked toward two men playing checkers in the far corner of the room. "Major, do you know if there's anyone in here from Rosecrans's army?"

"Can't say, Colonel. These men are mostly from the East."

"Who's winnin'?" Rose asked.

"I suppose I am," said a lieutenant. "What's the score, Jack?"

"You're ahead 1,021 to 940, best I recollect." The major jumped his checker three times. "Make that 941. Best make yourself comfortable, Colonel. You'll be here a spell. Set 'em up, Pudge," said Jack.

Rose walked uneasily up the stairs leading to the second floor. He turned at the landing and moved slowly down the narrow aisle between vermin-infested pallets that extended from one side of the room to the other and stretched to both ends. "I'm Colonel Rose," he said loudly. "Anyone here captured at Chickamauga?" No one answered. He squatted. "You, sir, how long have you been here?"

The man spoke without looking up. "Since Gettysburg, Colonel," he replied glumly, the cause of his sullen mood evidenced by the empty right sleeve folded upward from the elbow and pinned to his shoulder.

"I see you had a bit of bad luck, Captain. They been taking decent care of you here?"

"They don't take care of none of us, Colonel. I don't expect to get out'ta this place alive."

"That's no way to talk, Captain." Rose stood and walked on, shifting his eyes from side to side. Then he stopped. A lone officer huddled in a filthy corner drew his attention. The man wore no rank insignia. He's at the brink of despair, judged Rose as he watched the man sway rhythmically. Rose stared until the man looked up. "Sam, is that you?" He stepped gingerly across four rows of pallets and made his way toward the corner. "Sam Wade. I didn't know they got you, too."

Wide-eyed with fear, the man pressed against the wall. He shook his head vigorously. "You got me mixed up with someone else. Get away from me. Leave me alone."

"I'll be damned. It is you, Sam. I recognize your voice."

The man scrambled to his feet and ran to the far end of the room. When he reached the stairs he stumbled down them into the darkness below.

"What's the matter with him?" Rose asked a lieutenant stretched out at his feet.

The lieutenant pointed to his head and moved his forefinger in a circle. "He's a little tetched, Colonel. Says he doesn't remember his name. He got wounded in the head, up at Gettysburg."

"Gettysburg? Has he been here long?"

"Came some time in August," replied another officer. "A few days after they dumped me in this hellhole."

"August, huh? Guess he isn't who I thought he was."

Wade and Clinton stood silently, looking into the shallow grave. Two privates shoveled loose dirt onto Captain Post's blanket-covered face. His death had been difficult. Gangrene had begun eating away at the festering wound left when the surgeon removed his arm. Until then it had seemed that Post might recover. The infection had subsided slightly, and his fever had broken briefly. He had regained consciousness and swallowed a few spoonfuls of weak potato soup. The three men had talked in whispers about what they might do when Post regained sufficient strength for travel. About nine that evening, Wade and Clinton had returned to the convalescent barracks, where each had wangled a cot. They had gone to the hospital the next afternoon and found Post drenched in sweat and thrashing about in delirium. Three days passed before the blood poisoning ran its course.

Wade and Clinton turned solemnly and walked down the gentle slope from the temporary military cemetery. Neither felt like talking. Storm clouds began boiling overhead as they walked silently down King Street, turned south at Court Street, and headed back toward town. It grew darker by the minute as the sky turned rapidly from a dusty gray to nearly black. Rain began falling as they reached the livery at the corner of Court and South Streets. They stepped inside to wait for the storm to pass.

"What now?" asked Clinton.

Wade turned and examined the interior of the building. He waited as his eyes adjusted. They were alone. "There's nothing holding us here," replied Wade. "How would you like to take in a little plantation living?"

"That's askin' for trouble, Sam. She's goin' t'put two an' two together 'fore long."

"I think she's satisfied that I'm Thornton," Wade replied. He hesitated. "And there's something else, Jim. I think I love her. In fact, I'm sure of it."

"Look, Sam, I ain't got no business interferin' in your personal affairs, but she's what this war is all about. She's Southern aristocracy t'the core. I heard 'bout her while I was growin' up near here. Course we didn't travel in the same circles. I thought I recognized her back in Virginia, but it made so little sense that I let it pass." He squatted and looked out at the downpour. "For God's sake, Sam, I've heard they have more'n two hundred slaves." He turned away. "You don't understand these people any better'n anyone else up north." He shook his head. "That's why we're at war, I s'pose."

At half past two, Clinton pulled the reins and turned the wagon down the narrow, muddy lane leading toward the plantation mansion. As the wagon rolled noisily across the wooden bridge, two women in the distance looked up. They were on their knees at the edge of a weed-infested flower bed, cutting the last of the blooms that had survived the early frost. At the sight of the approaching wagon, the two women sprang to their feet and wiped their hands on their print dresses. One said something to the other and they giggled, then they ran toward the house. Wade saluted casually as the wagon drew to a stop at the base of the broad porch. Cathy Blair smiled and waved back.

Clinton vaulted over the side of the wagon and beat the mud from his boots as Wade stepped down. Clinton shifted his attention to the two women. He froze as they slowed to a walk and then stopped twenty feet from the wagon. The faint smile on the face of Cathy's companion faded when her eyes met Clinton's. At first she seemed unsure; then her jaw dropped.

"We're in trouble," Clinton hissed out of the corner of his mouth, barely moving his lips.

"You know her?" Wade whispered.

"Yeah, she's my younger sister's best friend—or was, 'fore the war."

Cathy, too, observed the strange encounter as she looked first at her companion, then at Clinton. She seemed momentarily distracted, then turned toward Wade and smiled. "I'm so pleased that you decided to come." Wade smiled and nodded. Cathy turned back to her friend. "Do you know Major Clinton?"

"He's Sally Clinton's brother. He went north before the war. The last I heard he had—"

"How are ya, Shannon?" Clinton said, cutting her off. "You filled out some since the last time I saw ya."

She half smiled and half frowned. "I should hope so, Jim Clinton. I'd barely turned sixteen when you left. What are you doing in that—"

Realizing that she intended to say, in that uniform, he interrupted nervously, "It's a long story, Shannon. I have t'talk with ya 'bout my family. Perhaps we can take a walk an' let these two get reacquainted." He rolled his eyes uneasily toward Cathy. "It's a pleasure seein' y'again, Mrs. Blair. The colonel an' I sure do 'preciate your invitin' us out like this."

"My pleasure, Major Clinton. I do hope you will stay awhile."

"Thank you, ma'am. Now, if y'all will excuse us, I have t'find out 'bout my family." He moved swiftly to Shannon's side and grasped her arm firmly.

"What was that all about?" asked Cathy, after Jim and Shannon had ambled off.

"Beats me," Wade said, shaking his head and shrugging. "No doubt, though, that they know each other well. Where do you want the wagon?"

"I'll have one of the slaves tend to it later. Shall we go for a stroll?" she asked.

Clinton and Shannon Morgan stopped at the top of the nearby knoll. She bent and clutched a handful of recently fallen leaves. "I just love this old tree," she said. "It has such a sense of permanence about it." She looked at Clinton and frowned. "I'm wondering if I should believe you, Jim Clinton." Her features softened, then she smiled. "But it is terribly romantic, the thought of you being a spy."

"That's why I went up north. War seemed pretty sure by then. They sent a bunch of us up so's we'd be in position t'go into the Union army an' report on their activities. I got found out an' had t'skedaddle. When I got back, General Jackson assigned me t'his staff."

Her eyes widened. "Stonewall Jackson?"

"The very same. The colonel served on the general's staff, too. He was a cap'n then an' sorta took me under his wing. After ol' Stonewall got hisself killed, the colonel an' me have been loners, workin' on secret missions wherever the gov'ment wants us t'go."

"So what are you doing here, Major Clinton? There aren't any Yankees here."

"There may be, Miss Shannon—'fore too long. It don't 'pear as likely our army'll whip the Yankees at Chattanooga as it did a short time ago. If those blue-bellies break loose, we'll need all the information we can get t'fight 'em off. The colonel an' I need t'be in place if that happens."

She thought for a moment. That seems natural, she concluded, but in what place, and to do what? Such things were beyond her—not that she really cared.

I sure hope my story doesn't clash too badly with the colonel's, Clinton thought. I knew we shouldn't come here. Women and war just don't mix. "Now, tell me 'bout my family. What happened t'Pa?"

Her expression darkened. "I'm sorry, Jim. Some hotheads got lickered up and went out to the farm one night in early '62. One thing led to another, and they hanged him. You know how he made his views known. He wouldn't keep quiet about his abolitionist sympathies."

Clinton turned and walked limply toward the swing. He squeezed his eyes shut, and the vision of his father dangling from a tree flashed in his mind. Tears streamed down his face. "The bastards," he said through clenched teeth. "They say they're fightin' for free speech, but it damned well better be speech the slavers want t'hear."

She walked to his side. "Don't say that too loudly, Jim. There's people around here who might doubt your story if they heard such words."

Clinton turned away and wiped his face with a sleeve. "An' the others?"

"They took off about a week later. They salvaged what they could from the fire and spent a few nights over at the Campbell place. They just rode out one night, and no one's seen them since. I think they went across the state to your aunt's place. Your sister hinted as much when I talked to her the day before they left."

"That's prob'ly for the best. What're *you* doin' here?"

"Mom and Dad both died the first winter of the war," she said solemnly. "Can't be sure, but the doctor said they were taken with some kind of fever. Jed's up near Knoxville someplace. Got a letter from him a couple of weeks back. He said he's disgusted with the way our army only half fights its battles. He's a sergeant in Stuart's cavalry. He's been wounded twice and captured once. When Cathy returned from Virginia, she was kind enough to take me in to help supervise the house servants. Before that, I'd been scraping by working in a dry goods store in Rome." She looked at him with watery eyes. "Everything's about to fall apart, Jim. Half the people from Rome have already gone farther south, or soon will. They know what's coming. Bragg had his chance and failed. Now there'll be the devil to pay. I think we'll lose the war, Jim. It scares me when I think what the Yankees will do to us."

Clinton cradled her in his arms and pulled her close. The warm, tender feeling of her breasts pressing against his chest gave rise to memories of a skinny, barefoot girl sloshing down the road the day before he journeyed north. He remembered teasing her about something, the specifics long since forgotten. The taunting had made her angry, so she had thrown a pebble at him before running. She had stopped shortly and reacted with disappointment when she realized he had not chased her.

"How long before you have to leave?" Cathy asked Sam as they strolled along the path toward the summerhouse.

"Can't say for sure. I sent a message informing my superiors that they'd have no way of contacting me for a few days." The lies emerged with less difficulty now; nothing in his real life meshed with the life she had forced him to fabricate. "I'll have to check back at the telegraph office before long."

"Just what do you do, exactly, Colonel Thornton?"

"I help fight this war, Mrs. Blair."

"Is that all you're going to tell me?"

"Seems so," he replied curtly. "Have you heard anything more from my father?"

"Only that he's still encamped just across the border in Alabama. You saw what it's like in Rome. Everyone expects the war to come crashing down on our heads shortly. There's a rumor that General Grant will replace Rosecrans. Everyone is scared to death of that man after what he did to Vicksburg."

Wade nodded. "I heard that rumor." He opened the door and followed her into the summerhouse.

"As a girl, I spent most of my time here. It's usually cool, even on the hottest days. Daddy had an old slave build me a dollhouse. It sat right there, in the corner, 'til it just fell apart one day." She turned toward him and unthinkingly grasped his hand. "I had such a pleasant childhood. I fear so for what my daughter will have to face."

"The Yankees aren't as bad as the stories make them out to be," said Wade. "It'll be a struggle for a while, but conditions will return to normal in time."

Cathy reacted instinctively, squinting harshly up at him. "You talk as if it's certain we'll lose!"

He bristled at the verbal attack, then relaxed. "Nothing is assured in war, Cathy, but only a fool would claim that it doesn't look bad. The weight of their material and manpower advantages will be difficult to overcome. It took them a while to crank up their war effort, but their factories run around the clock now. You know what it's like, even in Rome, and the war hasn't really reached here yet."

"I know you're right, but it's difficult to accept." She slipped her hand in his and led him out the door. "Let's go down by the stream. Do you mind?"

He followed without reply. He glanced at Clinton and Shannon talking on the nearby knoll and wondered how Jim was handling the situation.

Wade and Cathy walked a short distance in silence before she stopped. She looked pensively into his eyes. "What do you think of me?" she asked.

Wade stepped back. "Think of you? I think I'm pleased to see you, to be with you. I think I owe you my life—which, by the way, I never thanked you for saving. I guess I think you're special to me."

"That could apply to your horse. What else?"

He cleared his throat. "I haven't prepared myself for this, Mrs. Blair." He lowered his chin and blushed slightly, then reached out and fumbled with a small bow at her waist.

"What would you do if a hundred bluecoats came storming out of the woods right now?" she asked.

He smiled. "I'd run like hell. In fact, that sounds like a good idea, with or without bluecoats."

She clutched at his arm. "Not just yet. I know you've thought of me, else you wouldn't be here now."

"Not much," he said, trying to appear serious. "No more than three or four times a day. But that's usually at night, when my mind is free."

"As it should be, Simon Thornton."

"This morning, while we were waiting for the rain to stop, I told Jim we were coming here. He was opposed to the idea. Said women and war don't mix. I told him we were coming anyway." She smiled broadly and he felt her fingernails pressing inward through his coat sleeve. "Is he right? What do you think?"

"I think you should kiss me."

Wade cradled the sides of her face in his hands and leaned toward her. He kissed the tip of her lightly freckled nose, then pressed his lips against hers. She moaned softly as she slid her arms around his waist. They separated by a few inches. "This is a poor time for something like this," he said softly. "I may be dead tomorrow, and then where would you be?"

"I'd have had a full day of happiness, that's where I'd be." She shook her head slowly, thoughtfully. "I can't remember when I last had such a day."

Wade sighed. He had no experience in such things. He turned from her and clasped his hands behind his head. "This is probably the wrong thing to say, but I realized that I loved you that night in the barn, when you told me you had just learned of your husband's death. It suddenly came to me how fragile we are in such times. I still remember you sobbing . . . your warm tears dropping on my bare chest. I wanted to comfort you, to say something, but nothing seemed appropriate. So I just lay there, falling in love with you."

She pressed herself against his back and locked her arms around his waist. "You'll be staying in the summerhouse tonight, Simon. Jim can stay in the guest house. I hadn't planned on doing so, but I'll be making new arrangements for myself."

Samuel Wade, alias Simon Thornton, and Cathy Blair lay quietly under the comforter on the bedding she had spread on the floor. Other than their relaxed breathing, the only sounds were the distant croaking of a frog and the mournful notes from a harmonica drifting from the slave quarters.

Pearl Bowman had looked on in disapproving silence as her daughter collected the necessary bedding. Twice, as Cathy had carried the bundle toward the back door, her mother had fought the urge to protest. Cathy had seen the distress in her mother's eyes. Finally, hoping to ease her anguish, Cathy had placed the bundle on a table and pressed a finger to her lips, then smiled.

Her mother's mouth had tightened as she folded her arms firmly across her chest. She fidgeted uneasily but said nothing. In a world with so much suffering, she understood her daughter's need to reach out for love. Pearl and Cathy both knew that whatever would happen must happen that night. The next day, Cathy's father would return from a short business trip. His proud Southern breeding would not tolerate such wanton female behavior.

Six months had passed since Cathy had last made love with her husband. Barely three months had passed since she learned of his death. Perhaps it was less than a proper interval, she thought as she ran her finger through the folds of Wade's ear, but convention must yield in time of war.

She leaned forward and kissed him softly on the cheek. "Can I trust you completely, Simon Thornton?" she whispered in his ear.

Just her use of that name meant he must lie if he answered the question. In that sense, even their relationship was tainted by fraud. He regretted that. "The way you say that sounds quite ominous," he replied with a soft, sleepy voice.

"You didn't answer me."

"Trust me to do what?"

"Keep a secret."

What secret of importance could she possess? Making the promise seems safe enough. "You can trust me," he replied.

She rolled under the comforter and pressed her back firmly against his chest. He draped his arm loosely over her side. "What would you feel, Simon, if you learned that someone very close to you had become involved in a plot—a plot that meant the gravest consequences if it failed, or even became known?"

Already regretting his promise, he sighed. "I sense that your question is more than rhetorical."

"Perhaps. Perhaps not." She rolled her head toward him. "Just tell me what you'd think."

"I'd think that this person had probably considered the consequences and found the risk acceptable."

"My, my, Colonel. Your lack of curiosity is, well, curious."

"Is it? What would you do?" he asked.

"Ah, that's the problem, isn't it? What *am* I to do? I suppose that'd depend on how I personally felt about the act."

"Okay, so what is this hypothetical act that has you so troubled?"

"I'm wondering if I should even bother to tell you," she said poutingly.

She's stalling, he thought. "I'm interested now"—he placed his lips against her neck—"because you seem so interested."

"I'm having difficulty trusting you, Colonel," she replied more seriously than she chose to acknowledge, even to herself. "And you promised." Since the moment she had looked at Simon Thornton's picture and realized his identity, her interest in finding him had become an obsession. But there had seemed no place to begin the search. Fate must be on my side, she thought, but am I courting disaster? Can it be an accident that he ended up here, of all places in this vast land? She rolled and faced Wade as he placed his hand in the middle of her back. He ran his fingers lightly along her spine to the small of her back. She shivered and slid forward until her breasts pressed against his chest.

"Then don't tell me," he replied with a shrug.

"But I have to tell someone! I can't keep it inside me any longer." She looked into his eyes and tried to gauge his reaction. Seeing nothing, she added softly, "There's a plot to assassinate Abraham Lincoln."

Wade blinked. He felt his muscles tense, his breathing grow faster. "When?" he asked, hoping the inquiry conveyed inquisitiveness rather than cold shock.

"I don't know, Simon."

Wade let his head sink into the down pillow. "Why did you choose to tell me about this now, of all times?"

"Because of who's involved, Simon."

"What's the surprise? I'm sure nearly everyone south of Washington would prefer to see Lincoln dead." He resisted the impulse to grab her, to shake from her everything she knew. But he knew if he did, he would never learn another fact.

"Perhaps, but I fear for the wrath toward the South if the plot succeeds. There must be many people involved. They plan to eliminate perhaps a dozen Yankee politicians. The people behind this really don't care which side wins the war. They simply want Lincoln and these other men dead. They think they're bad for business, or that they will be once the war ends. There are some very powerful and wealthy men providing financial support. So far as I have determined, the men who are pulling the strings are all from up north. I'm frightened, Simon. They don't care anything about us. They're just interested in their railroads and high finance."

"How did you learn about this?" Wade asked calmly.

"That isn't important. But I'm sure it's true. I don't even know how many are involved, but I can give you the name of two Southern patriots who are convinced that they are doing the right thing." She rose up on one elbow and stared down at him. "One is my father. You'll meet him tomorrow. The other is *your* father."

# CHAPTER

# 18

Colonel Rose sat in a dark corner peeling small splinters from a larger splinter that he had stripped from a decaying wall beam. More than anything, he missed having his penknife. Whittling always helped him forget his troubles. He had chosen this spot, next to the massive rock fireplace, for a tactical reason.

Rose recalled that Sam Wade had told him about a man named Thornton, Wade's identical twin brother, and their separation at birth. The man who looked like Wade *had* to be Thornton. Nothing else made sense. What he couldn't be certain of was why Thornton, a Confederate, was in a prison for Yankees. Whatever the reason, it obviously wasn't something Thornton could do anything about. Thornton clearly was afraid of something, and Rose knew he had to overcome the man's fear before he could help him. Now Rose planned to test a carefully devised theory.

Thirty minutes passed before the man who looked like Wade found his way to the corner and leaned against the wall. After a few moments, he placed his face in his hands. Rose heard him whimpering from twenty feet away. Rose recognized the symptoms of a man who had given up. The man folded into his usual upright fetal position and leaned his head against the angle of the wall. Rose had peeled a small mound of splinters by the time the man fell asleep. Rose waited for a couple of minutes before easing himself up and moving silently to the dark corner, where he lowered himself to the floor and placed a hand on the man's shoulder. The gentle touch startled the man, who awoke immediately. He tried to stand, but Rose held him firmly in place. "We're going to have a talk," Rose said quietly. "First, I'll do the talking; then I'll give you some time to think about what I've said. You can talk later." Rose shifted to a more comfortable position. "I think I'll begin with a short story."

206

Sensing no immediate threat, the man relaxed and settled back against the wall.

Rose told the man what Wade had told him the night Wade arrived in camp. Rose wished he had asked more questions, but he had to make do with what little he knew. He told the man what Wade had said about twice seeing a man who looked just like him—once during a prisoner exchange the previous June, and again at the close of the battle at Gettysburg—a man who he assumed was his cousin until Wade's mother told him the whole story. As Rose laid out the story, the man grew more alert. The most telling change in his response came when Rose talked about how Wade's mother had taken Wade's wounded twin to her farm after the battle at Gettysburg.

Then Rose mentioned that Wade had lost all trace of his brother as a result of a prisoner exchange arranged by Colonel Thompson, Wade's immediate superior. Wade had expressed concern that with his brother's poor condition he might die if he failed to receive proper care.

Thornton turned and looked Rose in the eyes.

I may have reached him, Rose thought. "Well," Rose continued, "nothing much might have come of my conversation with Colonel Wade, if not for one unanticipated event: the next day I led my regiment into battle. We went forward at dark and slammed into a whole rebel brigade. I was captured and now I'm here in this hellhole with no obvious way of getting out."

Rose leaned forward and examined his puffy leg. "This damned gout is a terrible affliction," he said absently. "I couldn't even get my boot on the day they captured me. I had to take this one from a dead prisoner. It's two sizes too large—but I suppose that's better than too small." He shifted his weight and leaned against the wall. "You're Simon Thornton, aren't you?

"Now, before you say anything, think about what I've said. I might know some of these events from bits and pieces picked up here and there. On the other hand, I told you some things that I could know only if I'd heard them from Wade."

Rose leaned closer and spoke softly. "Now, here's the situation—at least as I see it. This war is a long way from its end. I think you've recovered your memory and realize just how precarious your situation really is. You're caught in the middle, with no place to turn. But what's more obvious to me is, it really won't matter in the long run, for as sure as there's sin, you won't be alive to see its end if you remain locked up in here. One day soon, you'll wander despondently to this little corner of hell, place your head against the wall, and go to sleep—but that time you'll sleep forever. It happens every day here, regular as the seasons. It has to do with giving up, I suppose.

"For my part, I aim to get out of here. I've even figured out a way of doing it. And if you'll let me, I'll take you with me. But first, I have to get a message to Colonel Thompson in Washington and tell him that you're here. Thompson will contact your brother, your brother will come here and contact us, and we'll see to it that you get home. Your brother is a resourceful individual. He'll find a way."

Rose elevated himself to a squatting position. "Well, that's the end of the story. You think about it and decide what's best for you. Every day you delay is another day you'll have to remain here. Communicating with Thompson will take some time and a bribe or two, but I know how to do that, too." He stood. "Sleep well, Simon. We'll talk more later."

The door swung open. "Here come those bastards with our daily swill," Rose said. "You eat hardy, now, Colonel. You'll need your strength. It's a long way from here to Birmingham."

A potbellied stove glowed red near the center of the small room. The few people scattered about the cramped, dockside dining room and bar had removed their light jackets. Although a slight chill hung in the air—the stiff wind had whipped the waves in Charleston Harbor into breaking whitecaps—the temperature had been a balmy sixty degrees since noon, about average for the last week in October. Steam from a cup of hot tea rose leisurely from its container for a few inches, hovered, then shifted direction and sprinted toward the hairline crack in the window. The albino, his arms tightly crossed at his chest, sat huddled at the table nearest to the stove with his coat collar pulled about his neck. As he waited, he reached up and pulled the flaps of his woolen cap over his ears. He turned at the sound of someone opening the door, pulled his watch from its pocket, and nodded. Two o'clock, on the nose.

A squat, red-faced, middle-aged man—obviously a man of means—walked toward the table where the albino waited. The floor squeaked under the pressure of his weight. The man wore a round planter's hat; his attire, which would have served him well for a day at the races, strained at the buttons with each movement of his pear-shaped torso. He clumsily removed his cap to reveal a totally bald head. The upper half of his left ear had been cut away at an angle. Rumor had it he'd lost it in a duel when an excited opponent had fired in haste. Others said a woman had bitten it off when she learned that he had taken another lover. Either way, thought the albino, it must have been a hell of a thing to witness.

Although they had never met before, each knew the other without introduction.

The obese man pulled up a chair and sat down, his ample posterior folding over the sides. "I received your message four days ago," he said. "I've come at two each afternoon for the past three days."

"Sorry for the delay," said the albino. "The military confiscated the train and left me stranded in Columbia."

The fat man leaned closer. "Does anyone know you're here?"

"Not that I'm aware of. I didn't even inform my benefactors of my plans."

"Are all of the pieces in place?"

"No. Only the middle links are solid. The Union army is camped in their backyard. It's only natural that they grew more receptive as the tension mounted. It's the stretch west of here that's been difficult. The West will fall in line later."

The frumpy man nodded. "We'll just have to wait and see. I have faith that the Union army will help us out. It might even be for the best. If Meade gets around Lee, or if Grant moves east from Chattanooga, the price of land options will plunge." He motioned to the waiter. "Whiskey, double." Then he turned back to the albino. "When do we move?"

"Probably no earlier than August or September. My people are patient. They want to see how the presidential nomination process progresses. Timing is everything. If events move too fast, the North might give up. That must be prevented. Opportunity would be lost if the South surrenders too quickly. Yes. Timing is everything." He glanced out the window and shivered.

"What do you need now?" asked the man, fingering the scar on his ear.

"I need men."

"How many?"

"A dozen, but I'd prefer a few more in case something doesn't work out with one or two."

"Any specific qualifications?"

"Yes, several." The albino reached into his pocket and withdrew a sheet of paper. "I'll give you this when I leave. I want you to memorize it and then burn it." He cleared his throat, then took a sip of tea. "The men must be unmarried and wholly committed to the Confederacy. All must be experts with musket and pistol, in good physical condition, and proficient horsemen. They must not have a criminal record, not even for a misdemeanor. Orphans would be best, but that's not required. Men who are estranged from their families would be desirable. They must have no distinguishing marks"—he glanced at the space where part of the man's ear had been—"such as visible scars or pox marks, and they must be willing to die for the cause if necessary. Oh, and one more thing: they must all be strangers to one another, preferably no more than two or three even from the same state. If any come from the army, make sure they're from units that haven't had contact. In short, sir, I want anonymous men who, if it comes to it, the world would never miss.

"There is one *special* qualification. I need a leader, someone who can both give and take orders. A man who has *earned* his commission rather than acquired it through political connections. Here's a name for you to consider, but use your own judgment. Move cautiously when making your selections. I'll contact you in February or March."

"You don't ask for much," said the fat man. "If I had a hundred such men, I could take Washington in a week."

"Surely your Confederacy has produced enough such men for my needs, sir."

The waiter set the glass on the table. "We shall see," said the fat man before gulping down the whiskey. "Such a search will be expensive," he added.

The albino slid his chair backward and reached down between his legs. He grasped a wooden box and set it on the table, covering the list of qualifications. He leaned forward and whispered. "Here's twenty-five thousand in Confederate currency and two thousand dollars in gold. More will be provided when the men have been selected."

"What should I tell them about the mission?"

"Nothing. They won't be informed of any details until the last possible moment. Simply tell them that their efforts may save the Confederacy. Any other questions?"

"Just one. If I must contact you, how shall I do it?"

"If you have an emergency, send a telegram to Richmond addressed to Mr. Q. Say that Mr. Butterfield needs assistance, and end with the first two letters of the name of the state in which you want to be contacted. Sign it Mr. Y. You will be contacted." The albino handed the man another small sheet of paper. "Here's a list of cities and the locations in them where you must go to be contacted. Starting two days after you send your message, attempts will be made to reach you between one and three in the afternoon. This will continue for five days. If no contact is made within that time, you will be presumed dead, and we will not respond to further messages." The albino turned and looked out the window. "If there's nothing else, then you should leave." He seemed mesmerized by the churning waves and failed to notice as the man secured the small but heavy box under his arm and walked toward the door.

A few minutes later, a second man entered, this one slender and bearded, his clothes badly worn. He slung his muddy leg over the back of the chair across the table from the albino.

"Did you see him?" asked the albino.

"How in hell could I miss seein' him?" the man replied. "He's as big as a house."

"You understand what we want?"

He glanced over his shoulder before whispering, "You want him dead, right?"

"*Only* if you receive instructions."

"And I get my money either way?"

"Of course, but *only* if you act on orders." The albino slid a small envelope across the table. "Here's a thousand in Confederate currency. That will keep you going. You'll receive the gold when the job is finished."

The man opened the envelope and counted the bills. He smiled as he leaned toward the albino. "When will you require my services, do you think?"

"Sometime in late spring, perhaps May or early June. You'll be told when and where." He turned his head and gazed at the waves. "Don't fail me, Mellen. Good day."

On the rainy Sunday morning of October 25, Wade sat at the breakfast table reading—for the tenth time, he guessed—an expanded Saturday edition of the *Courier*. "General Grant in Chattanooga; Rosecrans Relieved" the lead headline blared in inch-high letters. The first sentence of the story began with half-inch type: "Thomas Takes Field Command of Union Army." Nothing that followed added much; the headlines said it all. The beginning of General Bragg's end was written in those few words, and Wade knew it.

Grant's name conjured up hate and dread in the South. "Unconditional Surrender Grant" the press had dubbed him after he captured Fort Donelson in the late winter of 1862, and every battle the man had waged since only added to his mystique. The Confederacy could thank Grant for two of the greatest tragedies in its short existence: the defeats at Shiloh and Vicksburg.

Cathy Blair, in the course of several lengthy conversations with Wade, had unburdened herself of what she had come to refer to as "her terrible knowledge" of the conspiracy to assassinate President Lincoln and a dozen or so other Northern politicians. But it would have mattered little if she had never said a word about it. The plot apparently had been the worst-kept secret on the plantation. A simpleminded old slave had even approached Wade and naively asked, "What do assassinate mean, Master?"

But it had gone beyond that. The previous night there had been a celebration of sorts in the slave quarters. To get things started, the merrymakers had uncorked a couple of jugs of home-brewed corn whiskey. The spirits both numbed their minds and loosened their tongues. In their wanderings about the plantation, it seemed, they had overheard bits and pieces of the many recent conversations in the summerhouse. In time, they had fitted the pieces together sufficiently to understand the essential details. For the first time that night, the realization had collectively emerged that the Great Emancipator might be killed before securing their freedom for them. As the night progressed, talk of that, as well as the dulling effect of the liquor, had cast a pall over the gathering. Shannon had approached the slaves' party to watch and had overheard the talk. The next day she told Clinton. Cathy's only addition to this information had been the revelation of General Thornton's place at the center of the conspiracy.

Having gleaned everything possible from the paper, Wade folded it and placed it on the table. He looked first at Cathy's father and smiled. He did the same with her mother. Then he turned to Cathy. Her tight-lipped expression and the disappointment in her eyes let him know that she realized the time had come.

"You're leaving, aren't you?" she said.

"I'm in the army, Cathy. I've been here too long as it is." He turned toward Mrs. Bowman. "We can never adequately repay you for your hospitality, ma'am."

"No payment is necessary," she said as she placed her cup in its saucer. "I had begun to wonder if I'd ever see my daughter smile again. You have taken the pain from her heart. For that I am eternally grateful."

Cathy lowered her eyes. "Mother!" she said disapprovingly. "Please! Not in front of Simon." She glanced at Wade and smiled.

Clinton cleared his throat and slid his chair back. "I'll just say good-bye t'Shannon 'fore I hitch up the wagon. Mr. Bowman, Mrs. Bowman, this has been my best week in over two years. Mrs. Blair, if I may ever be of service . . ." He bowed.

Cathy placed her hand on his. "You will take care of Simon for me, won't you, sir? That is the only service I request."

"Ma'am," he said, smiling and shifting his eyes to look at Wade, "I'm already doin' that for three other people. One more won't add t'my burden a'tall." He turned to Wade. "I'll meet ya out front, sir."

Wade nodded. He placed the china cup to his lips and drank the remainder of the weak coffee. "I have a gift for you, Mrs. Bowman." He rose and moved to where he had draped his overcoat across a small table. Under the table lay a sack. He lifted it, returned to the breakfast table, and set the sack in the middle of it. "This isn't much, but I know how hard it is to come by coffee these days. There's five pounds of coffee beans in this sack, and six pounds of sugar-cured bacon."

Cathy's eyes sparkled with her smile.

"I'd have given these to you earlier," he added, "but I just figured you'd serve it all while we were here."

"My goodness, young man. It seems you've found a way to delight both the women in this family," said Pearl Bowman. She placed a hand on one of the exposed bacon slabs, almost caressing it. Her tongue instinctively slid across her lips.

"And for you, sir," he said to Bowman, "I have this old hand-carved pipe. Other than my watch, it's about all I've been able to salvage. A very special friend carved this and gave it to me shortly before he died. I never acquired the habit, and it should be put to good use."

As he finished distributing the gifts, Wade's gaze lingered on a family portrait atop the buffet. The picture, encased in an ornate brass frame, had obviously been taken before the war. He walked over to the hutch and lifted the picture. "You have a handsome family, sir," he said, looking at Bowman. Cathy moved beside Wade and identified the family members for him: Lucius Bowman sat stiffly erect in the middle; Arthur stood immediately behind him, to the right of Pearl Bowman. Her brothers flanked Arthur and Pearl. Cathy was at the far left. "The boys all look like you, sir," said Wade.

Arthur Bowman leaned sideways in his chair and turned to look at Wade. He smiled. "No, Frank looks more like his mother," he replied, a touch of sadness in his voice.

Wade did not reply. He had no basis for comparison. The first Mrs. Bowman had been dead for a quarter century. After a brief silence he looked at Cathy and said, "It'd be nice if I had a picture of you, Cathy."

Without answering she stepped over to the buffet, opened the bottom drawer, and withdrew a box. Inside was a small photograph that she tenderly took out and handed to Wade. "Frank had this picture of me made shortly before the war. The quality isn't very good but perhaps it will help you to remember what I look like." Her choice of words made it clear she expected many months to pass before she saw him again.

Bowman interrupted with a harrumph as he stuffed fresh tobacco into his new pipe, struck a match, and lit it. He inhaled deeply and blew a stream of smoke into the air. "God be with you, Colonel Thornton," he said finally as the smoke spread about the room. "Ten thousand more like you and the South would live for five hundred years."

Wade looked at the floor, embarrassed. Try as he might, he had been unable to develop any hatred for Cathy's father. It seemed the war had both hardened and softened Wade. Bowman had it in his mind to kill the president of the United States—but, then, so did Wade's own father. Both had acquired their values through a lifetime of breeding, reinforced by an abiding love for the South. Wade could never accept how they conducted their lives, but he had no trouble understanding it.

During the past few days Bowman and he had talked much about the war—when they weren't discussing Cathy. Never in those conversations had there been any mention of the assassination plot. The man mostly longed for solitude. That, given the times, was a futile yearning. Before many weeks passed, against all of his hopes and resistance, the war would sweep him and his way of life into the backwaters of history—perhaps even before Christmas if Grant had a say. The encroaching shadows of oppressive war threatened to ravage the citizens of Georgia, and Rome would experience the hard hand of Northern vengeance earlier than most. Arthur Bowman had rational cause for concern.

With the danger so near, the need for practical forethought had become urgent for Wade. The South's estranged brethren to the north had made their feelings clear. They passionately blamed their radical neighbors in the Deep South for this calamitous war. Yet in more than two years, the citizens of the Confederacy had avoided the essential measure of suffering that would stimulate them sufficiently to renounce their excesses. In such a climate, Cathy's safety depended entirely on her father's resourcefulness, thus conferring upon the man a particular, immediate value to Wade.

But that defined only Wade's short-term problems. He had grappled internally with his responsibilities. Now that he had sorted through his personal doubts and conflicts, he had arrived at an elemental conclusion: he would do everything within his power to assure that the plot involving Bowman and his father would fail. He had to get a message to Thompson, but to do that he would have to move unnoticed through the Confederate army and into Chattanooga. That would require a sturdy mount. He had already decided to go alone, leaving Clinton in Rome until he returned. Clinton would protest, of course, but conditions had changed. With Grant in Chattanooga, it had occurred to Wade that the Union army would soon be on the move. The more information Union forces had about Confederate troop strength south of Chattanooga, the better. Clinton knew the area and could move about freely. He made a mental note to tell Clinton of his plans on the way to town.

Colonel Rose and four other Union officers sat on the floor around a cracker box, talking in low tones. Thornton had been avoiding the colonel since the day Rose had cornered him. As the four chatted quietly, Thornton passed by a few feet away. He glanced at Rose and nodded faintly. Thornton continued toward the fireplace as Rose watched him from the corner of his eye. He waited a few minutes before rising nonchalantly and walking to where Thornton stood with his back to the room.

"Don't turn around," said Rose. "Are you in?"

"Do I have any choice?"

"No, not if you want to live."

"I guess I'll just have to trust you."

"I guess you will."

"You're right. I'm Thornton. How will you get the message to Colonel Thompson?"

"The sutler," Rose said. "He comes in every day about sundown. We've become well acquainted of late."

"Are you sure you can trust him?"

"No, but it's a chance I'll have to take. There are plenty of risks in this operation. Others say he's reliable if he's given enough money."

"How will we get out?"

"I'll tell you later. For now, we have to get the message out and wait for a reply. That'll take a week or more."

"I've placed my life in your hands, Colonel."

"I know, Colonel Thornton."

"I don't understand why my brother is so concerned about my safety. We've never even spoken to each other."

"All I know is, his concern seemed genuine. From the way he explained it, his mother invested considerable effort in keeping you alive. He may be thinking of her as much as of you. We won't talk again until I hear from Thompson."

An hour later, the sutler pushed his cart across the rough floor toward the center of the room. Word of his arrival spread quickly. Thirty feet away, two guards stood at the door.

The sutler lifted a soiled cover from the cart. Food that the prisoners would have discarded before the war now made them drool. The season for fresh fruits had passed. Most of what he had for sale appeared moldy or full of bugs. Even so, chances were good that he would push an empty cart out the door.

The system had been carefully designed. The sutler paid the guards for the privilege of entering the room. He paid them again when he departed. The men who were fortunate enough to reach the prison with money covered the two-way tariff by paying ten times the value of the goods. Nearly all transactions were in gold. A man who had managed to reach the inside with a ten-dollar or twenty-dollar gold piece concealed on his person revealed the size of his stash to the sutler. He then gave the coin to the sutler at the time of his first purchase and received paper credit slips in exchange. The process depended entirely on trust.

A cubic inch of corn bread cost fifty cents, three cubes a dollar. In season, an apple cost two dollars; white bread was fifty cents a slice, and so on. Few men had enough money to remain in the trading business more than a month, but the system rolled along. A new supply of prisoners arrived regularly. The new arrivals averaged about three hundred a month. The system had become self-feeding as men died, were sent to the hospital, or were transferred to other prisons. On a good day, the sutler cleared five gold dollars after expenses. His son came with him and kept the records.

Rose's plan called for twenty or so prisoners to get in line, with Rose near the rear. This would allow Rose a minute or so alone with the sutler before others wandered by to conduct their business. Fifty or more men were to mill around and block the view of the guards. Rose had planned well for this moment and had been waiting patiently to set the operation into motion.

Since arriving at Libby, Rose had solicited "investments" from a hundred of the prisoners. Each had provided a two-dollar credit slip against the remote chance of eventual escape. No promises had been made, and none were sought. It had been presented as a business proposition, with all the attendant risks of loss of capital. Since the sutler settled daily with the guards for the actual amount of sales, based on carefully inventoried wares upon entry and exit, the two hundred dollars in credits meant clear profit for the sutler—less his outside expenses.

"I must get a message to Washington," Rose said quietly when it was his turn. The sutler nodded. He had been playing both sides for more than a year.

He would pass the note to a Union contact in Richmond. Through a variety of channels, the contact would send it on its way to Washington. From there, depending on the need, the network had a variety of options. The process worked the same way in reverse. Money exchanged hands at every link in the chain.

"Hundred dollars in gold," the sutler replied. "Want anything to eat?"

"Four pieces of white bread," Rose replied.

"Two dollars," said the sutler. "Will you want a reply?"

"Yes."

"That's another hundred. Here's your bread. Not much mold today. I ought to raise the price."

As Rose handed the sutler the $202 worth of credits, he slipped in a folded sheet of paper with the address written on the outside.

"It'll take a week to ten days to get your reply," the sutler said. He handed two credit slips to his son and stuffed the other papers in his coat pocket. "Who's next?" he shouted. "I ain't got all night."

Rose walked slowly toward Thornton. "The message is on its way, Colonel." He hesitated before handing Thornton two pieces of bread. "Sleep well."

As Rose disappeared into the gloom of Libby Prison, Thornton smiled for the first time in four months.

# CHAPTER

# 19

The journey to Chattanooga had drained Wade's energy. The main roads to the city had been crowded with soldiers. The back roads and woods had been nearly as bad. Provost patrols were everywhere. By the end of the first day, he had decided he would have a better chance if he moved farther west, around the Confederate army. What should have been a two-day ride had stretched into five tension-filled days.

Now Wade sat limply astride the broken mare he had stolen from a drunken Confederate major. Lights were beginning to flicker in the sea of tents pitched on both sides of the Tennessee River. He looked wearily to his right, in the direction of Lookout Mountain. Hundreds of campfires dotted the slopes and crest. Fog shrouded the bottom two-thirds of Missionary Ridge some four miles across the valley. He dismounted and walked cautiously to the edge of the tree line, knelt, and brought the field glasses to his eyes. As the last light of day faded, he noticed a mounted patrol riding at a gallop along the river's near edge. He strained to discern the color of their uniforms. They could be gray, he thought, or just as easily mud-spattered blue. He lowered the glasses.

He huddled for an hour in the cold dankness. Sentry fires sparkled at fifty-yard intervals along the near bank of the river. Fewer than half as many fires blazed along the banks of Moccasin Point, but there were several company-sized encampments beyond. Probably a full brigade guarding the point, Wade thought. At this point, the river flowed south, made a sharp loop around Moccasin Point, then flowed north past Chattanooga. To get to the city, Wade would have to cross the river twice. The fires stretched along the inner banks of the river's bending path, then up to the outskirts of the city. There they blended with a maze of light that stretched through the city to the Tennessee River's

north bank and beyond. Those *must* be the Union lines, he thought. He untied the saddlebags, then removed the saddle and bridle and sent the horse
crashing into the underbrush. He then slid into a shallow gully to escape the
cold night breeze and waited another hour to give the army an opportunity
to settle in for the night. Just after eight o'clock, he reluctantly slipped out
of his Confederate uniform and tossed it aside. The biting cold sent uncon-
trollable shivers down Wade's spine. He bent into a crouch and scurried across
the rough terrain leading up to the river. He crawled through the gap between
the two nearest fires and edged his way to the riverbank. He secured his saddlebags
to a large chunk of driftwood and slid it quietly into the water. As he followed it in, Wade gasped and sucked in a deep breath before easing his body
completely into the cold river. With the current pushing him gradually south,
he began swimming toward the far bank.

Thirty minutes later, nearing exhaustion, Wade crawled onto the muddy bank.
He untied the saddlebags with shivering hands and ran in a crouch up the sloping
bank toward a stand of bushes thirty feet beyond. Pressing himself against the
damp, sandy earth, Wade lifted his head and peered over the rim of the ridge.
Ten feet away, two sentries huddled next to a fire. Wade opened the flap on
one of the saddlebags and quietly withdrew his pistol. The slight sound of his
movement blended with the slapping waves as he slid through the grass to where
the two soldiers sat with their backs to the river.

He pressed the pistol against the spine of the nearest sentry. "I'm your prisoner,"
Wade said in a whisper. "Now don't do anything stupid."

The soldier turned his head slowly as the other slid a hand toward his musket.
"I said, don't do anything stupid," Wade repeated more forcefully. The other
soldier relaxed and dragged his hand back. "I just rode in from Rome," Wade
said, rising to his knees. "My name is Wade. I'm a lieutenant colonel in the
Union army. I have to get across the river to our lines. You, the one with the
death wish, go over to that camp and get me an escort." The man rose apprehensively and backed out of the light. "You," Wade said to the other man, "I'll
trade you this pistol for something to eat and a little of your fire." He loosened his grip and flipped the handle toward the soldier.

After a few minutes, the second soldier returned with four other men, their
muskets leveled, trailing close behind. "That's him, Sergeant," said the messenger.
"Waltzed in here bold as you please and stuck a pistol in Augie's back. Said
he wanted to surrender, he did."

Without turning away from the fire, Wade continued munching on some
hardtack. "Any of you men got a blanket I can borrow? I'm freezing."

Moments later, a lieutenant ran forward. "Is this the man?" he inquired.

"Yes, sir," said the sergeant, pointing. "He's a cool one, he is."

The lieutenant pointed his pistol at Wade and motioned with the barrel.
"Get up, soldier!" he commanded nervously.

Wade patted the shoulder of the man seated next to him. "Thanks for the cracker, soldier." No one offered him a blanket.

An hour later, the small party had crossed the northbound leg of the river and was marching toward the headquarters of Brig. Gen. Richard Johnson, commander of 2d Division, XX Corps. Some kind soul on the ferry had draped a threadbare blanket over Wade's shoulders, and he pulled it tightly across his chest as he stooped to enter the general's tent. As Wade straightened his shoulders, he pulled his arm free of the blanket and saluted. "Lieutenant Colonel Samuel Wade reporting, sir."

The general raised his head and flinched at the sight of Wade. He examined him closely from head to foot. "Where did this man come from, Lieutenant?"

The officer cleared his throat. His voice broke as he tried to speak. He coughed. "Well, sir, he sort of—ah—surrendered himself, General."

The general glanced up at his aide. The officer smiled faintly and shrugged.

"Colonel Wade. I've heard that name before," said the general.

"Yes, sir," replied Wade. "I got here shortly before the battle last month. I was Colonel Rose's exec until the Rebs captured him."

"Hmmm," said Johnson. He motioned to his aide, who leaned forward so the general could whisper in his ear. The aide rose to attention, saluted, and moved quickly out of the tent. "Have a chair, Colonel. This may take a while. Have you had any supper?"

"Just a piece of hardtack, sir."

"Lieutenant," Johnson said, "go to my sleeping quarters in the next tent. There's a table with some food on it. Fix the colonel a plate and bring it here. Coffee, Colonel Wade?"

"I've dreamed of coffee, General. Thank you."

"After you bring the plate, please return to your unit." The lieutenant saluted.

"And, Lieutenant." The man froze, then turned.

"You did well, son."

Wade had just finished eating when the aide returned. He carried a bundle of clothing in his arms. A worn pair of boots rested precariously on the top of the pile. He placed the bundle on a small, unstable folding chair. "About five-nine, aren't you, Colonel?"

"That's close enough."

"Here's some long johns."

"Do you mind, General?" Wade held up the underwear.

"By all means, Colonel. I'm getting cold just watching you shiver."

Wade stripped and slipped into the underwear. "My God, that feels good. Pardon me, sir."

Johnson laughed. "You remind me of a prune, Colonel." He motioned toward the aide. "Is he here?"

"Right outside, sir."

Johnson nodded. "Bring him in."

Wade pulled on the worn trousers and shirt. "Thank you for the dry clothes, General. These fit better than the ones I lost."

A second officer stepped into the tent and saluted.

"Turn around so this man can see your face, Colonel." Wade turned and looked into the officer's eyes.

"Major Shead, do you know this man?" asked Johnson.

"Yes, sir. He's Lieutenant Colonel Samuel Wade." He smiled. "He's a bit wetter than when last I saw him."

"He's the same man you told me about?"

"Yes, sir. The last I saw of the colonel, his horse had collapsed under him. Right after that, Longstreet's men rolled over us. I never saw Colonel Wade again."

"Congratulations on your promotion, Major," Wade said.

"Thank you, Colonel."

"Thank *you*, Major. You are dismissed." Johnson looked sternly at Wade. "Where have you been, Colonel? You've been listed as missing for more than a month."

"Sorry, sir. It's a long story."

"I have all night, Colonel. Start from the beginning."

"Care for a touch of whiskey?" asked Johnson as Wade relaxed. "That's quite a story."

"Thank you, General. I'll have a sip. Then with your permission, sir, I'd like to get a few hours' sleep. I'll telegraph General Washburn in the morning and get my assignment."

"You *have* an assignment, Colonel, with the 77th Pennsylvania."

"I realize that, sir, but in light of what I've learned, General Washburn may have other ideas."

Johnson poured the glasses full. "This is the last of it, Colonel. Sip easily."

Wade nodded appreciatively. "Yes, sir. Thank you, sir." He touched the glass to his lips. They sat in silence for a few moments, enjoying the liquor.

"I know General Washburn, Colonel," Johnson said finally, "as well as his brother the congressman. If you don't mind granting me the privilege of reviewing your communications with the general, I suppose there's no harm in seeing where this leads."

"It would be my pleasure, sir."

"How's that whiskey, Colonel?"

"Excellent, sir." Wade drained the glass. "Now, if the general will excuse me, it's been a long day."

"Good night, Colonel. My aide will find you quarters."
Wade set his glass on the rickety table, rose wearily, and saluted.

Wade arrived at the telegraph room at seven. He prepared the first message and made himself a copy. He would need a record for General Johnson. He handed one copy to the telegrapher.

HAVE UNCOVERED A MATTER WHICH REQUIRES YOUR URGENT ATTENTION STOP I FEEL THIS MATTER MUST BE REPORTED ON IN PERSON STOP PLEASE RESPOND STOP

Three hours later, Wade received the reply.

WHERE HAVE YOU BEEN STOP WE HAVE BEEN SEARCHING FOR YOU FOR A MONTH STOP PLEASED YOU ARE ALIVE STOP A MESSAGE WILL FOLLOW FROM COL THOMPSON STOP HE HAS NEWS STOP

Eight minutes passed before Thompson's message arrived.

WELCOME BACK TO THE FOLD STOP RECEIVED MESSAGE ONLY YESTERDAY STOP YOUR BROTHER IS IN LIBBY PRISON STOP YOUR FRIEND R SENT WORD STOP HE IS THERE TOO STOP WHAT NEXT STOP

Wade folded both messages and stuck them in his pocket. His anxiety rose as he hastily scribbled a reply.

THANK YOU FOR YOUR EFFORTS STOP MUST RETURN TO WASHINGTON STOP CLINTON STILL IN GEORGIA STOP MUST FIRST GET HIM OUT STOP NEED YOUR ASSISTANCE STOP REQUEST THAT GEN WASHBURN SECURE TRANSFERS FOR US STOP PLEASE REPLY SOONEST STOP

He paced anxiously as he waited. I need to be three places at once, he thought, and none of them is here.
"Beggin' your pardon, Colonel," said the telegrapher, "but you're drivin' me crazy pacin' back an' forth like that. Go on out an' get some air, sir. I'll call you when I receive the reply."
Wade nodded. "I won't be far."
"Gotcha, Colonel."

Wade walked to the end of the block, then returned. He stuck his head inside the door.

"Nothin' yet, Colonel. Only 'bout five minutes have gone by."

Wade nodded. I'm a pain in the ass, he thought. He would need a horse soon. He sloshed toward the stables two blocks west. Mangy bunch of nags, he thought. He would need a horse with CSA markings. He walked around the corral but saw none. He pulled out his watch, then headed back to the telegraph building. He got there in time to see the telegrapher stick his head out the door.

"Message comin' in, Colonel," shouted the clerk.

Wade rushed inside. The clerk wrote the last word and handed the flimsy to Wade.

WORKING ON DETAILS STOP CAN YOU CONVEY URGENT MATTER BY WIRE STOP

Wade wrote the reply and handed it to the telegrapher:

NO STOP WILL AWAIT YOUR REPLY STOP

"You must have somethin' real important goin' on, Colonel, if you'll excuse my sayin' so. I go off duty in a few minutes. I'll tell my relief t'watch for the reply t'this message. Why don't y'get somethin' t'eat an' come back this afternoon?" He turned and began tapping the key.

"Sounds like a good idea, Corporal. Thanks for your concern."

"Don't mention it, Colonel," the man said without missing a tap.

Torn between joy and fear, Wade walked into the crisp, late morning air. Libby, he thought. Can Simon survive there? How long do I have? He had no doubt of the accuracy of Thompson's message. Knowing that Rose—he at least assumed the "friend" was Rose—had been sent to Libby was favorable news, of a sort. Rose had all the qualities of a leader. He knew men. If anyone could keep Simon alive, Rose would. His speed in getting a message to Thompson—in spite of what must have been challenging obstacles—confirmed the man's resourcefulness and initiative. Now Wade faced his own challenge, one requiring him to resist one of the strongest elements of his own nature: he must be patient and wait. He yearned for the more straightforward elements of war. How much simpler life would be if I had command of a regiment, he thought. Then I'd know the enemy. No confusion, no uncertainty—just win or lose on the field of battle, doing what West Point trained me for.

As he stepped onto the muddy street, he heard his name.

"Samuel? My God, I've been looking high and low for you."

Wade turned at the sound. "Is that you, David?" He flashed a grin.

"In the flesh," replied David Healy Jr. "Where have you been? Colonel Thompson sent me here to search for you. I'd reached a dead end and planned on returning to Washington tomorrow."

"It's a long story, David. How's your father?"

"Bored, Sam. The war's reached a standstill in the East."

"I don't suppose you'd know where a man could get a thick, juicy steak around here?"

Healy laughed. "There hasn't been a steak around here in more than a month. Grant opened the trail for resupply only two days ago. I know where there's some fish, though. A young quartermaster captain I met knows a thing or two about fishing. Care to join us?"

"Are you sure it's okay?"

"Oh, there's plenty. It'll only spoil if we don't eat it. I'm on my way there now. Come along and tell me what happened to you."

"Very well, but I must be back at the telegraph office in an hour or so."

Following lunch, Wade leaned back and patted his stomach. "Captain Hughes, permit me to commend you. I never ate a better plate of fish in my life. Fried to perfection. All that's missing is a bit of brandy."

"Thank you, sir. Come around tomorrow and I may have another one." He wrinkled his nose. "This one was rather puny. Only about two pounds dressed weight. I can't help with the brandy, though. Sorry. Perhaps after we take Atlanta."

"You may have a long dry spell, Captain."

"I don't know, sir. Word is that General Grant plans to break out in a couple of weeks, soon as Sherman arrives and we're fully resupplied."

"You're a quartermaster, Captain. What are the chances of getting me a couple of good horses with Confederate brands?"

"Could probably be arranged. When do you need them?"

"Can't say. I'm waiting for a change in orders. Day or two, I reckon."

Wade stood and patted his stomach again. "Thanks for the fish, Captain. I must return to the telegraph office. Can we meet later, David?"

"I'll be here, Sam. Now that I've found you, I'm without a job. Will you ask Colonel Thompson what my instructions are?"

"Consider it done."

Wade arrived at the telegraph office at a quarter past one. A new telegrapher sat at the key. "Do you have a message for me? Name's Wade."

"Came in a few minutes ago, Colonel. Here y'go, sir." He handed Wade the message. Wade unfolded the flimsy. It was from Thompson.

UNDERSTAND YOU MUST FETCH COMPANION STOP ORDERS RELIEVING YOU BOTH ARE BEING PREPARED STOP WILL BE

SENT TO GENS JOHNSON AND SHERIDAN BY TOMORROW
STOP CANNOT PROVIDE FURTHER ASSISTANCE STOP YOU
ARE ON YOUR OWN STOP REPORT HERE WHEN MISSION
COMPLETE STOP

Wade nodded his approval and then wrote his last message:

RAN ACROSS LT HEALY THIS MORNING STOP REQUEST YOU
ASSIGN HIM TO ME STOP WILL TAKE HIM WITH ME STOP
THAT IS ALL THE ASSISTANCE I NEED STOP

It's time to report in to General Johnson, Wade thought as he inserted the last message into his pocket. I need to get the captain working on those horses while I'm at it.

Wade stood in the shadows of the dilapidated bar. Before heading for Chattanooga, he had instructed Clinton to come here each day at noon beginning a week after he left Rome. He pulled out his watch. Ten minutes until noon.
"Think he'll show?" asked Healy.
"He'll show. Any problem getting the horses shod?"
"None, other than it cost a fortune. Confederate currency will be worthless in six months."
"We're watching a fading cause, David. The value of money always drops first." Wade turned toward the sound of footsteps. "I think that's him coming now. Stay in the shadows until he gets closer."
Clinton glanced over his shoulder as he approached the bar. He bent and pulled a chunk of mud from his boot, glanced around again, then leaned against the corner of the building.
"Do you have a horse handy, Jim?" asked Wade softly.
Clinton stiffened, then relaxed. "Thought you wouldn't return, Sam. Never thought I'd say so again, but it's been gettin' borin' 'round here. Are we comin' back?"
"Not this year."
"Then I'll have t'steal a better horse. Mine's skin an' bones. Sound mounts are gettin' rather scarce."
Wade nodded, then said, "You remember Lieutenant Healy, don't you?"
"Sure, Sam. How are you, Lieutenant? How'd the colonel drag y'into this mess?"
Healy saluted. "I got lucky, Major. I'm well, and you, sir?"
"I'll tell y'when I'm back amongst blue uniforms."

*       *       *

Conditions in Rome, Georgia, had deteriorated visibly in the short time Wade had been away, and winter loomed barely six weeks distant. Every week, on average, another store closed for want of wares to sell. The last of the three ferries that had served the town had developed a leak ten days earlier. As the townspeople watched nostalgically, the weathered boat had settled to the bottom by its dock.

The Southern people were confronted with an onerous decision, just one of many that placed in doubt the prospects for their survival as a nation. In recent weeks, much of the livestock had been unceremoniously confiscated for military purposes. Only through desperate action did any remain: as word of the approaching Southern raiders flashed from farm to farm, horses and mules had been spirited away to the deep forest and hidden in the winding draws and craggy gullies. Most of their owners knew that they were only delaying the inevitable. As the north winds grew chillier, the farmers collectively sensed a dreary future. The war, which until then had been largely an eastern affair, had turned on them. The theft—none saw another name for it, for they received no payment—of the principal means of their livelihood steadily dulled their patriotism. More to the point, without animals to pull the plows, fields lay fallow. Without planted fields to provide feed for the rapidly dwindling herds, the circle of despair would tighten.

The trip from Rome by Wade and his companions had required twice the expected time. The stolen horses had tired quickly from a prolonged period of short rations. Three miles west of the plantation, the men dismounted and led their gaunt animals alongside the waterlogged road. They found themselves uncomfortably close to Southern troops. It seemed that General Thornton had led an advance across the Georgia border five days earlier. His men had made camp recently in the woods along the road. The anxiety of Wade and his companions grew more intense as they strolled uneasily toward the lane leading up to the plantation turnoff.

"There must be at least two regiments," Clinton whispered to Wade.

"More like a division," Wade replied softly.

"Wonder where they came from?" commented Healy.

"They're militia troops from Alabama," said Clinton, shaking his head. "Look at 'em. Some of 'em still have converted flintlocks. Wait 'til Colonel Wilder's horse infantry crashes down on 'em with those new repeatin' rifles. That'll sap their enthusiasm in a hurry."

"My brother is with Wilder," said Healy. "He says those rifles will end war forever."

Clinton and Wade glanced at each other skeptically. "No chance of that, David," said Wade. "They'll just hike up the casualty count."

Wade led his horse to where a knot of men squatted around a fire. "What unit are you men with?" he asked.

"First Regiment, Alabama Militia," replied a sergeant proudly.

"You're part of General Thornton's command?"

"None other. We've been waitin' nigh onta two whole years t'get those damn Yankees inta our sights. We'll show 'em what fightin's all about."

As Wade returned to the road, he leaned toward Clinton. "More likely they'll show them how fast an Alabaman can run," he whispered. "You know what this means, don't you?"

"Yeah, Sam. It means we'll be stayin' a spell."

"It's necessary, Jim."

"I know, but that doesn't mean I have t'like it."

Wade handed his reins to Healy and strolled casually toward another campsite. "Anyone know where General Thornton might be?"

"Where else, Colonel?" replied a corporal. "He's joned t'other of'cers down at the plantation house. Seen him gallop by a couple a hours afore sundown."

"Much obliged, Corporal." Wade resisted the urge to ask if they had anything extra to eat. Their frail frames needed every mouthful.

"Change in plans," Wade said as he drew alongside the others. "We'll camp in the woods south of the summerhouse. I need time to think—and I don't need any distractions."

"I can't imagine what'd distract you at the plantation house," Clinton responded with a sly smile.

Bathed in the soft light of a lantern, Maj. Gen. Henry Thornton conversed with two younger officers a few feet beyond the summerhouse's front door. Their gestures became animated at times, signaling their disagreement. Several minutes passed before the youngest of the three saluted and strode briskly toward his mount. The remaining two talked quietly for a few minutes more; then the second officer saluted and followed the first. Thornton stood alone for a moment, then turned into the darkness and strolled leisurely through the dew-laden grass.

With hands clasped behind his back, his head slightly bowed, Thornton was thinking of his wife, Victoria, as he eased up the slight grade toward the solitary giant oak that grew on the knoll. But only briefly did he manage to embrace Victoria in his mind. For weeks now, hope had been slipping from his grasp with agonizing deliberateness. To preserve his peace of mind, he had mastered the art of self-delusion, a mental state that increasingly pervaded the Confederate high command.

Nothing in his disposition counseled acceptance of fate as the master of man's destiny. It seemed that God somehow had decided to have sport with him, to let the war drag on until all that he had known of beauty and contentment was ruined. With Grant now in Chattanooga, he realized that the war soon would take another turn for the worse. He wondered how many more such turns the South could endure. He suspected that the answer was few. Union forces were closing in from three sides. He already regretted his decision to go along with the hopeless conspiracy. Realizing he had been used, he clung to the only redeeming rationalization—that the war had been responsible for propelling him grimly, if hesitatingly, toward this desperate, last-gasp attempt to ensure the South's survival.

Thornton stopped next to the trunk of the majestic old tree. As a thick cloud slid across the quarter moon, he leaned forward, head bowed, and sighed. A firm pressure against his spine was the first indication that someone had drawn near. He instantly sensed the malevolent nature of the pressure, the need for apprehension confirmed by the sound of a pistol cocking. He considered a variety of actions, but in the end remained motionless.

"Your present position is just fine, General. Just remain calm and nothing will happen." The whispered voice was clear and crisp in the still night air.

My God, thought Thornton, it's Simon! One does not forget the sound of a son's voice. But just as surely as he recognized the voice, he also knew that his mind had manipulated his hopes again. "I'm going to turn," he said calmly, reluctantly. "If you feel you must shoot, you'd be doing me a favor." He sighed, then let his weight shift slightly backward as he lowered his arms. He turned awkwardly in the calf-high grass. The surprised expression froze on his face as he peered into the eyes of the bearded young man. Common sense rejected what his senses wanted to make him believe. But it had to be . . . "Samuel?"

"Why not Simon? Would it surprise you to see your son standing here?" asked Wade.

"Yes," Thornton replied, "if he were holding a gun to my spine."

"Walk to the other side of the tree, General. I want to talk to you in private."

Thornton complied, then asked, "What are you doing here?"

"I've been waiting a lifetime to speak with you, sir."

"Whatever for?"

"You don't know, do you?"

"Know what?"

"I'll tell you later. Did you know my father?"

"No, I never met him."

"But you knew who he was—what he was?"

"For the most part, yes, I knew. I hated him for what he did to your mother and your aunt."

"So, Victoria did tell you about that night."

"Yes, but not until years later."

"Did she tell you who saved her life?"

"She said one of Caroline's farmhands rescued them."

Wade shook his head. "Untrue, General. They aren't visible from here, but off behind that stand of trees at your left are two men, among the most important people in my life. One is a young lieutenant. He's my recently acquired stepbrother. He's an intellectual young fool who still thinks this war is some grand and glorious adventure. We know better, don't we, sir? The second is a slice of fine Southern stock, born no more than a half-dozen miles from here. Unfortunately for your side, he's a major in the Union army now. He has a clearer understanding than anyone I know of the meaning behind this damnable war. There is a third man among those whose relationships I treasure most. He's an eighteen-year-old soldier in the Union army. He's what this war is all about. Coincidentally, he's the son of the man who saved your wife and my mother. His name is Washington Petree. His father, Jefferson, died a few years back. Remember him? He was the slave who accompanied your wife on that visit. At my mother's request, Victoria returned to Alabama without him."

Thornton sighed. "I knew of Jefferson's devotion to my wife. That's why I sent him with her that summer. What I don't understand is, why did she decide to keep that part from me?"

"I'm sure she had her reasons. I suspect that she withheld much of the story. Tell me, sir, if I had the power to grant you only one wish right now, what would it be?"

Thornton smiled at the irony of a Northerner asking that question. "I have so many, young man. I wish that this war would end—that much is certain. I wish that you and your people would leave us in peace." He hesitated. "No, more than anything, I'd ask for my son's safe return."

"You amaze me, General. I expected you to be different. I see I have misjudged you. You have just defined the essence of Western philosophy: we start with futile yearnings for the world and invariably return to the only elements in life that are important—the flesh of our flesh. Yet, knowing that, you and so many like you have sent your sons to war, possibly to die, for something as vile as slavery." Wade had an insatiable need to understand this man, to peer into the deepest recesses of his mind. Had his natural mother been correct in her assessment of him—judging him publicly as shallow and superstitious, a man willing to reject a son for so trivial a flaw as a birthmark? He doubted that. He always had. Still, Wade had a gnawing urge to provoke Thornton, to anger him, to test his character. But what would that require? He seemed so calm, so controlled. "What would you be willing to sacrifice to get your son back?" Wade finally inquired.

"Anything," Thornton replied without hesitation.

"Your own life?"

"If I could see him, confirm his safety, yes." He drew a deep breath. "Where is this leading, Samuel?"

"Be patient, sir." He decided to try another tack. "Did you have Judge Wade killed?"

My God, thought Thornton, how can I answer such a question? "Why would I do that?"

"Just answer the question. I know what he plotted for my mother and your wife. Did he order my mother's abduction?"

"So far as I could determine at the time, he did," Thornton replied firmly.

"And you had him killed for that, didn't you?"

Thornton stepped back. "That's an unfair question, Samuel, with you holding a gun pointed at my chest."

"Trust me, sir, I won't shoot you, regardless of your answer." He waited in silence.

"Very well then, yes, I had him killed." Thornton hesitated before adding, "My only regrets are that I delayed so long and that the man I sent to carry out my order never returned."

"I have the power to grant your wish," said Wade, suddenly changing the subject.

"What? How? Is Simon alive?" The facade of control faltered. "Have you seen him?"

"No, sir, but I have been in contact with those who have."

The guise of restraint faded completely. "Where is he? Is he well?" Thornton instinctively reached out to Wade.

Wade retreated two steps. "I wouldn't say he's well, but he's alive. For how long, I can't say. As for where he is, I'll keep that to myself. I'm going to test you, General. This test will have difficult answers." He lowered the gun. "Let's go for a walk down the hill. I'd like you to meet my companions."

They strolled for a while in silence, Thornton with his hands clasped behind his back, Wade with the pistol dangling at his left side. With the general's fifty-pound advantage, he could have disarmed Wade with minimal effort. Wade sensed no urgency for such drastic action. They approached the trees. Even in the faint light, the forms of the other men stood out against the darker rise beyond the stream. Both men held carbines propped against trees, their barrels pointed at Thornton.

Thornton yielded to his curiosity. "What's the test, Samuel?"

"I'm aware of your conspiracy to kill President Lincoln, General."

Thornton stopped abruptly, then turned toward Wade. Despite the increased risk, disarming him suddenly seemed a more attractive option.

Wade smirked and added, "It's a real dilemma, isn't it, sir?"

"You're speaking in riddles. What's a dilemma?"

"You were wondering if you should try for my gun."

"You're mother raised a perceptive son. Yes, I suppose the thought crossed my mind."

"Why did you hesitate?"

"Because of what you said about Simon."

"Very good, General. You passed the first part of the test. Now for the more difficult part. I'll make a trade with you, a life for a life. I'll bring you your son. In return, you will tell me everything you know about the conspiracy. More than that, you will help in any way I ask to foil the plot."

"What makes you think I know anything about such a plot?"

"Simple, General, because you were considering the risk of taking this gun from me. You didn't object, you didn't feign surprise, you simply considered the more direct solution to the problem. But, then, I already knew of your involvement. So let's stop wasting time. What is your answer?"

Thornton shook his head. "I can't make such a promise."

"Then you have lost two sons this day."

"What do you mean? I have only a son and daughter."

"No, *Father,* you have *two* sons. Your wife gave birth to triplets—identical twin boys and a girl. She had to give *me* to her twin sister. It's quite an interesting story. You'll have to ask Victoria about it. I don't have the time to explain the details." Wade slid the pistol into its holster, turned his back on Thornton, and walked toward the trees. Five yards away, he turned back. "I'll bring Simon to you, but not because I have any desire to fulfill your wish. I'll do it because he's my identical twin. I almost killed him at Gettysburg. I've slept poorly ever since. I guess it's as much for me as anything. But mostly it's for Caroline. She found Simon at the edge of death that night after the battle and convinced General Meade that he should let her nurse your son back to health. She saved his life. I figure that evens things. She took one of your sons, and now I'll give back to you the one she saved. Is that fair enough?"

"And the other?" asked Thornton quietly.

"Other what?"

"My other son. Is *he* lost to me forever?"

Wade moved a few steps closer. "I don't know. I oppose nearly everything you believe in. I need more time to be able to accept what I've only recently learned. But no purpose of this damnable war will be served with Simon's death, so I'll bring him to you. That's all I know to do for now."

Thornton paused before responding. The shock of learning that Sam Wade was his own flesh and blood had yet to sink in. Just as important as the revelation of their paternal kinship was the fact that Thornton's newfound son had forced him to confront his deepest values. He was being given a way out of this impossible assassination scheme, a chance to redeem his honor, if only he had the courage to act. He *had* to take it. "What do you want to know?"

"Does that mean what I think?" Wade asked. "You're going to help me?"

"If possible. I know far less than you probably suspect, but I'll provide whatever assistance I can—short of betraying my friends."

"And who are these friends?"

"A few men from around here—Arthur Bowman and others. They know even less than I do. But the men behind the plan are wealthy Northerners with plenty of money. What information do you need?"

"We'll get into that." Northerners? That complicates things even more, Wade thought, but I should have guessed. They want to pluck the South and know that Lincoln will stop them. Did he have enough time to implement the whole plan?

Wade had considered simply telling his father that Simon was in Libby Prison. It would be simple enough for a general to get him out. But just as his father had faced a dilemma earlier, Wade faced one now. Trust comes with difficulty, and Wade had no guarantee that he could trust his father. Nothing Thornton could say at this stage of their relationship would guarantee that trust. For now, there were too many obstacles in the way, and the stakes were too high to yield to sentimentality. Lincoln had to be saved, so Wade had to do this the hard way and hope that the act would forge a bond between his father and him that no words ever could.

As Wade turned, he glanced toward the mansion. Only one window on the south side had a light shining—a second-story window near the left corner of the house. In it he saw the silhouetted figure of a woman. Can she see us? Wade wondered.

"Father, I need a small favor."

"What's that, Samuel?"

Wade pointed toward the lighted window. "Cathy Blair. *My* one wish is to marry her when this war ends. The problem is, she thinks I'm Simon."

"Why not simply tell her the truth?"

If only it were that simple, Wade thought. "There are complications. I can't handle more than one war at a time. When the subject comes up, as it inevitably will now that she's seen us together, will you confirm that I'm your son? It's not as though it'll be a lie."

Thornton nodded. I've known him for only a few minutes, he thought. How quickly lives become entangled. "I'll see what I can do, Samuel."

"Thank you, Father."

Wade leaned against the telegraph counter, pencil in hand. Best keep it short, he thought as he scribbled a message for Thompson.

LEAVING CHATTANOOGA TODAY STOP IF TRAIN ON SCHED-
ULE WE SHOULD ARRIVE IN FIVE DAYS STOP INFORM MY
MOTHER STOP

The clerk accepted the paper and tapped out the message.

Wade rubbed his rump, yearning for everlasting relief from sitting a horse. He pushed open the door and edged between Clinton and Healy, placing an arm around each of their shoulders. "Well, gentlemen, shall we go? It's a long way home."

From the diary of Caroline Wade-Healy

*November 19, 1863*

*This has been among the most memorable days of my life. I've heard so much about President Lincoln's rough language and homespun humor. Some even say he's a baboon being manipulated by those around him. I think not. I believe that no leader has ever been better placed to address the trials of his people. To-day, here at Gettysburg, he spoke the most beautiful words I've ever heard. I've never witnessed such a solemn occasion. Thousands were gathered to dedicate the new military cemetery. The local paper published a special one-page edition this evening. The editor said little about Mr. Everett's two-hour harangue; he recorded Lincoln's remarks in their entirety. I've read the words a dozen times and find that they are now etched in my mind. Perhaps for the first time we know the meaning behind this conflagration that is tormenting our nation.*

*This has been a doubly good day. A telegram arrived late this afternoon. Colonel Thompson informed me that Samuel will arrive in Washington this weekend. It's a blessing that he and his friend Major Clinton are out of Chattanooga. Rumors are flying that General Grant will attack the Confederates in the next few days. The newspaper editors have no shame. They report even the most minute details of our military plans. Our soldiers' lives are placed in jeopardy so that the papers can sell a few more copies. The price of freedom is high.*

*As pleased as I am to learn of Samuel's homecoming, I can't resist wondering. It must be important for Colonel Thompson to bring him home at such a critical time. Each turn of this war seems to place my son in danger again.*

*Still, I shall sleep peacefully this night.*

---

# CHAPTER

# 20

From the diary of Caroline Wade-Healy

*November 27, 1863*
*It seems that General Grant is our only true warrior. The account of the Battle of Missionary Ridge is uplifting. Our brave soldiers climbed up an eight-hundred-foot-high mountain and sent the rebels running, and all the while they were being fired on every foot of the way. It is reported that the men charged up that hill without orders. How does Grant inspire the men to such feats of bravery? Two months ago it appeared all was lost in the West, that the Confederates had recovered from the defeats at Vicksburg and Gettysburg. Now the rebel army seems all but destroyed.*

*How can the Confederacy withstand three such devastating defeats in less than five months? It seems to be turning into a war of attrition. Will we have to kill them all to bring this war to an end?*

*There are rumors that the president wants Grant transferred east to go after Lee. I suppose that is the only way we will find out how great a warrior Grant really is.*

*Now that winter is approaching, I suppose the war will be on hold for a while.*

*I still haven't heard from Samuel. He should have arrived in Washington already. I hope nothing is wrong.*

The three men strolled briskly into the warehouse and went straight to Thompson's office. Thompson heard them coming and met them at the door. "I'm glad you finally made it back," he said. "You're two days late. What caused the delay?"

Wade shook his head. "Our train was sidetracked so many times I lost count, sir."

"That's hardly surprising, Sam. Now that Grant has driven the rebels away from Chattanooga, every available transport will be shipping supplies for the push toward Atlanta."

"So I've heard," Wade replied. "Missionary Ridge comes about as close to being an impregnable natural fortress as I've ever seen. And the Rebs just broke and ran. It's difficult to believe."

"This is the beginning of the end, Sam. It's obvious that General Bragg lacked the resources to follow up his victory at Chickamauga. The South is scraping the bottom of the barrel just to keep its soldiers supplied with basic needs. A year from now, perhaps sooner, the end will be in sight. There's talk here of giving Grant command of the entire Union army."

"Doesn't surprise me. The man's about done it all."

Thompson motioned them into his office. "Have a seat while I get General Washburn."

"Gentlemen," said Washburn as he preceded Thompson into the office a few minutes later. Wade and his companions turned and started to rise but Washburn held up his hand and said, "Please, remain seated. How are you all doing?"

"Fine, General," they answered in unison.

"We're glad to be back, sir," Wade added.

Once they were all seated, Wade looked at Thompson and asked, "Have you given any thought to a plan to free Simon?"

"It's already in progress on that end. They're going to dig a tunnel. But there's time to discuss that later."

"Did you tell my mother I'd be in Washington tonight?" asked Wade.

"She's at Willard's Hotel. Your father's there, too, Lieutenant Healy." Thompson turned to Clinton. "You pulled it off again, Jim. You brought him back alive."

Clinton grinned. "Either I'm gettin' smarter, sir, or he's gettin' luckier."

"Unfortunately, there's still a long way to go." Thompson opened a cabinet. "I think this reunion calls for a little refreshment." He set a bottle and glasses on his desk and poured. "Gentlemen," he said after everyone had a glass, "a toast, to a speedy and successful end to this infernal war."

Thompson poured himself another drink and set the bottle in the middle of his desk. "Help yourselves, gentlemen." He gulped down the second glass of whiskey. "All right, Sam, what is this urgent problem that you were so reluctant to tell me about by telegram?"

Wade looked first at Washburn, then at Thompson. "There's an elaborate plot to kill President Lincoln and perhaps as many as a dozen other government officials."

Thompson flinched, then regained his composure. "Who told you that?"

"I first learned about it from a Southern woman—"

"Well, there you go," interrupted Thompson. "Probably wishful thinking."

"No, sir. It's much more involved than wishful thinking. Actually, she was adamantly opposed to the idea."

Thompson leaned forward. "Listen, Sam, this goes on all the time. This is the fifth conspiracy I've heard of in the last three months. The president and a dozen men! Do you have *any* idea what that would involve? My God, Sam, the president is under constant guard. He's been shot at twice in the last six months. Rumors of assassination plots flourished even before he took the oath of office."

"But sir—"

Thompson lifted his hand. "Forget it, Sam." He smiled unevenly and poured himself another drink. "Besides, it's not planned for tonight, is it?"

"No, sir. I really don't know when they plan to do it."

"Well, then, relax. You've earned it. Concentrate on rescuing Simon and leave politics to those who have time for it. Now, tell me about this woman you found. What's her name? Is she pretty?"

Wade glanced at Clinton, who shrugged. Wade realized he could do nothing more, but he refused to dismiss the plot that easily. "Do you mind if we discuss that tomorrow, sir? I'd like to say hello to my mother before she goes to bed."

"Of course, Sam. There'll be plenty of time to talk later. I'll keep Jim entertained while you go see her."

Wade rose and turned to Healy. "Do you want to come along, David?"

"Tell my father I'll be over shortly. I'd like to discuss my next assignment with Colonel Thompson while I'm here."

Wade nodded. "I'll tell him you'll be right along."

Ten minutes later, Wade arrived at Willard's. He asked for his mother's room number, then bounded up the hotel's main staircase. When he reached her room he paused to straighten his coat and brush the dust from his uniform before knocking.

The door opened. "Samuel." Caroline Healy's eyes lit up; then she pulled him toward her by his coat sleeve and kissed him on the cheek. "You look well. Southern cooking must agree with you."

"So Colonel Thompson has already told you what happened?"

"I had to apply a bit of pressure, but you know how persistent I am. Come in. David's here."

Wade stepped into the room as Caroline closed the door. Healy extended his hand. "How is it down there, Samuel?"

"The South is coming apart. . . ." He hesitated. "Congratulations, *General* Healy. I hadn't heard. Colonel Thompson neglected to mention your promotion."

"Just came through Congress yesterday. I doubt he knows."

"Oh, he knows, sir. Trust me, he knows. My guess is he isn't looking forward to—how shall I say this?—addressing you as a superior officer."

Healy chuckled. "He'll adjust." His smile faded and he added in a more serious tone, "Actually, Sam, there are many far more deserving. You, for instance."

"Me? A general? No thank you, sir. Generals have too much responsibility. I'm more of a loner. I've been with two different regiments, and those associations combined lasted less than a week." Wade turned to his mother. "Has Colonel Thompson told you about Simon and our plan to free him?"

Caroline's worried look revealed that she knew. "I ought to tell you to let it be, but I can't. I want Simon to live, Samuel, and he won't if he remains in that prison."

"I'd have gone after him even if you were opposed. Besides, I promised someone I'd do it."

"Who?"

"My father."

She recoiled in shock. "Your *father?* How could you promise him that?"

"It's a long story. At the time I was holding a gun on him, but it wasn't necessary."

"You actually *saw* General Thornton?"

"On a plantation east of Rome, Georgia. Exactly eleven days ago."

"Dare I ask? Why did you promise such a thing?"

"It's personal, Mother. I never kept anything from you before, but this must remain between my father and me."

She wanted to ask more, but resisted the temptation. His reasons must be sound, she thought. "When will you leave?"

"I haven't had an opportunity to discuss the details with Colonel Thompson yet." Wade glanced at his stepfather. "I'll want to take David Jr. with me when I go. We'll be discussing the plan in more detail soon—perhaps tomorrow." He looked back at Caroline. "Will you be here long?"

"Until the first of next week," she said. "Your stepfather is on leave until his new assignment comes through." She turned to her husband and smiled. "He's moving up to the army staff."

"Congratulations again, sir. If you'll excuse me, Mother, General, I'm very tired." He leaned forward and kissed Caroline on the cheek.

"Take care of David, Sam," Healy said as he stepped back. "Is he here?"

"Oh, I'm sorry, sir. His plan was to come here after he discussed his next assignment with Colonel Thompson. He's probably in the lobby waiting for me to leave. I'll send him up. I like that young man, General. He's done well."

"With someone like you to guide him, he has. You're his hero, you know."

"Well, he could have done much better in his selection, sir."

"I doubt it, Sam."

"Well, it's time I was going." Wade squeezed his mother's hand. "Good night, Mother."

She held his whiskered cheeks in her hands. "Go with God, Samuel."

"Thank you, Mother. Sir, may I talk with you for a moment—out in the hall?"

"Certainly." Healy followed Wade out the door and closed it behind him.

"Sir, what I have to say is highly confidential. May I rely on your discretion?"

"Of course, Sam. What is it?"

"While I was in Rome I got wind of a plot by Confederate business and political leaders and Northern businessmen to kill President Lincoln. I have reason to believe it's serious."

"How did you learn about it?" asked Healy.

"From several sources, sir. When I told Colonel Thompson about it, he seemed unconcerned. He told me there have been several threats on Lincoln's life, dating back to when the president first arrived in Washington."

Healy nodded. "He's correct. Even Lincoln has become more concerned of late. Security has been increased in the past several months."

"Then this information should increase Colonel Thompson's concern. I don't understand his dismissing it as though it were nothing more than idle gossip."

"Give it time to sink in, Sam. Perhaps he's preoccupied with other matters. Is there reason to believe the attempt is imminent?"

"No. Quite the opposite. I think the conspirators will be guided by political events. If Lincoln fails to get renominated, I don't expect anything to happen."

"Then my advice is to wait and see what develops. Discuss it with Jason later, when the opportunity presents itself."

"All right, sir, but I won't let it drop. And sir, I'd appreciate it if you wouldn't tell my mother about this."

Healy grasped Wade's arm. "Consider it our secret, Sam. It's so good to see you. Caroline has been worried sick with you being so far away."

"Yes, sir. She does worry about me. Well, good night, sir. I'll send David right up." He saluted.

Healy returned the gesture. "Good night, Sam. We'll talk more later."

Wade and Clinton sat on the edge of their beds at the temporary officers' barracks. "I don't know, Jim," Wade whispered. "Colonel Thompson's reaction to my information about the assassination plot is perplexing in the extreme."

"Why's that?"

"You heard him. He acted as if the idea had no credibility at all. He didn't even want to know the details. That's strange behavior for him. He's usually curious to a fault. His repudiation of something like that is totally out of character."

"Maybe he's right, Sam. If these rumors surface so often, he's prob'ly gotten tired of hearin' 'em. Besides, it's not his job."

"Then *whose* is it?"

"Confounds me, Sam. The way Lincoln rides 'round town, *anyone* could shoot him full of holes. It wouldn't take much of a plot if'n someone really wanted t'kill him."

"That may have been true before," said Wade, "but now he never goes out without an escort. It's obvious that there's more concern for his safety than there used to be."

"Well, Sam, you've done ever'thin' *you* could. Colonel Thompson's right 'bout one thing: we need t'concentrate on the task at hand. Have you given any thought t'where we're headin'?"

"Richmond, of course. Why?"

"I was just wonderin' how many people you'll run inta the first hour in that city who know y'have a death sentence hangin' over your head."

"I've tried to avoid thinking about that."

"Well, y'better *start* givin' it some thought. Y'can't go traipsin' 'round down there as if y'was on a holiday."

The sun had already set when the 45th U.S. Colored Infantry Regiment prepared to leave the firing range. The men had been there most of the day, and they were tired and hungry. Except for the white officers who led them, no more than two dozen of the eight hundred men could read and write proficiently. Those who could wore stripes on their sleeves. One of them was Sgt. Washington Petree, the ranking noncommissioned officer in a small, select company of sharpshooters under the command of 1st Lt. Frank Bixby. This had been their final day on the practice range, and the men were joking and boisterous as they waited for the regiment to form.

"The men did well today," Bixby said to Petree.

"Yes, sir. Every one of them can consistently hit a man-sized target at a hundred yards. I'd say they've earned a few days off."

"I agree, Sergeant Petree. I'll see about getting passes for the men."

"Sir, pardon me for asking, but . . ." He hesitated.

"Go ahead, Sergeant. What is it?"

"Sir, when do you suppose they'll let us do some fighting? The men are ready and eager to do their part."

"I know they are, Sergeant. These things take time."

"Yes, sir, I know. But it'd be a shame if all of this training went to waste. We can shoot Rebs as well as anybody else can."

"Patience, Sergeant. Your turn will come. It looks as if we're about ready to head back. Get the men settled down."

From the diary of Caroline Wade-Healy

*December 31, 1863*
*11:30 P.M.*
*What a lovely Christmas season this has been. Samuel and his friend Jim left by train for Washington this morning. I know it will be a long time before I see him again. It's a comfort knowing he has such a close friend. I know they look out for each other.*

*Samuel will be disappointed. He left without Cathy's picture. She is a lovely girl. Perhaps I will have grandchildren after all!*

*In a few minutes it will be 1864. I will close by wishing this year good-bye. And may there never be another with so much pain and suffering for our poor nation. It is with God's bountiful blessing that we are all alive to see the new year. May the same be true a year from now.*

# CHAPTER

# 21

Colonel Rose maneuvered the top stone, jiggling it carefully from side to side. The rock resisted movement at first, then slid unevenly forward. Major Andrew Hamilton grasped two corners, and together they lifted the heavy stone and placed it gingerly on the floor. Then they lifted a second rock and placed it on the floor next to the first. The removal of a third rock created an opening roughly twenty inches square. While they were removing the stones, another officer, Capt. Issac Johnston, scooped a handful of ashes from the hearth and let it sift through his fingers into a rusty can containing a half inch of water. He blended the mixture with a splinter from a beam until it formed a lumpy paste. When the rocks were replaced, he would use the mixture to fill the gaps around the edges. Only by close inspection could anyone distinguish the substance from the original mortar.

"I'm going down with the first shift," said Rose as he removed his shirt. "We have to find a way to dig faster. I want to see what's going on."

Even without an inspection, Rose knew the problem. The men were about played out. Despite that, or more probably because of it, every time a guard kicked a man or slammed him to the floor with a musket butt, the man demanded the next turn in the tunnel. The hole had become an obsession for others who had nothing else to cling to. Despite their hitting dirt as hard as granite, the tunnel had become their hope.

It brought tears to Rose's eyes to see these ashen, wasted men—nearly two hundred had volunteered and were sworn to secrecy—struggle against such long odds, with no promise of reward. He knew better than anyone that the probability of being detected was high. Even if they escaped, the chance of reaching Union lines was slim. Still they went in, where they had no room for maneuvering, where the air hung as heavy as lead after two minutes of digging. Working at arm's length, there was no way to get any leverage. The only option was to shave paper-thin layers of dirt with a chisel. During the past three days, each rotation of three men had barely filled a cigar box before they crawled out exhausted. Allowing for the time it took the men to get in and out, digging four pints of dirt required forty minutes.

Rose muttered to himself as he prepared for the descent. "When we began, I thought we'd reach the fifty-foot mark in three or four days." He looked at Hamilton. "What's it been now, twenty-five days?"

"Six, sir," replied Hamilton. "Twenty-six. Today's February second, and we're still ten feet short of our goal. I calculated it this morning. We've averaged less than eighteen inches a day. We dug ten feet during the first two days, but now we're down to less than a foot a day."

"Well, I'll take a look," Rose said, straining to pull himself into the narrow opening.

"You shouldn't go into that hole, Colonel. It's too risky. Leave that to a younger man. We had to pull three men out during the night shift. We nearly lost Colonel Hobart."

Rose glanced at Hamilton and grinned. "Are you saying I'm too fat, Andy?"

"No offense intended, sir, but it's a practical thing. The heavier you are, the more air you require and the more difficult it is to pull you out if something goes wrong."

"No offense taken, Andy."

The escape plan had evolved slowly. Rose had needed more time than he first realized to organize the tunneling efforts from within the prison. Hardly a man among the twelve hundred prisoners even approximated normal strength or endurance. The deplorable physical condition of many of the officers rendered their manual efforts ineffectual. Simply climbing down to the tunnel required physical strength and mental determination possessed by less than a fifth of the prisoners. Months of breathing stale, germ-laden air and eating only half rations had weakened everyone until even prolonged standing resulted in a malignant weariness that sapped the strength needed simply to think. If the men were confined much longer, many would lack the strength to escape. Rose believed that Thornton was approaching that stage in his confinement.

Rose grabbed a rock used for a handgrip and swung his legs into the opening. He slid his feet forward until his body lay horizontal and his back pressed flatly against the rough stone base of the hole. He had completed the second-worst part of this tedious exercise. Now he had to turn facedown and let his legs and torso descend into the darkness while he held onto the edge of the outer stone face. Once he was hanging vertically, Rose worked his way down the knotted, six-foot-long rope fastened by a hook to an oak rafter. The lower end dangled nine feet from the bottom of the shaft, for they had no more rope. Rose lowered himself until he was clinging by one hand and his feet were within about three feet of the floor. This was the worst part.

Several badly sprained ankles confirmed the hazard of making that three-foot drop into total darkness. He took a few deep breaths, thus preparing himself mentally before loosening his grip on the rope. No matter how many times one did this, the jolt resulting from abrupt contact with the floor never ceased to be a surprise.

Rose gasped for breath. The major's correct, he thought. I *am* too old for this—he had just turned thirty-four. But propriety demanded that he do his fair share.

He lit a match and held it to the candlewick. In the dim glow, he saw a second pair of legs slide through the hole in the mantle. Nine more men, eleven in all, would join the shift. Rose had concluded that, if the guards called for an unexpected head count, the others could cover for that many. To date, they had been lucky. Tunneling operations had always been shut down or in transition when surprise inspections were called. But Rose realized that time and fate were working against them. They had to finish the job and take their chances on the outside.

As the others made their descent, Rose moved closer to the tunnel opening. He leaned against the wall and waited as the men dropped down, one by one. When they were all at the base of the shaft, Rose lay on his chest and peered into the tunnel. Major Hamilton crowded in next to him. The tunnel, lit only by the dim candlelight, extended too far for them to see the end. "I'm going in," Rose said. He tied a handkerchief over his nose and mouth before sliding the length of his body into the narrow hole. The slow, slithering motion necessary for forward movement caused a powdery dust cloud to swirl up the inward-sloping sides and fold back toward the middle. A moving man thus encountered a constantly circulating barrier of dust. Even with the filtering cloth, Rose's breathing immediately became labored. He coughed. "This dust is the problem," he observed. "It has the consistency of talcum powder." He coughed again.

"What do you suggest, sir?" asked Hamilton from behind.

"Have you considered sprinkling some water on the floor? That should hold most of the dust in place." The time required for a man to move in and out of the tunnel had slowed the process more than all the other delays combined. If they could improvise a way to extend a man's time in the tunnel as much as four minutes, they could dig twice as fast.

"It's worth a try," said Hamilton.

Rose moved two body lengths into the hole before he looked back over his shoulder. "Have the men fan the air, Andy, the way they normally do it." As the tunnel had extended, forcing fresh air along its length had become the most difficult technical problem. Constant fanning of hats had been effective at first. Now, forcing fresh air forty feet into a hole little more than a foot across approached the impossible. Fatigue quickly diminished even this feeble effort. Maybe more men in rotation would reduce the fatigue factor. He'd have to think about that. "Are they ready?" asked Rose.

The men began fanning. Instantly, a dense cloud of dust swirled into the hole. "That's enough," said Rose. "It's a wonder anyone can stay in here for a minute, let alone three or four." He wriggled backward. "We have to get some water down here or we'll never finish."

"We'll get right on it, Colonel," said Hamilton.

Transporting the water proved to be a problem. They had no buckets—or anything else nonporous and transportable—within the prison compound. Again, the men resorted to what they had at hand: their hats. Although the process was slow and tedious, within two hours the tunnel floor was coated with a thin layer of mud. Rose watched as the first man slid into the tunnel. "It's a might muddy," said the young captain, "but the water cuts the dust. I think it'll work, sir."

Rose walked to the corner of the room and retrieved a warped wooden plank. He handed it to one of the men waving air into the tunnel from the base of the shaft. "Here," Rose said, "two of you men substitute this for your hats."

The change in tactics had immediate effect. "Hey," shouted the man, his voice muffled from thirty feet inside the tunnel, "I don't know what you're doin', but there's fresh air comin' back here."

Rose smiled. One of the officers patted him on the back. "Let's get this over with," Rose said. "I want to go out on the eighth—the ninth at the latest. Can we make it?"

"We just may now, sir," said Hamilton.

"Good. I'll see what we can devise to keep a steady supply of water coming down here. That's the key. Stick with it, men. Freedom is through ten feet of dirt."

Outside, large, fluffy snowflakes skittered through the frosty February air. In the six hours since sundown, nearly three inches had accumulated on the porch roof below the ice-encrusted windowpanes. Sitting stiffly next to a bedroom window in a darkened, two-story house, Wade pressed a pair of field glasses firmly to his eyes. He frequently lowered the glasses and wiped his sleeve across the frigid pane to clear an opening. The window provided the only direct line of sight across the intervening rooftops to the massive building nearly four hundred yards south. In between rubbing the window and blowing on his hands to stimulate circulation, he had studied every visible facet of the structure during the past forty minutes—as he had done a dozen times before during the past three weeks of mind-numbing boredom.

Slowly, methodically, he turned his head right, then left, then right again, panning the full length of the dark mass of Libby Prison that loomed menacingly against an even darker sky. From this angle, the structure completely blocked the view to the ice-laden James River, only a stone's throw away on the other side. Three days earlier an unusually bitter cold wave had washed over central Virginia. Soon afterward, the city's civilian population retreated into virtual hibernation. For the first time in the memory of many residents, the river's surface had frozen solid.

Wade shifted his attention from the prison to the ground outside the house. He familiarized himself with the landscape, with how it looked in the dark, with the barriers that might impede a hasty retreat. He made mental notes of alternate routes leading from the place where the prisoners would surface. Only one thing bothered him: it would be easy to track the escapees in fresh snow.

Except for one small glimmer, all of the prison lights had been extinguished. A single foot-square pane glowed next to the entrance. The guards used the small opening to visually identify those seeking entry. The door provided the only access from the street, and the guards methodically searched everyone who entered and exited. Except for Clinton. Wade watched as the door opened and light flooded the crystalline white surface outside. He saw a dark form walk into the deserted street, stand for a moment, then move silently through the snow toward Wade's window perch. That must be Jim, he decided.

Wade lowered the field glasses and sighed. So much can go wrong, he thought. He forced the uncertainty from his mind. Too much time makes the imagination run wild. Time had become the one commodity he possessed in abundance.

In the company of Clinton, Healy, Sergeant Willis, and six other enlisted men—all Southern born but battle-tested veterans from the Union cavalry— Wade had departed Washington before dawn on January 11. The evening before, a message had reached Thompson, informing him that the long-delayed tunneling had commenced five days earlier. Wade and his companions had been prepared for weeks. Aware of the chronic food shortage in Richmond, they had brought along a forty-day supply of provisions. Following five days of hard riding, circling wide around the fringe of the Confederate army, they had, at dusk on the sixteenth, arrived within sight of the Southern capital's outskirts.

While the others made camp in the trees, Clinton had ventured into the city in search of more permanent shelter. He had rented the small, furnished house for two thousand Confederate dollars a month and made arrangements for some firewood.

By the time Wade's group arrived, Rose had begun to mistrust the sutler, forcing Rose to consider an alternative means of communication. The problem had been solved more by accident than anything else. The sergeant in charge of the night watch had an expensive weakness for stud poker. During the day, when off duty, he often played in the back room of a nearby saloon. In Clinton's search for useful information, he, wearing a corporal's uniform, had wandered leisurely into the bar three days after arriving in Richmond. As he nursed a whiskey and watched the game, a private asked if he wanted a seat. Before long, the sergeant owed Clinton nearly a thousand Confederate dollars. The sergeant, hoping to win back his money, invited Clinton to join him and the other guards for a game inside the prison. A strained friendship had developed, giving Clinton virtually unobstructed nighttime access to the facility. Clinton thus unintentionally became the key to the operation.

Hardly any heat reached the second-story bedroom where Wade sat watching and waiting. With nothing of importance visible in the bleak darkness, he crept gingerly down the squeaky L-shaped staircase. As he descended, he blew on his stiff fingers. The others were huddled together around the stove, fast asleep. The sound of snoring filled the long, narrow room that had served as both sleeping quarters and parlor since their arrival. It's just as well they went to sleep early, thought Wade. Boredom and close confinement had made relationships contentious during the past few days.

The sound of muffled footsteps preceded Clinton's opening of the door. He stepped quickly into the small foyer, brushed the snow from his uniform, and shivered vigorously. "God!" he exclaimed. "It's colder'n a witch's teat out there."

"How did it go?" inquired Wade.

"I managed a few words with Major Hamilton," Clinton replied as he fumbled with the buttons on his coat. "He thinks they'll be ready tomorrow or the next day—the ninth at the latest"—he blew into his cupped hands—"provided the weather breaks. No better clad than they are, half of 'em will freeze t'death 'fore they walk a mile in this weather. There's one piece of good news, though. Rose says they've solved the dust problem. They're making good progress an' anglin' upward t'the surface now."

"Did the guards take the bribe?"

"Slick as the James River."

"The twenty thousand Confederate dollars was enough? That's a surprise."

"I had t'up the ante with five hundred in gold, split among 'em, but it's a bargain if'n it'll buy a few extra hours. But Rose has t'take them out by Tuesday. The guards rotate on the tenth."

"Any word on my brother?"

"I didn't see him, Sam, if that's what y'mean. But Hamilton says he's holdin' up fairly well. The men drew lots yesterday, so he had t'take his chances with the others. His number is thirty-three. Rose goes out first, followed by Hamilton and Johnston." Clinton draped his coat over a chair and made his way through the bodies to the stove. "There's a problem, though. There's this colonel—name of Streight—who outranks Rose. He's tryin' t'take charge. Rose thinks he might try t'break out 'fore ever'thin's ready."

"Is there any advantage in your trying to get more information in or out before the break?"

Clinton shook his head. "I doubt it. We've been instructed t'be on the alert each night at nine, startin' tomorrow. We can see enough from here t'know if'n the escape's in progress."

"How fast can they move through the tunnel?"

"It'll be slow. They have t'crawl on their bellies in single file. If we're ready t'move when the colonel comes out, we'll have plenty of time t'get there 'fore Simon makes it through."

Wade nodded. "I guess there's nothing to do now but wait." He thought for a moment, dreading to raise the next subject. "I've decided on a change of plans."

Clinton winced. "Isn't that risky at this late date?"

"No, I don't think so. It doesn't affect anyone but our group."

"What do y'have in mind, Sam?"

"Once we've got Simon, we'll come back here. I know we agreed earlier that if we rode north, the confusion would work to our advantage. But that's where the Rebs will concentrate their search. I think we'll have a better chance if we go south first. We'll hole up here for a couple of days—just long enough to let the tension subside—and then drift down to the railroad station and catch a southbound train. You'll need to check the schedule tomorrow. It's a straight shot to Wilmington, North Carolina. From there, we'll go to Atlanta, then circle up to Rome and on to Birmingham."

Clinton shook his head. "Colonel Thompson won't like that, Sam."

"With any luck he won't even know what happened 'til we're in Rome. Besides, our orders are discretionary."

"What's the advantage in that, Sam? If we skedaddle back t'Washington, then cut over t'Chattanooga, there won't be much Confederate territory Simon'll have t'cross t'get home. That seems safer t'me."

"Frankly, Jim, I've had doubts all along about Colonel Thompson's plan. Letting one of Thompson's spies smuggle Simon all the way from Chattanooga to Birmingham—that's well over a hundred miles—strikes me as rash. I'd rather escort Simon myself. Then I won't have to wonder if he made it. He's been in this hellhole for nearly half a year on quarter rations." Wade sat in a chair and leaned back against the wall. "I'll admit that I don't have everything worked out yet. We'll just have to assess conditions when we get to Rome. One thing's certain, though: I'm not turning Simon over to anyone else."

"Okay, Sam, but there's still the problem of us crossin' a thousand miles of enemy territory."

"The issue isn't the distance, it's what might happen during the journey. It's not reasonable to expect a total stranger to take the risks inherent in a trip to Birmingham. Simon won't be of much help in an emergency. Prison breaks a man's spirit, slows his reflexes. I had only one thing on my mind when I thought they were taking me to my execution. Let it be completed quickly and painlessly, I said to myself—and I was in prison for less than a month. Simon has been in Libby for six months. I have to consider this from his perspective. It'll be better for him to be with me than some spy of Thompson's."

A long silence ensued between them. Clinton trusted Wade's judgment—up to a point. The man seemed fearless when confronted with danger. But sometimes, when his passions came into conflict with his judgment, passion prevailed. Clinton sensed that this might be such a situation. "I know y'believe yours is the best choice, Sam, but tell me one thing—honestly now. It's not that y'just want t'see Cathy again, is it?"

Wade hesitated. Clinton's assessment was accurate, but only in part—and a small part at that. There had been too much time for thinking during the long, tediously monotonous days. Discontentment nurtured by idleness and mounting tension had distracted him from the task at hand, allowing concern about the assassination conspiracy to return to the forefront of his thoughts. More specifically, Thompson's cavalier dismissal of the plot increasingly distressed him. He had never doubted Thompson's high regard for the president. If possible, Thompson's concern for Lincoln's welfare had been proven greater than his own. Knowing this, Wade had even prepared himself for Thompson's insistence on a delay, before fully developing the escape plans. This seemed logical, since it would have allowed time for Wade to gather more information about the plot. Thornton wasn't going anyplace; the escape could wait—or so Wade's reasoning had suggested. Instead, Thompson had dismissed the plot as another harebrained Confederate scheme that had no chance of succeeding.

But where could Wade begin? Obviously he could not ask questions of those who would dance in the streets upon learning of Lincoln's untimely demise. General Thornton had added almost no information to that previously revealed by other sources. True, Wade now had a better understanding of some of the reasons behind the plot, but he was nowhere closer to learning when the attempt would be made. Thornton had, however, divulged the central element of the plot. Ten targets had been identified: the president, Secretaries Stanton and Chase, and the three senators and four congressmen who formed the Committee on the Conduct of the War. In Wade's mind, the grand scope of the plot only added to its credibility. Thompson had concluded precisely the opposite. "How in God's name," Thompson had asked him, "will the conspirators get all of those people together at one time?" That's a fair question, thought Wade. But still, if someone had thought of a way . . . He had thought about options for accomplishing such a grandiose task. Nothing seemed credible.

The cloak of secrecy seemed impenetrable. But that cloak, more than specific knowledge of an event that he passionately believed to be in the offing, had become the source of enduring anxiety, a problem that his agile mind
refused to displace for long.

"I'll admit that I would like to see Cathy again, Jim. But there's more to
it than that. I want to speak to my father again about the assassination plot.
Our chances of running across him are best if we travel this route." He walked
absentmindedly to the window, then turned. "That, and I personally want to
return Simon to his home, just as I promised. Then my conscience will be at
ease. There's one other thing, something I've never mentioned, not even to
you. I—"

"You want t'meet your natural mother."

Wade nodded. "How did you guess that?"

"Common sense."

Wade sighed. "This war's far from over, Jim, and I'm a soldier. There's
no assurance any of us will survive. This is a task I want to complete—have
to complete. Caroline would understand. I'll worry about the consequences
later." He returned to where the men lay sleeping. Looking in silence at the
forms sprawled about the room, he wondered how they had slept through the
discussion. "I see no sense in endangering the men. After things settle down,
I'll let you take them back to Washington."

"The hell you will!" Clinton exclaimed. Two of the sleeping men flinched
but didn't awaken. "Just the two of you, travelin' 'cross the width of the Deep
South? You'd never make it, Sam. Two men who look 'xactly alike—you'd
stick out like, well, y'know what I mean. These men may ride back if'n they
wish—Lieutenant Healy's sound enough t'lead 'em—but I'm comin' with ya."

Wade smiled. "Are you countermanding my order, Major?"

Clinton's face reddened. "Don't make me go back, Sam," he pleaded.

Wade patted his shoulder. "We'll see, Jim." Wade returned to the window. "It's stopped snowing." He tilted his head upward. "The moon's coming out. One way or the other, it won't be long now." He turned and looked
at Clinton, who stood facing him, his hands clasped behind his back. What,
Wade wondered, did I do to deserve such a friend? "Have we overlooked
anything, Jim?"

"Prob'ly. It seems we always do."

"Where are those captured Confederate order forms Colonel Thompson
gave us?"

"In my saddlebags, in the kitchen," replied Clinton.

"I'll talk to the men in the morning; then I'll decide who makes the trip
south. After that, have Lieutenant Healy fill out the forms. Tell him to forge
Secretary Seddon's signature. Colonel Thompson gave me a copy of the stamp
used to emboss his seal."

"I'll take care of it, Sam."

"Let's get some sleep, Jim."

"Sam?"

"What is it, Jim?"

"Thanks."

"For what?"

"For lettin' me tag along. Whatever happens from now on, I've had a high time this past fifteen months. It's been a real pleasure."

Wade stood speechless. He had placed Clinton's life in jeopardy more times than he dared to remember. "It *has* been interesting, hasn't it?" Wade finally muttered. He ought to say more, he knew, but what? "Good night, Jim."

"Good night, Sam. I'll see t'the orders after y'decide if any of the others're goin' with us."

"No, Colonel," said Healy, "I won't go back to Washington. If you're going to Birmingham, I'm going with you."

Wade extended his hand, the thumb and index finger almost touching. "Lieutenant," he said, "you are about this far away from a court-martial for insubordination. It's only out of respect for your father that I don't have you sent back in chains."

"Damnit, sir, you're going to the home of the woman I love. I must go with you."

Wade turned toward Clinton, asking him with his eyes for help persuading the impetuous young officer. "Beats me, Sam," Clinton said with a shrug. "I can't imagine *anyone* wantin' t'expose himself t'so much danger for the love of a woman." He grinned.

"You're no help," Wade replied, his anger softening. Clinton had recognized Wade's inconsistency.

"All right," Wade told Healy. "But I doubt we'll have to worry about you on the way back."

"What do you mean?" asked Healy, puzzled.

"After what you did to Nancy Caroline, she'll take one look at you and shoot you between the eyes."

"I'll take that chance," said Healy defiantly.

Nearly ten months has passed since the incident. Nancy Caroline no doubt had a more striking term for it. Healy had been inducted into the army for a single mission. His father was being sent to contact General Thornton. The stated reason was to purchase cotton; the unstated reason was to secure the release of Caroline Wade-Healy. She had been kidnapped several months earlier. No one knew where the rebels had hidden her. Thornton had refused to return Mrs. Healy, stating only that the matter had been removed from his control.

Young Healy's mission began where his father's failed. He had ridden to the Thornton plantation, guided by secret orders to find and release Caroline and transport her to Union lines. A less likely savior never existed. He had learned to ride a horse on the way to Thornton's headquarters, and learned how to load a pistol properly only months later. He had just one advantage: he knew Caroline's niece and namesake, Nancy Caroline Thornton. He knew her intimately. He had met her in Boston, where she attended a finishing school while he was at Harvard.

The general had been correct when he had stated that Mrs. Healy had been placed outside his control. Only upon arrival at the plantation had Healy Jr. precisely translated the meaning of this statement. Confronted with the fact of Caroline's absence, he had no options for a continuation of the search. Almost without thinking, he socked his former intended in the jaw, threw her into the back of a wagon, concealed her under some hay, and drove the team north. The abducted Nancy Caroline, together with Lt. Col. Simon Thornton, who had been captured months earlier, added weight to the Union demand for the release of Caroline and Samuel.

Young Healy and two hundred other observers had been at the misty glen at the time of the exchange. He had watched from where he sat uncomfortably on a large mare as Nancy Caroline had climbed from a covered wagon onto the rain-soaked trail. She had glanced at him briefly, her icy stare boring into his eyes. Across a space of eighty feet, her disdain for him had been obvious to everyone within sight of the star-crossed encounter.

He had no reason for believing that her attitude had changed. Still, he had to learn that for himself. It had been a long war. She must know by now that the South's cause is lost, he persuaded himself. Perhaps she's given thought to the remainder of her life. Perhaps her plans included him.

"I'll take the court-martial, Colonel, in exchange for the opportunity to see Nancy Caroline again. Please, Sam. I wake up in a cold sweat at night thinking about the suffering I caused her." He hesitated. "But I brought her north for a noble cause, don't you agree?"

"That's hitting below the belt, David," snapped Wade.

Healy stiffened and elevated his chin. "Yes, sir, it is."

Wade softened again. He respected his stepbrother's tenacity. He sighed gently and let his shoulders slump. "I won't have time to look after you, David. If anything happens to you, your father will kill me. I've often thought I might die in this war, but I'd prefer it not to be by a Union general's hand." He jabbed his finger at Healy. "Do I make myself clear?"

Healy smiled broadly. "Yes, *sir*. I'll do everything possible to stay alive."

"What about you others?" Wade asked, turning to face the enlisted men, who had stood listening, amused by the exchange.

"Let me see if I's got this straight," said Sergeant Willis. "It's either ride back to Washington on our own, through Lee's whole army, or take a train ride halfway across the Confederacy so's we can hobnob with a Reb general whose daughter wants to shoot the lieutenant here in the head. Is that our choice, sir?"

Wade shook his head and chuckled. "Doesn't sound very appealing, but that about sums it up."

"Well, I'll give you one thing, Colonel," added a corporal named Chapin, "your war's a heap more interestin' than the one I been fightin'. I think I'll tag along, if'n the colonel don't mind." He turned to Sergeant Willis. "What about you, Jack?"

Willis shrugged. "I have too much respect for Lee to go that way. Reckon I'm goin' on that train ride, Colonel."

"Good. What about you other men?" The murmurs and hesitant nods answered Wade's question.

"Then it's settled. We'll leave as soon as things calm down after the escape." Wade turned toward the corpsman. "Private Littlemore."

"Yes, Colonel?"

"I want you to bandage up my brother so it looks like he has a head wound. You'll stay near the whole time, understand?"

"Yes, sir." Littlemore waited a moment before adding, "Why don't I give all of you wounds, sir? It'll be less suspicious if you look like a bunch of wounded goin' home for a spell."

Wade turned to Clinton, who shrugged. "That's a fine idea. Where do you plan on scraping up the medical supplies?"

Littlemore grinned broadly. "I'll do it today, sir. I'll have no trouble makin' my way 'round. I'm from Florida, sir—more Southern than these damned Virginians ever dreamed of bein'. And thank you, sir, for havin' confidence in me."

"You just take care of my brother, Corporal, and everything will be fine."

Littlemore snapped to attention. "*Corporal,* sir?"

"That's correct, Corporal," Wade said with a serious expression and a sharp, official nod. "I'll have more confidence with a corporal in charge of this operation." He patted Littlemore on the shoulder. "Now, men, get everything packed except for two days' rations. If anything goes wrong, we must be prepared to move on a moment's notice. Don't make any loud noises—nothing that will attract attention. Be alert and everything will work as planned."

# CHAPTER

## 22

Three days and two nights passed without incident. On February 9, nearly a month after Wade and his companions had ridden south from Washington, a new moon and an overcast sky combined to make for an unusually dark night around Libby Prison. Wade sat at the window again, this time without the snow and frost-covered glass obstructing his view. A brisk, southerly wind had been blowing for the past eighteen hours. Most of the snow had melted. Now, mud presented a problem. Worse still, people moved more freely with the warm weather. Wade watched through field glasses as the guard changed at Libby. Clinton stood silently behind Wade, snapping his fingers nervously. There's so much activity, Wade thought.

"It'll be tonight," Clinton said confidently.

"I think you're right," Wade replied without lowering the glasses. "Is everything packed in case we have to move in a hurry?"

"Has been for three days, Sam. Frankly, I'd just as soon be headin' out tonight."

"I know, Jim." Suddenly alert, Wade leaned closer to the window. "Two men just sprinted across the street. I think that's the first of them." He waited a moment, then announced, "There goes another one." He let the glasses drop before he stood. The chair tipped and crashed backward to the floor. "Let's go."

They rushed down the stairs, the noise alerting the others. "This is it, men," instructed Wade. "Douse the lights. Check your weapons. Anything's possible from here on. Remember, after Major Clinton and I leave the house, you men move out in twenty-second intervals and take your posts. Be calm. Don't draw attention to yourselves. It should be over in less than an hour. If you think you've attracted attention, don't come directly back to the house. Move in a wide circle, until you're certain you aren't being followed." He took in a deep breath. "Let's get it over with." He instinctively drew his pistol and spun the chamber to ensure it was fully loaded. He eased the weapon back into its holster before turning, grabbing a sack and a pile of blankets, and striding rapidly to the door, Clinton a step behind.

Wade struggled to obey his own counsel; the urge to run nearly overwhelmed him. Clinton softly whistled a tune. Wade's anxiety subsided as he settled into a firm, steady gait. It took nearly ten minutes to cover the distance to the street in front of the prison. Wade stopped at the corner, looked both ways, then walked casually across the street to the fence. Two days earlier, Clinton had pried two adjacent boards nearly loose. Tonight he slid them back, and Wade stepped through the hole.

Colonel Rose turned with a start when he saw the two men. For a moment he thought the escape had been foiled before it had hardly begun. Then he recognized Wade. "How did you know we were coming out, Colonel?" asked Rose.

"We've been watching for you for three nights, sir. The problem is, if we noticed you, so could anyone else who happened to look this way."

"There's nothing we can do about that now."

"It's good to see you, sir. You've met Major Clinton."

"Yes. Thanks for your help, Major."

"Don't mention it, sir. I reckon it's been a rough four months for ya."

"I've spent better," sighed Rose. "I can hardly walk, what with this damned gout." He turned and looked toward the tunnel's exit. Men were climbing out at the rate of one every thirty seconds. "It'll be a few minutes before Colonel Thornton comes through. We'd better get back against the fence."

"At this rate, it'll take all night," said Wade.

"It's a marvel they can move this fast. That tunnel is barely big enough to wiggle through. We had no wood for shoring, so we had to keep it small."

"Where are you going from here, sir?" asked Wade.

"North. That's all I know. Some of us will get caught, that's for sure. But many will make it."

"Here, sir, I brought you a few blankets and a sack with some food. Sorry I couldn't bring more."

"Thanks, Sam. I'll distribute them."

"Sir, you're welcome to come with us. One more or less won't make much difference. We're going to hole up for a couple of days before I take Simon to Alabama."

"No, Sam, I promised some of the men I'd help them get through this. I've traveled this country before. That may give me an edge. Most of these men have had whatever nerve they had beaten out of them. But thank you just the same. Besides, the thought of going south doesn't strike my fancy."

"I understand, sir. What's that noise inside?"

Rose looked at the prison. "It's to cover the sound of our escape. The men who are staying behind are putting on a performance, a little music, a play, and just generally making a ruckus."

"Good idea, sir."

"Here comes Simon now," said Rose. "You better be on your way."

"Good luck, sir. I hope you all make it."

"Same to you, Sam. I give us a better chance than I give you." He glanced to his left. "Simon, over here. This is your twin brother."

Thornton crawled closer. He rose to his knees and looked into Wade's eyes. Neither man knew quite what to say to the other, so they said nothing. With tears running down his cheeks, Wade reached out and grasped Simon's arms. "We'll have time to talk later," he finally said. "Let's get you to our hiding place."

Simon Thornton sat at the kitchen table, stuffing himself with salt beef and canned peaches. A single candle flickered on the counter across the room. The other men were all in the parlor, some sleeping, others talking in low tones, waiting for the tension to subside. Everyone had made it back safely, with nothing unusual to report. Wade sat across the table, silently waiting for his brother to finish his first solid meal in nearly six months. Outside, all remained quiet, with no evidence that anyone had become aware of the prison break. Occasionally, the faint sound of music drifted into the house.

Finally, his hunger satisfied, Thornton pushed the plate aside. He leaned back and stared into his twin's eyes. "Why did you do this?" he finally asked. "You don't even know me. These men have risked their lives for a stranger."

"They're soldiers," replied Wade. "They're here because they were given the chance to perform an important mission. For most, it's a sort of a home-coming—they're all Southern born and bred."

"Is that how you explain *your* involvement, Samuel? We may be broth-ers—looking at you, I have to accept that as a fact—but we're also enemies."

"Fighting for different beliefs, perhaps, but we're not enemies. Wars have come and gone throughout history, but they always end. Eventually, con-ditions return to normal. I simply feel I'd like it best if we were both alive when this war ends. Besides . . ." Wade let the thought drop.

"You were about to say something?"

"It's not really important, just a bit of guilt. Everything that's happened to you during the past fifteen months has been my fault, one way or another. Colonel Thompson never should have sent you back. He did it to protect me, but he acted without my knowledge. He knew I never would have approved. I prefer to take care of myself." Wade rose and walked to the window. In the distance, two men dressed in ragged blue uniforms hurried uneasily across the yard of the next house. How many will make it? he wondered. "Then there's my mother." Wade turned toward Thornton. "She has quite an investment in you. She doesn't like wasted effort. In some respects, it seems she's made surviving this war a personal challenge. I suppose she'll do anything to have her family alive and safe when it ends. Like it or not, you're a part of her family, and she asked me to get you out of prison if possible."

Thornton nodded. "I owe her a great debt of gratitude. It's impossible to repay her."

"You've done that already, Simon. You're alive."

Wade's comment surprised Thornton. He should have known why his aunt had gone to such great effort to save his life. She was his mother's identical twin sister, and *his* mother would have done the same had circumstances been reversed. Now *his* twin had acted for the same reason. There was more than charity in what they had done for him, more even than love. To Caroline and Samuel, Simon's life was as precious as their own, and they would risk everything to save it. Were there words powerful enough to explain that, to make others understand, to make him understand? Perhaps one: family. More than conviction, higher than cause, greater than nation, family was unquestioning, enduring commitment, and let the devil assign the consequences. That was something to think about. "What do you plan to do with me?" Thornton finally asked. "Northern prisons are no better than Southern ones."

"I'm not going to return you to any prison." Wade went to the stove and poured a cup of coffee, then carried the steaming pot to the table. "I'm taking you back to Birmingham. I promised General Thornton I'd see you safely home. After that, you're on your own."

"You've met my father?"

"*Our* father," Wade said pointedly.

Thornton stared back numbly.

"Yes, we've met. It's a long story. We'll have plenty of time to talk about it on the way to your home." Wade yawned. "I don't know about you, but I'm tired. There's some bedding in the corner. When you're ready to go to sleep, just find a place on the floor and make yourself at home. We'll be staying here for a couple of days. Then we'll have a long train ride."

"I think I'll just sit here and drink some more coffee. I can't remember the last time I had real coffee. It's strange what you think about when you're locked up. I thought a lot about coffee and apples." He slid his hand across the table. Wade hesitated a moment before he clasped it in his own. "Thank you—Samuel," Thornton said quietly. A tear ran down his cheek.

Wade grinned nervously. "You owe me one, Simon. I plan to collect when the war's over."

Thornton nodded, his eyes overflowing.

Two weeks had passed since the escape. Every available Confederate unit had responded to the shock as reports spread that more than a hundred starving Union prisoners were on the loose in and around Richmond. Within two days a quarter of the prisoners had been rounded up. Wade had been correct in his assessment that it never would occur to anyone that the fugitives might go south. Even so, the frenzy of activity had convinced Wade that their chances would improve if they remained in seclusion longer than originally planned. By the fifth day, as the search expanded to the area north and east of the city, the tension in and around Richmond itself subsided. That evening, Wade and his companions—most of them in bandages—made their way casually to the railroad station. Prior to boarding, Clinton had heard someone comment that the number of recaptured Union escapees had risen to nearly half, and that it was likely that most of those still on the loose had reached Union lines. Wade nodded as Clinton whispered the information in his ear. "I heard another civilian say that a rebel patrol returned Rose in chains this morning," Wade replied softly. They never discussed the escape again.

The train left the Richmond station at sundown on February 14, and the roundabout journey from Richmond to Rome progressed without incident. Compared to the preceding months, the time they spent on the train was more boring than anything else. The forged papers served their purpose the two times they were questioned officially. For the most part, however, no one bothered to acknowledge the eight injured officers and men accompanied by two uninjured officers and a corpsman as they journeyed to Rome for long-term medical treatment. The train entered the Rome station at 7:00 P.M. on Saturday, February 21, two days behind schedule. The Southern railroad system was in near chaos. Wrecked and burned-out cars were being pushed from the track, left to rot like so many dead carcasses, with only their metal parts removed for reuse. Those cars that remained in service would have been discarded in better times. But for now there was nothing with which to replace them. It had been an instructive journey, an opportunity to observe firsthand the depth of the despair that was eroding the fervor that had previously sustained the Southern people. Only the absence of a viable alternative kept them going.

Wade's men were among more than forty Confederate soldiers, most of them wounded, and a few civilians who left the train at Rome, the end of the line.

Wade stood on the platform—Simon on one side, Clinton on the other—as the men climbed down with Lieutenant Healy in the lead. Wade smiled at his young stepbrother. He's turned into a damn fine soldier, Wade thought, one who was worthy of a promotion. He'd see to that when they returned to Washington.

"What now?" Clinton asked, his eyes roaming up and down the street.

Wade hesitated before answering. He knew that Clinton objected to his desire to take a side trip to see Cathy. But what harm would it do? With the plantation only a dozen miles away, he could go there and return in twenty-four hours. As a practical matter, most of them were more at ease in the South than in the North. Besides, this left more time to round up the horses they would need for the journey across half of Alabama. They were deep in enemy country and the danger could not be ignored. It had been different when there were just the two of them to worry about. Now the safety of ten men depended on Wade's judgment.

Wade wrinkled his nose. "For openers," he said, "get the men cleaned up. They're getting ripe."

Clinton smiled. "Y'all ain't 'xactly a rose yourself, Sam." He slapped the flat of his hands against his chest, and a cloud of dust and soot boiled outward. "But I'll see to it. You still thinkin' 'bout goin' ta the plantation?"

"I *have* to see Cathy, Jim, even if only briefly. You get the men settled in someplace for the night and I'll look around."

"Sam—"

"It's settled, Jim. It's something I must do."

Clinton nodded. "I know, Sam. I just wanted to ask a question 'bout the men. I think they'll be able t'move easier without these bandages. With all of the doctors here, someone may want t'examine 'em. That'd be downright embarrassin'."

"I agree," Wade replied. "Men, dispose of those bandages first chance you get. From here on, stick together. Talk to strangers as little as possible." He placed his hand on Simon's shoulder and smiled. "We're in your hands, Brother." Their eyes met. Simon understood that Sam might question his trust. Were circumstances reversed, he probably would have felt the same way. "Let's go for a walk, Simon." Wade turned to Clinton and pointed. "We'll meet in front of that bar in two hours, Jim."

"Whatever y'say, Sam. Get inta formation, men. You may as well look like soldiers. Two hours, Colonel." He saluted.

Wade returned the salute, then turned and walked toward the river.

"Why don't you strike out for Cincinnati?" asked Simon. "Your own people are only fifty miles away. I can make it home from here."

"I know," Wade replied, "but there's more to it than that. I want to meet Victoria and Nancy Caroline. I may never have another chance. I've been eye to eye with death a dozen times in the past three years, and I may be again. I have to speak to our father again, too, if we can find him. Simon, I haven't mentioned this, so I don't know what your thoughts are. There's a plot to kill President Lincoln, and our father is part of it. I intend to do everything possible to stop it."

"What can you do here in the South?" asked Simon.

"I don't know just yet. I have to find out more. Our father may be able to help. I'm sure he doesn't want to see Lincoln die any more than I do."

"I don't know, Sam. He's a hard man—Southern to the core. He won't let his way of life slip away without a fight."

"I'm not asking that of him. But killing Lincoln won't help the South, and he knows it—I think. I've met Lincoln, talked with him. To the president, every man in uniform is an American. He doesn't even recognize the Confederacy as a country, for God's sake. He simply refuses to believe that the country can be divided, legally or otherwise."

"And that's the point of disagreement, isn't it?"

"I realize that, Simon, but dwelling on that issue obscures the central point. Lincoln doesn't think of the South as an enemy. He never has." He stopped and placed his hand on Simon's shoulder. "The South can't win this war, Brother. It never could. It's true that the Union had its share of command problems at the beginning, but those are being resolved. We have twice as many men under arms now as we did a year ago, and supplies are coming out of the factories faster than they can be shipped. And what's the condition in the South by comparison? I think you know. After what we saw on the way here, you'd have to be blind not to see that your cause is futile. The Confederacy can't even replace its losses in men and materials, let alone respond to the growing threat. Your countrymen will make the road difficult, of course, and the war may drag on for another year or so, but what then?

"That's why Lincoln is important, perhaps more to the South than to the North. The country has to be put back together, Simon, and Lincoln will be your friend in that process. Without him, there's no way to predict what the Congress may do. There are many in the North who want to make the South pay for what's happened."

They walked on in silence, stopping finally at the river's edge. Wade looked inquiringly at Simon and said, "Will you do me a favor?"

"You know I will," Simon replied.

"Wait with Major Clinton for me. I'm going to try to find a horse and go to the Bowman plantation tonight. When I return, we'll be on our way to Birmingham."

"Consider it done."

Wade patted Simon on the back. "Thanks. I'll be back tomorrow. Help Jim and David Jr. keep the troops in line, Simon."

Midnight came and went as Wade rode on his stolen horse down the lane leading to the mansion. A single light flickered faintly in the parlor window; the second floor was dark. The gentle clomp of the horse's hooves sounded like a hammer beating on tin in the calm night air. Wade dismounted near the corner of the house. Better to let them sleep, he thought as he led the horse toward the summerhouse. He wrapped the reins around the hitching post and entered the place of fond memories.

He stopped just inside and looked back toward the mansion. He noticed the faint glow of a match in an upstairs room, then the soft shimmering of lantern light. He saw the outline of a figure at the window just before the room darkened again. The light moved across two windows before disappearing, only to appear moments later in the first-floor kitchen window.

The figure of a woman was visible in the window. A few minutes later, a man opened the door and stepped outside. He held a lantern in his right hand; Wade could make out a rifle dangling from his left. The dark form of a woman was barely visible in the background. Wade's attention turned to where his horse stood blowing mist through its nostrils into the cold night air. The animal seemed not to notice as the man approached from its rear. The man moved warily forward as he struggled with both the lantern and the cumbersome weapon, finally stopping at the gelding's right flank.

"Kind of cold out for a stroll, isn't it?" Wade asked calmly.

The man dropped the lantern and brought the shotgun to his shoulder. The lantern shattered against the stone walk, and dancing blue flames spread along the rocks and into the dried grass.

"Who's there?" asked Arthur Bowman, peering over the barrel into the darkness.

"How are you doing, Mr. Bowman? Want some help putting out that fire?"

Bowman stood the rifle against the wall of the summerhouse and began stamping on the flames. "What the hell you doing creeping around here like that?" Bowman asked, obviously perturbed.

"I didn't realize I was creeping," Wade said, helping to douse the last of the fire. "I didn't want to wake anyone. Someone in there certainly has good ears."

"It's Cathy. She doesn't seem to sleep much, what with all the worrying she does."

"And what's worrying her?"

"You, mostly. She wakes up each morning with a certainty in her mind that you're dead. Then there's her brother Frank. He's home, recovering from a badly broken leg. Still doesn't get around much. Added to all of that, we received a letter a few weeks back from Pervis informing us that he lost his right leg just below the knee. Bad things keep happening to the men in Cathy's life." With the last of the fire out, Arthur placed his hands on Wade's shoulders. "It's good to see you, son, but if you don't mind my asking, what are you doing here?"

Wade thought for a moment. "Just moving through, sir. I'm taking some men over to Alabama to help train their militia." He could think of nothing better to explain his presence. "We stopped over in Rome to rest our horses and round up some provisions. There isn't much to be had."

"I know. At least having you here will put a spark back in Cathy's eyes. Are you all right?"

"As good as can be expected with this damn war dragging on," said Wade. "I don't imagine we'll be able to absorb much more."

"It's our own damn fault, what with the army taking all our stock and winter provisions. We're defeating ourselves, and the politicians can't see it. I heard the other day that the population of Rome is down nearly fify percent and dropping daily. I was for our independence as much as anyone, Simon, but I'll be damned if I see how we can keep going much longer. The will to fight is about gone."

"All Jeff Davis has to do is send a letter to Lincoln and tell him it's over," said Wade.

"There's a better chance of a tidal wave washing over Tennessee than of that happening." Bowman realized he had lost Wade's attention. He turned and saw his daughter standing twenty feet behind him on the walkway. "Well, I'm going back to bed." He pursed his lips, then added, "It's warmer in the house, Cathy, why don't you two come inside?"

"I'd like to talk to Simon out here, Father—if you don't mind."

Bowman looked at Wade, then back at his daughter. He sighed loudly. "I suppose you're both old enough to know what's best." That was as close to granting his permission as convention would allow. "I guess I'll have to walk back in the dark," he added as he approached Cathy. "Watch out for the broken glass, Daughter." He turned. "Damn, Simon, you scared the wadding out of me." He placed his hand gently on his daughter's shoulder and squeezed.

She placed a hand on his and looked into his eyes. "Good night, Father. I'll be fine."

He nodded. "Perhaps now you will."

They watched Bowman return to the mansion. When he was back inside, Wade pulled Cathy firmly to his chest and kissed her hard on the mouth. He felt the dampness of her tears as they gathered where their faces pressed together. "My God, you feel good to me," he said, hugging her tightly. She leaned back, then kissed him again without replying.

He felt her shiver. "Let's go into the summerhouse and light a fire," he suggested.

She nodded, then kissed him again.

Wade stacked the wood in the fireplace while Cathy went to a storage room to fetch a pile of old blankets. She spread them on the brick floor in the brightening light of the fire, then she sat on the makeshift bed and leaned against the wall. As the light spread across the room, Wade stood and looked at her. He noticed her dress folded over a nearby chair and smiled as he watched the shadows dance on her face and arms.

Cathy reached up and pulled him beside her. He pressed against her and kissed her wantonly. For a blissful moment, the war faded from his thoughts. It would return again, he knew, with all of its vengeance and horror; but there ought to be more, had to be more, and he had to reach out and take it or the war would consume him. A man has only so much killing in him before his soul turns to rot. But this woman stood for life; she was his bridge back to humanity.

"Simon, this is my older brother, Frank," Cathy said the next morning. "Major Frank Bowman."

"It's an honor to meet you, Major. The last I heard, you had been captured at Vicksburg."

"It was the worst day of my life, Colonel."

"I can imagine, Major. It looks like your injury will take you out of the war."

"Not likely, sir. The South needs all of its men, now more than ever."

"All of us have our limits, Major. From the way Cathy described your injury, you'll be fortunate to walk without a limp."

"The leg seems to be healing nicely, Colonel, and a limp won't limit me when I'm astride a horse."

"Well, don't push it too fast. Full recovery can be slow."

"Frank has been in training for a special mission," Cathy interjected.

"What mission is that, Major?"

"I'm not at liberty to discuss it," Bowman replied, glaring at Cathy.

"You two can get better acquainted later," Cathy said hastily, changing the subject. "Right now, I'm starving. Mother has breakfast cooking. I'll go help her. Don't be long."

"Can I help you down the stairs, Major, or can you handle that?" asked Wade.

"I'll make it, Colonel. Just let me put my arm around your shoulders. Will you hand me that crutch?" With the aid of the crutch, Bowman pushed himself to a standing position. "You seem to be on the move a lot, Colonel."

"It does seem that way, doesn't it?"

"What exactly is your assignment, sir—if you don't mind my asking?"

"No, I don't mind," said Wade. "Mostly I gather information that the generals use in their planning. I guess they need someone who knows what to look for."

"You're a spy?"

Wade hesitated. The conversation was getting out of hand. "Only if I have to be. There are many ways of getting information, Major. Sometimes I get it by interrogating those on the other side. The thing is, I try not to let on what I'm doing. It's interesting work, but it usually keeps me on the fringe of the war." He breathed deeply as they entered the kitchen. "That certainly smells good, Mrs. Bowman."

"It's nothing, Simon. We don't get guests much these days."

The family ate as if it had been days since their last meal. Wade realized that they usually had less than this to eat during most full days. He ate sparingly, knowing they would salvage what remained.

After breakfast, Wade led Cathy to the top of the hill near the mansion. "Can't you stay for a few days?" Cathy pleaded.

"No. I'll be leaving this afternoon." He brushed the hair from his forehead. "Can't say when I'll return, but it probably won't be for a long time."

"And what am I to do in the meantime?"

"Survive until I come back for you."

She turned her back to him. "Where are you going?"

"North of Birmingham. It's a long journey on horseback, so I have to get on with it."

"And what will you be doing?"

"Can't say. There are ten men waiting for me in Rome. They don't think I should be here now, but I insisted. Since I'm a colonel, they didn't have enough votes to overrule me." He smiled; she frowned. She was in no mood for levity. "What kind of mission is Frank supposed to be on?" he asked, changing the subject.

"I don't know," she answered. "He won't say much. You two are peas in a pod. Whatever it is, he thinks it's important, though. He's in no shape to do anything strenuous, but he says he'll be leaving by the first of April." She waited. "There is one thing. He knows the albino. He described him perfectly, and the other man who was here, too."

Wade stiffened. "What do you make of that?"

"I don't know. I was afraid to ask more."

Wade turned away and closed his eyes. What better way to keep the father under control than to involve the son? These conspirators seldom engaged in frivolous planning, or failed to execute their plans. They had planned well. He swung around and grabbed her by the shoulders. "Think about it, Cathy. It's not a coincidence at all. From the conspirators' point of view, it makes perfect sense. With the whole family involved, that improves their chances that no one will disclose the plan for fear of causing harm to the others. These are dangerous men playing for huge stakes. My guess is they want to control the country after the war ends. They know that Lincoln will be concerned about the damage done in the South, and they don't give a damn about the South. You have to make Frank understand that. If he's involved, convince him that it's a fool's errand. He may be in a position to stop it. You have to make him think about that."

"Sometimes you scare me," she said, her eyes wide. "I bet I have welts on my arms."

"I'm sorry, Cathy, but this is important. I can't talk with Frank about this, but you can. You may be saving your father's life in the process. Think about it! If you were these men, would you want several dozen people who could send you to the gallows running loose?"

"My God," she said, turning toward the house and raising her hands to her mouth. "Oh, my God."

\*     \*     \*

"Where are they, Captain?" Wade screamed. "I want them out here—now!"

"That's impossible, Colonel. These men have no papers. For all I know, they're deserters, or worse. Until I identify them, they stay in the stockade."

"You want to know who they are? I'll begin with the colonel. His name is Thornton. Lieutenant Colonel Simon Thornton. He's the son of Gen. Henry Thornton, commander of the Alabama militia. He's my twin brother. Our father will have you boiled in oil for this. The major was raised less than fifteen miles from here, on a scrubby piece of land that a goat could walk around. His name is Clinton, James Clinton. The others are from all over the South, from Texas to Florida. You want their pedigrees? I can give you those, too." He pounded on the desk. "I want them out, Captain."

"By whose authority, Colonel?"

"By the authority of Secretary of War Seddon." He reached inside his pocket, removed a wrinkled document, and slapped it on the desk. "Read this."

The captain unfolded the paper. He read it slowly, then carefully studied the seal. It seemed authentic. Then again . . . "I'll send a letter, Colonel, and try to clear up this matter. Until then, they stay where they are."

"Come with me, Captain."

"Where to, sir?"

"The telegraph office."

"What for?"

"I'm going to send a couple of telegrams."

"To whom?"

"You ask a lot of questions for a captain. You want to clear things up? We'll clear things up. You just ignored a signed order from the secretary of war. That's punishable by death in time of war. We're going to send a telegram to Secretary Seddon."

The captain tried to speak. "Sir—"

"Shut up! If you question me again, Captain, I'll have you put in chains, and the sergeant can carry you over to the telegraph office. Now get up and get out that door."

"Sir, perhaps I didn't understand the significance of that document. It's best that I be cautious, don't you agree?"

"What are you suggesting, Captain?"

The captain motioned. "Sergeant, come here."

"Yes, sir." The sergeant rushed across the room.

"Look at this. Tell me what you think."

The sergeant examined the document. "It appears authentic, sir. There's a seal and all. I'd say it's real enough, sir."

"I seem to have made a mistake, Colonel," the captain said.

Wade snatched the paper from him. "Captain, do you see that clock?"

"Yes, sir."

"What time is it?"

"Ten after seven, sir."

"I'm going to sit in that chair over there until ten after eight. By that time, I expect to see eleven horses, with saddles and provisions for five days, hitched in front of this building."

The captain threw his arms into the air. "Where am I going to get eleven horses, sir?"

"You're the provost, aren't you?"

"Yes, sir, but—"

"Find a way, Captain. Your department must have nearly that many. Start there. You've delayed me long enough. An hour, Captain. Time's wasting."

"Sergeant."

"Sir?"

"You heard the colonel."

"Yes, sir. There'll be hell to pay, sir."

"Make them good horses," Wade said. "They have to make it all the way to Birmingham. I want to be in the saddle by eight-fifteen."

"Yes, sir," snapped the sergeant. He saluted and left.

"Now, Captain. Get my men."

# CHAPTER

# 23

The troop turned down the single-lane road that led to the Thornton mansion. Once off the main road, Sam Wade pulled out his watch. It was precisely 9:00 A.M. on March 1. Wade raised his hand and the others halted in place. Wade sat quietly as the scrawny mounts pawed the ground, their hot breath misting in the crisp morning air. Jim Clinton leaned easily forward and rested a forearm on his horse's neck. Simon Thornton shifted his weight uneasily from one side of the saddle to the other, growing more agitated with each passing moment. David Healy Jr., ever eager to disconnect himself from a horse, dismounted and relieved himself by the side of the road.

Wade, his gaze locked on the weathered, three-story mansion, turned sideways in the saddle, pressing his left foot against the stirrup. The saddle shifted a few degrees to the left, breaking the silence as leather rubbed against leather. He waited for he knew not what. The enlisted men lingered in silence as the mystifying delay dragged on. Finally, Wade sighed loudly and straightened himself in his saddle. The horse responded to the gentle nudge of his heel by advancing at a slow walk.

As they approached to within eighty yards of the mansion, a woman strolled easily onto the veranda. Wade again raised his hand to signal a halt. Thornton dismounted and handed his reins to Wade. He hitched up his trousers and buttoned his tunic, then stood for a moment before advancing slowly toward the house.

As he drew closer, Victoria Thornton flung her hands to her mouth. "My God!" she screamed, "it's Simon." She ran down the steps and along the lane toward the solitary figure. She stopped ten feet away and smiled broadly as her son closed the space between them. As he neared, she lunged forward and flung her arms around his neck. Thornton lifted her from the ground and swung her around, hugging her firmly.

Nancy Caroline rushed from the house and stopped on the first step. She shaded her eyes and smiled, then ran to greet her brother. The three talked excitedly for a few minutes, their comments muffled by the breeze. After a time, Thornton turned and pointed at Wade. Victoria stepped to where she had a clear view, then folded her arms tightly across her chest. She said something to her son, then began to cautiously advance to where Wade still sat relaxed on his horse.

He had equally dreaded and yearned for this moment. Hundreds of hours on the road had provided sufficient time for thought about this first meeting with his physical mother. Now the moment was at hand. He swung his leg slowly over the horse's neck and settled to the ground. He handed both sets of reins to Clinton and beat the dust from his uniform before stepping forward. When they were five feet apart, they both stopped and looked into each other's eyes, waiting for the other to speak. "My mother sends you her love," Wade said finally.

"And how is my twin sister?" Victoria asked politely.

"She's well." Wade kicked nervously at a clod. "This war's worn her down some, but she's resilient." He glanced up and pointed at the balcony. "She told me about a conversation she had with you up there, shortly before the war began."

Victoria turned to hide the tears sliding down her cheeks. "I remember it well," she replied softly. She sniffed, then wiped her face with a worn sleeve. She kept her face turned from him. "I've had no time to prepare for this moment, Samuel. I'm afraid I'll say the wrong thing. When did Caroline tell you what we did?"

"Not long ago. One question kept running into the next. In time, I was able to figure out most everything for myself. She only filled in the details. I assumed the general told you—"

Victoria spun around. "General Thornton? My husband? He knows?"

"Yes. I told him everything, late last fall. We had a long talk under less than favorable circumstances. Mostly, I talked and he listened."

"My God! Why did he keep this from me?"

"Several reasons come to mind. It was then that I told him I'd bring Simon home. He probably didn't want to raise your hopes. My guess is, it seemed wise to him to avoid the matter entirely."

"And he knows he's your father?"

"Yes. He seemed less surprised than I expected." Wade turned at the sound of hoofbeats. A lone rider had pulled onto the road and was advancing at a trot. "Is that the general now?"

Victoria shaded her eyes. "Oh, my Lord!" she exclaimed. "It seems impossible that he'd arrive at the same time as you. He hasn't been here in weeks, not since he escorted the Bowmans through here."

"The Bowmans? What were they doing here?" Why hadn't Cathy mentioned it? he wondered.

"They stayed just one night. They were on their way to Mrs. Bowman's sister's home, down near Mobile, after her brother-in-law died."

General Thornton pulled his horse to a stop. He smiled as he looked down at his wife. He dismounted and took her gently in his arms, then he kissed her hard on the lips. A mixture of anger and fear clouded Victoria's thoughts—anger that he had kept such a secret, fear that he might hate her for her secret. Thornton turned and extended a hand to Wade. "Thank you, Samuel," he said, his face growing serious. "I never doubted you'd bring Simon home." He turned as Simon approached, placed his hands on his hips, and examined his son carefully. Then he nodded approvingly and extended his arms. Simon stepped into his embrace. Shortly, he extended an arm to Victoria and pulled her to him.

After hugging them both, the general stepped back and placed his hands on Simon's shoulders. "I felt some bones through that sorry excuse for a uniform," he said. "Where have you been?"

"Prison," answered the younger Thornton, "Libby Prison."

"Libby? But how—"

"It's a long story, Father. There'll be time later."

The general's eyes connected with his daughter's. She had advanced cautiously toward the gathering. There had been too many surprises in such a short time. Thornton motioned with his head. "Come here, Nancy Caroline." He took her hand. "It's my pleasure to introduce you to your other brother." He knew they had met briefly once before, but that had been under stressful conditions. They hadn't even spoken. He had watched from the seclusion of the trees as that distant drama unfolded, the same as he had watched this morning. He had been watching and waiting for some time now, since late the previous evening.

A week earlier, one of his staff officers had informed him that a troop of men had ridden through camp. They had stopped at headquarters and asked to see the general. He had been miles away at the time, inspecting his troops. The men had ridden on, but Thornton had concluded from the men's description that Wade and Simon were in the group. The officer had reported seeing two lieutenant colonels who looked enough alike to be twins. The next morning, Thornton had passed command temporarily to Brig. Gen. Tilton Graham and ridden out alone, pushing his stout horse to close the distance between his sons and himself. As much as he wanted to see Simon, he had thought it best to delay the reunion until they arrived at the plantation. He had taken a shortcut and camped in the woods south of the house. He had sensed Wade's anxiety as he watched the long delay on the road. He had waited, however, knowing that Samuel would eventually sort through his feelings. Finally, he had been unable to wait any longer.

At her father's urging, Nancy Caroline edged uneasily toward Samuel. She smiled nervously as she approached.

"Can't be much different than hugging Simon," he said, breaking the tension. She blushed as she slowly extended her arms.

"I feel as if I know you," Wade whispered, then kissed her softly on the cheek. "My stepbrother has told me so much about you."

She reared backward and frowned. "Your stepbrother?"

"Yes. You know him well. Perhaps too well." He pointed. "See that bearded young lieutenant sitting nervously astride that gray nag? That's David Healy Jr." Nancy Caroline gasped. "He's ridden a long way to find out for himself exactly how you plan to kill him. He's been dreading this moment, but still, I couldn't keep him away." Wade placed his arm around his sister's shoulders where she stood frozen in place.

It was all too much. Her lower lip quivered and tears streamed from her ice blue eyes. Slowly, she brought a hand up and pushed the blowing hair from her face.

Wade leaned closer. "I hesitate to ask a favor so early in our relationship, but please go easy on him. You can't say anything that he hasn't said to himself more forcefully." She looked into her newly discovered brother's eyes. "There's been so much hate," he added. "Now it's time to love."

At that precise moment, Maj. Gen. Ulysses S. Grant leaned limply against a tree two hundred miles to the north. In his hand he held a telegram that had just arrived from Maj. Gen. Henry W. Halleck in Washington. Considering its import, the message was brief. A week earlier, on February 24, Congress—at the president's request—had approved the creation of the regular army rank of lieutenant general. That done, Lincoln had instructed Halleck to summon Grant to Washington. When he arrived, Lincoln would appoint Grant to the new rank and make him general in chief of the Armies of the United States. The telegram informed Grant that the president would, at eleven that morning, send a message to Congress informing both houses of Grant's nomination. The leaders in Congress had promised immediate action on the nomination.

Grant dreaded the responsibility almost as much as he dreaded going to Washington. But Grant knew a soldier's duty, and he always followed orders. Many would come to rue that day, foremost among them Gen. Robert E. Lee, commander of the Confederate Army of Northern Virginia.

As the sun settled gently on the horizon, Wade walked easily down the steps of the veranda. It had been a good homecoming, more graceful than he had expected. Only Caroline's absence made it less than perfect. Perhaps as important, it had become apparent during the long ride by train and horse that the South faced defeat before many months passed. The South's resolve was fast dissolving, and no power on earth could reverse the inevitable progression toward its surrender. People talked openly of the coming of the end, as though they almost welcomed it. But the Southern armies remained in the field, largely unbeaten and totally unbowed. More young men would have to die before it could end.

Wade turned at the sound of footsteps. He smiled as Simon and his father approached. Victoria stood on the veranda, watching as the three men came together. *I wonder what she's thinking?* mused Wade.

"How does it feel being home?" Wade asked, looking at Simon.

"Strange," he replied. "It'd be easy to forget that I'm a soldier."

General Thornton placed his arm around Simon's shoulders. "After he's had a long rest, I'll be looking into having him reassigned closer to home." He turned to Wade. "And what about you? Will you be returning to Washington?"

"In a few days. As soon as the horses regain some strength. There's not much chance of getting fresh mounts around here. These'll have to do."

"You'll need an escort to Yankee lines, of course," said the general. "I'll see to that. I'll send a telegram tomorrow requesting a cavalry troop for that purpose. They should be here in a couple of days. You can stay until then, I hope."

"I suppose. My men are nervous, as I'm sure is obvious." Wade placed a hand on Henry Thornton's arm. "I've been meaning to ask you, Father. This morning, Victoria told me that the Blairs spent a night here several weeks back. She said nothing about them mentioning me, even though Cathy thinks I'm Simon. I don't understand, sir."

"They never mentioned you because they never met Victoria. She was in Birmingham tending to a sick friend. The Blairs remained only one night before traveling on to Mobile. I had offered them an escort this far. Victoria told you only what I told her. The Blairs returned by another route after the brother-in-law died."

Henry Thornton gently grasped Wade's arm. Their eyes met. "Now that we've resolved that," Thornton continued, "I'd like some information. Tell me about your Colonel Thompson, the man who sent Simon to Libby Prison."

From the diary of Caroline Wade-Healy

*March 1, 1864*
*10:00 P.M.*
*I had the strangest sensation to-day. It settled over me like a gentle breeze.*
*I felt as though my life came together for the first time, as if some distant*

voice was whispering in my ear that the reason for my existence on this earth had been satisfied. I still haven't concluded whether I'm at the beginning or the end.

Two months have passed since I last heard from Samuel. Even Colonel Thompson seems mystified as to his whereabouts. The prison break made all the headlines. More than half of the men reached our lines. The papers reported that 109 escaped. Simon's name was absent from the list, but I know he's free. It's satisfying that my son had a hand in something so important.

Finally, something has happened that the Boston Globe didn't report before it occurred. I hate that paper!

I heard to-day that Mr. Lincoln nominated General Grant for promotion to lieutenant general. I think it's a hopeful sign. I understand that Grant will be the first to hold that rank since George Washington. How can Grant fail, with the father of our country looking over his shoulder?

I watched a parade in Washington last week. My, how the times have changed—and for the better I might add. The men were all Negro recruits, marching there beside the railroad, with sticks instead of muskets balanced on their shoulders. It made me think of Washington. I shall have to inquire after him when I return to Gettysburg.

I must begin thinking of the future; I have to contain my hatred for the South. My family will come together again—whole this time, with all the secrets washed away by the blood of war. There are enough problems in the North. Already, powerful men are plotting the rape of the South. A strange man without any pigment in his skin approached me in Washington. He wanted to know if I was interested in investing in Southern railroad development after the war. I told him I was satisfied with riding the railroad, and that I preferred to let others build it. He pressed quite forcefully before I made him understand that I truly had no interest in his proposal.

There is so much money in the hands of so few people. I feel guilty with my own accumulation. I'm tired of the strain of watching after it. I know Samuel wants to remain in the army when the war ends. I hope he'll reconsider and run my shoe business. I'm ready for a long rest.

I have no passion for what I must do now. I have to take the train to Chicago next week. There have been severe cost overruns in the expansion of the factory there. I suspect that my manager is not being entirely honest with me.

Spring's in the air.

Godspeed on your return home, Samuel. Be safe.

———————————

In Washington, the political mood was shifting. Lincoln wanted the war to end, and he hoped Grant would make the hard choices needed to run General Lee and his army into the ground. Lincoln also knew that he could expect the full cooperation of the Congress in doing what had to be done. One of the most dramatic shifts in attitude had been with respect to the Negro and his part in the war. Gradually, and against great resistance, it had become an accepted fact that the black man could perform as well as the white man in an army uniform. Only two conditions were necessary: the first was the ability to learn how to fire a rifle with reasonable accuracy; the second was the willingness to face danger and, if necessary, die in the process. Both of those requirements had been difficult enough to find in white recruits, especially at the war's outset.

Now, as the fourth year of the war drew near, no one could see exactly how the changing views of war, and the part of the Negro in those views, might evolve. But one fact was evident: there was no shortage of young black men willing to test their abilities in the effort to kill those who had held their race in bondage for more than two centuries. Many of them were the equal of the best of their white counterparts in their abilities. Among them was the company of men in which Washington Petree served as a sergeant. Their training now completed, they were eager—and a bit anxious—at the prospect of getting into the war in a way that counted for something.

With spring approaching, the Army of the Potomac was deep into its preparation for what everyone knew was coming when the trees began to green. Several Negro regiments were joining the ranks of that army, and Petree was excited about the prospect. On March 1—an unusually warm day for that time of year—there had been a parade of sorts, a formal exhibition of the marching skills that were essential for an army on the move. Petree knew they had done well because everyone had cheered as they marched by, columns aligned, ranks so straight that at ground level they appeared as one when they drew even with the officers on the reviewing platform. Petree's thoughts were on the day's proceedings when Lieutenant Bixby approached from behind.

"How are you this evening, Sergeant Petree?" Bixby asked.

"I'm fine, sir," Petree said, turning. "And you?"

"I'm proud of you and the men, Sergeant. That's how I am. You did well today."

"Thank you, sir. But will they let us fight now that we've had all of this training?"

"I think so—now that they can see that you *are* prepared. Today was the clearest possible example that all of you are soldiers, which is what I wanted to discuss with you."

"Yes, sir?"

"When the spring campaign begins, there's talk of putting the men's skills as sharpshooters to the test. I've been asked to develop a plan for how we can best serve those needs. I'm good enough at the planning part, but my superiors want a full report on how we will carry out our duties in the field. I'm not very good at that sort of thing. I'm aware of your skills in that area. I'd like your help."

Petree smiled. "You want *me* to prepare the report, sir?"

"If you wouldn't mind, Sergeant—*and* assist me with the planning, of course. What do you say?"

"Sir, it would be my pleasure. When do we begin?"

"Tomorrow, Sergeant. Everything has to be ready by the first of May."

"Sir?"

"Yes."

"I know these men, sir. They believe in what they're fighting for."

"I'm aware of that, Sergeant."

"They won't let you down, sir. They won't let the army down. I'll see to that."

Bixby reached out and patted Petree on the back. "We'll begin tomorrow, Sergeant. Get a good night's sleep."

# PART 4
# LINCOLN

# CHAPTER

# 24

The late winter storm blew in from the west, totally unexpected. That morning a warm southerly wind had washed over the city, and people had accepted the change as a signal that they should emerge from their winter hibernation.

Stewart Webb found the warm weather refreshing after the freezing gales that had pummeled the ship during most of the trip from England. The ship had docked in New York Harbor three days earlier, on March 1. Then, at about two that afternoon, the wind shifted to the north and the temperature began to drop. By five, an inch of snow had accumulated and the temperature had fallen to ten above zero. Now it took all of Webb's energy to push against the wind and move his feet through the swirling drifts. The cabbie would go no farther than the bottom of the hill, leaving him two long uphill blocks to walk. He had been feeling poorly anyway; now his cough had returned, and he shivered from the piercing wind as he trudged upward to the hilltop mansion.

Webb hated the American aristocracy. They were ever so much more crude than their English cousins, who generations before had come to an easy alliance with their money and shiftless way of life. In England, the rich pretended at power, content to terrorize only those poor, ignorant wretches who rented their land. The rich seldom attended the university anymore, and their women never did. Squandering the necessary four or five years of prime youth to get a degree had become the province of those in the middle class who wanted what the rich would never relinquish.

Americans, on the other hand, were always unsatisfied. They wanted more— more of everything. He saw nothing of grace in their existence. Perhaps it had been the same when the noblemen's wealth had been new, but he doubted it. These men were so—well—primitive. To them, a million dollars was nothing more than a stepping-stone on the way to the second million. He suspected that the absence of titles caused the difference. Titles added to a man's prestige, gave him a sense of worth and dignity beyond the size of his estate and bank account. Here, the rich wanted money for the sake of having money. And he had to deal with them as equals, or nearly so. It galled him. He so much more preferred the Southerners, with their life of grace and style—and honor. They had transported their English values with them more than two centuries before, and they lived by them still.

Perhaps if England had recognized the fledgling Southern government earlier, back when the war began, he would have no need to be here now. But the Southern noblemen had clung to that abominable and peculiar institution of slavery. They were as much within its grip as the slaves themselves. It had fed on itself, consuming reason first, then the whole land. He had warned them back in '58, but they refused to listen. So now he had to hasten their destruction, and it caused a pain deep in the pit of his stomach. Or perhaps the discomfort came from the roast beef he had eaten for supper. The life had been cooked from the stuff. He yearned for the tenderness of a juicy kidney pie; he yearned for the tenderness of sweet Julie Ross. He wondered what she might be doing at this minute.

Webb lifted the brass knocker and let it drop. A few seconds later, the door swung open and the doorman, momentarily jarred by a blast of wind, quickly regained his composure and stood stiffly at the entrance, his nose stuck in the air as if a bad smell had rushed past him. They overdo everything here, Webb thought. "Webb," he announced, "Stewart Webb." He omitted his title.

"Welcome, Sir Stewart," called out a young man with slick, wavy hair wearing a silk smoking jacket. Webb stepped past the doorman, and they shook hands. "We've been waiting for you, sir. You must be eager to get out of that terrible weather. With any luck, this will be the last of winter."

"I certainly hope so," Webb replied as he brushed the snow from his coat.

"Everyone is here, waiting in the library. Joseph, take the gentleman's coat and hat. Would you like a glass of port, sir?"

"Thank you, no, but do you perchance have any brandy? I seem to have developed a chill. A spot of brandy might be just the thing."

"Of course. Thomas, see to it, please." The young man nodded at the butler, who stood nearby.

"I'm Ira McFadden."

"Call me Stewart."

"Stewart it is."

McFadden directed Webb to the library. "Gentlemen, this distinguished gentleman is Sir Stewart Webb—Stewart to his friends. We're all friends here, so I suppose it's Stewart. Let me introduce you to my guests." Standing left to right were Henry Livermore, of the railroad Livermores; R. C.

Waxelman, of the banking Waxelmans; and, of course, Fermin Cox, of everything that involved money. Beyond him stood Ray Goodwider and Charles Pitcurry, followed by Henry Weyhooper, Gus Smith, and Old Pete Field's youngest and most worthless son, James. Sterling Andrews rounded out the circle. Ten in all, counting Ira McFadden. Two men were missing. Perhaps they would arrive later in the evening, or perhaps they had been caught unaware by the storm.

Webb nodded as McFadden called each man's name. Among them they had or controlled enough money to finance the operation of the U.S. government for three months, war and all. In truth, they *were* financing it, through the purchase and sale of bonds and other securities, and they had enriched themselves handsomely in the process.

The butler entered the room carrying a glass and a bottle of brandy. "That will be all, Thomas," said McFadden. "Please close the door as you leave." McFadden turned to the others and motioned with his hand. "Please, gentlemen, be seated. With the weather as it is, you will want to stay here for the night. Your rooms have been prepared, so we have all the time we need." He turned to Waxelman. "I'll let you begin, R. C."

Waxelman cleared his throat. "I'll get to the point, Stewart. Is there any plan for England to recognize the Confederacy?"

Webb smiled and shook his head. "Gentlemen, I think I can give you assurance that England has no plan to recognize the Confederacy. I'll admit we were thinking along those lines prior to Gettysburg and the fall of Vicksburg. Last August, however, my government engaged in a full analysis of your situation. We reached a firm conclusion: the South will lose the war. As far as we're concerned, the sooner the better. Then life and commerce—especially commerce—can return to normal."

"What assurance do we have of your government's position?" asked Field.

Webb shrugged. "You have my word. I have no reason to deceive you. But I must say, those with a lingering doubt about the outcome will have their dreams shattered by Grant. I think we're about to witness one of the bloodiest summers in the history of warfare. Lee will resist with everything at his disposal, but in the end he will succumb to superior force. Grant will pound Lee's army into the Virginia dust. I see no other possible outcome."

"I agree," said McFadden. "Everything is in place. The only requirements are spring weather and decent roads. By fall, Lee will be beaten or forced to flee into the Deep South. All of the indications are there."

Weyhooper leaned forward and poured his glass full of port. "Which brings us to the larger question. Rumor has it that Grant will want Sherman to lead the western army, with Atlanta as his objective. Once Atlanta is captured, even the politicians will know that the end is near. That brings us to the elections. What do you think will happen in the elections, Mr. Webb?"

"I haven't the slightest idea, sir. To be frank, I don't understand your politics. With all that time between the conventions and the November election, who can say what will happen?"

"It's a matter of timing," said Cox. "If Grant has Lee in his grip by late summer, or if Atlanta has fallen, Lincoln will win the Republican nomination and probably the election. Otherwise it may be Simon Chase on the ticket, or who can tell? McClellan, on the other hand, is certain to win the Democratic nomination."

"I think McClellan can beat Lincoln," said Livermore.

"On what platform?" asked Goodwider harshly.

"On an antiwar platform, sir. What else? It's his only chance."

"He'll have no chance under the conditions described by Fermin," said Andrews. "Lincoln is the best politician of our age. He sometimes looks like an idiot—and usually talks like one—but he knows how to win votes. In times of war, the perception of winning is everything. Lincoln's supporters will scatter across the country displaying maps of the Confederacy, comparing 1860 to the present. With the Trans-Mississippi lost to the South, even a fool will see that the war is all but over. As a practical matter, there is nothing to settle with the South, or won't be by the end of summer. The South has lost everything south of Tennessee and west of Louisiana. When Atlanta falls, Alabama and Mississippi will be lost. By September the South will be down to Virginia, the Carolinas, Florida, and whatever part of Georgia Sherman hasn't captured. Even if we let them go, they will be begging to come back into the Union within five years. Besides, what chance will McClellan have of making a case for giving up with so many lives already lost? Not even the soldiers will vote for him. And if McClellan *does* win, Congress will ignore him. I predict he won't win a single state, with the possible exception of New York."

"I disagree," said McFadden. "New York will go for Lincoln."

"The Irish hate Lincoln and this war," countered Pitcurry.

"That's nonsense, Charles. They simply don't want to *fight* in this war anymore. There's a difference. Besides, they aren't alone in their opposition."

Everyone laughed—except Webb. He hated the Irish. It seemed to him that they always wanted something for nothing, and maintaining peace in Ireland had drained the English treasury for the past century. "No one knows what the Irish will do," snapped Webb, "least of all the Irish."

"Do I detect some resentment in your tone?" asked McFadden.

"Nothing personal, sir. It's just a general observation supported by a hundred years of fact. No offense intended."

"None taken," said McFadden. "My people settled here three generations ago. But we're straying from the central issue. Are we in general agreement, then? With Grant in command, and if Lincoln turns him loose as he surely must—Congress will tolerate nothing less—can we assume that Lincoln will be nominated and win the election, unless something completely unforeseen prevents it?"

"That's obvious," said Cox, now fully convinced.

"I want a vote," said Livermore.

"Very well," said Cox. "All who think that Lincoln will win, raise your hand." He counted. "Eight. And I make nine. Nine for, one against. So Lincoln wins the election." He said it as though the deed had been accomplished.

Webb shook his head. Such arrogance, he thought. They pretend that the people don't matter, that they hardly have a say in the outcome. Perhaps they don't. With all of the money these men have, who is to say what they can accomplish?

"So what do we do about it?" asked Pitcurry.

"What will England think, Stewart, if Lincoln wins?"

"It will present certain problems."

"Such as?" asked Waxelman.

"Such as, what will happen when the North wins the war and four million slaves are set loose to do and go as they please?"

"I don't see that we can do much about that," said Field.

"Perhaps not directly," the Englishman replied, "but from our perspective, we'd think it best if they remained where they are. The world needs cotton, gentlemen, and the best cotton comes from the southern part of your country. Without cheap labor, the Southern economy will dry up completely. Then where will we get our cotton? If the South is treated like a long-lost brother— if there is an easy peace as promised by Lincoln—the South will prosper and be in a position to use machinery for farm production. What will the Negro do then?"

"Come north, perhaps," said Waxelman. "What a disaster that would be."

"Or head west," said Goodwider with disgust, "there to become self-sufficient and acquire political power, which would be even worse."

"My God," exclaimed Livermore, "that'd be terrible! Do you have any suggestions, sir?"

Webb sipped at his glass. "The problem is your Mr. Lincoln, gentlemen," he said softly, just enough to tickle the issue. "You know him better than I. Will he be able to resist the will of your Congress? By our assessment, the majority in Congress, left to their own desires, will vote to impose stiff penalties on the South, repress their natural leaders, and limit their authority to control their own affairs. But none of that will happen without Lincoln's cooperation."

"And they won't get it," said Smith, speaking for the first time. "Lincoln will commit every possible resource to the passive reconstruction of the South. One need only examine his plan for Louisiana. With only 10 percent of the voters willing to declare allegiance to the Union, Lincoln is ready to treat them as though they had never seceded. It's disgusting, I tell you, disgusting. No, gentlemen, we can't have that. The future is in the West, and the settlers there must be white, not black."

Silence followed his stark analysis. As the men filled their glasses, Webb added an afterthought. "It would benefit *all* of us if Mr. Lincoln should suddenly pass from the scene. If he were to be assassinated, it would not only clear the way for the radicals in your Congress, it would also cause a furor in Washington and make him a martyr. That would eliminate any chance of your moderates letting the South off."

The clatter of glasses ceased as all eyes turned toward the Englishman. Why had that possibility been overlooked? In an instant, it became obvious that Lincoln would have to go. They had considered it early on, but only as a remote alternative, never seriously. They had left the details to McFadden. He had told them at the outset that any plan involving the Southerners that failed to emphasize the Southern goal of victory in the war would never gain their support. Lincoln's assassination offered them at least the illusion that the North would become demoralized and let the South go its own way. McFadden never believed that for a minute. But he wasn't a Southerner. So the grand design for the plan had included a contingency option for the assassination of Lincoln. The details of the application of that part of the plan were nearly in place, so much so that all McFadden had to do was send word to the albino to carry them out.

What a curious social analysis, thought McFadden. Perhaps they had misdirected their attention all along. Back in 1861 and early 1862, with the South's long string of convincing victories in battle behind them, their fortunes had seemed to be favored. How things had changed. Once Congress approved the construction of the intercontinental railroad, business's attention turned to the West. Almost overnight the South became a backwater in terms of economic interest. Expansion west would energize the nation, and all that energy would produce undreamed-of opportunity, with money generated at every turn, the cornerstone of which would be land for the taking at 10 percent of its value. Settlers would have limitless opportunity, with no one looking too closely if deals were being orchestrated that enriched those willing to take a few chances and cut a few corners. Only one thing could get in the way: Indians. It would take a decade, perhaps a bit more, to clean up the Indian problem. But all in all, what a time to be alive!

If these men could eliminate Lincoln, they could control the nation's destiny, McFadden thought. But no one had tried to assassinate an American president before. Somehow, the very idea seemed difficult to grasp, perhaps because there had never been a sound enough reason. Now the reason had been articulated, and by an Englishman no less. What an irony! Lincoln had to die, if not in the near term, then certainly before the end of the war. Everyone present knew it, and all except one accepted it. And for the act to have any meaning, it had to appear, beyond question, to have originated in the South.

But McFadden had to admit, if only to himself, that the thought of assassinating the president tied a knot in his stomach.

Across the room from McFadden, the Englishman breathed easier. The meeting had gone better than expected. Webb could read the resignation on the Americans' faces. As men of action, they never dwelled on the consequences of a decision once made. These men were ready to be convinced, ready to conspire in the murder of their president. They simply needed a slight nudge.

Webb smiled inwardly. His mood had nothing to do with cotton—or with who won the war, for that matter. That perspective, at least, applied to Britain and him equally. Britain had an interest in ending the war, true enough, but it also had a general indifference to which side won. The island nation thrived on commerce, and nothing cooled commerce so much as a civil war in a major trading country. So his government wanted the war over. But Webb's perspective was that of a conservative member of Parliament. At this critical stage in his life, he found himself outside the ring of power. That galled him. At the age of fifty-six he more frequently envisioned his own end. He had to move events along more quickly if he hoped to fulfill his lifelong dream. He wanted to win the prime minister's seat. To do that, he had only one option: he had to work both sides of the Atlantic and, hopefully, bring down the British government in the process. Then he planned to be available to move into the vacuum. He had a simple enough plan; unfortunately, its execution was beyond his direct control.

The first phase had just been completed. There had to be a plausible reason for these men to seek British assistance. He had provided it. But the second part was more tricky. The conspiracy had to leak into the open, but only at the proper time and in a way that would not implicate him. The British government had to be caught and be vulnerable to being held accountable for its treacheries—as seen from the perspective of the U.S. government. Intervention by one country in the internal politics of another was among the few inviolable, if unwritten, rules of international behavior. It just wasn't done unless one was willing to risk war. A firestorm of protest would rise up in the United States; if everything worked as planned, an upheaval in Britain would follow. The sitting government would fall and, as the leader of the Loyal Opposition expressing his indignation, he would become prime minister.

These Americans were new to the art of infidelity; they were virtual neophytes and remarkably easy to manipulate. He, on the other hand, had learned the skill from kings who were masters of the art and had refined the process for more than four centuries. Recognizing his advantage made him smile again, this time more openly.

But attention had shifted from the Englishman. He was, after all, a bit player in the high drama that promised as a reward unfettered control of the economic destiny of a nation with the potential to become a premier world power. These men, too, had learned from kings—and they had learned as well as any king the need to kill those who sought to extinguish their ambitions. They were about to demonstrate their commitment to their goal.

"What about our prior plans, gentlemen?" asked McFadden. "What do we do about our Southern friends?"

"Is this the time to discuss that," asked Andrews, "with Mr. Webb in the room?" Andrews rose and began to pace. "We are going too far. People are bound to suspect us. Gentlemen, we need to rethink this."

McFadden glanced at Waxelman. Andrews was becoming a problem. His commitment obviously was weak. But McFadden could not decide alone. Waxelman nodded once, and McFadden answered the same way. He would tell the others later, if they were told at all. They were all equal in the deliberation process, doing nothing without consensus, but Waxelman was first among equals. McFadden turned to Webb. "Sir, we have only two choices. We want a new president in office in '65. We either take steps to influence the election and thereby ensure that Lincoln loses the nomination or the election, or—"

"Or what, Ira?" Field asked.

"The alternative is obvious," replied Webb.

"We may need your country's assistance, sir," said McFadden. "If we try the less direct approach first, then we must have a plan."

"And if that fails?" asked Webb.

"We already have a plan for that eventuality, sir. I need only give the order."

"I see."

"There is only one problem," said Waxelman, his attention turning to the issue of their "Southern friends," as McFadden had put it. "The foundation and the house don't match."

"I fail to see your point," Webb said.

"At the time we put that plan in motion, we had limited our attention to the South's economy. That meant we had to gain control of as much of the railroad system as possible down there. Now, such an effort is unnecessary, even counterproductive. The goal has changed." Waxelman turned to McFadden. "We have to clean up that problem, Ira. Don't you agree?"

"I agree, R. C., but I think we need a vote."

"Are we fully prepared to carry out the new plan?" asked Waxelman.

"Everything is ready," McFadden answered. "All of the soldiers are carefully selected and trained Southern boys. Since they know nothing about us, there can be no trail leading back to us from them, even if some are caught. It will be a simple matter to ensure that federal authorities recognize their heritage and conclude that they were the vanguard of a Southern conspiracy. I'll take care of that."

"Good," Waxelman said. "I move that we authorize Ira to sever our ties with a certain group of Southern gentlemen of which we are all aware, and that the separation be . . . permanent."

"What other choice is there?" said Cox with a shrug. "Regrettable, but necessary."

"These men have given us their support," said Andrews. "We can't simply kill them."

"Not only *can* we," answered Cox, "but we *must,* as regrettable as it may be. They know too much. Just think how angry they will be when we fail to help them rebuild their railroads. They will disclose everything they know at the first opportunity. This is a matter that we must put behind us, Sterling. It's the only safe option."

"How can they harm us?" asked Andrews. "They don't know our names."

"Are you willing to gamble everything," asked Field, "your fortune, your life, your lovely daughter's life? If they connect one of us to the plot, they connect us all. I'll sleep better if we put it behind us once and for all. I call for a vote."

All hands rose, even Andrews's.

"You'll see that it's done?" Waxelman asked, looking at McFadden.

"It'll take some time to clean things up down there, R. C. I expect until middle or late spring. There are some other loose ends that need knotting at the same time. I'll take care of everything, say by the middle of June." At twenty-eight, McFadden was the youngest in the group. While the others were interested only in money and power, McFadden reveled in the intrigue and the danger. He had unbounded confidence in himself and in his ability to organize and carry out complex tasks. The others were content to let him, reasoning that McFadden's solitary association with the men in the field added another layer of insulation if something went wrong.

"I assume, gentlemen, that Ira should keep his young Southern soldiers ready," said Field. "I think we will need them before this concludes."

The others nodded in agreement.

"Well, Stewart, that brings us back to you," said Waxelman. "It appears that our first course of action is to try to regulate the election. That will require your cooperation. I assume there is a price for your nation's services."

"Nothing much, but there *is* something of future concern," replied Webb. "What's that?"

"Cattle production. The demand grows each year. A million acres of prime ranch land in the West would ease my—our concern."

"You don't want much," Waxelman said sarcastically.

"Not really. There's millions of acres out there, sixty-five million in the Colorado Territory alone. What's a million when you have so much?"

"We may have to purchase it," said Cox to Waxelman, unwilling to spend more time on the subject.

"Done," said Waxelman, "provided the others agree."

The others smiled and nodded. It amounted to their profits for less than a month.

"What land do you have in mind?"

"Our survey team reports that land in the northern Colorado or southern Wyoming Territories would meet our needs. There's sufficient water, the grass is chest high, and it's unoccupied." Almost. He failed to mention that a hundred thousand Indians of various tribes relied on unrestrained passage through the area to feed their families. "I can show you a map tomorrow. It's at the hotel."

"That won't be necessary," Waxelman said. The others nodded in agreement.

Webb sighed. "One final matter, gentlemen. I'm not interested in your solution to your problem down south. But for our part, my government won't be pleased if we provide our cooperation and things don't work out as we agree, regardless of the success of your plans. We will want immediate access to our share of available cotton once the war ends, at least a hundred thousand bales to begin with. And there is one other concern. Unlike with your Southern friends, your identities are known to several in my government."

In McFadden's mind, the Englishman's stock plummeted. He frowned. He had brought Webb into their confidence, and now, in the first two hours of their association, he had issued a threat. It made him unreliable. It made him worse than that.

"Your point is taken, sir," said Waxelman, with no obvious concern in his voice or expression—only a side glance at McFadden revealed his displeasure—"and you have nothing to worry about. But you must remain patient. There will be political complications to untangle in the wake of the war." He breathed deeply before adding, "I see no reason to delay the cotton delivery, however. I even know the man with the ships to deliver it." He took several swallows of wine. "It's cold in here, don't you agree?" The nods confirmed his observation.

If not for his self-obsession, or if he had known Waxelman better, Webb might have sensed, even expected the shift in temperature. But his perception failed him. "We're practical men, R. C. We'll watch and wait, for a reasonable time."

"Excellent," said Cox. "We shall have to devise a plan to send Mr. Lincoln back to Illinois. But there's time for that later. It's a pleasure doing business with you, sir."

"And with you," replied Webb.

"Well, that was fairly painless," said McFadden, rising to his feet. "I do believe I'm in the mood for a poker game. Will you join us, Stewart?"

"A minnow with sharks. No, sir. I'll watch, though, if you don't mind."

"Perhaps Sir Stewart would agree to deal," said Livermore. "Five-card stud."

They don't even trust each other, Webb thought. "If the others wish," he said aloud.

McFadden handed Webb the cards, then distributed the chips. "Thousand-dollar ante, ten thousand limit, three raises."

Webb gasped when he heard no objections. He might have felt less comfortable had he recognized the metaphor in the level of the stakes. He took a sip of wine and acknowledged to himself that he had never felt better.

# CHAPTER

# 25

From the diary of Caroline Wade-Healy

*Thursday, March 6, 1864*
*12:00 noon*
*My God! Will this destruction of our nation's seed corn never end? My poor Gettysburg has suffered so, but no more, I suspect, than any other community across our tortured nation. They buried young Tony Langley this morning. That makes twenty from this small town. A quarter of those died here last July.*

*I grieve when I think that Samuel is a part of this terrible killing. Here comes the train. I truly dread this trip to Chicago. I seldom have omens, but I sense a bad one.*

*March 10, 1864*
*6:00 P.M.*
*Nothing works anymore! I have just squandered four days of my life riding on this dreadfully cold train. Schedules mean nothing in time of war. The most insignificant of military needs takes precedence over the most pressing of civilian matters. At least I'm here. I have only a few minutes before the train arrives at the Chicago station.*

*My, how everything has changed! This must be the fastest growing city in the country. Large vacant tracts of a year ago are filled with factories of every size and description. When this war ends there will be an explosion of westward migration. The jobs and the land will be here. When I was a girl, this was the frontier. No more.*

*It sometimes seems that every young man in the nation wears a uniform. There will be so much disruption when they all come home. I don't know much about business, as I freely admit, but I know one thing about people: they all need shoes—even those poor souls who have lost a leg in the war. At every stop I was struck by the large number of young men with artificial limbs. They shouldn't have to beg the way they do. I will have to think about that. Something must be done.*

---

"It's been a long time, Mrs. Healy," said the desk clerk. "It's so good to see you again."

"Thank you, George. Is my room ready? I sent a telegram nearly a week ago." She truly hated this city, the source of so many bad memories. But if she had to be here, she might as well dwell in comfort. The Stockman's Hotel had been built at the edge of the stockyards, a matter in which she had some direct financial interest. Cattle produced hides, and hides were necessary for shoe production. The immediate availability of cheap leather had prompted her to build her largest factory here. A blind person could find the hotel simply by following the smell of the stockyards, yet the dining room, its kitchen staffed by French chefs, served the best meals anywhere on the continent. That alone made the trip worthwhile—if anything could. Caroline truly relished the mushrooms stuffed with crab that was shipped in ice all the way from New England. What kind of world will we live in by the turn of the century? she wondered. She doubted she'd be around to find out.

On March 1 her accountant had wired her that her fortune had surpassed six million dollars. Her worth almost made the purpose of the trip seem ludicrous. The immediate problem involved mere thousands of dollars—hardly a week's profit. But take care of the pennies, someone had said, and the dollars will take care of themselves. Besides, she despised a thief.

"Everything is ready, Mrs. Healy, just as you requested. The Governor's Suite. I must inform you, ma'am, the rooms are more expensive than the last time you visited. We haven't had an open room in months."

"It's to be expected, George. What with the war, everything costs more. Even shoes."

"Will you have dinner in your room this evening?"

"No. I need to move around, get my circulation going again."

He passed the registration book across the counter. She signed and slid it back. "How long will you be staying with us?" the clerk inquired.

"Do I have to tell you right now?"

With the suite in such high demand, he wanted to say yes. "Of course not, Mrs. Healy. Can you give me a rough estimate?"

"At least a week, perhaps two or more. This is a business trip, and I don't want to leave until everything is resolved." It would surprise Mr. Pendergrass, the factory manager, to see her. She purposefully had kept her visit a secret.

Then she remembered: he won't know me when he sees me. Her first choice
as manager had been Isaac Bullock, her Boston manager. But he had declined,
giving as his reason an unwillingness to relocate his family. Perhaps, she had
thought, but not quite accurate. Bullock had an invalid wife, so he kept a
mistress. Everyone knew about it, but no one discussed it. He presented the
outward appearance of being a loving husband who doted on his wife—a totally possessive witch with never a kind word to say about anyone. Don't
judge, Caroline reminded herself. No one could know the suffering she had
endured.

So Bullock had recommended his assistant manager for the job. She trusted
Bullock implicitly, so she had hired James Scott Pendergrass solely on
Bullock's recommendation. She had never met the man. Perhaps that had
been unwise. Maybe he *was* a crook, or perhaps the job had simply overwhelmed him. It made no difference, she thought. Or perhaps the discrep-
ancies were reasonable what with the supply problems and inflated costs. She
had to discover the reason for herself.

After unpacking her luggage and taking a bath, Caroline descended the
stairs to the dining room. Even at a quarter past eight, there were few empty
tables. She stood at the entrance, waiting to be seated. As she waited, she
felt as though she was being watched. She turned sharply, and a man seated
alone at the far side of the room turned away. Had he been looking at her?

"This way, Mrs. Healy," said the maître d'. "Your table is ready. How's
the general doing?"

"He's fine. He's serving on General Meade's staff."

"I always liked the general," he said as he pushed her chair closer to the
table. "I met him many years ago, when I worked at Miss Charlotte's—"

Caroline raised her hand to silence him. "Don't look now, but there's a
man on the far side of the room, seated beneath the picture of the mill. Do
you know his name?"

The maître d' stole a glance. "He turned away, ma'am. I think he might
have been looking at you."

"Do you know who he is?"

"Yes, ma'am. He comes in here occasionally. His name is Sterling Andrews."

"Do you know what business he's in?"

"Something to do with mining, I believe. He also manufactures utensils
for the military—you know, tin plates, knives, spoons, that sort of thing. He
usually has a young woman with him when he comes in here. He's alone
this time."

"Does he live around here?"

"No, ma'am. He's from Philadelphia, I believe. I could check if you'd
like."

"Don't bother. Is he still looking this way?"

The maître d' stepped aside as a waiter poured a glass of water. He glanced across the room. "He's looking this way, Mrs. Healy. I'd say he is staring."

"Thank you." She glanced up at the waiter. "I'll have some of those scrumptious stuffed mushrooms to begin with—and coffee. Then I'll have one of those delightful marinated steaks, with corn and carrots. I'll have wine with the meal, something red and dry. Cherry pie for dessert, if you have it."

"Very well, Mrs. Healy." He wrote down the order and left.

"He keeps looking this way off and on. Shall I do something, ma'am?" asked the maître d'.

"No. I don't want to make a scene." She reached inside her bag and handed him a dollar. "That will be all—and thank you."

"Thank *you*, Mrs. Healy."

Caroline resisted the temptation to look across the room as she savored the mushrooms. She had a vague memory of the face, what she had seen of it, but nothing she could place. Where have I met him? she wondered.

An hour passed before she finished the meal. The mysterious man paid his bill and left the dining room while she was eating her pie. She hated herself for gorging that way, but she had eaten so sparingly on the journey—and she had always had a weakness for good food. She smiled as she remembered the prize she had won for making the best peach pie at the county fair. That had been when—1835 or 1836? Before the war, before Samuel—before everything. Even before Porter Wade. She shuddered. All the memories, good and bad, were mixed together. How frail we are, she thought, and how much we are at the whim of fate. I wonder who that stranger is? And what is his interest in me?

After writing her room number on the check, Caroline placed a generous tip on the table and flicked the bread crumbs from her dress. She touched the napkin to her lips, slid her chair back, and strolled slowly into the ornate lobby. She thumbed through a magazine for a moment, then walked down a hallway. About halfway down, she turned and walked through an open door. She stopped and waited. Soon, she heard muffled footsteps on the carpet. She stepped sharply into the hall.

"Who *are* you, sir?" she demanded.

Surprised, the man stepped back. He glanced over his shoulder. They were alone. "I didn't intend to frighten you, Mrs. Wade—I guess it's Mrs. Healy now, isn't it?—but I confess my surprise at seeing you here."

She waited.

"I suppose you don't remember me," he added nervously. "I'm Sterling Andrews. We met only once. You may recall a gathering of businessmen in Philadelphia, shortly after the war began." He chuckled. "I'll never forget how you knocked the props from under that pompous quartermaster colonel. I think about it often."

"I do remember you—vaguely," Caroline said noncommittally. "Why were you staring at me, back in the dining room—and were you following me just now?"

"I confess to staring, but not to following you. My room is just down the hall." He hesitated. "But I must speak with you, only someplace else. May I come to your room later?"

"Certainly not!"

"Then could we meet someplace, perhaps in a bar or another restaurant?"

"I'll have to check my schedule. What's this all about, Mr. Andrews?"

"Not now, not here. You *must* trust me, it's important. I just don't know what else to do. Everyone knows your reputation, Mrs. Healy. No one is more respected or thought of as being more honest and patriotic."

Caroline blushed. "You make me sound like a saint. I assure you I am not, sir. I'm simply a businesswoman trying to get along in a man's world. It's sometimes a struggle, I might add."

"I'm certain it is, Mrs. Healy. There's a fine little dining room down the street. Their pancakes are delicious. Perhaps you would permit me to buy you breakfast."

Although miserably full just now, she knew that would pass. Besides, what harm could it do? "As you wish, Mr. Andrews. I'll meet you in the lobby at seven-thirty tomorrow morning."

"Excellent. I'll be looking forward to it. Until tomorrow." He smiled, nodded, and walked past her down the hall. He stopped near the end and inserted a key into a door. As it opened, he glanced at Caroline, who was still standing there. They both smiled.

Well, she thought, at least he told the truth about his room.

As Sam Wade prepared to jump on the train, he slapped his exhausted horse and sent it galloping into the bushes. The other men had already filed into the empty railroad car. A search for clothing other than their Confederate uniforms had delayed them. In desperation, Wade's men had subdued a Union lieutenant and four enlisted men stationed as guards at a railroad bridge. The humiliated soldiers had objected strenuously when ordered to remove their uniforms before being bound and gagged. The remainder of Wade's men had found various pieces of civilian clothing along the way before reaching the wood and water station. It had taken some convincing before the engineer reluctantly agreed to let them board the train out here in the middle of nowhere, some sixty miles west of Chattanooga.

They had been in the saddle for nearly forty-eight hours, and the thought of sleep pushed everything else from Wade's mind. Several of the men were already stretched out with their eyes closed as he walked on unsteady legs down the narrow aisle.

"Wake me when we reach Chattanooga," Clinton said as Wade approached. Without waiting for a reply, he placed his head against the side of the car and closed his eyes.

Wade dropped into an empty seat and shivered. His body had passed beyond fatigue and hovered on the verge of rebellion. Nothing worked right anymore, least of all his mind. He curled up on the hard seat, which felt more like a featherbed, and fell asleep immediately.

Wade bolted upright at the sound of the whistle. Too bad the train didn't break down before we arrived, he thought. Now he would have to look for another place to sleep. It was dawn and there were signs of life stirring in the battered city. The train chugged laboriously toward the station. The wheels screeched as the engine jerked to a stop. He turned around and shook Clinton. The major, dressed as a corporal, groaned as he rubbed his eyes.

"Already?" he asked.

"Wake up the men," Wade said. "Take them to that hotel we slept in last fall when we first arrived. I'll find someone to report to and meet you there. Try to get a few hours' more sleep before we look for some fresh uniforms." He walked down the aisle and stepped out into a gentle drizzle. Through the windows, he saw that Clinton had his hands full, trying to wake the others. How could this war have lasted so long, he asked himself, when we have such men as these? There were none better in the army, and they had been selected at random. Perhaps by the end of summer, he thought. This goddamn war has to end sometime. It seemed that every muscle in his body ached as he stepped onto the water-soaked roadway. He noticed the flags hanging limply from two windows of a building down the street. Probably headquarters, he thought. I wonder who's in command now?

Thirty minutes later he left General Thomas's office. It had been difficult convincing the general of his activities since late January. Thomas made Wade reduce it to paper, then questioned him on every point. Finally, in exasperation, Thomas said something about the story being too crazy to make up and sent him from the room with orders to report back later. In the meantime, he would attempt to confirm the idiotic account with Washington. Then Wade had found the telegraph office and sent a message to Colonel Thompson:

ARRIVED IN CHATTANOOGA THIS MORNING STOP MISSION ACCOMPLISHED STOP WE ARE EXHAUSTED AND NEED A COUPLE OF DAYS REST STOP SEND INSTRUCTIONS STOP GENERAL THOMAS HAS DOUBTS ABOUT MY ACCOUNT STOP EXPECT HE WILL WIRE YOU THIS MORNING STOP

A sergeant shook Wade from his deep sleep. He saw the sergeant's lips moving, but the words were garbled. Wade shivered as he rolled on the damp, cold floor. He opened his eyes wide in an effort to let some light in and fully awaken. He felt no better than when he had gone to sleep. "What time is it?" he asked, rubbing his eyes.

"Quarter after eleven, sir. You're Colonel Wade, right?" The sergeant's confusion was understandable. Wade still wore a lieutenant's uniform, and it fit him poorly.

"I'm Wade. What can I do for you?"

"Sir, Colonel Sorrel is downstairs. He wants to see you right away."

Wade rolled up on one elbow and rotated his once-wounded shoulder in a futile effort to ease the stiffness. He had felt numb when he left the train. That had been preferable to the aches that nagged him now. "Tell the colonel I'll be down in a moment. Thank you, Sergeant."

The sergeant stood and saluted. Wade managed a nod. He sat up and looked to his left. All except Clinton were still asleep. "I have to go downstairs, Jim," Wade told his friend. "Let the men sleep a bit longer."

Clinton nodded and let his head drop back to the floor.

Wade trudged sleepily down the stairs. "I'm Colonel Wade, sir."

"You're out of uniform, Colonel."

Wade examined his attire and shrugged. "You wanted to see me, sir?"

"I've been instructed to give you this telegram. It's marked urgent."

Wade accepted the flimsy from the colonel and read Thompson's reply:

PLEASED YOU ARE ALIVE STOP CONGRATULATIONS ON THE SUCCESS OF YOUR MISSION STOP YOUR MOTHER IS IN CHICAGO STOP NECESSARY THAT YOU GO TO HER AT THE STOCKMANS HOTEL BY NEXT TRAIN STOP GO ALONE STOP SHE IS WELL STOP WIRE ME WHEN YOU ARRIVE STOP

"That's all?" asked Wade.

"That's all, Colonel." He frowned. "General Thomas asked that you report to him as soon as possible." He hesitated as he attempted to analyze this sorry excuse for an officer. The man obviously needed some discipline. "Colonel, I suggest that you report to the quartermaster and secure a proper uniform before you present yourself to the general."

Wade shrugged. "The general has seen me in this uniform before, sir."

The colonel's features hardened. "That's an order, Colonel Wade."

"Yes, sir." Pompous son of a bitch, Wade thought. "Since none of my men are in proper uniforms, either, I'll just get them and we'll *all* go get properly attired."

"As you wish. I'll tell the general to expect you in an hour."

"I trust you will also inform him of the reason for the delay, Colonel."

"One hour, Colonel. Don't be late."

Wade saluted without replying.

He followed his men as they stumbled down the stairs. Proper uniforms were the least of their concerns. As their bodies adjusted to motion, they realized how long it had been since they had eaten last. There had been nothing but a paltry portion of hardtack and jerky in nearly three days. Wade nudged them along, but his thoughts were on the telegram. Chicago? Why Chicago? And why report to his mother? He sighed. He yearned to see her again. His success would please her. But it seemed a long way to travel for a chat. He followed his men into the open. The rain continued—one of those gentle soakers that farmers love. Wade eased his way to the head of the procession and led the men to the hastily constructed warehouse.

"I'm Colonel Wade," he said to the quartermaster captain inside. "This fine-looking gentleman is Major Clinton, and this is Lieutenant Healy. The others are enlisted men. Colonel Sorrel thinks we need some new uniforms."

"We ain't seen a new uniform around here in weeks, Colonel. We've got some used ones, though. Sergeant, fix these men up with what they need. You'll have to sign for everything, Colonel."

Wade nodded.

The uniforms weren't much, but at least they were clean and fit properly—for the most part. Wade slipped into a fresh pair of boots. A little loose, he thought, but better than too tight. "I'll need a pistol and holster," he said as he buttoned the coat.

"How about a sword, Colonel? Got one here that has hardly been used."

"Just the pistol, Sergeant. If the Rebs get close enough to stab, I'm a goner for sure."

The sergeant smiled. "Yes, sir."

"And some ammunition, and weapons for the other officers."

"Comin' right up, sir."

The sergeant faded into the dimly lit aisle. He returned a few minutes later and dropped the pistols and ammunition on the table. "Is that all, Colonel?"

Wade nodded. "Where do I sign?"

"I'll have to fill out the forms, sir. It'll take a while."

Wade glanced at a large clock standing in the corner. "I have to be at General Thomas's headquarters shortly. Major Clinton will sign your forms."

"I don't know, sir."

"Then you'll have to explain my delay to the general."

"I'll make do with the major's signature, sir."

"Thank you, Sergeant. It's been a pleasure doing business with you."

Major General George Thomas motioned Wade into his office. "Have a chair, Colonel." Thomas walked behind his desk and sat down. He rested his forearms on a wrinkled folder. "Following our meeting this morning, I sent a clerk over to personnel to look for your records." He slid the folder across the desk. "Are you *this* Colonel Wade?"

Wade opened the file and glanced at the first page. "Yes, sir." He placed the document back on the desk.

"Impressive, Colonel. You get around, don't you?"

"More than I sometimes prefer, General."

"I might add that your Colonel Thompson thinks highly of you, also. He has requested that I post orders sending you to Chicago for a short time. Highly irregular, you know, sending a lieutenant colonel to see his mother."

Wade reached into his pocket. "I received this telegram a short time ago, sir. I have no idea what this is all about."

Thomas nodded. "I've seen your telegram, Colonel. The word *urgent* caught the attention of one of my staff officers. So you don't know the reason for this—urgency?"

"No, sir, I don't. Colonel Thompson seldom does anything without a good reason, though."

"I've had your orders prepared, Colonel. I remind you that you are to notify Colonel Thompson immediately upon your arrival."

"Yes, sir. What about my men?"

"They will remain here for the time being. We'll find useful service for them in your absence."

"Will that be all, sir?"

"Yes. Have a safe trip. You may pick up your orders from the adjutant."

Wade stood and saluted. "Thank you, General. May I say something personal?"

"Of course, Colonel."

"I was on Snodgrass Hill that afternoon. You made a magnificent stand, sir."

"You were *there?*"

"Yes, sir. I brought about a dozen men up the back side of the hill, around midafternoon. We arrived just in time to be chased off, but that made us no less proud to have been a part of it. I just wanted you to know."

Thomas smiled. "That means a great deal to me, Colonel." He walked to the front of his desk and extended his hand. Wade hesitated for a moment, then grasped it. "I must confess, Colonel, I didn't know that any reinforcements made it through that afternoon."

"A dozen tired men hardly constitute reinforcement, sir."

"Nevertheless, you are to be commended. Good luck to you, sir," Thomas said, patting Wade on the shoulder.

Wade straightened. "Thank you, sir. Guess I'd better go see about a train."

The albino sat stiffly erect in the horsehair chair, shivering slightly from the lingering effects of the cold March wind. He balanced his hat on his knee and pulled his collar tightly around his neck. He hated the cold, not to mention heat. Perhaps that explained his mercurial temperament.

An elegantly polished marble staircase, the centerpiece of this spacious Philadelphia mansion, spiraled upward behind him. Beautiful young maidens in coal black dresses accented with white aprons scurried here and there, polishing this and adjusting that, hardly making a sound. When required, each provided a wide range of personal services. But such things were of no interest to him. Everything seemed precisely placed, with hardly a speck of dust in sight. No less care had been given to the other parts of the mansion. He had been here several times before, always at night, never without a scheduled appointment. Why had he been summoned this time? he wondered. Had the time arrived?

He appreciated the neatness, the perfection of planned orderliness, the symmetry of predictable form. Those conditions suited his own temperament. In a dreadful sense, that explained why he felt so uncomfortable, so apprehensive, as he sat waiting for Ira McFadden's summons. Twenty minutes had elapsed since his arrival. Uncertainty made him nervous.

"Mr. Whitey," the butler announced, "the master will see you now."

Whitey—it wasn't his real name; in his business it didn't pay to advertise his true identity—tightly gripped the brim of his hat with both hands. He blinked unceasingly now, a condition that had developed beyond his control as the stress had increased. There had been no letup for more than a year. He sighed loudly, then rose and followed the butler down the length of the great room. Stepping lightly on the polished marble floor, he advanced toward the large double doors at the far right.

The butler opened both doors simultaneously and stepped two paces inside. "Mr. Whitey, sir."

The room's occupant stood in a far corner swirling brandy in a snifter. He drained the remaining liquid. Only in his late twenties, almost boyish in appearance, he looked oddly out of place in the opulence evidenced by every appointment of his surroundings.

Whitey stood stiffly, six feet inside the room. The butler closed the doors as he backed out. The albino rotated his hat nervously, waiting for some acknowledgment of his presence.

The young man, dressed in black silk trousers and a red velvet smoking jacket, peered at his nervous guest. He frowned as he stooped and set his glass on a small side table. Every move he made bespoke power—all without a word.

Whitey heard the sigh from across the room. "You're late, Mr. Whitey," McFadden said quietly, his voice barely audible.

"Sorry, sir. It's the trains." He took a quick step forward. "Is there a problem, sir?" His anxiety had gotten the best of him.

"Not so much a problem as a concern." McFadden moved to the point slowly. He preferred to ease into discomfort. "You have served me well.

You organized matters in the South with care and frugality. We appreciate that more than you know."

"Thank you, sir." He breathed easier. McFadden seldom praised anyone.

McFadden walked to the bar and poured himself another brandy. He motioned toward Whitey.

"No thank you, sir."

McFadden nodded. "I forgot. You don't drink spirits, do you?" He walked to the center of the room. "As I was about to say, we have a concern. Actually, everything has changed. We are moving in a new direction, and the old plans have to be abandoned."

Whitey stiffened. "Everything, sir?"

"Not everything, Whitey. The men you have trained will be put to good use in time. No, my concern is with all those fine Southern gentlemen who want to go into the railroad business when the war ends. How many of them are there altogether?"

"Twenty-eight, sir, counting those on the fringe."

"And you know them all?"

"Yes, sir. I've slept in most of their homes at one time or another."

"What is your judgment of them?"

"I beg your pardon, sir?"

"What kind of men are they?"

"They are Southerners, sir. Proud, dedicated to their cause, intolerant of anyone who does not share their point of view."

"I assume they would be displeased if something happened to eliminate our plans involving their railroads."

"I think they would be quite angry, sir."

"Vengeful, too, don't you think?"

"Almost certainly, sir. They will interpret it as a betrayal of their honor."

"Hmmm, I see." McFadden swallowed the last of the brandy. "Just as I suspected." He placed the glass on a table and crossed his arms over his chest. "Well, Mr. Whitey, that's the concern. It's quite irreversible, our change in plans. We can't have vengeful Southerners running all over the place, can we?"

Whitey sighed. "No, sir."

"So I suppose the concern is a problem, after all, and problems have to be solved."

"*All* of them, sir?"

McFadden nodded. "That's right, Mr. Whitey. As quickly and efficiently as possible."

"Sir, I don't have to remind you that these are important, powerful men."

McFadden shrugged. "Not *that* important, Mr. Whitey. Not *that* powerful." He popped a horehound candy into his mouth. "What will you need?"

"I can't say for certain, sir. It'll take some planning. Some of the men we send won't make it back."

McFadden shrugged again. Did Whitey truly think that concerned him? "What are your chances of getting them all, Mr. Whitey?"

"Depends, sir, on the amount of time I have. I don't know where many of them are at present. The men I send will have to track them down in what may be very hostile surroundings."

"That's your problem. We don't want them to figure out what's happening. Make it look like an accident wherever possible. Pick your men carefully."

The albino was sweating now—for only the second time in several years. Unlike other people, he had very few pores. He had been given an impossible task, one that was doomed to fail. McFadden abhorred failure. But then, Whitey had been given an important responsibility, one that would test his skills to the limit. He might find twenty of the men, perhaps one or two more. With so much of the South in turmoil, freedom of movement was next to impossible. His agents would have to find men totally unknown to them. The first few would be easy enough, but the others would hear rumors and be on the alert.

"Coordinating this across half the continent will be difficult, sir."

"I told you that was *your* problem, Mr. Whitey."

"Do I have a budget, sir?"

"I think not. I can only guess at the cost, but I have established a $250,000 line of credit at our bank. Let me know through the usual channels if you need more." He walked closer, to emphasize the next point. He placed his hand on Whitey's shoulder. "You shall not fail for lack of funds, my friend. This is too important. Do I make myself clear?"

"Yes, sir."

"And not a word of this to anyone. No one. When this is finished, I won't want to see any of those men alive. Not a soul."

Whitey's eyes closed. "I understand. Will that be all, sir?"

"Yes. Good day, Mr. Whitey. Provide me a copy of your schedule when you have it prepared. Bring it personally; don't use the mail."

Whitey nodded, turned, and walked solemnly toward the door. His clothes were nearly soaked through with sweat.

"Oh, there's one other thing, Mr. Whitey." The albino froze. "Do this first, and take care of it personally. I want you to take a trip to Chicago. There is someone there who has become a problem. You'll find him staying at the Stockman's Hotel."

# CHAPTER

# 26

Wade took the spur line west and changed trains thirty miles outside of Chattanooga, then traveled through the rugged hills to Nashville. By dawn two days later, the train had reached Louisville, where a second engine and several empty cars were added following a lengthy delay. Something was being planned. Trains crammed with soldiers and war supplies pulled from the station every thirty minutes, heading south toward Chattanooga. Following several delays, the train for Indianapolis pulled from the station and rolled across the rugged Tennessee countryside. Nearly forty-eight hours later, it reached the outskirts of Chicago. The time was three in the afternoon on Monday, March 22, 1864.

Wade decided to report to the headquarters of the Military Department of Illinois before going to the hotel. But first, he went to the telegraph office and sent a telegram to Colonel Thompson. "Arrived Chicago at three this afternoon," the brief message read. "Will wire as soon as I know more." After having his orders stamped, Wade went to a barbershop and had his beard trimmed and took a hot bath. Feeling more refreshed than he had in weeks, he arrived at the hotel at six, just as the sun set on the first full day of spring. A man jostled him and knocked him off stride as he walked through the door. The man never looked back as he disappeared down the windswept street.

"Will you direct me to the room of Mrs. Caroline Healy?" he asked the attendant.

"And who might you be, Colonel?" the attendant inquired.

"Lieutenant Colonel Sam Wade. I'm Mrs. Healy's son."

"Ah, Colonel Wade. She's been expecting you. I'll show you to her room myself."

Caroline seemed surprised when she opened the door in response to the attendant's knock. She quickly recovered and reached out for Wade, placing her arms around her son as the attendant retreated down the hall. "I'm so happy to see you alive and well again, Samuel." She stepped back into the suite and looked into his sparkling eyes. "I've questioned myself a hundred times, asking you to go on that dangerous assignment."

"It had to be done, Mother. You look well."

"I felt well, until I arrived here. What has Colonel Thompson told you?"

"Nothing. He sent me a telegram and said it was urgent that I meet with you here."

She looked down the hall but saw no one. "Come in. I have so much to tell you. Have you had dinner?"

"No, although I did have a bath and a trim."

Caroline walked to the window and looked out across the city. She had grown no fonder of the place in the past two weeks. Where to begin? she wondered. With the worst part, she thought. "I've learned of something dreadful, Samuel." She turned from the window. "A man approached me the day I arrived here. He had been staring at me all during supper. He immediately expressed an urgent need to talk with me in private. The next morning, I met with him in a small eating establishment. What he said knocked the breath from me. He said he knew of a plot to assassinate President Lincoln and some congressmen. He was quite convincing. He even admitted to being a member of the group that is planning this terrible thing."

"Did he tell you his name?" asked Wade. "What group of men?"

She told him everything she knew. "I felt such distress that I came back to my room and stayed here until midafternoon. I was filled with such anger that I wanted to scream. I couldn't think, and I had no idea what I should do. That evening, I decided to send a telegram to David. I constructed the message very carefully, saying barely enough to alert him that something terrible was in the offing. Early the next morning—it was only a little over a week ago, but it seems like a year—an officer knocked on my door and woke me. He asked me to accompany him to headquarters. Another officer took me directly to General Burnside's office. He told me he had received an urgent message from General Halleck, and he instructed me to write out everything I knew. The message was sent to Washington by courier.

"When I was done I went back to the hotel. That was on the twelfth, I believe. I heard nothing more until five days later. Then I received a message informing me that someone was coming to Chicago to meet with me. Two days ago I received another message, this one informing me that you had reported in at Chattanooga and would come here by the most direct route." She froze at the sound of a knock on the door. Wade moved cautiously across the room.

"Who is it?" he demanded.

"Major Lewis Winslow of General Halleck's staff. May I come in, sir?"

Wade opened the door a crack. Anyone could get a major's uniform. "Let me see your papers, Major."

Winslow slid his orders through the crack in the door. Wade shut it and read the document, then he opened the door. "Come in, Major. Please excuse my caution."

"Are you Colonel Wade?"

"Yes, I am. This is my mother, Caroline Healy."

"It's a pleasure, Mrs. Healy." He turned to Wade. "Begging the colonel's pardon, sir, but when did you arrive?"

"This afternoon, Major."

"Then may I assume your mother has informed you of our concern?"

"She has, but we haven't had time to discuss the matter."

"I was informed that you have independent knowledge of this affair, sir. Is that correct?"

Wade turned to his mother. Her mouth hung open. "Yes. I learned of it some time ago, but no one took the information seriously."

"You may be assured, Colonel, that it is being taken seriously now."

"Explain something to me, Major. How did this matter reach General Halleck's ear?"

"As I understand it, sir, General Healy went to a congressman friend the night the telegram arrived from Mrs. Healy. Following a brief discussion, the congressman and General Healy went to see Col. Jason Thompson. General Healy informed Colonel Thompson that you also were aware of a plot.

"During the course of the discussion, Colonel Thompson recalled that you had mentioned hearing much the same thing, but he had dismissed it because he had heard of so many plots and it was impossible to investigate them all. Given the similarities between your comments and what Mrs. Healy had learned, Colonel Thompson concluded that the situation needed more thorough investigation. Colonel Thompson also revealed that more recently he had gotten wind of some possible undercurrent of activity among some high-placed businessmen who are dissatisfied with the way the war is being run. They apparently want to try to influence events to their advantage. He discovered nothing definite there, so he didn't make a connection—until this surfaced.

"Satisfied that they could no longer ignore the rumors, Colonel Thompson and General Healy woke General Halleck a little after midnight, and they all went to the White House. They met with Mr. Lincoln for about thirty minutes; then General Healy gave me a message to send to Chicago. By then it was about three in the morning. In the end, everyone concluded that it was best to wait until the detailed letter from your mother arrived before taking further action."

"So what do we do now, sir?" asked Caroline.

"We move as quickly as possible, ma'am, to find out as much as we can. Do you have any suggestions, Colonel? I have orders to give you every possible assistance. The same will come from General Burnside, as soon as I meet with him in the morning. What do you suggest for the next step?"

Wade shook his head. "I have to think about this some more, Major. I haven't had time to discuss it with my mother, to think about how her information corresponds to what I already know. Let's meet in the dining room for breakfast. I'll let you know then what I think we should do next."

"Very well, sir. I need to find a room for the night. Is seven-thirty acceptable?"

"That will be fine. See you then, Major."

Winslow saluted and turned to leave. He stopped at the door. "Sir, do you know the cause of that disturbance downstairs?"

"What disturbance?" asked Wade.

"When I entered the lobby, I noticed a large gathering at the end of a hallway. Several policemen were present. I just thought you might know what was going on."

"No, Major. I saw nothing unusual when I arrived."

"Very well, sir. Good night, Mrs. Healy. Colonel Wade."

"Good night, Major."

As the door closed, Caroline reached out and touched her son's arm. "You'll remain here, of course. There are two bedrooms."

"I'd stay here if I had to sleep on the floor, Mother. Do you have any idea of the danger you're in?"

"Of course, Samuel. I've thought of little else since learning about this. And why didn't you tell me that you knew?"

"You know why, Mother. I'm a soldier. I don't gossip about matters I'm uncertain of. I couldn't even make Colonel Thompson believe me. But that's not the problem now. The problem is, what do we do next?"

"I can think of one thing. The man I spoke with, Sterling Andrews, is still here in the hotel. I think it would be helpful if you talked with him. With the information you have, you might learn more than I did."

Wade nodded. "That's an excellent idea. I'll try to see him tomorrow. Right now, I'm going to see about room service. After that we'll go through this again in detail. I want you to tell me everything he said, no matter how insignificant."

Wade and Winslow arrived at the telegraph room at ten the next morning. They spent the next hour carefully composing the wording of the telegram. It was divided into two parts. The first read:

THE MATTERS CH BROUGHT TO YOUR ATTENTION  AND
WHICH WE DISCUSSED LAST YEAR ARE THE SAME STOP
COMPARING THE TWO EVENTS LEADS TO THE CONCLUSION
THAT THE PRINCIPAL ACTS RELATED TO THE SUBJECT WILL
BE CARRIED OUT IN TWO PARTS STOP THE FIRST IN EARLY
JUNE THE SECOND IF NECESSARY AT ANY TIME FROM
EARLY JUNE UNTIL EARLY NOVEMBER STOP PARTIES
CONCERNED SHOULD BE ADVISED OF THIS AND
APPROPRIATE MEASURES TAKEN STOP YOU ARE ALSO
ADVISED THAT THE GENTLEMAN WHO SURFACED THIS
MATTER DIED LAST NIGHT STOP HIS DEATH WAS RULED
A SUICIDE STOP MAJOR IS LEAVING FOR WASHINGTON
TODAY AND WILL PROVIDE DETAILS STOP

The second part, sent a few minutes later, read:

I BELIEVE AN ATTEMPT IS IN PROGRESS TO CLOSE OUT
THE SOUTHERN OPERATION BY ELIMINATING THE
PRINCIPALS STOP THIS RAISES GRAVE PERSONAL
CONCERNS THAT I CANNOT IGNORE STOP MAJOR WILL
CARRY MY PERSONAL DETAILED CORRESPONDENCE
ON THIS MATTER STOP DO NOT FEEL IT PRUDENT TO WAIT
FOR YOUR REPLY STOP AM LEAVING FOR CHATTANOOGA
BY FIRST AVAILABLE TRAIN STOP WILL GO FROM THERE
TO TAKE APPROPRIATE MEASURES TO PREVENT THE
WORST STOP I HOPE FOR YOUR DELAYED CONCURRENCE
AND NOTIFICATION OF GENERAL COMMANDING ARMY OF
THE CUMBERLAND STOP IF OPERATION GOES AS HOPED I
WILL BE IN POSITION TO OBTAIN INSIDE INFORMATION AS
THE EVENTS UNFOLD STOP MUCH IS UNCERTAIN AT THIS
TIME STOP MY LETTER WILL EXPLAIN STOP WILL CONTACT
YOU UPON MY ARRIVAL IN CHATTANOOGA STOP DO NOT
EXPECT MY RETURN TO WASHINGTON UNTIL APPROX ONE
MONTH FROM THIS DATE STOP HOPE TO HAVE A PLAN BY
DATE OF MY RETURN STOP

"That should do it," Winslow said. "Are you certain it's for the best that
you return to Rome?"

"I have no choice, Major. These people are making this war personal, so
I have to fight them on their terms. I have one name and I intend to make
the most of it. I depend on you to make my case to Colonel Thompson."

"You can count on me, sir. I wish I were going with you."

"It's more important that you fully brief the people in Washington, Major. My guess is that Colonel Thompson will want you to talk to Lincoln. If you get the opportunity, make Lincoln believe that this is not a half-cocked plot by some disgruntled Southern diehards. Planning has been in progress for many months now. They *will* act. I believe that the events of the next few months will determine the destiny of this nation for generations. Lincoln must understand that he is the pivot on which our future will turn. He must win in November; he must survive." Wade looked at his watch. "What time does your train leave?"

"Two-fifteen."

"Then I must return to the hotel and compose my letter. I'll meet you in the hotel dining room at noon."

Wade had struggled in his mind with the content of his letter to Thompson. Should he provide only the details of direct interest to the conspiracy? Or should he also explain his emotions, his personal feelings, so that Thompson would fully understand why he had to go into the South one last time? In the end, he decided on a compromise, leaving out the matter of his father, even though he knew he had to try to warn the general, either in person or through a messenger. War or no war, Wade was determined to save his father's life if possible.

He sat at the desk and sighed deeply as he rubbed his eyes with thumb and forefinger. His mother was humming as she packed in the adjacent room. She had purchased a ticket on the same train with Winslow. She and Wade would say their farewells at lunch. Wade focused his thoughts on the task at hand and began to write:

The death of the man named Sterling Andrews is unfortunate. I believe
he had more to tell me, perhaps the names of all the conspirators.
Although the death has been ruled a suicide, I am certain it was murder.
I do not assert my beliefs on this matter lightly. As I entered the hotel,
I was momentarily distracted by a man who bumped into me on his way
out. My thoughts were on other things, so I paid no attention to him at
the time. I remembered only after learning of Andrews's death that the
man had certain unusual features. Although he had his face mostly
covered by his coat collar, I saw enough to record in my mind that he
was an albino. I had never seen him before, but his involvement in the
plan has been described to me. I believe he had already killed Andrews
by that time and was leaving the scene of the crime.

This brings me to my trip to Rome. I have previously explained
the personal reasons that compel me to make this trip. There also

is a practical reason. I am convinced that Cathy's brother, Frank
Bowman, is the man assigned to lead the assassination attempt.
I believe they selected him specifically because of his relationship
to the men involved in the Southern arm of the conspiracy. His
involvement would provide obvious advantages to the primary
conspirators. If he has not left the plantation, I may be able to
convince him of the futility of his mission, especially now that
it is known. I have to persuade him that he must play along but
find a way to communicate with me or you when events are about
to unfold. This offers our best chance to foil the plot.

Now that you know my feelings as well as the available facts,
I pray for both your understanding and your support. Major Winslow
will fill you in on anything I have overlooked.

I need to take Major Clinton with me to Rome. If you receive
this letter before I leave Chattanooga, I would appreciate having
orders waiting for us to carry out our task. If not, I suppose we will
have to make do.

Your obedient servant,
Lt. Col. Sam Wade

The orders were waiting when Wade arrived at Chattanooga. Lieutenant Healy and the others who had assisted with the prison break in Richmond had been recalled to Washington. With nothing to detain Wade and
Clinton, they donned Confederate gray and set out for Rome. Since the day
the war began, both of the men had spent more time behind enemy lines
than with their own troops. The prospect no longer caused them fear; they
felt as comfortable dressed in gray as they did in blue. The difficulty had
become one of maintaining vigilance. Long exposure to dangerous conditions dulls the senses.

They crossed the Tennessee River at dusk on March 27 and rode at an
easy pace down a narrow lane south of Lookout Mountain. Throughout the
next two days, they were never out of sight of rebel soldiers. No one seemed
to notice them. They spent the second night with an Alabama cavalry troop
assigned to picket duty. It rained that night and continued the next morning as they saddled their horses and began the last twenty-mile leg of their
journey. Since Rome was out of the way, they turned east five miles north
of the city. The rain stopped around ten that morning, but the day remained
dreary. Wet, tired, and hungry, they arrived at the plantation at four in the
afternoon.

All things considered, it had been an easy journey, as easy as eighty miles
in the saddle could be. They walked the horses down the lane leading to
the mansion. The sun broke through the overcast for a few minutes; then

the light faded again as a gentle mist began to fall. They had given up trying to remain dry, and Clinton had developed a cough.

Arthur Bowman walked onto the front porch as they approached.
"Never expected to see you again so soon, Simon. What brings you back
this way?"

"A mission of some urgency, sir. Is Cathy here?"

"No. She went with Frank to Rome early this morning. We're almost out
of supplies. They thought they might buy what they could, although I doubt
it will be much."

Wade and Clinton stamped their feet on the first step to jar loose the mud,
then went to the top. "So Frank is still here. I thought he might be gone by
now. Sir, you remember Major Clinton."

"Of course. How are you doing, Major?" They shook hands.

"Passable, sir. It'll be nice to get out'ta the rain for a while."

Bowman turned back to Wade. "Frank plans to leave day after tomorrow,
Simon. Do you have a particular interest in seeing him?"

"I do, sir, and the rest of your family. I'll discuss it with everyone when
they return."

"I expect them back sometime in the morning. I'll tell Mrs. Bowman to
add two plates for supper."

"That won't be necessary, sir. We brought our own food. I won't let you
waste what you have on us.

"We can't have—"

Wade raised his hand. "That's all there is to it, sir. Otherwise, we'll have to
leave and come back later. You will need every scrap. If it's all right with you,
sir, we'll just settle down in the summerhouse, dry our uniforms, and talk later."

"You're always welcome, Simon. The summerhouse hasn't been touched
since you were here last month."

After lighting a fire and hanging their clothes to dry, the two men stretched
out for a nap. Just before dark, Clinton heard a noise. He rose and peered out
the window. "Better put your pants on, Sam. Looks like we've got company."

Wade rubbed his eyes. "Who is it?"

"They must've cut their shoppin' trip short. It 'pears t'be Cathy an' her
brother."

The two men dressed and went to the main room just as Cathy ran down
the walk. "Simon, are you decent?" she yelled as she opened the door, a broad
smile on her face.

Wade touched a match to the lantern, reached out, and caught her in his
arms. They kissed, then she squeezed him tight. "God, you feel good." She
looked up at him. "You'll stay longer this time?"

Wade shook his head. "I'm afraid not. Now that you're back, I'll be leaving tomorrow."

She squeezed him again as he ran his fingers through her hair. "I have to know something, Cathy. Did you talk with Frank?"

She backed away. "About what?"

"About his mission."

"I worked around to it, but it wasn't necessary. Father had told him about the plot and his part in it. Frank figured out the rest."

"Where do they stand?"

"I don't know. It's not something they talk freely about around mother or me."

"They'll *have* to talk about it now. Have you had something to eat?"

"We ate on the ride home. We went to look for supplies, but the town is about scraped clean." Cathy caught a glimpse of Clinton and added, "Hello, Major. I hadn't seen you standing there."

"Good evenin', ma'am."

"I'll tell them you're coming in," she said as she stood on her toes and kissed Wade on the cheek.

"Cathy tells me you won't be staying long," Arthur Bowman said as he touched a lighted match to his pipe. He had built a roaring fire in the fireplace, as much for the relaxed mood provided by the flames as for the heat. They sat in a half circle around the hearth.

"We have to leave tomorrow, sir. We're here for a specific reason."

"What's that?" Bowman asked.

"It's mostly about Frank, but what I have to say will affect all of you." Wade turned and looked at Frank. "I understand you're leaving the day after tomorrow."

"I'm as mended as I'll ever be," Frank replied. "What's this about, Simon? You've piqued my curiosity."

Wade sighed. "It's hard to know where to begin. Do you recall telling me that you had been training for a mission of unknown purpose?"

"Yes."

"I am convinced you are involved in the plot to assassinate Lincoln that has been so much discussed here."

Frank squirmed. "What? How did you arrive at that conclusion?"

"That will become clear soon enough. I only hope you don't decide that you need to kill the major and me." Wade shifted his position and looked at the senior Bowman. "Sir, before I begin, do you have any of that smooth sippin' whiskey left?"

Arthur smiled. "I believe I do, Simon. Mother, will you get the glasses?" They waited while Pearl fetched the glasses, then Bowman poured. "To health and safety," Arthur said. "Now, Simon, what is it you have to tell us?"

"A week ago," he began, "I was in Chicago with my mother. . . ." An hour passed before Wade finished his story. He told them everything: about his own past, about the prison break, about his two families, about his twin brother. The tension mounted as Wade exposed the full extent of his deception. Then he told them all he knew about the plot to kill Lincoln and of the threat to their own lives. As the Bowmans listened they passed through a range of emotions, seldom the same for any two at a given time, feelings evidenced only by the silent expressions in their eyes and their facial distortions. They each had different reasons to hate Wade. Their lists grew as the time passed.

Obviously numbed by Wade's disclosures, at times they simply listened, absorbing the words as though they were part of an impossibly wild tale, a story too improbable to be true. He had lied to them, after all, deceived them and taken advantage of them in countless ways. Why should this story be any different? The changing expressions left him wondering what they really thought, how they might react when he finished.

Cathy sat silently through it all. By the time he finished, tears were running down her cheeks. Pearl Bowman seemed spellbound. More than once, Frank glanced at the rifle hanging over the fireplace, but he obviously knew he would never make it. Clinton sat to his far left and behind, his holster unfastened, ready to react at the first hint of violence. No one had raised a question during the account, but there had to be many.

The only thing Wade omitted was his plea for Frank's assistance. Wade expected opposition to the request. He wondered how he would react if the circumstances were reversed. There was so much for them to grasp!

Arthur sighed as he rose and walked to the table where the nearly empty bottle sat. "It's about all gone. I surely do hate to see it go"—he hesitated as he looked into the fire—"but all things must end." He brought the bottle to where the others sat and distributed the remainder of the precious liquid as evenly as possible. All of the glasses were quickly emptied.

"So what do we do now, Father?" asked Pearl, clearly bewildered.

"I think that is obvious, Mother." He patted her hand. He could not say the words. He could not tell her that they must leave and perhaps never return. Where would they go?

South Alabama, perhaps, to his uncle's plantation. No. They would find him there—sooner or later. He couldn't live that way, always in fear. He had a friend from his school days who lived in Baton Rouge. Perhaps they might go there for a while and think about a plan. Perhaps they should go west, to California.

"How much time do you think we have?" Arthur asked solemnly.

"Based on what I know, sir, I'd leave within the next twelve hours. I've had to travel all the way from here to Chicago and back since they put this plot in motion. The albino may have been temporarily distracted by the murder in Chicago. Now he'll give full attention to this part of his assignment. The killers may be a few days behind me, but I wouldn't depend on it."

"Did you come all this way just to warn us, Simon—Samuel? Damnation! Just what *do* I call you, sir?"

"Sam will do fine."

Cathy rose and looked down at Wade with a pained expression before turning and running from the room.

"You certainly know how to test a woman's love, Colonel," said Arthur Bowman.

"I thought of that, sir. In the end, the decision seemed simple. I had to risk losing her love to save her life."

Bowman blinked, then smiled wryly and nodded. "I suspect she will figure that out on her own."

"You asked why I came," said Wade. "Warning you was one of *two* reasons."

"I think the second is obvious," said Frank, glaring at Wade. "You want me to expose my companions. You want me to become a traitor." He slammed his fist against the arm of the chair. "*That* I will never do, sir. I will die first." He rose and stormed from the room.

Clinton started to go after him, but Wade raised a hand to stay him. Without Frank's help, Wade had little chance of identifying the men behind the conspiracy. Without that information, the president's life would remain in constant jeopardy. Lincoln needed contact with the people; he would risk the danger and, in the end, pay with his life. So Frank had to sort through the problem. Had the war worn him down sufficiently to let him examine it rationally? How had his experiences at Vicksburg affected him? Only Frank Bowman knew the answer to those critical questions. A variety of options were open to him, with none of the consequences predictable.

Wade leaned forward. "It appears we are through for tonight, Mr. Bowman. I urge you to prepare for immediate departure. I suggest that you keep your destination a secret, even from your friends. And there is another matter. If you decide to leave, would you please try to find my father and warn him? I have to return to Washington as soon as possible. If you will agree to look for the general, I will write him a letter for you to deliver. Otherwise, I will have to mail it and trust it reaches him in time."

"Write your letter, Sam. I'll let you know our decision in the morning."

"Fair enough, sir." Wade leaned back and rubbed his eyes. He had been wise to dread this moment. Lives were in ruin, but now, at least, these people might survive. "Suddenly, I am very tired. Major Clinton and I will retire to the summerhouse. Thank you for your gracious hospitality, Mrs. Bowman. You have been very kind under difficult circumstances. I wish you the best." He rose, took her hand, and kissed it. As he backed away, he looked into her eyes. She smiled wanly, then nodded.

"I'm not goin' t'sleep a wink tonight," said Clinton as he walked with Wade to the summerhouse.

"We'll take turns keeping watch. Frank could go either way."

"Well, all I know is, six months ago there would've been no doubt which way he would go. He would've gone for the nearest gun an' tried t'blow our brains out."

"You're right, Jim, but much has happened in those six months. The best hope is that he will recognize that they selected him for dishonorable reasons, that he will see this as a Northern conspiracy. He need not think of himself as a traitor if he turns on them. I think he'll join us."

"I hope you're right, Sam. Just the same, I'll take the first watch."

Cathy Blair approached first, strolling down the walk with her hands behind her back. She had been thinking all night and still did not know what to say. She stopped at the door and sighed, then pulled on the latch. She stepped inside. Wade stood six feet away, one knee bent, his weight on one foot. She looked at him with damp, red-rimmed eyes. She had cried most of the night.

She closed the distance and slowly placed her arms around him. She pressed her face against his chest and the tears began to flow again. She sniffed as she looked up at his sad face. "I guess I have always known," she said softly, "or at least known something was awry." She squeezed him hard. "It's just that you lied to me, right from the beginning. I'd be a fool not to wonder if you really love me."

"That's the only spark of truth in this whole damn mess, Cathy," Wade said. "I was prepared to come here against orders to warn you. I'd take you with me if that were possible. But I'm a soldier. I have my duty to perform."

"Did you know I was here when you came back in September?"

"No. Jim and I were cut off during the battle. Jim's knowledge of the area made this the logical place to come. Then you got in the way and everything became complicated. We were Union officers in Confederate uniforms. How could I reveal that? Once the lies began, I saw no way to stop them. Nothing has been the same since."

"What are you going to do now?" she asked with a sniff.

"Whatever I can to prevent the assassination of President Lincoln. I should be in Washington at this moment. I've let personal considerations get in the way of my duty."

"What about Frank?"

"He knows the truth now. It's up to him. If he attempts to go through with his mission, he'll be captured or killed. If he's captured I will testify against him and the government will hang him. His only hope is to assist me. But it's his decision. Either way, I have to leave at sunup."

"Are we in as much danger as you say?"

"Let me put it this way, Cathy. There are men who want to kill every white person living on this plantation. In time, they will come. If not today, then next week. When they do, it will be too late to do anything."

"Then we really must leave?"

"Today if possible. Preferably this moment."

"Mother is packing now. None of us slept much. It's just so hard to leave a lifetime of work on a moment's notice, perhaps never to return."

"The South started this war, Cathy. So far, only the people in the border states have suffered much. But the fighting will go on until the bases of supply are destroyed. That means coming into the Deep South. Rome will be one of the first places attacked. Your plantation is right in the path the Union forces will take on the way to Atlanta. I doubt the plantation will survive whether you leave or stay."

She bristled. "But why? All we ever wanted was the right to preserve our way of life."

"Yes, but you purchased the privilege to live your way at the expense of four million Negroes. I'm sorry I can't feel sympathy for what's happening now. You should know that I didn't tell you everything about myself. A former slave was the only father I had. He worked for my mother after she bought him and freed him. He was smart, capable, and honorable. How he acquired those qualities, after being raised as a slave, is beyond me. I've seen what they live through down here. Those feelings are a part of me, as much a part of me as my mother, or you. I can't simply pretend they don't exist. If my feelings are a barrier between us, then I shall have to learn to live with it. But no matter how you or I feel, slavery is dead, and the South will have to find a way to survive without it." He had meant to avoid the subject. His blood always rose when he got on the subject of slavery. The Bowmans were one of the largest slave-holding families in Georgia. That had threatened to be a barrier between them from the moment he learned of her heritage. She *was* the South, as were her parents and Frank. Men were dying because of their commitment to defend a vile institution. If he could forgive her for that, then he expected no less in return. Their life together required the removal of this barrier. Better to resolve it now, or find that the walls were too high to breach. "For now," Wade added, pushing aside his personal thoughts, "the important thing is to save Lincoln's life. That is the best thing I can do for the South."

He turned, walked to the door, and opened it. "It's going to be a good day for traveling." He sighed. "The sun is coming up." He looked at Clinton, who was leaning against the far doorjamb. "Jim, it's time to pull our gear together and be on our way. It appears that Frank wasn't convinced."

"You're not the only man with passions, Samuel Wade." Cathy's anger flared at his impatience. She felt compelled to defend herself, her family.

"Are we simply to say 'Oh, too bad,' and let everything slip from our grasp without even mourning the loss? Frank has suffered, too. He has been badly hurt and captured. He saw his life shattered in those rat-infested caves at Vicksburg. He still has nightmares about that. And now the final humiliation confronts him: joining forces with a Yankee to save a Yankee president. And you can't even wait until after breakfast to hear what he has to say." Her face was flushed, nearly as red as her eyes. But anger helped. It pushed back the sadness, the worst of all her emotions. Love was her best, and she loved Sam Wade. Despite all the lies, she trusted him now. She believed he had told the truth, and in doing so had revealed his true character. She liked what she had seen. She liked that it had bothered him to lie, even though the lies had been necessary at the time.

Wade stood with his arms crossed, looking out the window, as Frank came around the corner of the house. He walked toward the summerhouse first, then turned and climbed up the hill to where the giant oak stood. Wade went outside and followed him. Clinton appeared at Cathy's side, and she jumped at the realization of his presence. She leaned her head on his arm as the two of them watched Frank and Wade meet. The two men talked for a while, only their movements suggesting the mood of the discussion. It was apparent that Frank was still struggling with the hardest decision of his life. The sharp kicks at the air, the chin dropped against his chest as the full importance of the choice he must make pressed upon him, conveyed the image of a man in turmoil.

Frank did most of the talking; Wade listened, speaking only when necessary. Finally, Frank turned and shuffled through the brown grass to the tree. He extended both arms and leaned against it for a long moment before nodding his head twice. He removed his hat and looked far past the horizon, his arms limp at his side. Wade walked closer, stood still for a moment, then extended his hand. Frank hesitated, fully aware of the commitment that taking Wade's hand would signal. His hand drifted up; their flesh met. Wade clasped Frank's hand with his other. The bargain was sealed. In a very small sense, North and South had met and found, as they joined, that the other was less onerous than either had thought.

The sun slid serenely toward the glowing horizon on an unusually pleasant early spring evening. The long shadows of twilight stretched across the woods. Such weather was common at this time of year. General Thornton might have enjoyed the warm evening breeze had not his dreams been so thoroughly dashed. The coming of spring assured the advance of the Union army. Alarm and vexation, nourished by a sense of dastardly betrayal, were common ingredients in a Southerner's view of events, no less here in the West than anywhere in the South. Henry Thornton still honored the cause, but the honor of the nation's leaders had been sacrificed somewhere along the way. He ascribed the fault to those who regulated events—the politicians and the generals, such as himself. The burning hope for victory had been replaced by the chilling fear of impending defeat. Had it been a futile effort from the start? he wondered. He brought his arm to his face and wiped the mist from his eyes.

Everyone from the newest fourteen-year-old recruit to himself sensed that Sherman's legions would strike out soon and roll across Georgia. There weren't enough men in three states to contain his army. But they must try, regardless of the human cost. Even some of the diehard Southern optimists had abandoned hope that their fledgling nation might somehow survive through the spring and summer now that Grant had assumed command.

The misery they endured would have broken the spirits of lesser folk. But the South hung on, the people collectively praying for a miracle. Thornton had a more urgent prayer. He needed more men. The nation had linked its fortunes to General Lee, but Thornton knew that the South would win or lose the war here in the West, against Sherman.

Thornton looked out through the trees at a thousand campfires. Although the days were warm now, the chilly nights would linger for a month or so more. The men sat close to the fires. They talked softly, as though they feared they might call the enemy to their positions if they spoke above a whisper.

Thornton lifted his weary body from the camp chair and strolled toward the fire. His adjutant, Maj. Tom Drew, reclined near the flames, roasting an ear of corn suspended on a stick. He rose to his knees as the general approached.

"At ease, Major," Thornton said. "Not much of a supper, is it?"

"I'll make do, General. We all will." Drew shifted to a sitting position. Thornton sat beside him, extending his hands toward the fire.

As the ground cooled, a thin layer of fog rolled up from the stream. In the distance, Thornton heard the muffled sound of horses. In the fading light and drifting mist, he saw two men approaching, leading their mounts behind them. They stopped for a moment at the nearest fire, perhaps thirty yards away. They spoke too softly for the words to be understood. His eyes shifted back to the fire. He hardly noticed as the two men drew closer.

"Pardon me, gentlemen, but we're lookin' for General Thornton."

Thornton rose to a crouch. "I'm General Thornton, Captain. May I help you?" The nearer of the two moved in front of the other and saluted as his companion slowly drew his pistol. Major Drew was alert enough to sense the danger and quickly stood. He saw the pistol slip under the closest man's arm. As the major lunged across the fire, a bullet pierced his heart. He fell into the flames.

Thornton rolled to his right as the intruder pulled the trigger a second time. The bullet missed. The man jumped into the clear as the captain drew his own weapon. They both fired at the same instant. One bullet grazed Thornton's arm; the second passed through his inner thigh.

Thornton pulled his pistol as he rolled. He fired, hitting the captain in the bridge of the nose. The fatal blow drove the man backward, the force knocking the other man to one knee. As Thornton raised his gun to fire again, he heard the distinctive crack of muskets. The second man's head jerked to the side, then sagged slowly as he went limp. Even in the pale light, Thornton saw the unmistakable glassy-eyed stare of death as the man slumped forward across Major Drew's legs.

Thornton clutched at his leg and tried to stand. The muscles revolted, and he crashed to the ground. A wave of nausea rolled up from the pit of his stomach as he strained to make sense of what had happened. Nothing that could explain it came to mind before the darkness in his head blended with the gentle Alabama night.

Wade sat limp in the soft chair, his legs fully extended before him. Thompson had told them to be seated when he entered the room and closed the door. The colonel's work quarters had been changed during the long months Wade had been away. Wade had grown accustomed to the stark appointments of the dark warehouse office with glass walls covered with shades. Somehow, the more elegant surroundings removed some of the mystery that had given Thompson such an aura of power. The sense of convention seemed to command a more formal association. Wade liked the old way better.

"You men must be tired. Have you had an opportunity to find quarters?"

"We don't require much comfort," Clinton replied. "Jus' havin' a roof over our heads seems a luxury."

Wade looked at Thompson. For the first time, he noticed the stars on Thompson's shoulders. "General? I didn't know, sir." He straightened himself in the chair. Clinton did the same.

"The promotion was approved by Congress five days ago, Sam. The army insisted that I move into this building." He looked at the freshly decorated room. "Rather fancy, don't you think?"

"Different," Wade replied. "More fitting for a general officer, I suppose."

Thompson seemed nervous. So much had passed between Wade and himself that had nothing to do with rank. Stars on a man's shoulders seemed to push people away. He did not understand it, but he had felt the same way. "Yes, well, only the coat has changed. I honestly like the look of the eagles better. A symbol of power and grace, the eagle. So, how did it go in Rome?"

"Frank Bowman has returned to his men. He had not been told of his assignment. He has agreed to assist us. It will be difficult. There is no way to keep track of him. He will communicate by letter. A trusted friend will carry his messages into Maryland and send them to general delivery here in Washington."

"Did you make him any promises?"

"Should I have?"

"Well, Sam, the man *is* involved in a plot to kill the president."

Wade leaned forward. "I will testify, if it comes to that, that he at no time was consciously involved. As a Confederate officer he was subject to orders, orders limited to training men for a mission of an unknown nature. Once he learned the full extent of his assignment, he agreed to cooperate fully. Major Clinton will support my testimony."

"You haven't gotten soft on the South during all that time you've spent down there, have you, Sam?"

"If you believe that, sir, then I suggest you relieve me. I will submit my resignation immediately."

"That won't be necessary, Sam. I meant nothing personal."

"That's precisely the point, General." Wade's lips tightened and his ears twitched. "This is personal in about every way. The general will recall that, when the general was a colonel, I informed him of this plot. The general chose to dismiss it as some half-baked rumor. Now there is this urgency to make up for lost time. The woman I love has had to go into hiding to keep from being murdered by Northern men who have grown wealthy from this war. My father is the target of murderers and about to be trampled by General Sherman's army. My mother has information that could lead to her murder. And I've got this boil from endless hours in the saddle. Personal, General? Yes, sir, this war has become intensely personal."

"Feel better, Sam?" asked Thompson.

Wade sighed. "Some."

"Are you ready to be killed, then?"

Wade blinked. "Sir?"

"As you can guess, the war is about to heat up. General Grant will be heading south in no more than a month. He's looking for trained officers. You've been offered a brigade, if you want it. A colonel's eagles go with the job."

"What about Major Clinton?"

"With all the reorganization, there will be room for seasoned veterans as regimental commanders. It's all been arranged. You just have to say the word."

"What about this other mess?"

"It's under control. We'll have to set a trap, but the president's life won't be put in jeopardy. We'll get to the bottom of it, in time. Now, do you want that brigade or not?"

"I simply don't know what to think, sir. Have I earned this, or does it come from someone throwing his weight around?"

"You might say that, Colonel. President Lincoln initiated the appointment. He appears to have some influence around this town. All that's required of you is a smile, and the job's yours."

Wade grinned broadly. There were no frowns in him now. A colonel's eagles and a brigade, and him barely three years out of West Point, he thought. "You know I want it, General. May I make two requests?"

"Of course."

"Lieutenant Healy. I think he's earned a shot at command. I would recommend his promotion to captain and assignment as a company commander. And then there is Major Clinton."

"Healy can be arranged. And as for you, Major Clinton, here is a set of silver leaves to replace those gold ones. I never quite understood military rank. Gold leaves for majors, silver for lieutenant colonels. Lieutenant generals outrank major generals. One wonders if the army knows what it's doing." He stood and extended his hand. "Congratulations, gentlemen. You've earned it. Now, before you go back to the war, I want a detailed briefing. Let me get someone to record this conversation. Following that, we have an appointment at the White House with the president. You can tell your story a second time there."

# CHAPTER

# 27

What a terrible ten days! The wagon carrying General Thornton home to Alabama had become a torture chamber. Every bump, no matter how slight, jarred his leg and sent pain to the top of his skull. He had nearly died from the wound. An artery had been creased, and the surgeon, drunk at the time, had difficulty stopping the bleeding. The standard remedy for such wounds was amputation.

Through the fog in his mind, Thornton had heard the surgeon discussing the operation. Thornton's head cleared long enough for him to ask a nearby major for his pistol. Thornton placed the barrel in the pit of the surgeon's stomach and strained to push the words out. "I may live, or I may die," he told the doctor, "but either way, I'll leave this earth with both legs attached." When the surgeon failed to answer immediately, Thornton jabbed the pistol deeper into the soft flesh of the man's belly. "Have I made myself clear, Captain?" The doctor swallowed with difficulty and managed a single word: "Understood." Then Thornton had drifted into unconsciousness.

Finally, a young corpsman had come to Thornton's rescue and kept the last of his blood from draining onto the floor—or so it had seemed from the volume already underfoot. Thornton really didn't remember much. He had watched groggily as men circled the operating table like so many vultures. When the commanding general dies, everything changes. Promotions usually follow, as a new commander brings his own ideas to the assignment. The doctor, more butcher than surgeon, had removed the bullet and bound the wound. Two days later, when Thornton's fever had subsided, some men carried him to a wagon filled with hay, covered him with blankets, and sent him on his long journey home.

When the weathered mansion came into view, Thornton let out a loud sigh. Another day in that wagon and he would have walked the remaining distance, regardless of the wound, to avoid the mind-numbing pain. He doubted he would ever ride in a wagon again.

Victoria rushed onto the veranda as the wagon approached. Racked with worry, she lifted her skirt and ran down the stairs to greet it. She had expected the worst and hoped for the best—all that a wife could do in time of war. "I've been half out of my mind!" she exclaimed as she reached over the sideboard and grasped her husband's hand. "I've thought of nothing else since the telegram arrived. How bad is it?"

"Painful," Thornton replied, "but not serious. A few weeks' rest and I'll be as good as new." He began sliding along the wagon bed toward the back end. Much of the hay preceded him over the edge. He eased himself out and came to a standing position on his good leg. "Help me into the house, Lieutenant, and then we'll see what we can do about getting the men some food." A detail of one officer and ten enlisted men had escorted Thornton.

"Yes, sir. I'll bet you're pleased to get out of that infernal wagon."

"You'll never know how pleased, Lieutenant." Thornton grimaced as he let his weight settle. "Just move easy, men, and everything will be fine." The two men supporting him half carried him up the stairs. "Into the parlor," Thornton directed. "There's a sofa there." Simon met them as they approached the front door. "Good to see you, son. Your old man has been damaged some, but it will mend." They eased the general onto the sofa, and he sighed with relief. Everything felt better now; he had made it home.

Thornton fell asleep soon after his arrival. It felt so good to stretch out on something soft that he slept the night through. Only an urgent call of nature woke him at dawn. He could not believe how much better he felt. The leg remained stiff, but the pain had mostly faded. He was sitting on the edge of the sofa, rubbing where it felt most stiff, as Victoria entered the room wearing her dressing gown.

"It's about time you woke up," she said with a smile. "You've more than slept the clock around."

"That's what I've needed, more than anything," he replied, "a good night's sleep." He motioned to his wife. "Come here, woman, and let me touch you." He patted the sofa beside him. "How have conditions been here?" he asked, knowing the answer from the brief visual inspection upon his arrival.

"We're making do. Most of the slaves ran off, but it's just as well. Food is becoming scarce. Tulip is still here. She keeps the household working. I feel so useless. When I was a girl, Caroline and I did everything around the house. Now I'm simply an inept twitterbug. Simon has become more and more withdrawn as time has passed. He can't figure out why his country has abandoned him. He thinks of himself as a bad dream that they would just as soon forget."

"I don't understand it either," Thornton replied. "He's done nothing wrong. I'll have to make some inquiries. How is Nancy Caroline?"

"Unhappy. She mopes around all day, mostly doing nothing. Many of her friends are gone now. Rebecca went to Europe. Her father must have kept a stash of gold hidden somewhere. They say he's gone to California to wait out the war. It's not much of a life here for a young lady."

"Nor is it much of a life for a young man, Victoria. I've seen suffering that no one would have believed possible three years ago. Now it's commonplace."

"I know, but Nancy Caroline lives her life here. All she knows is that her world has collapsed and there's no hope of rebuilding it. She would think differently if there were young men around. She talks frequently of going north when the war ends. She has decided that she's again in love with David Healy Jr."

"She could do worse."

"If he survives. She's certain he's in the thick of the war."

"Well, none of this can be helped. Say, do you remember when Simon broke his leg? He had a pair of crutches. Do we still have those someplace?"

"I had them stored in the attic. Shall I send Tulip for them?"

"No. Send Nancy Caroline. There will be no slaves when this war is finished— servants, either. She may as well get used to fending for herself, and others."

"It won't be easy, Henry."

"If the choice comes down to starvation, it'll be easy enough. Call her down. I want to get out and get some fresh air."

Thornton hobbled about the barn, feeling more frisky with each passing hour. He savored the contentment of home, with no army of men to worry about feeding and supplying. With the slaves gone, the place had become run-down. The feed was nearly gone. Much of the fall crop had rotted in the field. The army had confiscated the remainder. Without draft animals, spring planting was impossible. The cycle of life had been broken. For Henry Thornton, the South was dying, the victim of self-inflicted wounds. In the effort to save everything, it had all been lost.

Balancing on his good leg, Thornton pitched a light fork full of hay into a stall—just to feel that he was doing something productive. The army had lost much of its glamour. Being a general meant the promotion of death. He sighed as he looked around the spacious barn. Only three old mares remained of his once prized stable of horses, and they were long past the age for foaling, of no use even to the army. Not even the gold stars on his collar had given him the influence to prevent the confiscation of the other horses. The barrel full of oats would last a month if rationed. What then? With spring here, life should be returning to the South. Knowing that made the fallow fields seem that much more drab.

In a nearly field he saw Simon walking. The young man had stopped, grasped a handful of soil, and squeezed it, then opened his hand and let the sandy loam filter through his fingers. He rose and stuck his hands in his pockets before strolling listlessly on.

Henry Thornton pulled his suspenders onto his shoulders and draped his coat over his arm before hobbling into the late afternoon glow. He watched as the one-armed mail carrier drove his wagon along the circular lane leading to the house. Tulip limped to the edge of the porch, talked to the man for a moment, then pointed toward the barn. The mail carrier wheeled his wagon around and drove toward Thornton. "How y'doin', General?" he yelled as he approached.

"Making do," Thornton replied. "You're out kind of late, Daniel."

"Mail's been stackin' up, General. With my route doubled these past months, I don't get the mail delivered as often as I should. You're gonna be here for a while, so's I heard. Glad to see you're up an' around."

Thornton leaned on the side of the wagon. "What do you have for me today?"

"Just one letter, General." Daniel reached precariously over the edge of the seat and handed the envelope to Thornton. "Mailed nearly a week ago."

Thornton wiped his hand on his trousers and accepted it.

"See ya in a couple of weeks, General." Daniel pulled on the reins and the horse trotted down the road.

Thornton broke the seal and turned his back to the half circle of sun above the horizon. He unfolded the paper and held it to the light. Glancing at the signature, he noticed it was from Arthur Bowman.

April 9, 1864
Dear General Thornton:
I am in southern Alabama, Henry. The exact place is better left unstated.

I pray that this letter reaches you in time.

I wish I could say we are doing well, my friend, but I cannot. I'll get right to it.

Early this month, your son paid a distressing visit to my plantation. He came to warn us of a plot to kill all of us—you, John Ward, myself, everyone. At first it seemed incredible, something out of a nightmare. Then he told us his true identity, and followed with a story that, if I had not known some of it to be true, I would have found unbelievable.

It seems our "friends" from the North have had a change in plans. Their sights have shifted to the West, and we have become a liability. Men have been sent to kill all of us and, I suspect, every member of our families.

John Ward's son is dead, as are Tom and all of the others who remained in the Rome area. You know who I mean. John was on the run with his family. He stopped only long enough to give me a warning.

He said that he would have been dead, too, if he had not accompanied his wife to visit a sick relative in a nearby county. He returned late at night and found his son dead in the barn. Sam had already departed by that time. We did not respond as we should have to the urgency of his plea. We nearly paid with our lives for the delay. Needless to say, the panic in John's eyes urged us to action. We were already half packed at the time. Our plans were to leave the next day and try to find your headquarters as we moved deeper into the South. Instead, we left at sundown.

When we reached your headquarters, we learned what had happened to you. From what I heard, I suspect that you have no idea of the reason for the attempt on your life. I told no one. The purpose of this letter is to let you know that the attempt was part of a plot to kill us all. If you remain alive to receive this, you will realize the urgency of your immediate departure and the elimination of any clues to where you have gone.

As would be expected, John originally assumed the murder had been committed by robbers, probably deserters. A short time later (that night, I presume, or early the next morning), Erin Cheatham's son ran to John's house sobbing, saying that his mother and father had been shot for no apparent reason. Later that day, John took the bodies of his son and the Cheathams to Rome. Once there, he learned that there had been seven other murders, all in the previous twenty-four hours. Every one of those killed was involved in the conspiracy. Only John, you, and I are still alive as I write this letter.

Pearl is with me. I sent Cathy up north with the child. Her destination is Washington or New York—or maybe Gettysburg if she thinks that wise—where she hopes to find sanctuary until the war ends. Then she will search for your son. I gave her three hundred dollars in gold—half of everything I had left in the world. It won't stretch far, but she is a resourceful young lady. She will survive, somehow. If I were honest with myself, I'd accept that I will never see her again.

Mass murder is only part of their madness, Henry. I neglected to inform you that they recruited Frank, my son, to lead the men who are to kill Lincoln. He was at the house when Samuel arrived, and he left only hours before John arrived. He was very bitter after his capture at Vicksburg. He wanted revenge for the humiliation he felt. I now think he will try to stop the plot. According to Cathy, apparently he and Samuel have reached some sort of agreement. I realize now that the murderers will not let him live. If they will go to the difficulty of searching out all of us, and take the risk of killing us on our home ground, they won't hesitate to kill those more directly involved. No matter how this turns out, I fear they will spare no effort to hunt us all down and hang us.

Henry, we have been used by both sides in this terrible war. May God forgive us for our wickedness.

Good-bye, old friend. We really made a mess of it, didn't we? We hung on too long. Now we have become relics of a best-forgotten past. The world will not miss us. We have nothing left to offer—except, perhaps, an honorable death.

If you remain alive to read this, do not delay. You know too much. They will find you and kill you.

Good luck, Henry, and may our offspring restore honor to our proud names.

Thornton slumped as he finished the second, more careful, reading of the letter. The last ounce of hope drained from his weary limbs. He returned to the barn and, with great difficulty, pulled the carriage from the corner. He had exerted himself too much, and the pain returned to his leg. Supporting himself on one crutch, he removed an empty grain sack from a hook and slapped it against the cracking leather of the seat. Dust boiled into the still air. The carriage had been used sparingly of late. He dragged it into the aisle between the stalls. He slid back the boards that closed the horse stall and led the youngest of the three old mares through the opening. Simon would have to string the harness. Thornton led the animal out the barn door into the chilling air. The mare nudged him with her nose, and he placed an arm around her neck. He had raised her from a gangly colt, almost losing her at birth. Now she snorted and pawed the earth, and he patted her on the forelock. Then he returned to the barn.

Minutes later, he led out the older mares. Simon would have to pull the heavier carriage from the barn. Thornton dropped the loose reins. Then it hit him. "What have I done?" he said in a soft whisper. "My God, what have I done?" His legs began to shake, then his arms. Sharp pain ran through his groin and up his back. He sank to his knees and sobbed as he rolled onto his side. A range of feelings overwhelmed him all at once: hate, sorrow, fear, determination, regret, hopelessness. As much as anything, he mourned for his dead South, as if it were a grand lady that he unwittingly had helped to kill. Somewhere along the way, in the effort to save her, he had abandoned both reason and his values—had become willing even to sacrifice his son and his honor to preserve her life. He had failed on all accounts, except one: Simon remained alive. The fate of his beloved South was for the best. She had demanded too high a price of him. If he retained the slightest doubt of that, he needed only to look around. Unplowed fields stretched to the horizon. Most of the paint had peeled from the grand old house. The livestock was gone. The slave quarters were empty and silent. The darkies had taken their pain with them—he wished them well in their effort to heal their wounds—but also they had taken their songs. He missed the songs. He had often wondered how those wretched souls could sing of hope. Now he realized they had been right to endure.

A hawk screeched in the distance. The first star sparkled in the evening sky. The smell of smoke from the chimney filled his nostrils. He felt the damp earth. Soft sounds of desperation rose from someplace deep inside. His senses still worked, which meant that the spark of life remained. What a shame. His presence had become a blight on the planet. He lifted his head and wiped away the tears. He nearly screamed from the pain as he scaled the crutch; then he shuffled back to the barn. One at a time, he filled several buckets with grain. He placed the buckets under the seat of the carriage and lashed them in place before his energy failed him completely.

"Simon," he called out weakly. "I need your help, son."

Hearing his father's voice, Simon ran toward the barn.

"Help me to the house," Thornton instructed, "then come back after supper and prepare the wagon and carriage for travel. Don't ask why," he added hastily, hoping to discourage Simon from asking questions. "Just trust that I know what I'm doing, and don't delay."

"Supper's ready," Tulip announced as they approached the house. Inside, the women stood in the kitchen, ready to take their seats.

Henry stumbled into the room and gripped the back of his chair. He looked down at the meager fare on the table. He closed his eyes and sighed, the sound of his despair so loud that the others turned and looked at him. He sighed again. "Please be seated. I have something to say."

Victoria took a step toward him, then stopped. Henry saw the mixture of fear and confusion in her eyes. He nodded encouragingly at her, and she slid the chair from beneath the table and sat down. The others followed her lead.

"You, too, Tulip. Pull up a chair." Thornton's brow furrowed deeply as he rubbed his aching leg. How would he ever make it in a wagon?

"But Master—"

"This is my last order to you, Tulip. Please be seated." He eased himself into a chair.

Tulip wiped her hands on her apron and dragged the spare chair from the corner.

"Listen to what I have to say. I'll be brief. You have five minutes to eat. When you've finished, I want you to gather whatever you'll need for a long journey. Nothing else. The horses are too weak to pull a heavy load. I'm sorry to tell you, but this will be a one-way trip. Tulip, you pack the remaining food. Don't leave anything behind that we can carry. Simon, after you get the transportation ready, gather your mother's fine china and silver. Wrap the china carefully and place it in a chest. Take it out back, someplace out of the way, and bury it deep. Hide all traces. Then prepare a small map of where you buried it and give it to your mother. We'll take the flatware with us. We may have to sell it. Victoria, if there's anything else you want to try to preserve, put it in the chest with the china. Nancy Caroline, you go to the library and open the safe. There is nearly three thousand dollars in gold and another thousand in Yankee greenbacks. Get it all. You may as well bring the Confederate currency, too—despite its worthlessness. Victoria, you and Nancy Caroline pack what will fit into one large trunk, no more."

Victoria opened her mouth to say something, but her husband lifted his hand. She settled back in her chair.

"When you finish packing, carry everything out front and place it on the wagon."

"Henry, it's dark outside," Victoria said when he paused.

"I can see that, Victoria. I want to be a dozen miles from here by sunup. I'll explain everything later. For now, just do as I say. We'll travel in both the wagon and the carriage until one of the horses gives out. That probably won't be long. All right, that's it. Let's get to work." He grimaced as a sharp pain shot up his thigh. He wished he had rested during the day. Too late to worry about it now. Damn that wagon.

Victoria rose silently and walked toward the great room. Nancy Caroline followed. In good time, she would have answers for the hundreds of questions. After all, Henry was a rational man, so he must be acting with good reason. He deserved her trust. Still, he had placed a difficult challenge before her during a time of profound stress. She walked ponderously up the stairs and into the bedroom. She pulled the trunk from the corner and slid it into the middle of the floor.

"Mother," Nancy Caroline said.

Victoria had no time for questions. "Later, Nancy Caroline." She sniffed, then wiped her nose. "Just do as your father has instructed."

Down in the kitchen, Thornton looked at Simon. "Go on, son. Prepare the wagon and carriage, then bury your mother's things."

Simon stood, his soft eyes fixed on the general. "Father—"

Thornton shook his head and lowered his eyes. Simon turned and walked out the back door. The elder Thornton watched as his son's slumping figure faded into the darkness. When he was gone, Thornton looked at the housekeeper.

"That leaves just the two of us, Tulip. I'm freeing you now, so you can do as you please. If you choose, you may come with us. If you want to go your own way, I'll give you two hundred dollars in gold. I wish I had more to spare, but we have a long way to go."

"Where are you goin', Master Henry?"

"North. A long way north."

"I'll start packin' the food. Ain't much, so's it won't take long. I'll pack some extra blankets, too." Her voice sank to a whisper.

"Tulip."

She turned her black face toward him.

"Once you've packed the food, bring all of the lamp oil and place it on the table."

She looked deeply into his eyes. He saw resistance there, something never evident before. "I's lived here all my growed life, Master Henry. This is my home. I can't watch this place burn."

She always knew what he would do, sometimes even before he knew. "Then you mustn't watch. After you've gathered up the oil, you take the carriage and drive Victoria and Nancy Caroline out to the main road. Simon and I will meet you there with the wagon."

"Master Henry—"

"Gather up the food, Tulip. We don't have much time. And don't call me master ever again."

She nodded.

Thornton looked at the table. No one had eaten a bite. For the first time in months, he felt no hunger either. He sat at the table and placed his head in his hands. No more, he thought. I'll resist no more. I have to guide them to safety, then take care of one last bit of unfinished business. Then it will be finished. He thought back to the letter, and about Cathy and Samuel. She may never find him, he thought. So much unfinished business.

His thoughts turned to his sister-in-law. She had more money than a banker. And she owed him. After all, she had taken his son. What's a son worth, Caroline Wade? If he could get his family to Gettysburg, they could begin a new life. She owed him that much. He rose on the crutch and hobbled to the hall closet. He opened the door and withdrew his one remaining dress uniform. He would wear it this one last time. The rank meant nothing now. He had lost his command. But he had earned the right to wear the uniform. He smiled to himself. In the broader range of his life, he hadn't done so badly. Starting with a few acres of brushland, he had built the plantation into an object of pride. He had become a state senator and commander of the state militia. Indeed! There were few in Alabama who had not heard of Henry Thornton.

He struggled into the dress uniform. It hung loosely on him. Too little starch in the diet, he thought, smiling wryly. Too little of anything in the diet. He sat and pulled on the brightly polished boots. He had broken into a sweat by the time he got the second boot on his injured leg. He stood awkwardly on one foot, straightened his coat, tied the sash, and fastened the sword to his belt. He looked up and admired himself in the mirror. As he studied the slightly foggy image, his mind drifted back nearly a year, to a rainy afternoon in late June. He had watched from the mist as Simon and Nancy Caroline were traded for Samuel and Caroline Wade. The Thornton line would continue because of that act. It was the best thing he had done in his life. He had worn this same uniform on that occasion.

Victoria cleared her throat. "We're ready to carry down the trunk, Henry. We also have a small carpetbag. Is that all right?"

He turned, smiled at his wife, and nodded. He heard noise in the dining room. "Nancy Caroline, go help Simon dig the hole to bury the china. Then we'll be on our way."

She opened her mouth to object, but her father's stern look made her think twice.

"My, my," said Victoria, "if you don't look handsome."

He looked down. "I plan to leave it here. Just an aging man's indulgence of himself. I wanted to wear it one last time." He supported himself against the wall and let the crutch drop. He stretched to his full height.

Victoria reached out and pulled at the corners of the coat. A tear ran down her cheek. "If you could only know the feeling I had when I first saw you in that uniform. Women have a special place to store those memories, you know. I have quite a few stored there, but that feeling was the best of all. I watched the governor shake your hand. I watched you sitting straight and proud on that black horse as the regiments marched by on parade. And I was your wife, the wife of Maj. Gen. Henry Thornton. God, what a day." She waited a long moment, then lifted her head and looked into his dark eyes. There, too, she saw the mist of fond reflection. "After being permitted to live such a day, I'd think it sinful to have regrets. So I won't have any." She poked at a shiny brass button. "And don't you have any, either."

He wrapped his arms around her and pulled her firmly to him. His lip quivered. As his eyes closed tightly, an involuntary sobbing sound rose from somewhere deep inside. He swallowed hard. Regrets? he thought. What possible reason could I have for regrets?

"What?" McFadden screamed. "How could that happen?"

Whitey's eyes were fixed on the floor. He had no answer. He had learned only recently that Frank Bowman had been absent from his unit for nearly three months, home in Rome with a broken leg. Now McFadden knew. Whitey wished he had kept it from him. But that was the least of their worries. Whitey knew from the outset, when McFadden had given him the assignment to kill all of the Southerners, that there simply were too many things that could go wrong with so vast an undertaking. But *these* men thought of themselves as infallible. If they wanted something done, all they had to do was order it, pay the bill, and forget it, as though that made it an accomplished fact. Well, Whitey thought, the real world was far more complicated.

McFadden gulped down a full glass of brandy, then poured another. "Tell me the rest of it," he said, his face still flushed with anger.

"Not everyone has reported in yet, sir, but most of the mission has been successful. The disposals in the East went off without a hitch, but we had difficulties getting our men into the West—Georgia and Alabama in particular. There were army units everywhere. Two men got into General Thornton's camp and shot him before they were killed. Unfortunately, the general survived."

McFadden threw his arms over his head, splashing brandy across the room. "Don't tell me he got away!"

"I'm afraid so, sir. His men transported him to his plantation. By the time word reached me and I sent another team after him, he and his family were gone and the mansion had been burned to the ground. They vanished without a trace."

"Damn," McFadden hissed. "What else?"

"The Bowmans, sir. They've also disappeared, as has John Ward and his wife. I suspect the mission turned sour with that. When our people arrived, Ward's son was the only one at the plantation. They tried to beat Ward's location out of him, but they got carried away and killed him. They panicked and ran. When they returned, his body had already been discovered. Ward evidently found his son, somehow pieced together what was happening, and warned the Bowmans before he fled the area."

"Do you have any *good* news for me, Mr. Whitey?"

"Yes, sir. We have developed leads on the Bowmans and Wards. I think we will find them shortly. Also, Frank Bowman apparently left the Bowman plantation before any of this became known. He's back with the unit, apparently unaware that anything has happened and none the wiser to his part in all this."

"How can you be certain?"

"It's the only thing that makes sense, sir. If he knew about the plot and realized who was behind it after discussing it with his father, he'd conclude by simple deduction why the others were being killed. Sir, reports appeared in all of the area papers. Frank Bowman grew up knowing these men. With knowledge of their deaths, and with a warning from Ward, it's inconceivable that he would return to the unit as if nothing had happened."

Perhaps, perhaps not, McFadden thought. Could anything more go wrong? Maybe it *was* time to pull back. Perhaps he should say as much to Waxelman. Then he remembered Andrews. Don't compound the disaster, he admonished himself. Whitey's theory seemed sound, as far as it went. But what if Bowman had returned *precisely because* he knew. He'd figure out that such an action would seem improbable, the same as Whitey had done. But why would he do that? Why? No reason came to mind. They had moved both too fast and too slow. He had to accept responsibility for that. He had personally approved Whitey's plan. He had insisted on prompt action. There should have been more planning. But time was growing short. It was April 22, with the Republican convention drawing near. No, he had to play the game with the chips he had. Frank Bowman was okay. He was sure of it. He poured another glass of brandy.

"The damage is done, my friend," he said, his voice under control. "Clean up the mess down there as best you can. Is there anything else?"

"That's it, sir. Since I am to proceed, I have to send some telegrams. I'll be on my way."

"There isn't any way for these telegrams to be traced back to us, is there?"

"Not a chance, sir. Everything is in code."

"Very well. Keep me informed."

# CHAPTER

## 28

Brigadier General Jason Thompson slumped forward in his chair and stared glumly at the pile of papers scattered about his desk. He now understood the dire meaning of the phrase "chained to a desk." That had been his fate since early April, shortly before Wade returned from Chattanooga. When Thompson had congratulated Wade on his new assignment and promotion, he had meant it, for he thought of the young man as a truly remarkable soldier. But that hadn't eased his personal disappointment. He would have traded places with Wade or Clinton in a moment. As the war moved relentlessly toward its conclusion, here he sat, wasting away, languishing on the fringe of history. Was his bitterness so unreasonable? He thought not.

Ironically, Thompson's power had diminished considerably with his appointment to general officer rank. In late winter, General Washburn's brother had decided against running for reelection to Congress and had resigned his seat. General Washburn resigned his army commission at the same time, and the brothers had returned to Illinois. With the war advancing toward what everyone sensed was its final phase, the Special Engineers Section dwindled in importance. Thompson had been certain that the army at last would honor his request for a field command. The rebels had been killing senior Union officers in wholesale lots. But when General Grant took command of the army, political officers were suddenly in less demand. Grant wanted professionals in the field, officers with formal military training and extensive combat experience, officers more interested in bringing the war to a quick, successful end than in personal glory—officers such as Col. Samuel Wade, now in command of a brigade advancing toward Richmond.

Reports were both good and bad. They were good because Grant had not fled after Lee whipped him soundly in the Wilderness. They were bad because the two most tenacious generals of modern times were asking so many young men to die to prove who was right. Maybe Grant *would* outmaneuver Lee. Maybe Grant *would* break into the open and force Lee into that one last, decisive engagement that would end this hellish war. But Thompson doubted it. Lee seldom made mistakes. He would make Grant pay in blood for every inch of Virginia soil. If ever Grant had doubts about it, they had surely vanished after reviewing the casualty figures from the week's proceedings at Spotsylvania Court House.

There had been one bright spot. Congressman Washburn, with Lincoln's support, had gotten Thompson promoted during his last week in office. Thompson still enjoyed looking at the star on his shoulder, but he hated the mundane War Department assignment that had accompanied it. The bureaucracy had closed in around him. He saw no hope of escape.

Thompson was now responsible for organizing and monitoring the flow of war materials. The job required skills few men in the Union military possessed; it required a man with an ability to remember everything about everything. In performing this mainly clerical task, Thompson analyzed war production needs and determined which businesses around the country were capable of increasing production in response to shortages *before* they developed in the field. As a result of his research, he had acquired an immense store of knowledge about the industrial capacity of the nation. He knew, better than anyone alive, the weaknesses and strengths of the national economy. It was knowledge that offered an insightful man the opportunity to become obscenely wealthy, provided he had the time and resources for investment and took advantage of the opportunities.

Thompson had the resources. Counting real estate holdings, government bonds, and the shipping operation he had inherited from his father, he measured his wealth at slightly more than two million dollars—and climbing. Time had become the problem.

Thompson glanced up at the large clock hanging over his desk. Half past four. He placed a large folder filled with papers in a leather case and bound it shut. Then he put it in the top drawer and turned the key. He rose and walked to the clerk's desk and told the sergeant seated there, "If anyone asks for me, tell them I've left for the day. I'll be in by eight tomorrow morning."

The sergeant nodded. "Yes, sir," he replied without looking up.

Thompson covered the four blocks of Pennsylvania Avenue to Tenth Street, where he turned into the brisk wind and walked past Ford's Theater toward his favorite bar. He had an appointment with the newest U.S. senator, William Sprague, of the Rhode Island Spragues. In the process, Thompson would have a drink or two before hopping a cab to the White House, where he was scheduled to meet with Lincoln and Stanton.

Thompson and the senator had finished their second glass of beer by the time the sun set. Thompson ordered another. Both men drank too much but neither ever admitted it, even to himself. "Won't Kate be expecting you, Senator?" Thompson asked.

Sprague shook his head and shrugged. "She won't think about me until after ten. Her social affairs keep her busy until then."

"She's quite a woman, Senator. Quite a beautiful woman. And how is her father?"

"Secretary Chase is doing well, all things considered. I think he really believed he would outmaneuver Lincoln and get the Republican nomination. He offered to quit the cabinet, but Lincoln refused to release him."

Thompson chuckled. "I know. Lincoln wants to keep him where he can watch him. That doesn't alter the fact that he's done a remarkable job financing this war. The nation's banking industry will never be the same."

Sprague drank deeply from his mug. "And how about you, General? How is Miss Healy? You do still see her, I presume?"

"Now and then," Thompson replied. "I suppose we'll marry after the war, although I would prefer a less willful woman."

Sprague had little sympathy for Thompson. Kate Chase-Sprague gave new dimensions to the word *willful*. "How is her father?"

"Doing well." Thompson nodded. "He's content with his assignment on Meade's staff. I fear he will get his fill of war, however, by the time Lee is through with the Army of the Potomac."

Sprague leaned forward. "Have you given any thought to my request?" he asked quietly, changing the subject.

"Yes. It might be possible."

"I need ten thousand bales, General. I need them as soon as possible. My mills are drying up."

"I'll be seeing Secretary Stanton this evening at the White House. I'll see what I can arrange."

"I won't forget it, Jason. Want another glass?" He motioned to the waitress. "I'd like you to meet someone," Sprague added, nodding toward the entrance.

Thompson turned. A neatly dressed young man stood just inside the door. Thompson had never seen him before. "Who is he?"

"His name is Wagner. Jeremy Wagner. Among other things, he's an accountant. He's associated with some men I think you should learn more about."

From the diary of Caroline Wade-Healy

*May 16, 1864*
*5:00 P.M.*
*I am filled with joy! It is so seldom that I get to write good news.*

*Victoria is out of the South. They are all here, her whole family, somewhere in the North. She doesn't say what drove them here, but I can read between the lines of her letter. Something terrible has happened,* and they had to escape whatever it was. Otherwise, she could tell me where she is. The important thing is that they are away from the war, alive and safe. She will reach out to me sooner or later, and I will be whole again, as our bleeding nation surely will be whole again.

Must go.

May 17, 1864
11:00 P.M.
My heart is breaking. A letter from Samuel arrived this afternoon. I tore it open eagerly, almost frantically, only to have my heart also ripped as a result of the effort. Tragic is the only word that applies to the carnage of these past two weeks. First the Wilderness, then Spotsylvania—places with no meaning, and to think it is only beginning. Samuel says it is necessary; David agrees. We had 17,000 casualties in the Wilderness— 17,000! And to think that the soldiers cheered when General Grant informed them that they were moving on with the single hope of making an extended fight of it with Lee. Now we wait for the final butcher's bill from Spotsylvania Court House. Insanity must be contagious.

Why am I drawn to it so? Is there some flaw in us that compels us to explore new, more efficient ways of making human waste of so many handsome young men? But drawn to it I am. I sit here and look at Samuel's letter—wrinkled, blood spattered, dirty from the Virginia soil where men were trampled into the ground by their comrades—and I cannot take my eyes from it. Why did he write it? Did he have a need to purge his soul? His mind? What is there that is worth this much suffering? A word, a life, a nation? Is freedom worth it, or the life of a president, or a nation that is exerting maximum effort—one part trying to rip itself from the other, the other to keep itself whole?

I have been frightened for so long. First for Samuel, then for Victoria and her family, then for David, and now for all of them. I no longer have feelings left over for myself. How can we ever repair ourselves, once this is finished? How can we lead normal lives again? The scars will be deep, that is for certain, with our affairs invisibly regulated by their legacy, until the last of our generation passes from this earth.

I must rest now, or this melancholy will consume me. Things always seem better under a new sun.

---

"Another round," General Thompson instructed the barmaid. "Make mine a double."

Thompson had spoken with Wagner only briefly the night before. His meeting with Lincoln had lasted nearly an hour, twice the usual twenty to thirty minutes.

Lincoln's interest in the reconstruction of the South increased daily. He said he could *smell* the end of the war, that he had to be ready to act before the Congress tied his hands. One major battle for certain, perhaps two, and it would end—if only Grant could pull Lee into the open. "I'll fight it out on this line if it takes all summer," Grant had said. Lincoln smiled when he repeated the words. He had waited long enough to hear that kind of talk, to see that kind of commitment.

Thompson had gained important insights from these conversations. Lincoln displayed his intellectual strength more in his vision than in his knowledge. He *felt* the right course of action. Others could fill in the details. Supplying the interconnecting structure had become Thompson's assignment, along with others, and Lincoln wanted to delve into it, to probe the possibilities, to know his options. What about the remaining four million slaves? he would ask frequently. How do we assimilate them? Were they capable of voting intelligently? How do we employ them at useful work without first providing them some level of formal education? Educating them would take years, generations. But without it, with those in the South left to formulate an internal solution, nothing would change. Lincoln saw the possibility of continued slavery, only by other names: repression, or perhaps exploitation. This would drive many Negroes north. Preventing that had become a priority, at least for the present.

But first Lincoln had to be nominated; then he had to be reelected. If the president bothered to read the papers at all, he had to know that his chances of either were universally judged to be between slim and none— and you could drop the slim when considering his chances for both. And this with the Republican convention less than two weeks away.

Unfortunately for Lincoln, others less burdened by the immediate stress of finding a way to end the war—many would have thought it better if the war dragged on for a while—had spent more time thinking about postwar problems, and opportunities. Jeremy Wagner represented such men, but he kept his personal views to himself.

"Have you found a way to assist the senator with his problem?" asked Wagner.

"It's a slow process," Thompson replied. He would say no more. He resented those who pried into other men's business.

"Multiply his problem by a thousand—make that ten thousand—and you have some idea of what we face once the war ends," said Wagner. "Some structure must be in place that will keep the nation moving forward."

From the moment he'd met Wagner, Thompson had struggled against a sense of uneasiness. Wagner was too slick, too knowledgeable, to suit Thompson. Such men were manipulators. They used words as others used money, to buy the souls of weaker men. So why was he drawn to the man? He had promised Senator Sprague that he would listen to Wagner. Beyond that . . . "And what are you suggesting, Mr. Wagner?"

"Nothing complicated, General. Certainly nothing improper. Men with both the vision and the resources to elevate this nation to the pinnacles of world power must be given the latitude to make the process work. Such men as yourself, General, can aid this process immensely."

Classic, Thompson thought. Classic manipulation. "When the war ends, sir, there will be many problems with no apparent solutions," said Thompson.

"Not really, General. Everything is linked to two things. One is industrial development. The other is politics. Each is fully dependent on the other, and they are linked by capital. Capital—nothing else—will lift this nation to its potential. We cannot have the industrialists and developers pulling in one direction while the politicians pull in another, now can we? That would drain everyone's energy, with nothing accomplished. There must be coordination. There must be an orderly process. There must be those who will produce and those who will work and consume. There must be expansion and, at the same time, concentration. It has all been thought through quite carefully. It's more a matter of freedom of action than of knowing the specific requirements."

Thompson shook his head. "You're losing me, sir. I sense you're trying to say something but can't quite spit it out."

Wagner laughed. "You're right, of course. I just don't know what you'll think about all of this. I'm trying to gauge your response without telling you what I want you to respond to. I'm giving you too little credit, General. I'm sorry I'm doing such a poor job.

"Now, tell me, sir, would you say you are close to the president?"

Thompson blinked at the conversation's sudden change in direction. "No, not really close. He listens to me. He listens to others. Then he makes his own decisions."

"Is he a man who can—how should I say this—be persuaded?"

"Many have tried, but few have succeeded. Others can persuade him to do only what he wants, and not before, not until, he decides on the right course of action. The politicians have never misjudged a man so completely as they've misjudged Lincoln. He's shrewd. He disarms lesser men with his crude, folksy talk and idiotic stories. Before they know it, he's telling them what to do— and it usually has nothing to do with what they set out to accomplish. He's smarter than they are. He sees through their petty maneuvering and is at the crossroads, waiting for them, when they think they have outflanked him."

"Hmmm." Wagner frowned. "You're right, of course. Many would prefer to see someone like McClellan as president. Tell me, General, you know Lincoln. How does he propose to restore the Union when the fighting stops? What does he hope to accomplish?"

Thompson thought for a moment before answering. Was he betraying some unwritten confidence by discussing Lincoln this way? It somehow seemed wrong, but not for any obvious reason. "That's difficult to say, sir. I suppose he wants to change the way people think about the outcome of the war. If possible, he wants to avoid punishing the Confederate leaders. He thinks they need their heroes, men such as Lee."

"Do you think his goals are realistic? Will the results be helpful?"

"I don't know. The Southerners will be a defeated people, difficult to lead. And then there is Congress, especially the more radical Republicans—Lincoln's own men. Those who have watched over the war—especially those serving on the Committee on the Conduct of the War—want to make a hard peace to match Sherman's idea of hard war."

"Just as I thought," said Wagner, nodding. "The way I see it, there's no guarantee that beating the men in the South will alter their view. It may do exactly the opposite. Defeat may harden their view or simply redirect their anger. The point is, General—and you see it clearly—reconstruction could drain the nation's energy and resources. The future is out west. Don't you agree?"

"I suppose. I know Lincoln agrees. But he won't abandon the South to Congress." Thompson downed his drink and looked firmly into Wagner's eyes. "Where is this conversation leading us, Mr. Wagner? Lincoln's views on reconstruction must surely be known to you. Besides, you don't strike me as a man who enjoys a discussion of the philosophy of politics."

"To the contrary, General, I enjoy both. But I do have a point to make. The people I represent feel that you are the type of man who'd fit easily into their organization. You see what's out there—waiting for those with the courage to take advantage of momentary opportunity—and make it work for the good of all, of course."

"Of course." That's hogwash, and he knows it, Thompson thought. "Enlighten me, Mr. Wagner. You persist in mentioning these people you represent. Who are they?"

"Very wealthy men, General. Very wealthy men. They are the men who will guide this country when the war ends. But they have a problem. They won't have time to look over their shoulders at the politicians. They need a president, and men in Congress, who will understand their vision of the country's future. They need men in high places who can provide them with the information necessary to make informed decisions. That's where you come in. You know as much as any man alive about the economic capacity of this nation, its strengths and weaknesses, what the people want and need. That's valuable information. It's worth more than you probably realize to men who need to minimize their risks and invest their capital where it will do the most good."

That had the sound of a bribe. Thompson had to set the man straight. "I have no interest in your money, if that's what you're suggesting."

"Oh, my heavens no, General. I wouldn't insult you by even suggesting—well, we both know what I mean. What I'm talking about, General, is power.

The power to shape a nation." Wagner leaned back and smiled broadly, then leaned forward and patted Thompson's hand. "Well, General, we'll talk again. I've enjoyed this more than you'll ever know. Permit me to buy you another drink, then I must be on my way."

Thompson had consumed more than his quota already. Wagner held his liquor too well. Trusting such men often meant trouble. Thompson studied the man as he slipped easily into his raincoat. The smile never left his face. To him, that easy grace and kindness was nothing more than a tool, a tool all too easily converted into a dagger if someone betrayed him. Thompson had seen such men before; Washington had been overrun by them. But Thompson had another reason for being frightened by this man: he was attracted by what Wagner had to say. The thought troubled Thompson deeply.

He watched Wagner walk toward the door and, with a tip of his hat, disappear into the night. Thompson had the feeling that he had been talking about one thing while Wagner talked about something entirely different. He just had no idea where the conversation had been leading. Still, he saw merit in where it had ended. The idea of power intrigued him. In retrospect, the war that he thought would never end was slipping by all too quickly, and he had touched only its fringe. Glory had eluded him, and he resented that. Such opportunities seldom present themselves twice. What would there be for him when the war ended? He hated the shipping business, yet he still owned the six ships bequeathed to him by his father. He had more money than a rational man could spend in a lifetime—two lifetimes—and lately had become a man in search of a purpose for his life. Marriage seemed like a correct next step. But then what?

He shook his head. He needed sleep. After gulping down the rest of his drink, he staggered into the cool night air and hailed a cab. He would have time enough to think about Wagner later.

Wade sat in the general's tent. The aide had said seven. It was a quarter past eight. Generals are probably busy, Wade thought. Colonels could wait. He heard talking outside. The voices moved closer.

"Is he here?" a voice asked.

"In your tent, sir."

"Very well." A short wait followed. "Ah, there you are, Colonel." Wade stood at attention. "Be seated, son. We're not much on formality here. Sorry to keep you waiting. How are things with you?"

"Fine, General Meade."

"I won't keep you long, Colonel." He reached out and grasped a folder. "This is an outstanding record, Colonel. It surprised me to see the entry from General Thomas. He says you led the only attempt to relieve his forces on Snodgrass Hill at Chickamauga. I didn't know *anyone* even tried."

"Just an accident, sir." Why did Thomas bother? Wade wondered.

"Accidents don't seem to be evident in your record, Colonel. But that's not why I brought you here. There's a general on my staff who is quite fond of you. I'm sure you know to whom I refer."

"Yes, sir."

"Well, as you are probably aware, we are receiving a large number of Negro regiments. I don't know how they will respond when they go into battle, but we will have to use them. If they perform poorly, it will be quite an embarrassment to the army and to the government."

"They'll do fine, General. They know better than any of us what this war is about."

"Hmmm. I suppose you're right. But whatever the case, they need leaders, trained leaders. Your stepfather thinks you have what it takes to meet the responsibility. I need a brigade commander. It's policy not to force officers to command Negro regiments and brigades, so it's strictly voluntary. If you don't want it, you can keep the brigade you have now. What do you say?"

"I have one request, sir."

"Name it."

"I want to select my own sergeant major."

"All right, Colonel. I'll prepare the orders today. Oh, and I suppose you'll want Colonel Clinton as your executive officer. General Healy told me you would probably ask for him."

"That's correct, sir."

"You'll both be transferred tomorrow."

"Is that all, sir?"

"Yes, Colonel, and thank you. You'll receive your orders tomorrow. Good night."

Wade saluted. "Good night, sir."


South and west, perhaps forty miles from the meeting between Wade and Meade, a fat man with a partially severed ear stood in a run-down Richmond bar. A shortage of whiskey forced it to be rationed at a rate of two ounces per customer per day. Even at that, except in a few favored establishments, the golden liquid soon became nearly nonexistent. Ginger beer had replaced it, but its smell made the fat man sick. He had nursed the second ounce of whiskey for the past thirty minutes. The bartender moved busily about, dividing his attention between the cramped barroom and the small storage space at the rear of the building. All the other customers had consumed their whiskey quota and left for the night. The fat man pulled out his watch to check the time, then gulped the last few drops in the jigger. Too bad, he thought.

The door opened and a rush of humid air blew through the bar. A slender man in tattered clothing entered the building. He brushed the rain from his jacket before seating himself on a chair at the nearest table. The man had piercing eyes and wore a full, scraggly beard. The bartender paid no attention as he poured whiskey through a funnel from one partially empty bottle to another. When he had accumulated six empty bottles, he gathered them in his arms and disappeared through the doorway to the back room.

When he was gone, the slender man rose and strolled nervously toward the fat man. He dug into his coat pocket and slipped out a small pistol, carefully keeping it concealed in his grubby hand. Without speaking, he placed the barrel against the back of the fat man's head. Looking into the grime-encrusted mirror that hung behind the bar, the fat man inattentively observed what was happening. When he saw the gun, he dropped his glass and began to turn. A sharp report filled the room. The fat man pitched forward across the bar. Blood flowed down both sides of his face and dripped from his chin and nose.

"What was that?" shouted the man from the back room. There had been no warning, no reason to suspect violence. Hearing no answer, he continued with his chores.

The slender man stuffed the weapon back in his coat pocket and strolled casually from the bar without having said a word.

The task approached completion. Only Bowman and Thornton remained, but Bowman and his wife were believed to be in Baton Rouge. The Bowman girl had slipped through their fingers, but what could she do? She would have nothing to offer but hearsay—Southern hearsay at that. The war had taken her family and she had become bitter, so someone had to pay. That's what they would say motivated her, if she tried to make anyone listen to her. What risk could she pose, alone and penniless, with no one of consequence the least concerned whether she lived or died?

They would have to suspend the search now. Only one task remained. Then they could concentrate on the main objective. And with him five thousand dollars richer in the bargain.

Thompson bolted upright in bed. Despite the cool night air, his naked body was covered with sweat. The time has come, he thought, and I failed to recognize it. He felt stupid, blind, unworthy. Such lapses could cost men their lives. Perhaps they knew him better than he knew himself. He looked too deeply into events, or not deeply enough. His reaction time had become slow. He thought back to his lone combat mission, his one attempt at real soldiering. It had worked in the end, but not because of anything he had done. Everything had gone wrong. Only dumb luck had led to its success. Even so, his bungling had cost the life of Captain Bottoms. They're right, he thought angrily. I have no business leading men into combat.

Thompson's thoughts returned to the present. It was time to bring Wade home. By now he would have whetted his appetite for action; he had given

honorable service out where the lead hornets flew. Now the time for the final mission was at hand—the reason for bringing him home.

Wagner had asked to meet at the same bar tomorrow. Thompson planned
to join him. As usual, they would talk about politics and business, and about
the president—especially about the president. Thompson's association with
Lincoln had become well known, and that made him the perfect target. He
had money; that made his contact plausible. He was a general officer; that
gave him the inside information and the power to influence events. He knew
Lincoln well enough to get close to him and influence his actions; that made
him the perfect scapegoat. They had forgotten only one thing: a man with
those qualities would not be totally stupid. But this time Thompson planned
to lead the conversation, to give Wagner what he wanted, the signal of his
willingness to be manipulated. He smiled. He realized a great lesson that he
supposed he had always known but had never really put into words: timely
information was the ultimate power, even more so than money. He let his
head sink back to the pillow, breathed deeply once, and fell asleep.

# CHAPTER

## 29

Thompson sat in a red chair, one of several that lined the wall of the foyer leading into the president's study. There were a couple of cabinet officers with Lincoln, so he expected a long delay. The president had to know that all hell was about to break loose with the convention drawing near. Lincoln seldom took a day off, even on Sunday. Thompson looked at his watch. Nine in the evening. He looked at the calendar hanging on the wall. It read May 22, 1864.

"The president will see you now," announced John Hay, Lincoln's personal secretary. Thompson's thoughts had strayed. "General Thompson?" Hay said more forcefully.

Thompson looked up, startled. "You said something, Mr. Hay?"

"The president will see you now, sir."

"Thank you. I seem to have been preoccupied."

"Yes, General, you were. Go right in."

Lincoln met him at the door. He smiled and extended a bony hand. "Good evening, General. Sorry I kept you waiting. This convention is truly a distraction from more important matters."

"I can't think of anything more important than your reelection, Mr. President."

"Why, thank you, General. What can I do for you this evening?"

"I'm afraid I'm here on political matters, too, sir."

"Oh, then perhaps I should ask Secretary Seward to remain. Would you mind, General?"

"Not at all, Mr. President."

"Please be seated, General."

"Thank you, sir. I'll get right to the point. I had a meeting with Representative Teal this afternoon. He made a special trip from New York to talk with me."

"I know Representative Teal well," said Lincoln. "He's been a good friend."

"He certainly supports *you*, sir. You will recall our conversation a short time ago, about evidence of a plot to discredit you shortly before the election."

Lincoln laughed. "Politicians remember such remarks, General." He leaned closer. "Are they coming after me, General?" Who isn't? he thought.

"I'm afraid so, sir. It appears they intend to use the press."

"The *Boston Globe*, I'll wager."

"Yes, sir, and the *New York Tribune*."

"There's a pair to draw to." Lincoln looked at Seward and frowned. The secretary of state licked his pencil lead and wrote something on a tablet. Lincoln leaned back and relaxed. "What are the particulars, General? Give it to me with the bark on."

"Mr. Teal says there are at least three charges. Apparently, the plan is to hit you hard; then, while you're reacting, to strike again with parts two and three. The idea is to have you so off balance by the time of the convention that a peace candidate can be nominated."

"They might consider General McClellan. I hear he's available." Lincoln chuckled at his own wit.

Seward laughed and winked at Thompson, who smiled disbelievingly as he shook his head. How does he do it? Thompson wondered. I can't imagine anyone carrying the weight of this war as he has and still having a sense of humor. "Sir, the first article is scheduled to appear within the next couple of days, in the *Tribune*."

"What will it say, General?"

"Mr. Teal thinks they will allege that you have struck a secret deal with the British in order to keep them out of the war. They will say that you plan to transport large numbers of Negroes to the North to work in English-owned factories for slave wages. The objective is—"

"I know the objective, General. They hope to make workingmen angry at the prospect of losing their jobs. It would make me angry, too. Go on."

"He also says they will accuse you of making a secret deal to give Britain access to all of the confiscated cotton they want, as well as first priority on new crops following the war. This will result, as they will tell it, in our own factories doing without and our laborers and returning veterans being unemployed. Basically, sir, the thrust of the charges will be to plant the idea that you've sold out to a foreign power simply to free the slaves."

"Are you certain of this, General?"

"If Mr. Teal is to be believed, sir."

Lincoln grinned, then broke into loud laughter. Seward leaned back and smiled, then began writing again.

"And what's the third part?" asked Seward, looking up from the tablet, poised to write.

"Land, sir. They will charge that you are sacrificing our sovereignty by offering certain British politicians three million acres of land owned by the United States. They will allege that you have come to think of yourself as the king of America because Congress has not had the stomach to oppose you on key war issues, and that you think you can give away the birthright of the American people in order to assure the freedom of the Negro and get yourself reelected."

Lincoln frowned. "This 'they,' whoever they are, ought to attend a meeting of the Committee on the Conduct of the War if they think I don't have to answer to the Congress. I sometimes think I would get a friendlier reception in Richmond. Is that it, General?"

"As far as I know, sir." He hesitated. "Sir, I don't understand."

"Understand what, General?"

"Your lack of concern, sir. I thought you'd be furious. You're acting as if it's, well, comical, sir."

"In a way, it is, General. Now that I think more on it, it's downright hilarious. What do you think, Mr. Seward? Did you get all of that down?"

"I have it, Mr. President, every word."

Seward looked at Thompson. "General, there are many rules in politics, but there is one that is an imperative: if you're going to fire your salvo at an opponent, you better make sure the first shot is fatal."

"But Mr. Secretary, they're trying to discredit this administration."

"I know what they're trying to do, General," Lincoln interjected. "Now, let me ask you a question. We crossed into Virginia on the fourth of May. How many men have we lost since then?"

"Thirty thousand, more or less." A perplexing question. What did it have to do with anything?

"That's what—roughly two thousand men a day, dead, wounded, and captured? That's a brigade each day. I've had to find a way to send a fresh brigade each *day*, General, just to replace the casualties. That's a division every four to five days. We've lost more men in the past fifteen days than we had in the whole army at the start of the war. And these people want to discredit me by accusing me of giving the British a few million acres of land, land that no one wants except the Indians? The Colorado Territory *alone* has sixty-five million acres!

"It saddens me, General, that these men think they are capable of directing the future of this nation. It truly saddens me. In another time and place this pitiful effort might have some small measure of success. But it means nothing compared to the magnitude of the catastrophe that confronts this nation today. Are the people going to sacrifice eleven states, occupied by thirteen million people, out of concern for the issues you have raised? Many of them may be uneducated, General, but they are *not* stupid.

"No, General, I may lose, and I may lose badly, but it will be because of those brigades, those divisions. It will be over the issue of freedom for four million Negroes in our midst. It has always been about that and nothing else. The people know what I stand for. Their decision is whether they, too, want the same for this nation as I do. More precisely, do they want this nation to remain a Union, or a gaggle of quacking states, threatening to disrupt the barnyard every time they don't get their way? This war is about the most fundamental of issues; it is about civilization, what is right and wrong. Even if we gave the South what it wants today, it would not prevent the end of slavery. Those poor souls would cross into the North in a flood, with no way to stop them now. They could line men shoulder to shoulder, from the Atlantic to the Mississippi, and still they would come."

Lincoln rose and walked to the window. "Still, we must do something, I suppose. I won't be at the convention, Secretary Seward, so you will have to address this problem. General, when did you say these allegations will first appear in print?"

"Probably day after tomorrow, sir. On Tuesday."

"How does Teal know all of this?"

"I asked him, sir. He replied only that he had a reliable source."

Lincoln nodded. He, too, knew the value of sources, and of keeping them secret. "Can you do something by then, Seward?"

"It will be a rush job, sir, but I think it can be done."

"Fine. Thank you, General. You've been a great help. I appreciate your service. I won't keep you any longer."

"Very well, Mr. President. If there is anything I can do, just let me know."

Lincoln nodded and extended his hand. "I will, General. Good night."

"Oh, Mr. President, one other thing I should mention. I think I've been contacted by the conspirators."

"You *think*, General?"

"It's rather strange, sir. Senator Sprague introduced me to a man a short time ago. I recently had a long conversation with him in a bar. He's articulate and seems to know a lot about finance and politically related issues. But he's also quite curious about you, sir. He inquired, from a variety of perspectives, about your views. It was more the way he talked than anything specific. I realized only later, as I thought back on the whole of the conversation, that he was more interested in my opinion of you than in any of the other subjects we discussed. I think he wanted to know if he could manipulate me in some way, to serve some hidden goal."

"May I make a suggestion, General?"

"Of course, Mr. President."

"*Let* him manipulate you. Give him the rope and see if he hangs himself. If his motives are innocent, no harm will be done. If they are not, I'm certain you'll know what to do."

"Very well, sir. He indicated that he wants to go further with these discussions. I'll just string him along and see where he leads." Thompson walked to the door and turned. "Good night, Mr. President, Secretary Seward."

After Thompson had shut the door behind him, Lincoln spread his long frame on the sofa. "Do you think they have any chance of success, William?"

Seward shook his head. "None, sir. By the time of the convention, it won't even be a matter of discussion." He thought for a moment. "That's what worries me."

Lincoln cocked his head. "What do you mean?"

"These men aren't very apt at politics, Mr. President. They are not likely to be the type of men to take a beating gracefully. By thwarting them so easily, you will only force them to find a more lasting solution."

Lincoln nodded. He sighed and laid his head on the back of the sofa. "I think you are right, sir." His eyelids drifted shut and in a moment his breathing became heavy.

Seward walked quietly to a shelf and retrieved a shawl given to the president as a gift. He spread it over Lincoln and shook his head slowly. What will become of us if we lose this man? he wondered.

The albino sat behind the bar, on a box in the filth-strewn alley. He had waited for more than an hour. Now, sitting there in the darkness, he knew he looked suspicious. For five nights in a row he had arrived here precisely at eight. He had waited until ten, then returned to the hotel. He had grown weary of the ritual. He realized he should have returned earlier. Something must have gone wrong. He huddled against the unseasonably cool air and waited. Just as he rose to leave, he heard the sound of footsteps to his right. He slid quickly back into the shadows. The figure drew closer. "Is that you, Mellen?" he asked in a whisper.

"Yeah, it's me."

"Were you successful?" asked Whitey, avoiding the preliminaries.

"Not entirely," replied Mellen. "We had some difficulty findin' John Ward, as you know. Not sure who he might've talked to 'fore we caught up with him. We killed him, though. We lost Bowman's trail in Mobile. By the time we arrived at the Thornton place, the house had been burned and the general'd vanished. No one knew he was gone. We still don't know where he is."

"Damn," snapped the albino. "My benefactors will be disappointed."

"To hell with your benefactors," Mellen hissed. "If they think they can do any better, let 'em do their own killin'. Ain't much chance of those two talkin' nohow. They'll stay in hidin' an' surface later on. Then we'll get 'em."

"What about the man in Richmond?" Whitey asked, apprehension evident in his tone. From his perspective, the elimination of the fat man had been critical. He had recruited the thirteen men who would kill Lincoln.

"Shot him in a bar. No witnesses. That fat, flop-eared old bastard never knew what hit him."

Whitey smiled. Could have ended worse, he thought. "And the men who went with you?"

"I took care of 'em all myself—at night, while they slept."

"So everything's cleaned up?"

"Nothing to worry about. You got my money?"

"Five thousand in gold, just as I promised. You sure there are no loose ends?"

"Sure I'm sure. I do good work. Those two gettin' away weren't my fault. Too much distance to cover. I'll get to 'em later."

"I'm sure you will." He handed Mellen a small wooden box. "Here's the gold."

Mellen's knees buckled under the unexpected weight. "This is heavy," he said, grinning broadly. "Never thought I'd be rich. Reckon I'll lie low awhile, maybe go to California."

"Is there anyone who knew about your mission?"

"Only you—and your damned benefactors."

Whitey reached up with his left hand and grasped Mellen behind the neck. Uncertain of the meaning of the action, Mellen clung to the gold. As Whitey pulled Mellen's head forward, he raised his other hand and pressed a double-barreled derringer against Mellen's right eye. Whitey pulled the trigger, blinking from the momentarily blinding flash and flinching as warm blood splashed on his face. Mellen dropped like a rock, still clinging to the container filled with gold. Whitey pried Mellen's fingers from the box before placing the small pistol against the man's other eye and again squeezing the trigger. He was nothing if not thorough. "I wish you hadn't been so careless," Whitey said softly. He pulled a handkerchief from his pocket and wiped the blood from his face. "You should have gotten the other two." He sighed. "Oh well, what's done is done." He turned and walked toward the street.

When Whitey reached the hotel, he stopped under a gaslight and looked into a window, then went inside. The night clerk nodded as he walked by, then returned to reading the paper. Whitey climbed the stairs to the second floor and knocked softly on the third door to the right.

When it opened, the man inside motioned for the albino to enter, then shut the door behind him. "Any problems?" he asked.

"Perhaps. They never did find General Thornton. He undoubtedly got a warning and went into hiding. Can't be sure. They never found Bowman, either. He was traced as far as Mobile, but he vanished."

"Must we always have these bits of unfinished business, my friend?" asked Ira McFadden.

"I'll take care of it. I always do," Whitey said in a wounded tone.

McFadden swished the brandy in his glass. "So you do. I have a meeting in the morning; then I must return to Philadelphia. It's time to prepare to move the men down from Baltimore to Washington. I'll entrust that task to you. Select your time carefully. Is the backup plan in place?"

"Yes, sir. But it involves only the president and the two cabinet members."

"We'll hope it doesn't come to that, but it's critical that we get Lincoln."

"If necessary, sir, I'll take care of it myself."

"You're a comfort, my friend. All of us appreciate your diligence. Tell me, what progress has there been with General Thompson?"

"Wagner says he's about ready. The general is a cautious man."

"Well, I trust Wagner to convince him of the benefits of joining us. I want everything ready to go no later than June eighth, when the convention ends. If Lincoln wins, have the men strike at the first opportunity after that date."

"It'll take a few weeks to conclude the preliminaries, but they'll be ready, sir. Have a safe trip home. I'll be leaving for New York City on the morning train, so I doubt I'll see you again before our task is complete."

"Report to me when it's finished."

"Yes, sir." Whitey set the wooden box on the table. "Here's your gold, sir." He turned and walked toward the door. "Good night, sir."

McFadden smiled as he ran his finger across the top of the box containing the gold. Whitey is correct in his self-assessment, he thought. He's thorough enough on his own behalf. His hired help is another matter. More's the pity.

# CHAPTER

# 30

McFadden smiled as he opened the *Tribune*. He expected to see a banner headline announcing that Lincoln had bargained away American jobs to free the slaves. The smile faded when he saw a less prominent headline that read: LINCOLN THREATENS TO NATIONALIZE FOREIGN BUSINESS. The story read:

Secretary of State William Seward's eyes flashed with anger last night as he discussed the nation's new labor policy with reporters at the Baltimore Pavilion. The secretary made a surprise visit to the city to engage in preliminary discussions with members of the Republican Party platform committee. The Republican convention is scheduled to open here in two weeks.

The secretary's comments were in response to rumors that a secret agreement had been reached with Great Britain to allow the employment of former slaves at greatly reduced wages once the war is won. Sources identified the agreement as part of a secret protocol attached to a treaty recently negotiated between Great Britain and the United States. The treaty addresses a broad range of trade issues and remains to be ratified by the Senate.

The president this morning completed the first draft of a bill that, if ratified, will authorize the government to seize the assets of any foreign power seeking to exploit workers in this country as a result of disruptions caused by the transition from war to peace. Seward noted that the bill was specifically aimed at England, as a result of pressure from factions there attempting to obtain western land from the federal government in exchange for the British government's not recognizing the Confederate States of America. The secretary acknowledged that he, too, had heard the rumors and branded as a hoax a news article expected to appear in this morning's edition of the *Tribune*.

> Seward said that President Lincoln, angered by pressure from un-
> named factions in Great Britain, vowed to let the American people know,
> in the clearest possible language, that his administration will do everything
> within its power to help returning veterans find jobs that pay decent
> wages. Seward stated that he had come to Baltimore primarily to inform
> members of the platform committee that Mr. Lincoln wanted strong language
> in the Republican Party platform that would make clear the president's
> stand on this issue of vital interest to our soldiers and sailors.

Although there was more to the story inside, the essential facts were covered on the front page.

That wily old son of a bitch, thought McFadden. How did Lincoln find
out? It required little effort to imagine Waxelman's fury. Nothing angered
him more than being outwitted. Someone had leaked the information and
told Lincoln—or someone close to him. No other explanation made sense.
But who? And how had the president reacted so quickly? The final draft of
the official-looking documents had been reviewed on Friday and sent to New
York City by courier that same evening. They had arrived unopened. That
had been confirmed by telegram.

McFadden skimmed the remainder of the story until he reached the final
paragraph:

> Seward noted that Mr. Lincoln decided to withhold the treaty from
> the Senate until the source of the reported false documents could be un-
> covered. He added that the president would recommend that the treaty
> not be ratified if he discovered that the British had a hand in the affair.

"My God," McFadden said aloud. Several people in the dining room turned
and looked in his direction. This cannot be permitted to happen, he thought.
The treaty promised great benefits to his group. It would open a variety of
markets for businesses in which he and members of his group had purchased
large blocks of stock. Millions of dollars were at stake, perhaps tens of millions.
That single paragraph could send stock prices plummeting.

Something had to be done before the other two parts of the story appeared
in print. He first thought to direct that his stocks be sold immediately. But
such action was strictly forbidden. They had agreed not to act independently.
If he saved himself while others in his group lost millions, what would they
think? Most of the others might not find out, but Waxelman certainly would.
One way or the other, Waxelman always learned of every large financial
transaction. He would automatically suspect that someone had tried to manipulate the market for personal gain. That would alert him. Once the documents were revealed to be forgeries, as would surely happen within a short
time, stock prices would climb again. But if, in the interim, someone sold

high and bought low, a fortune could be made. McFadden had thought of that before, but he had never figured out a way to make it happen.

No. He had to sit tight and take the losses—if it came to that. He closed his eyes and imagined Waxelman reading the same news article. McFadden vowed to find out who leaked the story; someone would pay with his life.

He reached into his pocket and withdrew a small notebook. He jotted down a message and signaled to the waiter.

"May I help you, sir?" inquired the waiter.

"Yes, it's urgent. I need someone to get this to the telegraph office at once. Who might that be?" McFadden's thumb pressed against a gold eagle.

"That would be me, sir. I'm just going off duty."

"Hurry, man—and keep the change."

The waiter smiled as he grasped the note and the gold coin. He would make a month's wages in an hour.

The *Globe* printed its planned version of the story, revealing everything of importance in the forged documents. No reporter from the paper had been at the Baltimore news conference. An hour after the *Tribune* hit the streets, a *Globe* reporter telegraphed the complete text of the *Tribune* story to his Boston employer. Four hours later, the *Globe* published a special edition, printing word for word the text of the *Tribune* story about Seward's comments and stating its belief that the documents reported to be the secret protocol were a forgery. The *Globe* professed its indignation at being misled, of course, but the damage had been done. The stock market had closed by the time the special edition reached the streets. The *Globe* would headline its Wednesday edition with the report that the market had lost more than twenty million dollars the previous day, with a general decline in all stocks. The story made no reference to a possible relationship between this event and news coverage of the treaty.

At the Baltimore railroad station, the train from Pittsburgh ground to a halt in the early morning light. Cathy Blair stood at the top step of the second car. She had been on the run—the only word that seemed appropriate—and the stress had sapped her strength. Necessity now forced her to stop and find temporary employment. While sleeping in the Cincinnati train station two nights earlier, someone had stolen her luggage, including the bag that contained most of her money. She had cried for an hour upon discovering the theft. Thank goodness she had been resting her head on her daughter's bag. She had placed a ten-dollar gold piece in it wrapped with a note, in the event she and Sandra became separated on the long journey. For a reason she could never explain to herself, she had written Caroline Healy's name and address on the note. Perhaps that had been because she now envisioned the small town of Gettysburg as the only spot on earth that had a ring of permanence to it.

When Cathy had stopped crying, she had pulled herself together and boarded the train to Pittsburgh, where she arrived with only seven dollars and a one-way ticket to New York City. But she couldn't face being alone and broke in a large northern city, so she cashed in the ticket and bought one to Baltimore instead. At least it was close to the South. She had no idea where to turn. The idea of seeking out Sam's mother in Gettysburg kept popping into her thoughts, but instinct more than reason guided her southward. Seven dollars would last only days in the city.

Her daughter pulled at her dress. "Mommy, I'm hungry."

"I know, honey." She could offer the child no encouragement. With no luggage to wait for, she stepped down to the platform and began walking toward the center of the city. Sandy trailed close behind, holding her doll by a leg. The sun had hardly risen, but Cathy could feel the perspiration trickling down her back and chest. She was wearing the only dress she had, a garment better suited for winter than late spring in Baltimore.

For her daughter's sake, she fought to restrain her tears. The child did not understand her mother's sadness. Cathy stopped in front of a store, wondering which way to go. Then she turned and saw herself in the window. Despite every effort to hold them back, the tears flowed.

At seven that evening, Richard Fox, the editor in chief of the *Chicago Herald,* received a long telegram from his chief reporter in Boston. The telegram contained the full text of the *Globe*'s original story. Thirty minutes later, before Fox had decided what to do, he received a second telegram, this one containing the full text of the *Globe*'s special edition story. He walked to the front of the building, hailed a cab, and went to the home of James O'Connor, a close friend and Brig. Gen. David Healy's banker and financial manager. O'Connor answered his knock on the door.

"What are you doing here at this time of night, Richard?"

"May I come in?"

O'Connor shrugged and waved him inside.

"Read this," said Fox.

O'Connor smiled as he read. Finished, he looked smugly at Fox.

"Now, read this."

When O'Connor finished, he returned the second telegram. He smiled again, then nodded, as if blessed with a revelation.

"Well, what do you think?" asked Fox.

"I think this will be an interesting campaign, Richard."

"Do you think the *Globe* and *Tribune* were manipulated?"

"How long have you known Lincoln?" asked O'Connor.

"Oh, about twenty-five years. Why?"

"How many really stupid acts have you seen him commit?"

Fox thought for a moment. "None like this."

"Then you tell me."

"Someone forged the documents, hoping to catch Lincoln unaware and throw the convention into deadlock."

"That's my guess, only Lincoln found out and threw it back in their faces."

"What are you going to do?" asked Fox.

"First thing in the morning, I'm going to buy stocks for my clients. David Healy has a spare million, as does his wife. Then I'll wait a couple of weeks and sell it all. I'll be a genius, my clients will be a lot richer, and Lincoln will be renominated. What are *you* going to do?"

"I think I know what Lincoln would say. He would say that when one lie counteracts another, there's no story."

O'Connor nodded. "Care for a drink, Richard? I have this most magnificent bottle of Napoleon brandy, fresh off the boat from the Continent." He put his arm around Fox's shoulders. "You know, Richard, this is a wonderful time to be alive. Just so your trip won't be a waste, how about a game of cribbage?"

Early the next morning, Waxelman knocked at McFadden's hotel room. When McFadden opened the door, Waxelman rushed angrily in. "You received my telegram?" asked McFadden.

"That goddamn son of a bitch," Waxelman replied.

"What do we do?"

Waxelman exposed a bottle of Canadian whiskey. "Do you have some glasses?"

"For God's sake, R. C.! It's seven-thirty in the morning."

"I insist you join me," Waxelman said curtly.

McFadden got the glasses from the dresser and Waxelman poured. "Call a meeting. I want everyone present, even the albino. Is he in Baltimore?"

"I think so, but is it wise having him see everyone?"

"Get him here. You'll take care of it later, of course, after he has finished. We'll meet on Saturday at my home. Make it ten in the evening. That should give everyone time to get here. And I want that idiot Sir what's-his-name here, too."

McFadden nodded. "How bad were we hit?"

"Conservatively, ten million. And it's bound to get worse this morning. There will be no more of this game playing, Ira. Lincoln has to die. If this plan fails, we develop another."

"Are you that certain he'll beat McClellan?"

Waxelman drank the whiskey without answering.

"I suppose so," McFadden said, answering his own question.

Waxelman poured another glass. "I've stopped the second and third releases cold."

"How did you manage that? The press doesn't like to be told what to do."

"Wasn't much of a problem. First, I asked them not to print it. When they refused my request, I informed them that I would open a paper down the block from theirs and give the papers away free until I ran them out of business. They knew I'd do it, too. They immediately realized that they didn't have a story. Wish I had some seltzer." He took another swallow.

"The one remaining problem is getting Lincoln out of the White House without his guards. Work on that, McFadden, as fast as possible. I want everyone's agreement on this. When it's finished, I want everything cleaned up."

"Everyone? Even the Englishman?"

"Everyone." He drained the glass and poured another, then dropped into a chair. "God, what a mess," he said too softly for McFadden to hear. "Papa warned me never to take partners in business or prisoners in war." He nearly fell from the chair as he struggled to remove his coat, revealing a sweat-soaked shirt. It had been a lifelong article of faith with Waxelman never to drink hard spirits. It makes you do terrible, stupid things, he always said.

# CHAPTER

# 31

On June 8, Lincoln was renominated for a second term. Seward had been correct: the brief uproar resulting from the stories in the *Tribune* and *Globe* had been lost in the shuffle of high political drama. The stock market had rebounded quickly, and the promised piece of labor legislation had been placed in a drawer in Lincoln's desk. It would never surface again.

That same day, John Hunt Morgan captured the town of Mount Sterling, Kentucky, and robbed the local bank of eighteen thousand dollars. In the Shenandoah Valley, Generals Averell and Crook joined Maj. Gen. David Hunter in his drive on Lynchburg. At Cold Harbor, where Grant's army had suffered a terrible beating, the last of seven thousand Union dead were being laid to rest. Unbeknownst to Lee, Grant was building a strong defensive line in front of Lee's trenches to shield a dash by the bulk of Grant's force toward Petersburg, Virginia. Grant had one remaining chance to draw Lee into the open, to fight the all-out battle that would bring this bloody conflict to a close. If he failed, a siege would be inevitable, with the war dragging on indefinitely.

Also on June 8, a letter addressed to Col. Samuel Wade, care of general delivery, arrived in Washington. Thirty minutes later, Brig. Gen. Jason Thompson produced a document signed by General Halleck, authorizing the seizure of the letter to Wade for military censorship purposes. No one raised an objection. Thompson went to his office and opened the letter.

June 2, 1864
Dear Colonel Wade,
We have been alerted, but still remain in a town named Essex, just east of Boston. We are waiting for something, but no one has told us what. The men are growing restless, and drinking is becoming a problem. I plan to sneak this letter to a postal drop on my next trip to

town, probably day after tomorrow. Two of the men came down sick a few days ago. The people behind this may have decided to delay things because of that.

I don't know much about Washington City, so I asked some questions of a local resident. All she knew of the city was a place called Ford's Theater, where she once saw a play. I suggest that you and I attempt to meet there.

June 3

I was interrupted yesterday. We were told last night that we should plan on leaving this place on or about June 16, but not earlier. That means we'll arrive in Washington no earlier than the seventeenth, but it may be later. I will attempt to meet you at the theater between two and five in the afternoon. All I can suggest is that you post a man there to look for me, as I suspect you will have more important things to do than spend who knows how long waiting for the meeting. If you cannot be there, send a representative. I will provide in writing the information I have. Let me suggest a password, in the event I am contacted by someone other than you. How about Rome? You can figure out how to work that into a conversation.

We wait impatiently to be informed of the specifics of our mission. The men suspect we are wasting our time. Given the high degree of security we have encountered, I cannot assure you I will be able to sneak off to meet with you. In any event, I will not come unless I have specific information to deliver. The risk is too great for a useless meeting.

I tell you, sir, I'm frightened about this whole operation. If guns begin to blaze in open battle, how am I to avoid my own death? I console myself with the knowledge that I am a soldier serving my country. I suppose I can say as much without fear of eternal damnation, for the South has lost the war. Few among us deny the reality. The fight goes on from force of habit, bolstered by hope for a miracle, the nature of which no one can imagine.

If this information fails to suit your purposes, I am sorry. It is the best I can do under the circumstances.

I know nothing of my family. I fear the worst.

For my part, I live now to make certain that my mission fails. What a terrible admission that is, but it is the truth.

Good luck to you. I am
In your debt,

Frank Bowman,
Major, CSA

"How are things with you, Washington?"

Petree turned at the sound of his name. A broad grin spread across his face. "Sam," he said spontaneously, then caught himself, "I mean Colonel Wade, sir."

Wade reached out and pulled the young man to him. "It's good to see you, my friend. How is the army treating you?" Wade patted Petree on the back as the young black man looked up at him.

"Couldn't be better, sir." He pointed to his sleeve. "I suppose you already know that I'm a sergeant."

"Not anymore, Washington—at least not *just* a sergeant. You're to be my sergeant major. Do you think you can handle the job?"

"You bet, Colonel. I've been watching how things are done. We heard you were going to be the new brigade commander."

"Well, it's official now." Wade turned to Clinton. "This is Lieutenant Colonel Clinton. He'll be the new exec."

"Good to meet you, Colonel Clinton. We'll get along just fine."

"I know we will, Sergeant Major," Clinton said with a smile. "Colonel Wade thinks mighty highly of ya."

"Thank you, sir."

"And this is Captain Healy," Wade said. "He'll be a company commander. I understand the brigade needs several."

"Yes, sir. We've taken some casualties."

"So I heard, Washington. Now, I'd like you to inform all of the officers that I want a meeting at my headquarters at seven this evening."

Petree stepped back a step and saluted. "Yes, sir, Colonel." Then he smiled. "Good to have you here, sir. The men will make you proud."

From the diary of Caroline Wade-Healy

*June 8, 1864*
*Joy is in me again! I received a telegram from Victoria this afternoon. She and her family plan to come to Gettysburg as soon as possible. She says they have no other choice, but did not say why or precisely when. She asked that I not tell anyone that they are coming. How can I keep such a thing a secret in this small town? Oh well, I shall have to try.*

*I have many things to do, diary, so it may be a while before my next entry.*

On the afternoon of June 8, Frank Bowman and his men were playing cards when a carriage rolled into the courtyard. Bowman rose and walked to the nearest window. A second vehicle, a wagon, followed close behind. The albino and two men Bowman didn't recognize waited in the carriage for the wagon to pull alongside. After exchanging places, the wagon driver left in the carriage.

"I'll get the men," the albino told his companions. Bowman barely made out the words.

"They're here," Bowman said to the others.

The albino opened the door. "Good day, Major Bowman. Please bring your men outside." The house emptied in a matter of seconds. The albino waved. "Over here, gentlemen." They moved to the side of the wagon. A large canvas tent-half covered the contents. The albino pulled it off.

"Yankee uniforms?" asked one of the men.

"That's right. Find one that fits. Get them on and I'll inspect you in a few minutes. Pardon my manners. This is Jeremy Wagner." The third man stood twenty feet away.

"Gentlemen," said Wagner with a nod.

"Mr. Wagner will escort us to Washington," the albino continued. "He has secured a house for us at the end of a largely deserted street. We will be leaving as soon as it's dark."

"Pardon me, sir," said Bowman, "but you said we would not leave until the seventeenth or later."

"There's been a change in plans. We need to be in place as soon as possible."

Wagner retrieved a package from the wagon seat. "Here, Major, this is your uniform. It's new. Officers in grubby uniforms stand out in Washington, so I purchased this just for you. I think it will fit."

Bowman tore away the wrapper and held up the coat.

"I don't suppose you've heard anything from your family lately?" asked Wagner.

"They don't know where I am," Frank replied.

"Of course not. How stupid of me. How is Cathy?"

"Cathy? You know Cathy?"

"I spent several days at your family's plantation last year. We had a long talk one evening. Delightful young lady. I should like to have gotten to know her better, but I had to leave for England the next day."

"If you don't mind my asking, Mr. Wagner, are you connected to us in some way?"

"Only indirectly. I'm making the arrangements."

"Arrangements for what?"

"Surely you have guessed that by now, Major Bowman."

"Sir, I have been guessing at what's going on since the day I volunteered for this assignment. The men are tired of doing nothing, and I agree with them. Either let us do what we are expected to do, or send us back to the army. The South doesn't have men to spare."

Wagner smiled. Perhaps he *doesn't* know, he thought. "Your waiting is nearly over, Major. Just a couple of loose ends to tie up and you will be granted your wish. That uniform looks fine on you. Fine, indeed. No one would ever suspect who you really are." He turned and examined the others. "You all look fine, men. Major, there's a regulation Union army pistol and holster under the seat. Strap it on. I understand that you have wagons and horses out in the barn. Have a couple of your men hitch up the horses. We'll leave after supper. What's on the menu?"

Bowman pointed. "Who is he?"

"Don't concern yourself with him, Major. His name is Ira McFadden. He pays the bills." A minor indiscretion, he thought, but what did it matter? None of them would be in a position to identify McFadden later.

Three days later, two carriages approached from opposite directions on a lane that ran through the Pittsburgh city park. They stopped when they drew next to each other. "Is everything set, Ira?" asked one driver.

"So far as it can be, R. C. Wagner plans to meet with the men again this afternoon and begin the process of moving them to Washington."

"What about Lincoln's meeting with the committee?"

"Nothing has been set, R. C. Wagner thinks Thompson will be the bait. He hopes to be able to ask him to call a meeting soon. But everything has to be right. There has to be a good reason."

"I want this matter behind us, Ira."

"I know that, R. C. But the timing has to be right. I'll keep you advised."

"Very well, Ira. Very well. I have to trust in you. You got that other mess down south cleaned up in good order. Too bad a couple got away. I presume you are looking for them."

"Arthur Bowman should be taken care of within a couple of days. Thornton has simply disappeared. He'll surface in time. We'll be waiting."

Waxelman smiled. "This is going to work out, Ira. And when it does, what a glorious day *that* will be." He snapped the whip and the carriage jerked forward. He looked over his shoulder. "Keep in touch, Ira. Remember, there must be no link to us."

"It'll be taken care of, R. C."

"When did you receive this letter, General?" asked Lincoln.

"This morning, Mr. President," replied Jason Thompson.

"Well, this confirms it. I suppose I will have to cooperate. Who will lead the men who spring the trap?"

"I thought I'd have Colonel Wade do that, sir. He's been so deeply involved in this that it seems unfair to leave him out at the finish."

"He's a good man, General. He has my full support and confidence."

"Sir, will you sign the order? General Meade may be reluctant to release him from his brigade."

"Bring it by when you're ready, General."

"Thank you, Mr. President."

The train screeched to a halt shortly after sundown, thirty minutes ahead of schedule. Victoria smiled as she pressed her face against the window. Although the long journey had been wearisome, her excitement had grown with each of the last hundred miles. It's hardly the same as coming home, she told herself, but, still, there's a feeling of security in the name. Gettysburg. Over the years, Caroline had written of the town so many times that it had acquired a special image in Victoria's mind. Yet what she saw exceeded the idealized vision she had of the place. After a quarter century, everything in the North seemed strange. The rich, rolling farmlands, the small, well-tended homes, the sense of normalcy and tranquillity—everything seemed so different from the South. Even Simon's spirits seemed to lift once they had headed east from Cincinnati, where they had been hiding for more than a month.

Only Henry's mood remained sullen. The general's leg was largely healed, so one place of hiding was as good as the next. If they really wanted him, he had no doubt that they would find him. Perhaps they would think twice about offending a relative of Caroline Healy's stature. He had sat by himself most of the way, speaking only when spoken to. Victoria turned from the window and watched him as he slipped into his jacket, although she had no idea why. It must be eighty degrees out there, she thought.

They were nearly impoverished. They had no home to return to. She still shuddered at the thought of the flames licking up the side of their house. She had never felt such a sense of desperation. She sobbed for hours as they rode northward through the darkness, never stopping until the first light of dawn. By then they were thirty miles away, and she had stopped looking back at the rosy glow against the black sky. It had taken so long to get the house just right, and then, in the space of one dreadful night, it had been reduced to a pile of ashes. But by now, time had dulled the anguish.

Unlike her, Henry had looked only north. The more she cried, the more he whipped the horses. Even more graphic than the sadness she felt at the loss of her home was the fear evident in her husband's eyes. At the time, she hadn't yet realized the reason for that fear. Now she knew. That made it easier. She loved him more than any house, more than the South, more than her own life. He would always be the handsome young planter who swept her off her feet and carried her south, to a land of grace and beauty. The life had tarnished, but the dream remained vivid. Those feelings were securely stored in her memory. They would have to satisfy her for the remainder of her life.

The evening of their second day away from the plantation, they had stopped at a roadside tavern on the Tennessee border. Only then had Henry told them the reason for leaving. It had become a matter of survival. None of them felt safe. Vicious, unfeeling people were on their trail. If they found him, they would kill him and anyone associated with him. That had been the first and last time they had discussed it. One phase of their lives had been closed, another opened.

As the miles passed behind them, there had come a time in Victoria's mind when she concluded that worse disasters could have befallen them. Although still saddened by the feeling of what she had lost, her unhappiness was being replaced gradually with the excitement of what might lie ahead.

She stepped into the aisle of the railcar and walked sedately toward the exit. She carried a single carpetbag. The trunk was already on the platform. Henry stretched as he gazed into the clear evening sky. Simon stood at his father's side, his hands deep in his pockets, his shoulders hunched forward. This meant a chance for him, perhaps the last chance to regain his self-respect. Nancy Caroline looked around and smiled, her first real sign of joy in weeks.

Well, baby sister, Victoria thought with a sigh, you get to take care of my children and me again. You were right, and I was wrong. There was, after all, nothing down there worth the destruction of our family.

# CHAPTER

# 32

Between drinks and popping peanuts into their mouths, Wagner and Thompson had been discussing the nation's political and economic woes for nearly an hour. They had met three times before this, always edging closer to the objective but never quite reaching it. Why? Thompson wondered. Perhaps they were waiting for something. Nothing that justified the delay came to mind. But they had moved closer tonight. After five jiggers of whiskey, he had difficulty keeping his thoughts on any subject, let alone politics and economics. Wagner had left the room to relieve himself.

Thompson adjusted his posture but found himself slipping in his chair almost immediately. By the time Wagner returned, Thompson had nearly dozed off.

Wagner smiled as he looked down at the general. It's time for the last step, he thought.

Wagner cleared his throat. "I've been wondering, General, how often do you meet with President Lincoln?"

Thompson's head snapped upright. "Wha—what?" He blinked, then rubbed his eyes. "Oh, once, sometimes twice a week. Why do you ask?"

Wagner seemed surprised. "That's fairly regularly," he said, ignoring the question.

"I suppose so."

"Do you know any members of the Committee on the Conduct of the War?"

"Yes. I know Senator Chandler, of course, and Senator Wade. I've barely talked with Senator Johnson. I know Representatives Gooch and Julian quite well. I know the others to speak to them." Thompson squinted. "Why do you ask?" he inquired again. He wasn't going to let Wagner back away.

"And Secretary Seward? How well do you know him?"

"I have dinner with him occasionally. I'd say we are friends."

"And, of course, you know Secretary Stanton."

"Better than any of the others. I've spent many hours talking with Secretary Stanton—and Chase, too."

Wagner pulled a name at random, a committee member who Thompson had failed to mention. "We have been in close communication with Representative Odell of the Committee on the Conduct of the War. He's of the opinion that positive results will follow if the committee members meet with the president, as well as Secretaries Seward and Stanton, to discuss certain matters related to the end of the war. Do you think that might be arranged?"

"They know where the president lives." So it's true, thought Thompson. They want to wipe out the whole nest with one blow. "Let them get an appointment."

"That's the problem, General. They're eager to avoid the appearance of weakness, of going to the president with hat in hand, if you know what I mean. They would like to arrange a quiet meeting with the president and the two secretaries. They would prefer to keep it secret."

"For what purpose?"

"I think that's obvious, General. There are many issues that need to be discussed. Economic issues. Repatriation of Southern leaders once the war ends. Compensation for war damage. The Indian problem in the West. Railroads. The war is ending, General. Grant may whip Lee in a matter of weeks."

Thompson knew better. He had seen the dispatches. Lee had checked Grant's every move, and Grant's men were tired after more than a month of endless struggle without seeming to gain an advantage. In the wake of the Cold Harbor disaster, many of the soldiers wondered if *anyone* could whip Lee. With Lee's army entrenched south of Petersburg, Grant realized that he had a major problem on his hands. The siege might drag on for months, perhaps until next year.

"I don't have to remind you," Wagner continued, "that the business of business is business. There will be more than a million and a half unemployed soldiers going home in the next few months. The problem is, the president has been so preoccupied with the war that he hasn't given much attention to these issues."

"You do the president an injustice, sir," said Thompson. "I personally have discussed all of those issues with him, some of them several times."

"I'm sure, General, but this meeting will be fruitful. It's important that it be arranged, as soon as possible. Do you think you can do it?"

"Probably. Just where do you want this secret meeting to take place?"

"The Capitol building would be the best place, General. With Congress in session, a meeting can be arranged without attracting attention. They could have their discussion and that would be the end of it. One more thing. Representative Odell would prefer to remain anonymous. You know how it is. He doesn't want it to appear as though he's trying to outmaneuver the others."

"Which, of course, is all that politics really is," replied Thompson. "Maneuvering, I mean."

"Precisely, General, so there's no need to mention where the request originated. I ask again, General, is this possible?"

"I'll think about it over dinner. You're buying, of course."

"Of course. I hear that the lobster and clams at the National Hotel are delicious."

"Have a chair, Samuel," General Healy said. "This is Major Stratton. He's here from Washington. How have things been going with you?"

"As well as can be expected, sir."

"How have you adjusted to the command of a Negro brigade?"

"They're as fine a group of soldiers as we have, sir. They get scared the same, sweat the same, even bleed the same. And they do their duty the same. I'm proud to be associated with them."

"Have you heard from your mother lately?"

"Yes, sir. I received a letter last week."

"Then you know she has house guests?" Healy wondered what Wade would read into the question.

"Yes, sir."

"Which presents a problem, Sam."

"I thought it might, sir, but she informed me that she sent notice to General Thompson."

"Oh, I didn't know that. What was his reply?"

"She wrote me before she heard back from him."

"But the problem remains," said Stratton. "Her brother-in-law is known to have participated in a plot to assassinate the president."

Wade had anticipated this conversation, although he had expected it to be with someone else—Meade, perhaps, or members of the military legal department. He knew that Stratton was right, technically, but technicalities tended to be overlooked in time of war—unless they served a military purpose. Wade had made some inquiries. In terms of state of mind, General Thornton had severed all relations with the United States when he assumed command of an army unit of a foreign power. Although the South's secession had never been recognized by federal authorities, the fact of the separation was beyond dispute. But if the separation was not a *legal* fact, then every rebel soldier was guilty of murder or conspiracy to commit murder. Not the most clearly defined legal situation all around, for the North or the South. If there were trials, they would have to begin at the top—with Jeff Davis and Lee—and work their way down. Where would it end once it began? Even so, Wade knew that there were those who wanted to put all the rascals in jail.

Wade sighed and shifted his position. "We are at war, Major. Although you and I may abhor the very idea of a plot to assassinate Lincoln, I doubt it is a crime for a soldier of a country in a state of war to contemplate such action. Then there is the undisputed fact that General Thornton willingly provided the necessary information that has led directly to uncovering the plot. He is under a death sentence as we speak. You know that. My mother, on the other hand, has provided the only direct proof that this plot was the creation of Northerners, not Southerners. Some of these conspirators are making millions from the war, and receiving the blessings of the government at the same time."

Wade shifted his attention to Healy. "I'm no lawyer, General, but Lincoln is. I'll wager you he would say the same."

Healy looked at Major Stratton. Stratton shrugged. "Well, Sam," Healy said, "you shall have the opportunity to make your case to the president. He has asked to meet with you and General Thompson the day after tomorrow at seven in the evening. You will turn over command to your executive officer and prepare to leave at once."

"Sir, isn't this a bit irregular? Is the president taking a personal interest in my father—in my mother? If so, he's looking in the wrong direction."

"His interest is in meeting with *you*, Colonel," interjected Stratton. "It has something to do with a group of Confederates who are in training and a letter sent to general delivery, Washington, D.C. In the meantime, your father is being watched."

Wade smiled. "Thank you, Major."

"I beg your pardon, Colonel?"

"The men who are set on killing my father care not a whit for questions of law. They will kill him on sight. The thought that our men are watching him is a relief. That improves his chances, wouldn't you say?"

"I see. I hadn't thought of that." Stratton rose. "Colonel, I have been ordered to return to Washington with you."

"Am *I* being watched, Major?"

"Certainly not, Colonel. The president merely seeks your assistance—nothing more."

Wade rose. "Will that be all, General Healy?"

"Yes, Sam. Everything will work out. I hope you don't take this inquiry personally."

"Sir, I take this whole war personally and have for some time now. It has done everything possible to wreck my family, and yet we survive and grow stronger. I have confidence that this country will not abandon us when we need it most." He saluted. "Sir, if there is nothing further, I'll take my leave."

"There's a boat waiting for you at City Point. Major Stratton will fill you in on the details. Good luck, Sam."

\*          \*          \*

Wade stood in the shadows, across and down the street from Ford's Theater. Thompson had also posted a man upstairs, in a second-floor window. He had been there every day since June 15. No one approximating Frank Bowman's description had appeared during the intervening seven days. In the meantime, the meeting between the president and the members of the committee had been set for Tuesday, July 12, at one in the afternoon. It would have been better to hold it earlier, but a variety of problems had developed. Several committee members had obligations that would prevent their participation until then. Thompson had insisted that delay was best, until everything appeared legitimate.

This meeting with Bowman had only one remaining purpose: Thompson wanted confirmation that the assassination attempt was still scheduled. The president had insisted on it, in exchange for his cooperation. None of the committee members had been told of the plot. So far as they knew, the meeting with the president was wholly legitimate, and they were delighted. Lincoln had come to them, so their stature on the Hill had gone up a notch or two. It was about time, they thought.

As Wade waited, his thoughts drifted. The meeting with the president had gone as well as he had dared to expect. Once Lincoln knew all the facts, he said that he agreed with Wade's assessment of the legal issues pertaining to his mother and father. But he also acknowledged that legal issues tend to become fuzzy when mixed with politics—and these were political times. Thousands were in prison who had never seen the inside of a courtroom, some incarcerations dating back to the first days of the war. But in the murky waters of Washington politics, the president was the first among many equals. If he publicly expressed his gratitude for the service rendered by General Thornton, no one would ignore the implications.

But what if something happened to Lincoln?

At 3:15 P.M., a Union officer approached from the south. He stopped and peered into a window for a moment, then continued on his way. He carried a newspaper in one hand. As he neared Ford's Theater, he stopped and propped his foot on a wooden bench. A moment later he glanced over his shoulder, then sat down. He opened the paper and began to read. A few minutes later, he casually placed the paper on the bench, rose, and continued along his original path.

As the officer drew even with him, Wade recognized the man as Frank Bowman. The uniform had thrown Wade. He drew a deep breath and was about to move into the open when he noticed another man thirty yards down the nearly deserted street. Wade watched him for a moment, then looked back at Bowman. The stranger kept his distance. When Bowman walked faster, so did the stranger. Wade backed deeper into the shadows. He hoped that the observer at the second-story window of the building across the street had remained in hiding.

Bowman strolled down the street and turned the corner. The man following him kept his distance, accelerating only when Bowman had passed from sight.

Wade played back the sequence of events in his mind. As he thought about the time Bowman had spent on the wooden bench, he noticed that the paper remained where Bowman had laid it. Nothing else seemed out of the ordinary. Wade waited for several minutes, then walked down the street. A hundred yards beyond the theater, he crossed over and strolled briskly toward the bench. As he approached, he withdrew something from his pocket and dropped it. He retrieved the object and the paper before turning around and striding quickly down the street.

"Are you certain?" asked General Thompson.

"As certain as I can be about such a thing," said Wade. "I think he was being followed."

"Describe the man."

"Five nine or ten. Dark suit, well dressed, wearing a hat. He had a mustache but no beard. He appeared to have sandy blond hair, but it was difficult to see clearly. He carried a cane with a blunt head."

"Damn," said Thompson, tightening his mouth. "That was Wagner, my contact. Where did he go after that?"

"I don't know. I retrieved the paper with the letter inside and went in the opposite direction."

"You've read the letter?"

"Yes, sir."

"Is there anything new in it?"

"Nothing of any significance, other than that they are in Washington, staying in a house down by the river. That's a sleazy part of town. I wouldn't want to be caught down there after dark. I think it's time to bring my men up. I'll need Clinton, Healy, Petree, and twenty others."

"So many, Sam?"

"Yes, sir. I don't want to take any chances. The men I'd like to use are all trained sharpshooters. I've seen them in action. They can hit a six-inch target at more than a hundred yards. The plan I have in mind calls for experts."

"I don't know, Sam. I think this needs the approval of the president. If your Negro troops panic when the shooting starts, it will set back their cause by who knows how long."

"They won't panic. Besides, Lincoln is like a god to them. They'll all die before they back off one step."

Thompson nodded, but not in commitment. "I'll let you know tomorrow, Sam. One other thing before you leave. It's been decided that General Thornton will be detained as a prisoner of war. I doubt that your mother ever thought that there might be consequences if she took them in. She's beyond suspicion, so nothing more will be said about the matter."

"And Simon?"

"We have contacts in the Southern government who tell us that he was discharged from the army more than two months ago." Thompson smiled. "It appears he's free to do as he pleases—up to a point."

Wade sighed, then smiled. "Thanks, sir. I've been half out of my mind with concern. Where will my father be sent?"

"That hasn't been determined. He doesn't seem to be going anywhere, so we want to wait until this mess with the president is finished before we do anything. In the meantime, he's being watched around the clock."

"I know he's not a threat. He's a tired, beaten man."

"I hope you're right about that, Sam."

"I am."

"I'll let you know the decision on your men. There's one other thing before you go. The president will actually go to the Capitol building."

Wade stiffened. "That's insane, sir. It'll place him in great danger."

"Precautions will have to be taken. He feels that the conspirators might be watching him. If he doesn't go, he thinks they may smell the trap. Also, since none of the congressmen has been told it's a trap, the president feels he'll be viewed as having used them as bait while he remained safe at the White House."

"Then tell the congressmen, damnit. It's not worth the risk."

"You don't know Washington, Sam. Word of the conspiracy would spread all over the city within twenty-four hours. These men love a sense of high drama. One of them would let it leak for certain. It's already settled, Sam. Besides, the president wants the meeting. The committee members have been squawking about the casualty count in Virginia and Georgia. Word is that some of them are pushing to get rid of Grant."

"Are they serious? Nothing could be worse for the country."

"Lincoln knows that. He intends to convince them that the time has come to shut up and let the military take the necessary measures to end the war." Thompson rose and walked around his desk. "But that's *his* problem, Sam. You need a plan that will allow your sharpshooters to take out the assassins before they can harm the president. Security is *your* problem. That's part of my concern with using Negro troops."

Wade sighed and stood. "I'll work it out, General." He saluted and left the office.

# CHAPTER

# 33

History would record the summer of 1864 as one of the hottest on record. Certainly, everyone expected July to be hot, both politically and on the battlefield. At Petersburg, Grant and Lee were pounding each other with regularity as the siege moved toward a stalemate. In the West, Sherman was driving relentlessly to the southeast, with the aim of capturing Atlanta before summer's end and driving Gen. Joe Johnston's army out of the war. But July began not so much with heat, as was normal, but with the raw violence of an ocean storm.

At four in the morning on July 2, a massive squall line rolled violently inland from the Atlantic. By half past four, gale-force winds were battering the Carolina coastline and moving rapidly up the bay, heading inland at twenty-eight knots, gaining velocity as the storm advanced. Captain Miles Portlander had waited patiently for this opportunity, and he had no intention of letting it slip by. He had to make this last run. If he made it, he would retire to a comfortable squire's life some thirty miles from Liverpool—with more than 150,000 pounds in the bank, his wife at his side, and a burnt-orange pointer that he had raised from a pup. That dream had driven him to take the highest of risks for nearly three years now. With a modicum of luck, he'd realize his dream within the month. He might even run for Parliament—after a year or two of hunting and fishing. At fifty-nine, he still had plenty of time. Just one more lucky turn of the wheel and his children would inherit a lot of money in fifteen years or so.

He did not delude himself; he knew his chances were poor. First, he had to beat the weather; then he had to outfox the Union navy. The Union navy had become the second largest in the world, making blockade running almost impossible. Rarely was one picket ship out of sight of a warning rocket from another—from the Chesapeake Bay through the Florida Keys and across the Gulf of Mexico. He knew it would be difficult to get the sails up in these winds, but he had seen worse. At least the tide was well up. But without sails to complement the steam engine, he would have no hope of outrunning the frigate that would surely give chase once its captain realized that Portlander had slipped past. He planned to take the engine up to maximum revolutions, then break free of the coast into the channel and dash to the southeast, into open waters, staying just inside the storm's edge. Hopefully he'd be far out to sea before the Union ships on picket duty realized he had left the secluded inlet, a deepwater cove nearly invisible except when viewed directly from the southeast.

I'll give it five more minutes, he told himself as the sky grew darker and the driving rain lowered visibility to less than a mile. He stumbled along the deck with hardly a path wide enough to squeeze through. The hold had been stuffed full, and the decks were piled as high as was prudent with bales of prime Southern cotton. The mills in England would pay a premium for this load, bidding the price up to double the price of a year ago. If he held his cards close to his vest and remained patient, he might get as much as five shillings a pound, perhaps a little more. Some had reported better. He checked the lashings between glances at the boiling sky.

"Is everything ready?" he yelled at his first officer over the driving force of the wind.

"Aye, Captain. Don't know what will happen when we attempt to get through the breakers, though."

"We'll make it, Johnny. We simply have to keep our sights set on the prize waiting for us when we reach Kingston." Portlander looked toward the heavens again. What irony, he thought. To have any chance at all, he had to break into the open when the chances for the steamer's physical survival were the worst. He expected the first hour to be critical, as they steered the ship through the surf and felt their way in the winding channel. One more look upward. "Rev her up, Johnny. Get the men on deck. We raise anchor in five minutes. You take the helm."

"Aye, Captain. The boiler's red from the fire." He sucked in a great gulp of air before dashing along the deck, calling the crewmen to their stations. "The captain wants nothing short of our best," he screamed into the gale-force winds. "Move lively, there. Get to your stations and stand by to raise anchor."

The crew moved with practiced efficiency, without any wasted motion. They, too, had seen worse, but not often. Although wisely scared, they were equally eager to get it behind them and return home.

The first officer climbed the stairs to the pilothouse and waited for the captain's signal to weigh anchor. His glance bounced along the row of instruments, first to the wind direction indicator, then the wind velocity gauge, then the recently installed depth meter. Finally, he looked at the chart. He knew these waters as well as the wart on his little finger. The tide would never be better, while the wind indicator would never be worse. With the wind now at forty-six knots, it would fight against the ship for every inch it yielded. With full power until they set sail, the ship might reach seven knots, eight at best. Would that be enough speed to control the ship in such rough seas? he wondered. It would be a close call.

The captain's arm dropped, and the crew cranked the anchor chain upward.

The run through the surf proved easier than expected. Two miles into the channel, the wind dropped to thirty knots. It was both a good and bad sign. The ship was easier to steer, but the Union captain would find it easier to see the smoke as the dark, narrow plumes hung together longer before blending with the clouds. Not an even trade, thought Portlander.

The ship gained speed as the wind velocity subsided. An hour passed, then another. Dare he chance it? Portlander clenched and unclenched his fists as his anxiety grew. He studied the movement of the clouds. It appeared to be a large storm. He had to take the risk and raise sail. To do any good, the sails would have to be set at a sharp angle to the line of the ship—perhaps sixty degrees—but he had no way of knowing the location of the nearest Yankee vessel. He needed the added speed. He knew their schedule, but they might have shortened their runs across the mouth of the bay in anticipation of his desperate act. He checked his watch. If they had cut their runs in half, one or the other could be sailing directly in front of him at that very moment. "Raise the sails," he yelled, accenting the verbal command with an arm signal that drove the sailors into frenzied action. The ship rolled to port as the canvas caught wind. He held his breath; then the ship settled as the load shifted to compensate. He sighed and smiled.

The weather had cleared measurably by the time they passed from sight of land. The mouth of the wide bay lay just ahead, then it was open sea all the way to Jamaica. He had inched his way along the slippery deck to the bow and lashed himself to the railing, the crew driven to perform better by the courage of their captain. As a small sandbar slid by some one hundreds yards to port, he pumped his arm with clenched fist, then moved it in a giant arc: full steam ahead; trim the sails for maximum angle against the wind. They had practiced the drill a hundred times but never in winds such as these.

As the ship reached fifteen knots, it sailed into open water. All of the coastline had become shrouded in mist; there were broken clouds twenty miles to their front. Too soon, he thought. We need another two hours of foul weather. He heard the lookout. The sailor was yelling and pointing south. He had spotted smoke coming from a ship still below the horizon. But if Portlander could see their smoke, they could just as easily see his. Should he cut the engines and rely more on the sail? That would cut his speed in half. And what about to the north? With visibility less than three miles in that direction, the other

Union picket might be no more than fifteen minutes' steaming time away. Maximum speed, his instinct told him. It had never failed him yet, not in nearly fifty years at sea. He pumped his arm as he glanced up at the wild-eyed first officer. He loved the chase, the dominance of sailor over nature. Johnny grinned at the captain and ordered the *Rouen* full ahead.

That son of a bitch is out there, thought Comdr. Harold Crosby, captain of the USS *Keystone State*. I just know it. I would be. It's his only chance. Crosby strained his eyes to see through the driving rain. Nothing. Not even a gull. He tried to think as the wind buffeted the 280-foot craft. The storm had been at its worst between four and five that morning. That's when he would have taken the risk, when his smoke would have been nearly invisible beyond a hundred yards. He leaned over the chart and tapped his finger. Did the *Rouen* raise sail? Probably, but only after he cleared the surf. He checked his watch: 9:40 A.M. More than five hours had passed since the worst of the storm. At an average of ten knots, that would put the *Rouen* about . . . here. Crosby pressed his index finger against the chart. And I'm here, he thought, ten miles aft and fifteen miles to his port, thirty miles seaward from the cove where the *Rouen* had last been seen. He hadn't gone in closer because it would have done no good. If not blocked by rain, the cove where the *Rouen* had been at anchor would have been shielded by ground fog. The *Rouen,* an older ship, had been built for inland or coastal waters. Shorter and narrower than the newer navy vessels, the *Rouen* could turn faster and maneuver better in tight channels. But in open water, the *Keystone State* had the advantage in speed. In a long chase, nothing else mattered.

"Come port to two-seven-zero degrees," Crosby instructed the ensign. "Full steam ahead." Crosby locked the expandable compass. Unless I miss my guess, he thought, we'll overtake them by six this evening, seven at the latest. If I'm right, there will be just enough light for what has to be done. No rocking chair at the end of this run, Captain Portlander. He almost felt sorry for the *Rouen*'s captain—almost.

There she is! Crosby pulled out his watch and smiled, fully satisfied with himself. Missed it by thirty minutes, he thought. Not bad, but it's too dark to do anything now. "We'll follow them until morning, Mr. Young," said Crosby, "then close at dawn. With luck, the *Rouen* hasn't seen our smoke." The two ships were on either side of the horizon, more than thirty miles apart. "Log the sighting," he said to Lt. Hamilton Barber. "Maintain this heading for thirty minutes and confirm the distance separating us; then set our speed at eighteen knots and let's settle in for the night. I'll be in my cabin. Call me if anything changes." He looked at his watch. Nine hours until dawn. Just about right—unless the *Rouen* changed course after dark; then the chase would become more interesting. But Crosby was counting on his opponent to stick to the shortest line between two points. The wind, which was blowing from bow to stern, suppressing the *Keystone State*'s smoke and carrying it away from the *Rouen,* gave Crosby a second advantage perhaps as important as the speed. Jupiter's hand was surely set against Captain Portlander this day.

"*Fire!*" Crosby yelled when the range closed to four thousand yards. The shell from the eleven-inch Dahlgren gun, set at maximum elevation, rocked the ship to starboard. He counted the seconds until the projectile splashed silently into the sea a thousand yards aft of the distant ship, which was riding low in the water with its heavy load. With the *Rouen* still out of range, the shot had been intended as a warning. I could blow him out of the water at two thousand yards, the captain mused, if I got supremely lucky. He clenched his fist as dark puffs of smoke belched from the *Rouen*'s stacks. He's going to make a run for it, the fool! thought Crosby. What chance has he got, fully loaded? "Close the angle, Mr. Young. Maximum speed." Crosby blew into the pipe. "We'll run at this speed for another thirty minutes to close the range. Prepare to fire on my signal."

"We're ready to fire now, Captain," called an excited gunner from below.

"Patience, men, patience. We'll get him."

"Aye, sir," shouted a gunner's mate.

At eighteen hundred yards, Crosby again gave the order to fire. Two projectiles sent towering waterspouts into the air, landing a hundred yards aft and fifty to port. Nearly on target.

"He's dumping bales from the deck," said the first officer, who was looking through the telescope. "He's picking up speed."

"It won't do him any good," said Crosby. "We'll still best him by at least four knots. We can be nearly alongside in another two hours. We'll be able to reduce him to splinters by ten." He tapped the chart table. "I'll give him thirty minutes to think about it before the next shot." Crosby leaned against a bulkhead and lit his pipe. All of that good cotton, he thought, going to waste. But a load such as that would have enriched the Confederacy with enough supplies to sustain a brigade in the field for three months, maybe more. He had to keep that in mind if the fool refused to drop anchor.

At 9:00 A.M., Crosby ordered two more shots. One went long and the other fell short. The gun crews adjusted their aim and waited for the order to shoot. With luck, the next shot would be on target.

The chase continued for another hour, with the *Keystone State* inching ever closer. The *Keystone State* had drawn to within a thousand yards—nearly pointblank range for its eleven-inch guns. With a single solid broadside hit, the *Rouen* would sink in ten minutes. Crosby wanted to avoid that if possible. "Prepare to fire," the captain ordered. "Aim for the rigging. If he doesn't drop sail then, we'll aim for the waterline. Let me know when you're ready to fire."

"Aye, sir. Ready to fire in thirty seconds."

"Very well. Prepare to fire on my command." He tapped on the table. "Left, ten degrees," he said to the ensign at the helm. The ship listed slightly as it turned. The new course would give the gun crews a better firing angle. "Are the guns aligned?" Crosby asked, giving the gunners time to ready their weapons.

"Aye, sir."

"Very well. *Fire!*"

Two shells struck the top of the *Rouen*'s rigging. Ten seconds later the sails began to slide down, and smoke from the twin stacks began to thin. They've had enough, thought Crosby. The prize is mine. He smiled, then slapped the ensign on the back. "Well done, Mr. Young. You have a steady hand."

They had boarded the blockade runner shortly after noon. It was now nearly two. A skeleton crew from the USS *Keystone State* would sail the *Rouen* to Washington, while the *Keystone State* returned to its station along the Carolina coast.

"Look at this, sir," said a sailor. "It sure looks important." He handed the ensign a package covered with waxed paper. "It's from the British embassy, from some fella named Webb. I found it in the captain's cabin."

Ensign Young took the package and turned it over in his hands. It certainly appeared to be important, with its official seal and all. "I'll take it to Captain Crosby. You keep looking."

Three days later, Wade waited in a dockside building as the men gathered around. He had returned to City Point the night before and met with Clinton. After the two men discussed the foundation of a plan, Wade sent Clinton back to the brigade while he arranged for a temporary adjustment in the brigade command structure. Clinton, Captain Healy, and Sergeant Major Petree had selected twenty-two soldiers, all of them qualified sharpshooters, for the mission.

Wade motioned for the men to pull in closer. Spread out on a table were sketches of the Capitol and the surrounding grounds and streets. "Listen carefully, men," he said as he leaned forward and braced himself on the table. "I know that Colonel Clinton has told you that we have a very important mission. Now I want to explain how we will do it. In a few days, President Lincoln has a meeting scheduled with some senators and congressmen. They plan to meet inside the Capitol building. We have information that a dozen or more Confederate soldiers will attempt to assassinate Lincoln and the two cabinet officers accompanying him. Our job is to stop them. You may be wondering why the president doesn't simply cancel the meeting or hold it in another location.

The reason is simple. If that happens, these assassins will simply try again at a different time and place. That time, we may not know about it, as we do now. The president wants these men captured. Failing that, we will kill them. It's as simple as that. They have been planning this for months, so they won't give up until we stop them."

Wade motioned. "Make a circle around the table, men, so everyone can see the drawings of the Capitol building and the area surrounding it. After we arrive in Washington, we will go to the Capitol and become familiar with the area. We have two major problems. First, we don't know exactly how the assassins will approach their task. That means we have to be prepared for several possibilities. Second, we can't operate in the open. We want the rebels to feel secure so they won't suspect something and delay their plans. The major advantage is that their leader is on our side. If he can, he will inform me of the details of their plan. But we can't count on that."

"The area 'round the buildin' is pretty open," said Clinton. "What'll we use for cover?"

"We'll have to do the best we can with what's there. The most likely place for the assassination attempt will be in front of the building when the president and his companions are all together. The arrival schedules are being carefully arranged. General Thompson is handling that end. Our job is to get the assassins before they're in range of the president and the others. Lincoln will have a cavalry escort, and they know what is expected. But they can't appear too alert or they may scare away the assassins.

"That's about it. You're all volunteers, so I know you'll do your duty. We'll work on the details once we get to Washington. For now, I want you to get your personal things and your weapons. We'll board the boat at 3:00 P.M. That's a little more than two hours from now."

Wade pulled Clinton and Healy to a corner. "What do you think?" he asked.

"I don't like this takin' place out in the open," Clinton said.

"That's the president's choice. He feels it's easier to control events if he can see what's happening. We have to understand that the goal is to kill or capture these rebels, not just to keep them from completing their task."

"The men will have to hit their targets on the first shot," Healy said.

"You and Sergeant Major Petree selected them, David. If you have any doubts, this is the time to express them."

"No. They're as good as any I've seen. But the distance will be a problem, even for experts."

"That's why we have two men for each of the assassins. It'll be my job to decide when to shoot. There won't be room for any mistakes."

Healy nodded. He had a grave responsibility. Wasn't it normal that he would be a little nervous? "I won't let you down, Sam." He smiled thinly.

# CHAPTER
# 34

Sunday, July 10, dawned wiltingly hot and humid. The still, heavy air that hung over the city added to the sense of foreboding. The people in Washington were in a state of near panic. All were asking the same question: would General Early attack the city, and, if so, what would stop him? The simple answer to their question was: nothing, or nearly nothing. In the past three months, the capital's defenders had been systematically reduced from a bristling array of army brigades and artillery batteries to nothing more than a few understrength regiments of recovering wounded and shiftless no-goods. Even General Grant, who needed men more than anything, had judged them to be excess baggage. The large cannon gaped ominously over the walls of the forts that ringed the city, but hardly a man remained who knew how to sight, load, or fire them.

Six days earlier—on Independence Day—Lincoln, his confidence buoyed by his relatively easy victory at the Republican convention, had decided the time had come to turn his thoughts to the end of the war, which he expected soon. In a document made public that day, he revealed a skeletal plan for reconstruction. The rancorous clamor that followed was worse even than he had expected. Some in the Congress, especially the radicals in his own party, called for his impeachment. But the uproar faded quickly. A more immediate emergency arose. Jubal Early had driven the Union army from the Shenandoah Valley and had broken loose into open country. General Lee, locked in a siege, ordered Early to advance on Washington in hopes of forcing Grant's hand.

Two days earlier, shortly before dawn on July 8, Caroline Wade-Healy was sitting silently, staring into the darkness out the window of the Gettysburg train station. At one o'clock that morning, she and her house guests had loaded a wagon and silently led the team of horses through the thicket behind the barn until they eventually reached a seldom-used road. The day before, they had seen men moving stealthily through the trees south and west of the farmhouse. Henry Thornton quickly concluded that the men were the assassins sent to kill them all. He was able to convince Caroline that they had to leave immediately. The only place she felt safe was in Washington, their present destination. They grew more nervous as they waited.

Victoria sat at Caroline's right, and beyond Victoria sat Nancy Caroline. The young woman had shed her dowdy clothes and was aglow in the new, yellow satin dress purchased for her by her aunt. She had another dress in her bag—bright green, the color of summer. Both dresses had bonnets to match. She had nearly forgotten how it felt to be pretty and truly alive, but she soon rediscovered the joy.

Nearby, Henry Thornton stood at the window, looking south. How far his eyes were straining to see, none of the others knew. In the silence, however, he made a fateful decision.

Simon sat relaxed at his aunt's left, his arms stretched along the back of the bench. It was as if a great weight had been lifted from him. From the moment he first walked into Caroline's old farmhouse, he had felt at home. He had spent some of the worst days of his life there—and survived. Realizing that seemed to help. In time, he would thrive again.

The whistle blew from down the track. Caroline rose and walked toward the door of the station. She believed it was a mistake to leave Gettysburg. But Thornton had insisted. Caroline, aware of reports that Early's army was marching on Washington, had decided to take the roundabout route, through Baltimore. At least then, if they were cut off, they would have a place to stay. Despite all that had happened, or perhaps because of it, she could not deny her family.

As they waited for the train to pull in, Caroline allowed herself a brief glimpse into the future. She had plans that went far beyond the manufacture of shoes. There were crops for textiles in the South, with eager hands to run the mills. She had bought equipment in England, and it was in transit now. The purchase of land would follow the war; then she would build the factories. She had to do her part to restore the nation's ties. But she needed someone to manage her affairs in the South, someone who understood the people there. Perhaps Henry. . . .

"Time to go," she said aloud. "We have a long ride ahead of us."

Nancy Caroline touched her aunt's shoulder. "Will you find someone to carry my bag, Aunt Caroline?"

"*You* carry it," Caroline replied sharply. She glanced at Victoria, then back at Nancy Caroline. "It's high time you learned how to take care of yourself, like the rest of us." Tears glistened in Nancy Caroline's eyes as she reached down and grasped the handles of her bag. The costs of war were taught in many ways.

Caroline had kept a record. Since the war began, this would be her thirty-first trip to Washington, an average of once every five weeks.

Late in the afternoon of that same day, 3d Division, VI Corps, sent by Grant by fast steamer from City Point, unloaded and marched through the subdued Baltimore streets. Three and a half years earlier, when Lincoln was preparing to take the oath of office as the sixteenth president of the United States, another group of soldiers had marched through the city. Its citizens had thrown rocks and anything else within reach as the fresh, neatly dressed New York militiamen marched past. Several people had been killed in the riot that followed. Nothing of that sort happened this time. Perhaps that was because no one saw anything neat or fresh about these men. As one observer commented, this particular group of soldiers looked as though they regularly ate rocks for their main course and washed them down with fire. The long columns of soldiers marched silently through the city and went into bivouac in the fields on its outskirts.

Cathy Blair watched them tramp past as she waited at the station for the evening train to Washington. She had sent a telegram to Gettysburg but received no reply. She could not afford to send another. She had two silver dollars and two quarters remaining after she bought the tickets for Washington. She had no other choice. She saw no point in remaining in Baltimore to starve. Shortly after her arrival, she had done something she had vowed never to do: she had pawned the brooch given to her by her grandmother as the old woman lay on her deathbed. Cathy had nothing left to sell.

She had slept in a church pew with her daughter the night before. She offered to wash dishes for the noon meal at a dining room, but the owner had taken pity and given them food. As she prepared to leave, he slipped two quarters and a sack with a loaf of freshly baked bread into her hand. At least tonight they would have something to eat.

As the train screeched to a halt, Cathy lifted Sandra and climbed the steps leading into the front car. She moved to the first seat and settled in with her daughter to wait for the connecting train from Gettysburg. The exact location of Early's army remained unknown, so guards filed onto the train, just in case. The front car was full by the time darkness settled over the city.

"What a sorry spectacle," Wade said to Clinton. He was looking through the window at a makeshift company hobbling along the street leading toward the outskirts of Washington. Half were bandaged, one soldier was missing a leg below the knee and walked with a crutch, and two men had an arm missing. "I suppose they can fire a pistol, if it comes to that." He knew better. These men had fought their war. They might get off a shot or two, but they would bolt when confronted with anything resembling a committed attack. Everyone knew it, even Lincoln, and still he refused to leave the city. But General Early's army was shelling the outskirts of the city. The Union army had to make a show of force, its principal objective being the purchase of time. Hundreds of clerks, most of whom had never fired a rifle, and all of the wounded who could walk were being organized and sent to the trenches.

"Do ya think VI Corps will make it?" asked Clinton. "It takes a long time t'move that many men."

"The Rebs have been this close before," replied Wade. "My guess is they don't want to capture the city, just scare the hell out of everyone who lives here, especially the members of Congress."

"Give them credit," replied Clinton. "They've succeeded."

Wade smiled wryly. "Don't tell me you're scared, Jim."

"I'm not a street fighter, Sam. I like havin' room t'move 'round. Tryin' t'defend a fixed position is a one-way ticket t'hell." He shook his head. "I sure wish VI Corps'd get here."

"Come on, Jim, let's get over to the warehouse. I want to stop by General Thompson's office on the way. It's less than two hours before we go over the plan one last time."

"Everything is ready," said Frank Bowman. He and Whitey stood on the porch of the small house with the river as a backyard. "When do we get to shoot the bastards?" The words were right, but the feeling behind them had faded. General Early had an army less than ten miles away, yet he was afraid to attack the U.S. capital, a city defended by less than a quarter of his strength.

Bowman and the other twelve assassins had been briefed on the operation. Quiet settled over the room as Whitey told them the details of the plan. Nobody uttered a word, but their looks spoke volumes. Well, they had demanded action; now they would have it. The question had become: would any of them be alive to enjoy the fruits of even this shallow victory?

"Tomorrow," the albino replied. "The president will arrive at the Capitol precisely at 1:00 P.M. Secretary Stanton will be with him, and perhaps Secretary Chase. The congressmen will all be inside. That will make your job easier. All of you will be dressed in Union uniforms, so no one will notice you.

"If Lincoln follows his usual practice, an officer and eight cavalry troopers will accompany him. Jerry, you and your team will be responsible for eliminating them. Carl, Tom, Duke, and Claude, that's your job. This means each of you has to kill two of the troopers. They always move in a column of twos, so it should be easy enough to pick them off. Jerry, you take care of the officer. The quarters will be tight, so you'll have to use pistols. The confusion should benefit the operation. People will begin screaming and running once the first shot has been fired.

"Major Bowman, you and your men are to kill the president and his cabinet officers. Get Lincoln first, then the others. All of this should take no more than ten seconds from the time of the first shot. Every second beyond that increases the chances that other soldiers in the area will react and arrive on the scene. Ten seconds after the first shot, all of you should run for your horses and follow the agreed route to the house."

"What about our escape plans?" asked one of the men. "Is everything arranged?"

"Everything has been taken care of. Just concentrate on doing your job."

Making the escape arrangements had been Whitey's easiest task. There were none. When they finished the job, they would go to a house on the north side of the city. If they were cut off from that house, they would go to another a mile farther east. Two men had been assigned to prepare each safe house for destruction. Powder had been placed under both structures, enough to turn the buildings into flaming splinters. The fuses had been put in place and hidden from view. No one would know for certain how many people had been inside, let alone be able to identify the scattered pieces of bodies. As an added precaution, the men responsible for the demolition work would be eliminated. There would be plenty of evidence to convince authorities that Southerners had killed the president.

A few other killings would brush away the trail completely. Whitey had been giving thought to that lately. Had someone been assigned to kill him? He had to wonder if his benefactors would let him live. He would not, if he were they. But he had been so loyal, so reliable. Surely they would have other tasks for him to perform. No. Someone else would take his place. So this noble effort must be successful. It had to be his crowning achievement, a masterpiece of planning. But if the plan failed, he had one final, less complicated scenario in mind. Only he knew the details. Although the results would be less spectacular, the central objective would nonetheless be accomplished.

The men were seated on the floor, their rifles stacked in the aisle behind them. Clinton leaned against the doorjamb leading into what used to be General Thompson's office. Wade cleared his throat, and a hush spread over the gathering. Behind him, tacked to the wall, were crude drawings of the Capitol grounds, an area all the men had become familiar with during the past several days.

"Men," said Wade, "this will be your final briefing. Don't leave here today without everything straight in your minds. I just talked to General Thompson. Nothing has changed since the last time we went over this. He received a message from Major Bowman. The rebels will approach from the west, behind the president's carriage." Wade pointed at the drawing. "Now, here's the plan. . . ."

When he finished, Wade drew a deep breath and turned his head slowly, looking into the eyes of each man seated before him. He liked what he saw. They appeared relaxed and alert. More important, they knew their jobs. "Any questions?" He waited.

When there were no questions, Clinton stepped forward. "Men, you'll never have a more important duty as long as y'live." He hesitated as all eyes turned toward him; then he clicked his tongue. "I'm proud t'be one of ya, an' I know Colonel Wade is, too. Aim straight tomorra."

"That's all, men," said Wade. "No one leaves here until it's time to go to the Capitol." He looked at Clinton, who nodded grimly. They had done all they could.

# CHAPTER

# 35

The sound of cannon fire in the distance reminded Caroline of Gettysburg. With the Thorntons safely tucked away in the National Hotel, Caroline wanted to see the reason for all of the clamor. People were running down the street, yelling and laughing. It seemed so incongruous with the sound of cannon booming to the north.

In the distance, she heard the deep, clattering roll of what sounded like a thousand drums. She looked east into the rising sun, in the direction of the Sixth Street pier, and shaded her eyes against the brightness. She smiled, then broke into loud laughter. Marching down the avenue, eight abreast as far as she could see, was a sea of men in faded blue uniforms. The men of the VI Corps had arrived and were stepping with a gait like nothing she had seen before, toward the forts that ringed the city. She stood at the curb as they marched by, all ten thousand of them. Early would be lucky to escape with his life, as the corps's 3d Division was rumored to be moving on his flank. Caroline waved as the men marched grimly past, but they had no time for anything except the business that had brought them there.

She smiled as she pondered the legions of weathered men in soiled and tattered uniforms. My, how this war has changed, she thought.

At nine that morning, Tuesday, July 12, the English ambassador, Edward Cunningham, arrived at the White House. He had imagined any number of reasons for the summons. He had risen early and dressed in formal attire, as he always did when he went to meet with the president. He never suspected the real reason for the meeting.

He arrived alone. Secretary Seward greeted him at the entrance. They shook hands, talked of the crisis that gripped the city—Seward expressed no real concern—then entered the White House and walked up the stairs.

"In here, if you please, Mr. Ambassador. I believe you know Secretary Welles."

"Mr. Secretary," said Cunningham, nodding at the navy secretary. His brow furrowed. Where was the president? This proceeding seemed unusual, even a minor violation of protocol.

On a table in the middle of the room he saw a neatly stacked pile of documents two inches high. They were lying on a large piece of waxed paper.

"Have a seat," said Welles, pointing to the chair nearest the documents.

Cunningham flipped his coattails and sat down. "This is highly unusual," he said, looking quizzically at the pile of papers.

"Indeed, Mr. Ambassador," said Seward. "Exactly our thought." He seated himself across from the ambassador, with Welles beside him in an easy chair. "I'll come directly to the point, Mr. Ambassador. I'm sure you have heard of the encounter with the *Rouen*."

Cunningham squirmed. "That has nothing to do with my government. The captain of the *Rouen* is a privateer."

"Carrying cotton for English mills, Mr. Ambassador."

Cunningham remained silent.

"A curious thing happened when we searched the ship, sir. One of our sailors found in the captain's cabin the documents you see before you. Coffee, Mr. Ambassador?"

"I believe I will, Mr. Secretary."

Welles rose and went to the door. A few moments later a servant entered with a silver tray. He poured the coffee and left the room.

"I believe you know Stewart Webb, a member of your Parliament," said Welles.

"Of course I know Sir Stewart. What does this have to do with him?"

"It seems your Mr. Webb has been party to a plot to assassinate President Lincoln. Such behavior may be acceptable in England, sir, but over here we take a dim view of such treachery."

The ambassador stiffened. "I have known Sir Stewart for many years. He would never engage in such sordid activity."

"I see," said Seward. "How familiar are you with Mr. Webb's handwriting?"

"I believe I would recognize it if I saw it."

"Very well, Mr. Ambassador. I insist you examine those documents. Take your time. Secretary Welles and I will leave you alone with them. Major Gillis will be right outside. Summon us when you are ready to discuss this further." Seward rose and walked to the door, followed by Welles.

An hour later, Gillis went for Seward and Welles. As they entered the room, Seward said, "You are a rapid reader, Mr. Ambassador."

Cunningham had lost his composure. He slumped in his chair; his coat lay crumpled on a nearby couch. He sighed as he leaned forward and shuffled the pile of papers. "I don't know what to say, gentlemen. My government knows nothing of this—that I can assure you." He took a sip of cold coffee. "Do you have any tea?" he asked. Welles went to the door and whispered to Major Gillis, who nodded and left.

"Do you question the authenticity of these documents, sir?" asked Seward.

Cunningham thought for a moment, then shook his head.

"Then do you agree, sir, that we have a crisis?"

Cunningham nodded.

"Mr. Ambassador, I say this to you with all candor: Mr. Lincoln does not wish another crisis. He prefers only one at a time. I'm sure you would agree that General Early's presence in our front yard qualifies as a crisis."

The ambassador nodded.

"You know our situation, sir. I believe it is safe to say that we have the most powerful army in the world at present, not to mention our navy. With this war nearly over, that army and navy will be unemployed. Am I making myself clear, Mr. Ambassador?"

"Your point is well taken, Mr. Secretary," said Cunningham with a heavy sigh.

"Do you have any suggestions?" inquired Welles.

"May I take these documents with me, Mr. Secretary?"

"I think not, sir. You will understand our reluctance to let these papers out of our sight," said Seward.

Cunningham nodded. "Have precautions been taken to protect the president?" He seemed sincere in his concern.

"Read about it in the Wednesday newspapers, Mr. Ambassador."

"Then may I be permitted to take care of my government's end of this problem, Mr. Secretary?"

"How do you propose to do that, sir?" asked Seward.

"Might I suggest that you read the same newspapers, sir? I believe you will be satisfied." He sipped his tea, then said, "Mr. Secretary?"

"Yes, Mr. Ambassador?"

"Do *you* accept that my government had no knowledge of this affair? It appears to me that Mr. Webb let his ambitions get the best of him."

"I think we can accept that position—provided the loose ends are tied up immediately and we encounter no further difficulty."

Caroline returned to the hotel dining room and ate a light breakfast. At precisely 9:00 A.M., she motioned to the waiter to bring her the check. As she waited

for her change, she glanced toward the back of the dining room and noticed a woman with a young girl sitting at a corner table. Caroline smiled
at first; then her expression turned to sadness. The young woman was dressed
in a worn, wrinkled dress, a garment much too heavy for the season. The
child, too, was poorly clad.

"Here's your change," said the waiter, interrupting Caroline's thoughts.

"Thank you. By the way, is that woman sitting over there a guest here?"
She nodded toward the corner.

The clerk frowned. "I don't know, ma'am. She came in about seven this
morning and has been here ever since. She ordered only tea, and probably
doesn't have money enough for that."

"You've never seen her before?"

"Never. We've been getting more and more of her type lately, mostly Southern
women who have ventured north looking for work. Most don't have children,
though. They're becoming a blight."

Caroline shook her head. "It's so sad. With their husbands dead, what will
they do?"

The clerk thought he knew the answer, but he dared not speak such words
in front of a lady.

As Caroline walked toward the door, something about the woman caused
her to stop. She turned and smiled as her eyes met those of the young girl
across the spacious room. The child waved with her fingers, then rested the
side of her face on her chair. Caroline walked back into the dining room.
She quietly slid into a chair at the next table and waved the waiter away when
he approached.

"Mommy, I'm hungry," the little girl said.

"I know, honey," the woman answered. She offered no relief for the child's
plight.

"What a darling child," Caroline said finally. "May I hold her for a moment?"
The woman ignored her, but the girl smiled.

"Excuse me, young lady. I don't mean to intrude, but I heard the child
say she's hungry."

The girl shifted to her knees and rested her chin on the back of the chair.
She looked up at Caroline with sad eyes as she wiped her nose with a sleeve.

"We're not seeking charity," the woman said curtly.

"It takes a whole village to raise a child," Caroline replied, just as emphatically.

The woman turned toward Caroline. It was her first clear view of the woman's
face. Caroline blinked.

"Ma'am," said the woman, "if you have work, I'll be happy to discuss
our problems with you. Otherwise . . ."

Caroline lowered her eyes. She was reluctant to speak, afraid to be per-
ceived as a fool. The woman had a slight Southern accent, but no more than

half the people in Washington had. The resemblance *was* startling. But what could one tell from a faded photograph? Caroline resisted the temptation to accept the rebuff and leave. "My name is Caroline. What's yours?"

"Catherine. I go by Cathy."

"And I assume this little angel is your daughter?"

Cathy nodded at the child and smiled. "Yes, she is. Say hello to the nice lady, Sandy."

"Hello." The little girl turned away, looking embarrassed, then twisted around and peered through the slats of the chair.

"She's three years old today," Cathy said proudly.

"My goodness," Caroline said. She reached out and touched her finger to the young girl's nose. "You need a birthday party, don't you." Sandy smiled shyly. "I bet you're hungry, too."

"Ma'am," Cathy said sharply, the tone unmistakable.

Caroline nodded. The woman had pride, if nothing else; hardly the best attribute under the circumstances, thought Caroline. But still, she had been there—almost.

"Do you have a room here?" Caroline asked, knowing the answer.

Cathy sighed. She turned and took a sip of cold tea without answering.

"I know I'm intruding," Caroline acknowledged, "but my name is Healy, Caroline Healy. Does that mean anything to you?"

Cathy's eyes immediately filled with tears. "Samuel Wade's mother?"

"Yes, child. And you're Cathy Bowman."

"How did you recognize me?" Cathy asked.

"There's a picture inside my bag. It's of you, my dear. Samuel left it at the house the last time he was home on leave."

"Is Sam here?" Cathy asked.

"No, not at the hotel. But there *is* someone here I believe you do know."

Cathy seemed surprised. "Who?"

"General Thornton. He brought his family to Gettysburg, but we had to leave. It seems some men are after him."

"I don't know what to say, Mrs. Healy. More than once I thought of going to Gettysburg."

Caroline ran her fingers through Cathy's limp hair. "Welcome to Washington, Cathy. It's a historic place, you know. Capital of our country." A long pause followed. "Well, my dear, you won't want to see Samuel looking like that."

Cathy's face lit up. "Then he *is* in Washington!"

"Yes, someplace in the city. I don't know exactly where. My husband is here on a brief assignment. He told me that Samuel was in Washington." She reached for her bag, then opened it. "Here's my room key, Cathy. You and Sandy have some breakfast and then freshen up. I'll tell the waiter to provide you with whatever you want. There are toiletries in my room. Use whatever you need. I have some errands to run; then we'll all go shopping—just us girls. What do you say to that, Sandy?"

The child nodded and giggled happily.

Wade left the warehouse first, at ten past ten. Clinton would bring the others at eleven. Following the scare by General Early's soldiers, the city was gradually returning to normal, although most civilians still remained in their homes. That would make Wade's job easier. Early had canceled his planned assault when he realized that veteran troops were defending the city. At nine that morning, Wade had reassured the men one last time, but he knew they had prepared themselves long before. There had been a few refinements in the plan. The men would amble to their stations in small groups instead of in formal lines of march. Although that would reduce the chance of anyone noticing them, nothing Wade did would solve that problem completely. People were still getting used to the idea of black men in uniforms carrying rifles.

The temperature rose rapidly after sunrise. It would be another scorching day. A gentle breeze blew from the sea, and it, too, was warm. Even though Congress had adjourned the week before, a parade of clerks and assorted other government employees moved in and out of the massive Capitol building and along the adjacent streets, carrying on the day-to-day business of government.

It was shortly after half past eleven by the time everyone settled into place and Wade made his rounds. The men were divided into two groups: Petree and eleven men across from the Capitol, Healy and the other eleven at the top of the Capitol steps. Lumber was piled at both locations, intended to serve both as a hiding place and as a prop on which to steady rifles. To the casual observer it appeared that men were preparing to work on the buildings.

Wade stood in the shade of the building across from the Capitol, studying the scene one last time, wondering what he might have overlooked. Thinking of nothing, he turned to Petree. "Sergeant Major, when the president passes that corner"—Wade pointed at the nearest intersection—"soldiers will block the street in both directions and stop traffic. As you can see, you and your men are nearly a hundred and fifty feet away from where the carriages will stop, so get yourselves braced and ready to fire well in advance of the president's arrival." Wade turned to the rest of the men. "Sergeant Major Petree will give the signal when it's time to leave the alley and take your positions. The rebels mustn't see you. We don't want to spook them. Is everybody straight?"

"Yes, sir," they all replied.

"Good. Don't forget my signal. I'll drop my hat. That's the indication for everyone to fire."

Captain Healy and his men moved to the top of the Capitol stairs. The plan was for the president to get out of his carriage directly below Healy's station. It was more than a hundred feet to the street, but workmen had roped off the area to keep passersby off the steps. If everything went as planned, the soldiers would have a clear line of fire.

When Wade finished confirming the proper placement of his men, he moved to where he had a clear view of Pennsylvania Avenue. All he could do was wait, and wonder about all the things that could go wrong. He brought his field glasses up and slowly examined the area. Everything seemed normal. Nearby, Healy leaned against one of the Capitol pillars. All of his men were hidden behind the pile of lumber. Clinton stood near the main entrance, waiting to come down the stairs when the president's carriage aproached. He would guard the president, protecting Lincoln with his own life if necessary.

There was nothing left to do but wait.

At 12:58 P.M., Lincoln's carriage turned the corner and advanced slowly up the street, a cavalry officer and eight troopers riding close behind. They knew the plan and had orders to dismount and form a shield around the president and the others as soon as the shooting began. Wade turned and looked over the vast lawn beside the Capitol. A squad of soldiers had been sitting in the shade of the trees. As the carriages carrying Lincoln and his cabinet officers came into view, the soldiers rose and formed into two files of six men each. An officer led them quickly toward the street. Wade's anxiety increased as he watched the two contingents converge.

Wade turned and walked as casually as possible toward the spot where Lincoln's carriage was supposed to stop. There was still some slow-moving traffic on the street. That had been Wade's greatest fear from the beginning. What if a carriage blocked the line of fire? What if a pedestrian got in the way? He felt his pulse race as Lincoln's carriage drew near. Forty yards beyond, the two columns of Confederates dressed in Union blue neared the edge of the street, drawing a yard closer with each step. Wade glanced to his right. Petree's men were in place. He looked up the stairs. He couldn't see anything except the pile of lumber. He could only assume that everything was ready there. He looked over his shoulder and saw that Clinton was in place next to Lincoln's carriage, positioned between the carriage and the approaching assassins.

Without really thinking about it, Wade reached for his hat. He calmly lifted it from his head and let his arm drop to his side. Shots rang out and smoke boiled from the lumber pile to his right and down the stairs to his left. Eight of the would-be assassins dropped like stones. Two others staggered momentarily, then fell as Bowman dived headfirst to the cobblestone street. Two of the thirteen remained standing, but they were obviously confused by the startling explosions from their flanks. Before they could draw their pistols, the cavalry troopers had dismounted and drawn their weapons. All eight carbines roared, and the last two Confederates staggered backward and fell.

The scene was one of utter chaos, with people yelling and running in every direction. Lincoln and his cabinet officers had no intention of stepping into the open until Wade assured them it was safe.

As the smoke cleared, Wade ran to Bowman. He still hadn't moved by the time Wade knelt beside him. "Are you hurt?" Wade asked.

"It's the same damned leg I broke before," Bowman said through gritted teeth. "I'm shot just above the knee."

"Don't move. There'll be an ambulance here in a few minutes." Wade looked around at the carnage. "It doesn't look as if any of your men will need it." He reached across Bowman and removed his pistol, then stood as a crowd began to grow.

"There's nothing to worry about, folks," Wade said. "Looks like some of Early's men made it into town after all. Everything's under control." Wade turned to the cavalry officer. "Move these people away, Captain, before someone else gets hurt."

Wade turned and looked at the carriages. He was surprised to see Lincoln's head sticking through a window. A moment later, the door opened and Thompson stepped out, which was even more of a surprise.

"I assume it's all over," Thompson said.

"Yes, sir. I haven't checked the bodies, but it appears all but Major Bowman are dead."

Just then, two wagons pulled up and soldiers began tossing the bodies on the beds. A medical orderly tied a tourniquet around Bowman's leg as two guards stood close by.

"What do we do with him?" asked Wade.

"For now, we'll seclude him in some corner of a hospital and treat his wound," replied Thompson. "Then I'll decide what to do with him."

"We couldn't have pulled this off without Bowman's help," Wade reminded him.

"That will certainly be considered, Sam." Thompson glanced over his shoulder. "Right now I have a very anxious group of congressmen and senators wondering just what in hell this was all about. And the president still wants to hold his meeting. He's a wily old fox. He's convinced that this affair will put the fear of God into them and make them easier to deal with." He smiled and shook his head. "My guess is they'll be mad as hell and willing to let Grant have his way with the rebels."

"Which is what Lincoln is after, isn't it?"

"Precisely. But this is a hell of a way to get their cooperation. Get your men out of here, Sam. I'll handle the newspapers."

"Do you still plan to blame Early for this?"

"Who else? We might as well put his invasion to some practical use. It shouldn't be too difficult to convince the press. You were right, you know."

"About what?" Wade asked, surprised.

"About your Negro soldiers. They didn't bat an eye."

Wade grinned. "I'll tell them you were impressed, sir."

"By the way, Sam, the president asked that you come to the meeting with the committee members and explain what happened here."

"Now?"

"I'll tell him you'll be there as soon as you get things cleaned up here."

"Give me fifteen minutes, sir." Wade saluted.

Thompson responded in kind, then went to get Lincoln.

As the president walked up the Capitol steps with Stanton and Chase, Clinton approached Wade. "What now, Sam?"

"The short answer is, it's time to go back to the war. We've got a brigade that needs our attention."

"What about the men?"

"We'll give them a couple of days' leave before getting on a boat and heading back to City Point."

"I'll try an' settle 'em down. They'll relive this a thousand times durin' the years ahead."

"They have to be quiet for the present, Jim. Officially, this was nothing more than some of Early's soldiers who just happened to be in the area dressed in the wrong color uniform. That's the way the president wants it. Make sure the men understand that."

"I'll take care of it. Will ya make it back t'the warehouse later?"

"Probably in a couple of hours. I have to go try to make sense of this to the congressmen."

The briefing went as smoothly as Wade could reasonably have expected. The members of the committee reacted about as Wade anticipated. Some of them expressed gratitude that the attempt had failed. Others, judging by their expressions, were clearly incensed that Southerners would try such a thing. Whatever else, Wade could tell by the looks on a handful of faces that this wasn't the last of it. He finished his remarks and asked for questions.

"I want to know one thing, Colonel," said Senator Chandler. "Why did you use colored troops for such an important assignment?"

Wade recognized the political implications of the question. He looked at Lincoln. The president smiled and nodded once.

"It was a practical decision, Senator. As a general rule, white troops spend very little time learning how to shoot. Some go into battle the first time having never fired a musket. Many of the white troops are born in cities or come from other countries and have never fired a gun in their lives before joining the army. There seems to be an assumption that they'll learn how to use a rifle on their own. I might add that few ever become proficient at the task. Ironically, we make the opposite assumption about black troops. There's widespread belief that they can't do anything without extensive training. The result is that black troops *are* well trained. It naturally follows that a high percentage of them become expert marksmen. The men selected for this mission are from a special company trained as sharpshooters. As such, they are the best of the best. It was my belief that this mission was so important that we had an obligation to use the best riflemen we had."

He waited for a reaction. Judging by the way Chandler asked the question, Wade was prepared for the worst, so he was surprised by Chandler's conclusion.

"Well, Colonel, it seems to me we need to reevaluate our training procedures for all our soldiers."

"I agree, sir. The average Southern soldier is much more efficient with a rifle than our men. My guess is, if you ask a Southern soldier, he'd just as soon not come up against our Negro regiments. I might add, Senator, they are outstanding soldiers in most other respects." He waited while the committee members assessed his explanation.

Finally, Lincoln cleared his throat. "Thank you, Colonel Wade. You have our gratitude for a job well done."

"I'll tell the men, Mr. President. They'll be pleased that their work is appreciated." Wade came to attention. "If that will be all, gentlemen, I have a report to prepare."

"By all means, Colonel Wade," said Chandler, smiling for the first time. "You've given all of us something to think about."

Wade looked at Lincoln and saluted, then turned and left the room.

"Here's my report, General," said Wade to Thompson at a quarter after eight that evening.

"Have a seat, Sam."

"Yes, sir."

"I want to offer my apologies, Sam. I should have listened when you first told me about this plot."

"You had a lot on your mind, sir. The war has worn us all down a bit."

"That's no excuse, Sam, not where the president's life is concerned. General Halleck concurs. I spent some time with him this afternoon. We're in agreement that you've earned these." Thompson handed Wade a small envelope. "The promotion is brevet of course, and it means added responsibility as senior brigade commander of your division." He smiled before adding, "I suspect you'll handle that without much difficulty."

Wade breathed deeply as he removed the rank insignia patches from the envelope. He held one in each hand, looking down at the embroidered star in the middle of each dark blue field.

"Congratulations—*General* Wade."

"Thank you—Jason." Wade swallowed and allowed himself a smile.

"You should know, Sam, the committee was quite impressed with your presentation this afternoon. President Lincoln sent General Halleck and me messages expressing his personal pleasure."

"I'm just glad the president wasn't hurt," Wade replied. "I admire that man more than words can express."

"We all do, Sam. And now it appears there will be no more talk about relieving General Grant. The members of the committee are finally convinced that we must prosecute this war as hard and as fast as possible. And I think we'll see more colored troops in combat assignments. They might as well earn their freedom—as every generation has to do. Have you seen your mother lately?"

"No. I've been fairly busy."

"Take a couple of days off, Sam. You've earned it."

"Thank you, Jason—for everything."

Wade rose and extended his hand as he looked deeply into Thompson's eyes. They said nothing as their hands met. It had taken a long time, but the two men were now equals. No one was more pleased than Jason Thompson.

Wade and Clinton returned to the hotel and ate a light supper. At 10:00 P.M., Clinton went to the suite while Wade stopped at the front desk to see if he had any messages. Then he slowly climbed the stairs and shuffled down the hall, his legs near collapse from the tension of the day.

"Samuel?"

He turned at the sound of his mother's voice. "It's nice to see you, Mother," he said with a weary smile. "I didn't know you were in town." His stepfather stood in the doorway at his mother's side.

"I arrived day before yesterday. Will we have an opportunity to talk?"

Wade sighed. "I'm sorry, Mother—tomorrow. I'm exhausted."

"I met with General Halleck this evening," said David Healy Sr. "I understand there was a minor altercation outside the Capitol this afternoon."

Wade managed a smile. "It's been taken care of, sir."

"So I understand. The general seemed impressed with your work—*General* Wade."

Caroline gasped and turned to face her husband. "I guess I neglected to inform you, dear," he said, deadpan.

She turned back toward her son. "What did you *do,* Samuel?"

Wade lacked the energy to respond. "I'll explain tomorrow, Mother. I'll meet you for lunch. Okay?"

"Of course, Samuel. By the way, there's someone else here to see you."

"Who, Mother?"

Caroline motioned for Wade to come inside. Cathy stood across the room, dressed in a new, bright blue dress. Her hair had been freshly washed and curled. She smiled radiantly.

Sandy stood at her side, clinging to her mother's dress.

When Wade saw them he rushed forward and extended his hands. "How did you get here?" he asked in total surprise.

Cathy grasped his hands and pulled him closer. Without answering, she placed his palms against her cheeks. "Later. Now kiss me, before I burst."

A man sat alone on the bank of a small stream south of the city, his eyes fixed on the reflection of the oval moon dancing in the gently rippling water. He had been sitting there in the dark for over an hour. There was no point in waiting any longer. He slid down the bank and into the shallow water near the edge. He took a pistol from his coat, then removed his wallet and shook it hard, scattering the contents on the water. As he watched the items float away, he inserted the pistol into his mouth. He had no awareness of the sound that followed his gentle squeeze of the trigger. The albino's head snapped backward; then his body sank beneath the surface. Soon it bobbed back up and drifted lazily toward the Potomac. He had served his benefactors well, but he had failed in the end. Well, almost. He had left behind one last surprise. He had met a young actor in Richmond before the war, and they had developed a friendly relationship. The albino had provided the handsome young man with financial assistance from time to time and nurtured his hatred for Lincoln and the Union. It had been easy enough to convince the young man that something had to be done. Although the opportunity had yet to present itself, the actor knew the time would come.

As the clock struck eleven that evening, Stewart Webb walked into the office of the British ambassador. He had been away for several days, trying to find out what had happened to the *Rouen*. The news was not what he had hoped. It was unusual being summoned at this late hour. He took a seat and waited. He rose as Cunningham entered and closed the door.

"I assume you've heard the news," said the ambassador.

"What news is that, sir?"

"About the capture of the *Rouen* and the package that the Union naval officer found on board."

Webb started to protest, but Cunningham cut him off. "I was summoned to the While House this morning, Sir Stewart. As you may imagine, this has not been my best day." He lowered his head. "Only one thing will make it end right."

"Sir—"

"There is no point in discussing this further. The United States government can do nothing. You have diplomatic immunity. That leaves the matter to be settled internally. I gave my promise, Sir Stewart. I gave my promise to Secretary Seward. Do you have any thoughts as to how this matter can be resolved?"

"Mr. Ambassador, I was just thinking of the welfare of England."

"I don't want to hear that, Sir Stewart. We both know what you were *really* thinking. This is a grave matter, one that could lead to war. I've promised that a solution will appear in the paper tomorrow. I trust that you will provide me with that solution." He walked to the door. "The mail ship leaves tomorrow morning at high tide. I have prepared two letters, both addressed to her majesty, Queen Victoria. I hope you make the correct decision in instructing me which one to mail. Now, sir, I shall leave you alone while you consider your options." Cunningham shut the door behind him.

Webb sat at a nearby table. The ambassador had placed a piece of paper next to a pen and bottle of ink. Webb had read too much of English history and concluded erroneously that the same standards applied in the United States. He sighed as he dipped the pen in the ink. When the dust settled from this affair, someone else would become prime minister of Great Britian.

Thompson arrived at his office late the next morning. A pile of telegrams and reports confronted him. After reading a few, he pushed the others aside. An aide could handle them. He sat in his chair and leaned back.

A sergeant walked up to Thompson's desk and saluted. "Here's a letter for you, General. It was delivered yesterday after you left for home."

"Who's it from?" asked Thompson, casually returning the salute.

"I don't know, sir. It's just addressed to you. No return address."

Thompson accepted the envelope and opened it.

Dear General Thompson:
We've never met, but I've heard much about you. It is best, for the present, that I remain anonymous, but I would point out that we have common acquaintances. It is important that I meet with you as soon as possible. I have a matter of great significance that I wish to discuss with you. Your forbearance in this will be appreciated.
May I suggest a meeting on the thirteenth, at half past twelve in the afternoon. There is a small park just north of Pennsylvania Avenue, on Sixth Street. I will be wearing a gray wool suit. My business will require only a few minutes of your time. I will recognize you.
                                                    With kind regards,
                                                    An Admirer

Strange, Thompson thought. Who wrote this? "Sergeant, it appears I have a late lunch invitation for this afternoon. Cancel all my appointments before two-thirty."

"There's only the one at two, with Major Brisbane."
"Right. Tell him to reschedule."
"Yes, sir."

Thompson arrived at the small park ten minutes early. He closely scruti-
nized every man who came near wearing a gray suit. He hadn't noticed before how many men wore gray wool suits, and in the hottest part of summer, no less. Up the street, standing in a doorway, was a man who fit the
description in the letter. He had been there for a few minutes. Thompson thought
the man had looked in his direction several times.

Thompson glanced at his watch. Half past twelve. I guess he isn't coming, he thought. He rose from the bench and began walking north toward the
edge of the park. As he walked, the man left the doorway and crossed the
street, quickly closing the distance. He wore a neatly pressed gray suit and
military boots. The suit looked new, and the boots were polished to a bright
shine. He wore no hat. He had a neatly trimmed beard, also gray. He carried himself like a man of authority—and he looked familiar. Thompson
stopped as the man drew closer.

"General Thompson."
"Did you send me a note, sir?" asked Thompson.
"Yes," the man replied. "Do you know who I am?"
"I feel I should remember your face, but I can't."
"I'm Maj. Gen. Henry Thornton." He hesitated as he fingered the gun in
his pocket. Cold-blooded murder was more difficult than he had imagined.

"Now I remember. I saw you at the prisoner exchange back in the spring
of '63. Considerable distance separated us at that time." He warily observed
that Thornton had not removed his hand from his coat pocket.

"Why don't we go for a walk, General Thompson?" Thornton turned without
waiting for a reply and headed toward a stand of trees. Thompson sensed
that this was more than a casual encounter, and he suspected he knew why
Thornton was here.

"Is this about your sons, General Thornton?"
Thornton extended his arm and leaned against a tree. "I have thought about
this meeting many times, wondering what I would do. When I learned what
you had done to Simon, I swore I would kill you. I believed that would be
my last act on this earth. Now I find I want to live more than I thought I
did."

"General Thornton—"
"Hear me out, General Thompson. What you did was unforgivable. Even
in war, sir, there are limits."
"Another man said those same words to me, sir. It took a while, but I finally
realized he was right."

"And who was that, General?" asked Thornton.

"Samuel, your other son. He actually pulled a gun during the conversation, and he hardly knew Simon at the time."

"He did that?"

"Yes, and there was a general officer present. I was a colonel at the time. Sam was right then, and you are right now. Unfortunately, there are so few guidelines. War is cruel, General Thornton, civil wars most of all. You have my apology. And what about you, sir? You conspired to have Lincoln killed."

Thornton turned and stared into Thompson's eyes. "I was thinking of my country, General."

"As was I, General Thornton. It seems we can both justify our actions."

Thornton sighed. "I'm a marked man, General Thompson. Your government wants to see me dangling from a rope. And if that doesn't happen, the men who thought to use me and my friends will see that I die. They've already killed most of us."

"It won't be the government that hangs you, sir. The president is aware of your assistance. He is willing to let the matter pass."

"Why?"

"Because he understands, General. There is no other explanation. Now, either shoot me, or hand over the gun. It is my duty to inform you that you are to be taken into custody, to be placed in a prisoner-of-war camp with other captured Confederate soldiers."

"That is all?"

"That is all, General. For you, the war is over." Thompson extended his hand. He heard a dull click as Thornton eased the pistol's hammer forward. Thompson accepted the weapon and smiled tightly. "Thank you, sir. As for the other matter, steps are being taken to deal with the conspirators. We may not get them all, but those we don't will realize that we know who they are."

From the diary of Caroline Wade-Healy

*July 14, 1864*

*Henry has been taken into custody, to be sent, I understand, to a prison in New York. Jason assures me he will be treated with the respect due his rank. And what is that? Are they not all worthy of equal respect?*

*The purpose for this war has ended, but the killing continues. Lee is trapped with no hope of escape. Sherman draws closer to Atlanta each day. Samuel informed me this morning that he must return to his brigade. Even with all that has happened, I have a measure of contentment. Even after all of the hell of this war—God knows my family has endured its share—we are all still alive. When this war began, I prayed for no more than that.*

*We will be leaving for the railroad station in about an hour. Now that General Early has withdrawn, the trains are moving north again. Victoria and Nancy Caroline are coming to live with me in Gettysburg, as are Cathy and Sandy. I guess I will be building another house or two soon. Simon will remain in Washington for a short time, then will travel to Chicago to represent me in the factory there. He has no business experience, but he will learn.*

*As I sit here writing this, I hear sounds of laughter across the room. Cathy is tickling Sandy and the child is shrieking with delight. Children bounce back so quickly, despite the worst we can do to them. Somehow we all must bounce back, everyone in our fractured country. But for now, our duty is to endure.*

———————————